Staff Credits:

For EMC/Paradigm Publishing, St. Paul, Minnesota

Laurie Skiba
Editor

Eileen Slater
Editorial Consultant

Shannon O'Donnell Taylor
Associate Editor

Jennifer J. Anderson
Assistant Editor

For **Penobscot School Publishing, Inc.**, Danvers, Massachusetts

Editorial

Robert D. Shepherd
President, Executive Editor

Christina E. Kolb
Managing Editor

Sara Hyry
Editor

Allyson Stanford
Editor

Sharon Salinger
Copyeditor

Marilyn Murphy Shepherd
Editorial Advisor

Design and Production

Charles Q. Bent
Production Manager

Diane Castro
Compositor

Janet Stebbings
Illustrator

S0-AGD-210

ISBN 0-8219-1643-2

Published by EMC/Paradigm Publishing
875 Montreal Way
St. Paul, Minnesota 55102

4002000026195

Printed in the United States of America.
10 9 8 7 6 5 4 3 xxx 08 07 06 05 04 03 02

fRankenstein
with ReLated Readings

Mary Shelley

East High School

WAUWATOSA SCHOOL DISTRICT
Wauwatosa, Wisconsin

THE EMC MASTERPIECE SERIES

Access Editions

EMC/Paradigm Publishing
St. Paul, Minnesota

Table of Contents

THE LIFE AND WORKS OF

Mary Wollstonecraft Shelley

Mary Wollstonecraft Shelley (1797–1851). Mary Wollstonecraft Godwin was born in London, England, the daughter of two radical thinkers, William Godwin and Mary Wollstonecraft, a famous women's rights activist. Mary Wollstonecraft's death of puerperal fever eleven days after giving birth had a profound effect on her daughter Mary's life. During her first three years, Mary was cared for by Louisa Jones, a nanny who also tended to Fanny Imlay, Mary's half-sister. It seems that Mary's early years under Louisa's care and with Fanny's companionship were happy. In 1800, however, Godwin was angered by Jones's affection for George Dyson, a young man Godwin thought irresponsible, and forbade Jones to see his daughters again. Mary thus lost the only maternal figure she had known.

Mary Wollstonecraft
Shelley

Within a year of his wife's death, William Godwin began to seek a new wife and a mother for his daughters. In 1801 he remarried, and his new wife, Mary Jane Clairmont, brought two children, Charles and Jane, to live with the Godwins. Tension raged between Mary and her stepmother, who favored her own children and resented Mary and the attention she received from the followers of Godwin and Wollstonecraft.

During her childhood, Mary spent a great deal of time writing, reading from her father's extensive library, and listening to her father and his friends discuss philosophy, politics, literature, and science. She also visited her mother's grave, where she would read from her mother's works. In her early childhood, Mary feared her father would abandon her; as she grew she idolized him, although she found him distant and not the caring parent she so desperately needed. When she was fourteen, Mary was sent to Dundee, Scotland, to live with the family of one of her father's admirers. Her experience with the Baxters gave her a sense of belonging to a close-knit group. She lived there happily for two years and returned in 1814 to London at the age of sixteen.

During a brief visit to London in November of 1812, Mary met Percy Bysshe Shelley, a leading Romantic poet, and his wife Harriet. Percy Shelley admired the works of both William Godwin and Mary Wollstonecraft, and soon became an admirer of Mary Godwin as well. In March 1814, Mary returned to London, and in May she met Percy again. They began to spend considerable time together, professing their love for one another at Mary's mother's grave. In July they ran away together to France, despite her father's protests.

Mary's stepsister, Jane Clairmont, who had by that time changed her name to Claire, accompanied them on their travels through Europe. Although the couple found it natural for Claire, who had aided them in their secret encounters, to join them, she soon became a source of tension between them as Percy turned his attentions toward her. When they returned to London in September, Godwin refused to see his daughter. Mary gave birth prematurely to her first child, a girl she named Clara, on February 22, 1815. A few days later Clara died. Mary wrote in her journal of a recurring dream in which she held her baby, rubbing her before the fire and thus bringing her back to life. Percy showed little concern over the loss and left Mary to be comforted by a friend. The death of her first child is one of many tragedies Mary faced before her twenty-fifth birthday.

The early months of 1816 were a period of relative calm and happiness for Mary and Percy. On January 24, Mary again gave birth, this time to a son, William. In May, Percy and Mary traveled to Switzerland with Claire Clairmont to join Lord Byron, another Romantic poet with whom Claire soon became romantically involved. The four spent the unusually cold summer in Geneva. There they discussed philosophical and scientific ideas, read ghost stories, and, at the suggestions of Byron, attempted to write their own. In June of 1816, when she was nineteen, Mary began to write *Frankenstein, or The Modern Prometheus*. Almost a year after beginning the novel for which she is best known, Mary Shelley completed it in May 1817, and published it in 1818.

In the later part of 1816, Shelley experienced two significant deaths. In October 1816, Fanny Imlay, Mary's half-sister, took her own life. Two months later, Harriet Shelley, Percy's first wife, drowned herself. Her death allowed Mary and Percy to marry, which they did on December 30. Despite his efforts, Percy was never able to gain custody of his children by Harriet. Shelley again gave birth to a daughter whom she again named Clara; this time the child lived only for one year. The multiple tragedies in their lives, including the deaths of their children and several close friends as well as a miscarriage for Mary in 1822, caused Mary to retreat emotionally from Percy during his last years. As a result of this estrangement, Mary experienced deep guilt when her husband and coworker died suddenly in 1822 in a boating accident. She is largely responsible for preserving Percy's work by annotating and publishing several editions after his death.

Shelley's main comfort was her son Percy Florence, the only one of her children to live to adulthood. After her husband's death, Mary returned to England with her son. Her later travels with him and a friend were the source of *Rambles in Germany and Italy,* which she published in 1844. During the last twenty-five years of her life, Mary wrote five more novels, including *Valperga, The Last Man,* and *Lodore;* twenty-five short tales; and several volumes of literary criticism. She also made substantial revisions to *Frankenstein.* The daughter of two great thinkers and the wife of a well-known poet, Shelley created her own lasting fame. On February 1, 1851, Mary Shelley died from a brain tumor at the age of fifty-three.

Time Line of Shelley's Life

1797 On August 30, in London, England, Mary (Wollstonecraft Godwin) Shelley is born to William Godwin and Mary Wollstonecraft Godwin. On September 10, her mother dies of puerperal fever, an infection caused by treatment sustained during childbirth.

1801 Mary's father marries Mary Jane Clairmont. She brings two children, Charles and Jane (who is later known as Claire Clairmont), to live with Mary, her father, and Fanny Imlay, the daughter of Mary Godwin and Gilbert Imlay.

1805 William and Jane Godwin begin the Juvenile Library, a publishing firm specializing in children's books.

1806 Mary hears Coleridge recite "The Rime of the Ancient Mariner," a poem that will influence *Frankenstein*.

1810 The Juvenile Library publishes Mary's poem "Mounseer Nongtongpaw."

1812 In June, Godwin sends Mary to Dundee, Scotland, to stay with his friends, the Baxters. Mary visits her family in London in November and meets Percy Bysshe Shelley and his wife.

1813 Mary Godwin returns to Scotland.

1814 In March, Mary returns to London. Two months later, she again meets Percy and they begin spending time together. By June 26 Mary declares her love for Percy, and a month later Mary and Percy run away together to France, taking Claire Clairmont with them. They travel through Europe, returning to London in September. Godwin refuses to see his daughter upon her return.

1815 On February 22, Mary gives birth to a premature daughter, Clara, who dies a few days later.

1816 Mary gives birth to son William on January 24. In May, Percy and Mary travel with Claire Clairmont to Switzerland, where they join Lord Byron. In June, the events that inspire Mary to write *Frankenstein* occur. Mary, Percy, and Clairmont return to England in September. Fanny Imlay commits suicide on October 9 and Harriet Shelley, Percy's first wife, drowns herself in December. Percy Bysshe Shelley and Mary Godwin are married on December 30.

Mary finishes *Frankenstein* in May. In September, she gives birth to another daughter, whom she again names Clara.

Frankenstein is published. Clara dies in September.

William dies of malaria on June 7. The Shelleys move to Florence, Italy. Percy Florence Shelley is born on November 12.

Mary begins writing *Valperga*.

Mary miscarries and almost dies in June. On July 8, her husband Percy dies. Mary writes "The Choice," a poem.

Valperga is published. Mary returns to England with her son and views the first dramatic adaptation of *Frankenstein*.

The Last Man is published in February.

Mary becomes ill with smallpox.

Perkin Warbeck is published.

Revised edition of *Frankenstein* is published with substantial changes, despite Mary Shelley's introduction which claims that no substantive changes have been made to the 1818 edition.

Lodore is published.

On April 7, William Godwin dies.

Falkner is published.

Rambles in Germany and Italy, a work based on travels with Mary's son Percy and one of his friends, is published.

On February 1, Mary Shelley dies of a brain tumor at the age of fifty-three.

	1817
	1818
	1819
	1820
	1822
	1823
	1826
	1828
	1830
	1831
	1835
	1836
	1837
	1844
	1851

Frankenstein

Romanticism and the Gothic Novel

Romanticism was an artistic and literary movement of the late eighteenth and early nineteenth century. As artists, philosophers, and writers rebelled against the rational, orderly forms of Neoclassicism, they created works that celebrated emotion over reason, the individual over society, nature and wildness over human works, the country over the town, common people over aristocrats, and freedom over control or authority. William Wordsworth and Samuel Taylor Coleridge (author of "The Rime of the Ancient Mariner, see page 230) were two early influential poets of the Romantic Era. Mary Shelley's husband, Percy, and their friend George Gordon, Lord Byron, were major Romantic poets of the later part of the period.

Shelley's novel *Frankenstein* is also influenced by and an example of the Gothic novels that were popular during the late eighteenth and early nineteenth centuries. Gothic novels contain elements of horror, suspense, mystery, and magic, as well as dark, brooding descriptions of settings and characters. In her journals and in her introduction to *Frankenstein,* Shelley describes horror or ghost stories that she was reading when she wrote this novel.

Mythological and Literary Influences

Frankenstein is subtitled "The Modern Prometheus," referring to the legend of Prometheus from Greek mythology (see Selections for Additional Reading, page 229). The allusion in the title suggests that Frankenstein is like Prometheus, in that Frankenstein is a creator of human life and one who was punished for stealing from a more powerful force.

The epigraph to the novel is from book 10 of *Paradise Lost,* a twelve-book epic poem by John Milton that tells the story of the fall from grace of Adam and Eve:

> Did I request thee, Maker, from my clay
> To mold me man? Did I solicit thee
> From darkness to promote me?—

Adam speaks these words in *Paradise Lost,* and while Shelley links these words to Frankenstein's monster in her novel, she also explores ideas conveyed by Satan, the fallen archangel, who also figures largely for Milton. In fact, Shelley makes many allusions to Milton's work. Critics have noted that Shelley compares Frankenstein to Milton's Satan, as well as to Goethe's Faust, who sold his soul to the devil in return for magical powers.

Scientific Influences

The Romantic Era began at the end of the eighteenth century, a period of great advances in the scientific world. Sir Humphrey Davy, Erasmus Darwin, and Luigi Galvani were three major scientists whose studies influenced Shelley's work. Davy, a specialist in natural philosophy or chemical physiology, wrote *A Discourse, Introductory to a Course of Lectures on Chemistry,* the source of Professor Waldman's lecture that appears in *Frankenstein.* Davy saw nature as a female force, as Shelley emphasizes in this novel. While one of the two branches of Davy's science concerns itself with trying to understand the ways of nature, the other concerns itself with changing the workings of nature. In *Frankenstein,* Professor Waldman shares Davy's preference for the latter course of study and encourages Frankenstein to do the same.

Frankenstein not only shows the influence of the scientific exploration of Shelley's time but critiques it as well, as Shelley explores the dangers of Davy's intervening science. At the same time, she praised what she saw as positive scientific practices, such as those of Erasmus Darwin. The grandfather of Charles Darwin, Erasmus Darwin presented early theories about evolution, including his idea that sexual reproduction is a higher evolutionary function than asexual reproduction. Frankenstein's experiments defy the natural evolutionary process by relying solely on a male parent or creator and by trying to create a new being while bypassing the natural process of mutation and adaptation.

Perhaps the experiments of Luigi Galvani involving electricity to restore life to dead animals were the strongest scientific influences on *Frankenstein.* Galvani believed that electricity was the force that sparked and sustained life. In one well-known experiment, Galvani's nephew tried to revive the dead body of criminal Thomas Forster. The surge of electricity resulted in muscle contortions and contractions, suggesting the means of bringing the monster to life in the novel.

Frankenstein is one of the first novels of the science fiction genre. Science fiction is highly imaginative fiction containing fantastic elements based on scientific principles, discoveries, or laws. By critiquing scientific theories, experiments, or practices or by using scientific bases to create new worlds, science fiction allows an author to explore many aspects of human nature and human society.

Political Influences

In *Frankenstein,* Shelley examines human society and socialization. Her ideas may well have been influenced by her readings of the works of Jean-Jacques Rousseau (1712–1778) and John Locke (1632–1704). Rousseau was a French philosopher who believed in the idea of the "noble savage"— that in their natural state, people are good and that social institutions corrupt them. Rousseau's ideas about people and nature became central to Romanticism and Shelley's novel. Locke was an English doctor, philosopher, and writer who popularized the idea of natural rights. Locke also presented several theories of human learning and development. Mary Shelley had read his "Essay Concerning Human Understanding" and several of the ideas put forth are reflected in the monster's process of learning about his surroundings, himself, and human society.

Psychological Influences

Mary Shelley's own desire for a family and her concerns about motherhood may be yet another source for *Frankenstein,* as the novel is largely about trying to produce a human life. Some critics suggest that Shelley's concerns about her ability to give birth to a child who would survive and that she could love are reflected in Frankenstein's creation and subsequent rejection of a living creature.

Shelley's Revision of *Frankenstein*

In her introduction to the 1831 version of *Frankenstein* Shelley writes:

> I will add but one word as to the alterations I have made. They are principally those of style. I have changed no portion of the story nor introduced any new ideas or circumstances. . . . Throughout they are entirely confined to such parts as are mere adjuncts to the story, leaving the core and substance of it untouched.

Despite Shelley's declaration, comparison between the 1818 and 1831 versions show substantial changes. Many of these changes reflect Shelley's own evolving attitude following the death of several of her children and friends. In Shelley's revision, fate plays a larger role. Although she does not remove responsibility from Frankenstein for his actions, she places greater weight on the role destiny plays in his work. In the earlier version, Henry Clerval shows Frankenstein's better side and offers him a reminder of that aspect of himself; in the later version, Clerval, like Frankenstein, also is consumed by his studies and search for fame. Family relationships vary between the two versions as well. In the 1818 version, Elizabeth is Frankenstein's cousin; in the later version she is an orphan taken into the Frankenstein family. In both cases Frankenstein's mother plans for Frankenstein to marry Elizabeth when they should be of age, but in the later version, she presents Elizabeth to Frankenstein as a gift, which the young Frankenstein takes as a literal statement, immediately objectifying Elizabeth and claiming her as his own. Two passages in which Elizabeth presents her views opposing Frankenstein's father's plan for Ernest's future and denouncing the court system are removed as well. The text that follows is the 1831 revision.

Frankenstein Since Shelley's Time

The themes and issues raised by Mary Shelley's *Frankenstein* are still relevant today. These concerns include the reaches of science, our attitudes toward scientific exploration, the responsibilities of a parent or creator to an offspring or living creation, and the effects of being rejected or isolated from society. The story of Frankenstein and his monster has taken many shapes since Shelley first wrote her novel. Literary and film adaptations continue to be popular. A few of the many Frankenstein films are listed below.

Selected *Frankenstein* Film List

Frankenstein, directed by James Whale, Universal Pictures, 1931
With Boris Karloff as the monster, this classic film is responsible for one of the most widely recognized versions of Frankenstein's creature.

The Bride of Frankenstein, directed by James Whale, Universal Pictures, 1935
Many critics call *The Bride of Frankenstein* one of the best horror films of all times. Boris Karloff again plays the monster. More human in this sequel than in the preceding *Frankenstein,* the monster is promised a bride (as he is in Shelley's novel).

The Son of Frankenstein, directed by Rowland V. Lee, Universal Pictures, 1939
In this film, Wolf von Frankenstein, Victor's son, is a scientist in the United States. Upon inheriting his father's estate, he travels to Germany with his family. There he meets Ygor, a broken-necked shepherd who lived through an attempted execution by hanging. Ygor convinces Wolf

to revive his father's monster. Wolf agrees, seeing this as a chance to restore his father's reputation; Ygor's motivation is revenge on the jurors who found him guilty. This film marks Boris Karloff's last appearance as the monster. He would be replaced in upcoming films by Bela Lugosi, who plays Ygor here.

The Ghost of Frankenstein, directed by Erle C. Kenton, Universal Pictures, 1942
Yet another take on the Frankenstein myth by Universal Pictures, many critics find this a weak follow-up of the Frankenstein movies that preceded it.

Frankenstein Meets the Wolf Man, directed by Roy William Neill, Universal Pictures, 1943
In a previous movie about the Wolf Man, Lon Chaney, Jr. had been bitten by a werewolf and become a werewolf himself. The werewolf looks for Frankenstein, who has died, and finds Frankenstein's monster instead.

Abbott and Costello Meet Frankenstein, directed by Charles T. Barton, Universal Pictures, 1948
This movie includes four famous horror movie favorites: Dracula, Frankenstein's creature, the Wolf Man, and the Invisible Man. The four monsters are paired with the comedy team of Abbot and Costello for a film that is more humor and high jinks than horror.

The Curse of Frankenstein, directed by Terence Fisher, Hammer Studios, 1957
The first Frankenstein film in color is applauded for its fine screenplay, casting, and directing.

Frankenstein Conquers the World, directed by Inoshiro Honda, Toho (Japan), 1966
A scientist in Tokyo battles a new Frankenstein monster.

Spirit of the Beehive, directed by Victor Erice, Spain, 1973
A young girl becomes preoccupied by the monster in the 1931 film *Frankenstein.* Convinced the monster lives, she heads to the countryside to seek him.

Young Frankenstein, directed by Mel Brooks, Gruskoff/ Twentieth Century Fox, 1974
Young Frankenstein is an amusing parody of the three Universal Studios Frankenstein movies of the thirties. Gene Wilder plays a brain surgeon who unwillingly inherits his family's business and estate in Transylvania. He becomes bent on creating his own monster.

Frankenweenie, directed by Tim Burton, 1984
Victor Frankenstein owns a dog named Sparky in this light parody. When Sparky is killed by a car, Frankenstein uses electricity to bring him back to life.

Gothic, directed by Ken Russell, 1986
This movie depicts the story told by Mary Shelley in her introduction to *Frankenstein.* The storytelling contest, her dreams, the interactions between Mary, Lord Byron, Percy Shelley, and Dr. Polidori, are presented in a horrifying, nightmarish manner.

Haunted Summer, directed by Ivan Passer, 1988
Based on a novel by Anne Edwards, this movie shows the pleasure-seeking lives of Lord Byron, Percy Shelley, Mary Godwin, and Dr. Polidori during the summer in which Mary conceived *Frankenstein.*

Frankenstein General Hospital, directed by Deborah Roberts, 1988
In this spoof of Frankenstein movies, Victor Frankenstein's twelfth grandson creates a monster in a modern hospital basement. Many critics consider *Frankenstein General Hospital* to be the worst Frankenstein movie ever made.

Frankenstein Unbound, directed by Roger Corman, 1990
John Hurt plays a scientist who inadvertently travels back in time. He meets Mary Shelley (played by Bridget Fonda), and Percy Shelley (played by Michael Hutchence, the lead singer of the Australian band INXS). He also encounters their neighbors—Frankenstein (played by Raoul Julia) and his monster.

Mary Shelley's Frankenstein, directed by Kenneth Branagh, Sheperton, 1994
Kenneth Branagh plays Victor Frankenstein and Robert DeNiro plays the monster in this recent adaptation. Critics consider Branagh's attempt at a faithful rendering of the novel successful in some ways but lacking in others.

Characters in *Frankenstein*

Main Characters

Robert Walton. Walton, a scientist and explorer, is the narrator. Through letters to his sister, Mrs. Margaret Saville, he relates how he met Frankenstein and the fantastic story Frankenstein tells him.

Victor Frankenstein. After the title character of the novel learns the secret of animation, or of giving life to an inanimate object, he gives life to a human of large proportions. Frankenstein tells his tale of discovery and despair to Robert Walton.

Elizabeth Lavenza Frankenstein. Elizabeth is an orphan who is adopted by Frankenstein's parents and destined to marry Frankenstein.

Henry Clerval. Frankenstein's dear friend, Henry eventually follows Frankenstein to the university and nurses his sick friend to health.

The Monster. Frankenstein's creation is often referred to as the monster or the demon.

Justine Moritz. Justine is employed in the Frankenstein household. She cares for the dying Mrs. Frankenstein and is greatly loved by the family.

Agatha, Felix, and Mr. De Lacey. Mr. De Lacey is the blind father of Agatha and Felix, the young people who live in the cottage near the place where the monster hides.

Safie. Safie is a young Turkish or Arabian woman who flees her father to marry Felix.

Minor Characters

Mrs. Margaret Saville. Walton's married sister, Mrs. Saville, is the specified audience of the story.

Alphonso Frankenstein. Victor's father, Alphonso, unknowingly encourages his son's studies by a passing remark. Alphonso worries about Victor when their correspondence is infrequent.

Caroline Beaufort Frankenstein. The daughter of Alphonso's good friend, Caroline marries Alphonso after her father's death. Mindful of her own poverty-stricken past, she adopts Elizabeth Lavenza from the poor family who has been raising her.

Ernest Frankenstein. Victor's younger brother does not share Victor's passion for scientific study.

William Frankenstein. William is the youngest of the Frankenstein children.

Professors Krempe and Waldman. These two scholars influence Frankenstein's work at the university at Ingolstadt.

Mr. Kirwin. Mr. Kirwin is the magistrate in the village in Ireland where Frankenstein is accused of murder.

Daniel Nugent. Daniel is one of the witnesses against Frankenstein.

Echoes:
On Mary Shelley's Frankenstein

Nor are the crimes and malevolence of the single Being, though indeed withering and tremendous, the offspring of any unaccountable propensity to evil, but flow irresistibly from certain causes fully adequate to their production. . . . In this the direct moral of the book consists; and it is perhaps the most universal application, of any moral that can be enforced by example. Treat a person ill, and he will become wicked. . . . It is thus that, too often in society, those who are best qualified to be its benefactors and its ornaments, are branded by some accident with scorn, and changed, by neglect and solitude of heart, into a scourge and a curse.

—Percy Bysshe Shelley
from "On *Frankenstein*," 1817 (published 1832)

Upon the whole, the work impresses us with a high idea of the author's original genius and happy power of expression. . . . If Gray's definition of Paradise, to lie on a couch, namely, and read new novels, come anything near truth, no small praise is due to him, who, like the author of *Frankenstein,* has enlarged the sphere of that fascinating enjoyment.

—Sir Walter Scott
from "Remarks on *Frankenstein: or, The Modern Prometheus: A Novel,*" 1818

The subject [of *Frankenstein*] is somewhat revolting, the treatment of it somewhat hideous. The conception is powerful, but the execution is very unequal. . . . Still the reader will begin *Frankenstein* excited by the leading idea, and he will read it to the end, not only on account of its accumulation of horrors, but for the sake of its fine and varied scenes—I had almost said atmospheric effects—and its deep insight into the natural workings of the human heart.   —Hugh Reginald Haweis
from Introduction to the Routledge World Library Edition, 1886

Yet ere long our sympathy, which has hitherto been entirely with Frankenstein, is unexpectedly diverted to the monster who, it would seem, is wicked only because he is eternally divorced from human society.

—Edith Birkhead
from *The Tale of Terror: A Study of the Gothic Romance,* 1963

Mary Shelley, barely nineteen years of age when she wrote the original *Frankenstein,* was the daughter of two great intellectual rebels, William Godwin and Mary Wollstonecraft, and the second wife of Percy Bysshe

Shelley, another great rebel and an unmatched lyrical poet. Had she written nothing, Mary Shelley would be remembered today. She is remembered in her own right as the author of a novel valuable in itself but also prophetic of an intellectual world to come, a novel depicting a Prometheanism that is with us still.   —Harold Bloom
from Afterword to *Frankenstein*, 1965

[F]or the far-reaching implications of the main theme and for the grandiose scenery through which the mad chase takes place, Mrs. Shelley's novel ranks as the greatest achievement of the Gothic school, notwithstanding its frequent clichés of phrasing and situations and the occasionally disarming naiveté.   —Mario Praz
from Introduction to *Three Gothic Novels*, 1968

What Mary Shelley actually did in *Frankenstein* was to transform the standard Romantic matter of incest, infanticide, and patricide into a phantasmagoria of the nursery.   —Ellen Moers
from *Literary Women*, 1976

All three [Walton, Frankenstein, and the Monster], like Shelley herself, appear to be trying to understand their presence in a fallen world, and trying at the same time to define the nature of the lost paradise that must have existed before the fall. But unlike Adam, all three characters seem to have fallen not merely from Eden but from the earth, fallen directly into hell, like Sin, Satan, and—by implication, Eve. Thus their questionings are in some sense female, for they belong in that line of literary women's questionings of the fall into gender which goes back at least to Anne Finch's plaintive "How are we fal'n?" and forward to Sylvia Plath's horrified "I have fallen very far!"
—Sandra M. Gilbert and Susan Gubar
from "Mary Shelley's Monstrous Eve," 1979

Mary Shelley's *Frankenstein or The Modern Prometheus* is a remarkable work . . . and a unique blending of Gothic, fabulist, allegorical, and philosophical materials.   —Joyce Carol Oates
from "Frankenstein's Fallen Angel," 1984

Since the James Whale–Boris Karloff production of *Frankenstein* (1931) there have been scores of sequels, film adaptations, cartoons, parodies, and travesties of the Frankenstein story. . . . By now, the name Frankenstein represents, in the popular imagination, an instantly recognizable myth. That the myth was created by Mary Shelley in a novel she wrote when she was eighteen years old is not quite so well known.   —Leonard Wolf
from *The Essential Frankenstein*, 1993

Preface

The event on which this fiction is founded has been supposed, by Dr. Darwin,[1] and some of the physiological writers of Germany, as not of impossible occurrence. I shall not be supposed as according the remotest degree of serious faith to such an imagination; yet, in assuming it as the basis of a work of fancy, I have not considered myself as merely weaving a series of supernatural terrors. The event on which the interest of the story depends is exempt from the disadvantages of a mere tale of <u>specters</u> or enchantment. It was recommended by the <u>novelty</u> of the situations which it develops; and, however impossible as a physical fact, affords a point of view to the imagination for the <u>delineating</u> of human passions more comprehensive and commanding than any which the ordinary relations of existing events can yield.

I have thus <u>endeavored</u> to preserve the truth of the elementary principles of human nature, while I have not scrupled to innovate upon their combinations. *The Iliad*,[2] the tragic poetry of Greece—Shakespeare, in *The Tempest* and *Midsummer Night's Dream*[3]—and most especially Milton, in *Paradise Lost*,[4] conform to this rule; and the most humble novelist, who seeks to confer or receive amusement from his labors, may, without presumption, apply to prose fiction a license, or rather a rule, from the adoption of which so many exquisite combinations of human feeling have resulted in the highest specimens of poetry.

The circumstance on which my story rests was suggested in casual conversation. It was commenced partly as a source of amusement, and partly as an expedient for exercising any untried resources of mind. Other motives were mingled with these as the work proceeded. I am by no means indifferent to the manner in which whatever moral tendencies exist in the

◀ According to this Preface, what has the author tried to preserve? To what does the author compare this work?

◀ Why was the novel written? What does the author hope to have accomplished?

---

1. **Dr. Darwin.** Erasmus Darwin (1781–1802), physician who anticipated ideas about evolution, and the grandfather of Charles Darwin
2. **The Iliad.** Ancient Greek poem by Homer about the sacking of the city of Troy
3. **The Tempest** and **Midsummer Night's Dream.** Fanciful plays by William Shakespeare (1564–1616) involving sprites and fairies
4. **Paradise Lost.** Epic poem by John Milton (1608–1674) about humankind's original sin, fall from grace, and loss of paradise

---

Words For Everyday Use

spec • ter (spek´tər) *n.*, ghost or apparition
nov • el • ty (näv´əl tē) *n.*, freshness; unusualness
de • lin • e • ate (di lin´ē āt´) *vt.*, depict, draw, or describe
en • deav • or (en dev´ər) *vt.*, strive; attempt with great effort

sentiments or characters it contains shall affect the reader; yet my chief concern in this respect has been limited to avoiding the <u>enervating</u> effects of the novels of the present day and to the exhibition of the amiableness of domestic affection, and the excellence of universal virtue. The opinions which naturally spring from the character and situation of the hero are by no means to be conceived as existing always in my own conviction; nor is any <u>inference</u> justly to be drawn from the following pages as prejudicing any philosophical doctrine of whatever kind.

▶ What events led to the writing of this novel?

It is a subject also of additional interest to the author that this story was begun in the majestic region where the scene is principally laid, and in society which cannot cease to be regretted. I passed the summer of 1816 in the environs of Geneva.[5] The season was cold and rainy, and in the evenings we crowded around a blazing wood fire, and occasionally amused ourselves with some German stories of ghosts which happened to fall into our hands. These tales excited in us a playful desire of imitation. Two other friends[6] (a tale from the pen of one of whom would be far more acceptable to the public than anything I can ever hope to produce) and myself agreed to write each a story founded on some supernatural occurrence.

The weather, however, suddenly became serene; and my two friends left me on a journey among the Alps, and lost, in the magnificent scenes which they present, all memory of their ghostly visions. The following tale is the only one which has been completed.

Marlow, September, 1817.

---

5. **Geneva.** Major city in Switzerland

6. **stories of ghosts . . . friends.** Shelley, in a later introduction, explains that *Frankenstein* grew out of a story-telling contest she participated in with her husband, Percy Bysshe Shelley, and two friends, John William Polidori and George Gordon, Lord Byron.

Words For Everyday Use	en • er • vat • ing (en′ər vāt′iŋ) *adj.,* weakening; devitalizing
	in • fer • ence (in′fər əns) *n.,* conclusion drawn by reasoning from known facts

Introduction to the Third Edition

The publishers of the standard novels, in selecting *Frankenstein* for one of their series, expressed a wish that I should furnish them with some account of the origin of the story. I am the more willing to comply because I shall thus give a general answer to the question so very frequently asked me—how I, then a young girl, came to think of and to <u>dilate</u> upon so very hideous an idea. It is true that I am very <u>averse</u> to bringing myself forward in print, but as my account will only appear as an appendage to a former production, and as it will be confined to such topics as have connection with my authorship alone, I can scarcely accuse myself of a personal intrusion.

◄ What question does the author say she will answer in this introduction? Why might this be such a frequently asked question?

It is not singular that, as the daughter of two persons of distinguished literary celebrity,[1] I should very early in life have thought of writing. As a child I scribbled, and my favorite pastime during the hours given me for recreation was to "write stories." Still, I had a dearer pleasure than this, which was the formation of castles in the air[2]—the indulging in waking dreams—the following up trains of thought, which had for their subject the formation of a succession of imaginary incidents. My dreams were at once more fantastic and agreeable than my writings. In the latter I was a close imitator—rather doing as others had done than putting down the suggestions of my own mind. What I wrote was intended at least for one other eye—my childhood's companion and friend; but my dreams were all my own; I accounted for them to nobody; they were my refuge when annoyed—my dearest pleasure when free.

◄ Why is it not surprising that Shelley should turn to writing?

◄ What pastime was dearer to Shelley as a child than writing?

◄ What accounts for the difference between Shelley's dreams and her writing?

I lived principally in the country as a girl and passed a considerable time in Scotland. I made occasional visits to the more picturesque parts, but my habitual residence was on the blank and dreary northern shores of the Tay,[3] near Dundee. Blank and dreary on retrospection I call them; they

---

1. **celebrity.** Shelley was the daughter of William Godwin, a political theorist and novelist, and Mary Wollstonecraft, a feminist activist and writer.
2. **formation . . . air.** Creation of a fantasy world
3. **Tay.** Longest river in Scotland, flowing to the North Sea

Words For Everyday Use

di • late (dī´lāt´) *vi.*, discourse; comment on at length
a • verse (ə vʉrs´) *adj.*, not willing; opposed

were not so to me then. They were the aerie[4] of freedom and the pleasant region where unheeded I could commune with the creatures of my fancy. I wrote then, but in a most commonplace style. It was beneath the trees of the grounds belonging to our house, or on the bleak sides of the woodless mountains near, that my true compositions, the airy flights of my imagination, were born and fostered. I did not make myself the heroine of my tales. Life appeared to me too commonplace an affair as regarded myself. I could not figure to myself that romantic woes or wonderful events would ever be my lot; but I was not confined to my own identity, and I could people the hours with creations far more interesting to me at that age than my own sensations.

► Why didn't Shelley make herself the main character in her writings?

After this my life became busier, and reality stood in place of fiction. My husband, however, was from the first very anxious that I should prove myself worthy of my parentage and enroll myself on the page of fame. He was forever inciting me to obtain literary reputation, which even on my own part I cared for then, though since I have become infinitely indifferent to it. At this time he desired that I should write, not so much with the idea that I could produce anything worthy of notice, but that he might himself judge how far I possessed the promise of better things hereafter. Still I did nothing. Traveling, and the cares of a family, occupied my time; and study, in the way of reading or improving my ideas in communication with his far more cultivated mind was all of literary employment that engaged my attention.

► Who encouraged Shelley to write? Why?

In the summer of 1816, we[5] visited Switzerland and became the neighbors of Lord Byron. At first we spent our pleasant hours on the lake or wandering on its shores; and Lord Byron, who was writing the third canto of *Childe Harold,* was the only one among us who put his thoughts upon paper. These, as he brought them successively to us, clothed in all the light and harmony of poetry, seemed to stamp as divine the glories of heaven and earth, whose influences we partook with him.

But it proved a wet, <u>ungenial</u> summer, and incessant rain often confined us for days to the house. Some volumes of

► According to this introduction, in what way did the weather affect the creation of Frankenstein?

---

4. **aerie.** Nest or house built on a high place
5. **we.** Mary Shelley, Percy Bysshe Shelley, and their children

Words
For
Everyday
Use

un • gen • i • al (un jēn′yəl) *adj.,* unpleasant

ghost stories, translated from the German into French, fell into our hands. There was the *History of the Inconstant Lover,* who, when he thought to clasp the bride to whom he had pledged his vows, found himself in the arms of the pale ghost of her whom he had deserted. There was the tale of the sinful founder of his race whose miserable doom it was to bestow the kiss of death on all the younger sons of his fated house, just when they reached the age of promise. His gigantic, shadowy form, clothed like the ghost in *Hamlet,* in complete armor but with the beaver[6] up, was seen at midnight, by the moon's fitful beams, to advance slowly along the gloomy avenue. The shape was lost beneath the shadow of the castle walls; but soon a gate swung back, a step was heard, the door of the chamber opened, and he advanced to the couch of the blooming youths, cradled in healthy sleep. Eternal sorrow sat upon his face as he bent down and kissed the forehead of the boys, who from that hour withered like flowers snapped upon the stalk. I have not seen these stories since then, but their incidents are as fresh in my mind as if I had read them yesterday.

"We will each write a ghost story," said Lord Byron, and his proposition was acceded to. There were four of us.[7] The noble author began a tale, a fragment of which he printed at the end of his poem of Mazeppa. Shelley, more apt to embody ideas and sentiments in the radiance of brilliant imagery and in the music of the most melodious verse that adorns our language than to invent the machinery of a story, commenced one founded on the experiences of his early life. Poor Polidori had some terrible idea about a skull-headed lady who was so punished for peeping through a keyhole—what to see I forget: something very shocking and wrong of course; but when she was reduced to a worse condition than the renowned Tom of Coventry,[8] he did not know what to do with her, and was obliged to dispatch her to the tomb of the Capulets, the only place for which she was fitted. The illustrious poets also, annoyed by the platitude of prose, speedily relinquished their uncongenial task.

◄ *What plan does Byron propose? What do Byron, Percy Shelley, and Polidori create in response to this plan?*

---

6. **beaver.** Piece of armor that covers the face; helmet visor
7. **four of us.** Byron, Mary and Percy Bysshe Shelley, and John William Polidori
8. **Tom of Coventry.** Tom of Coventry, or Peeping Tom, was, according to legend, struck blind for looking at the naked Lady Godiva.

Words
For
Everyday
Use

plat • i • tude (plat´ə tōōd´) *n.,* commonplace quality

I busied myself *to think of a story*—a story to rival those which had excited us to this task. One which would speak to the mysterious fears of our nature and awaken thrilling horror—one to make the reader dread to look round, to curdle the blood, and quicken the beatings of the heart. If I did not accomplish these things, my ghost story would be unworthy of its name. I thought and pondered—vainly. I felt that blank incapability of invention which is the greatest misery of authorship, when dull Nothing replies to our anxious invocations. "Have you thought of a story?" I was asked each morning, and each morning I was forced to reply with a mortifying negative.

Everything must have a beginning, to speak in Sanchean phrase; and that beginning must be linked to something that went before. The Hindus give the world an elephant to support it, but they make the elephant stand upon a tortoise. Invention, it must be humbly admitted, does not consist in creating out of void, but out of chaos; the materials must, in the first place, be afforded: it can give form to dark, shapeless substances but cannot bring into being the substance itself. In all matters of discovery and invention, even of those that appertain to the imagination, we are continually reminded of the story of Columbus and his egg. Invention consists in the capacity of seizing on the capabilities of a subject and in the power of molding and fashioning ideas suggested by it.

Many and long were the conversations between Lord Byron and Shelley to which I was a devout, but nearly silent, listener. During one of these, various philosophical doctrines were discussed, and among others the nature of the principle of life and whether there was any probability of its ever being discovered and communicated. They talked of the experiments of Dr. Darwin (I speak not of what the doctor really did or said that he did, but, as more to my purpose, of what was then spoken of as having been done by him), who preserved a piece of vermicelli in a glass case till by some extraordinary means it began to move with voluntary motion. Not thus, after all, would life be given. Perhaps a corpse would be reanimated; galvanism[9] had given token of such things: perhaps the component parts of a creature might be manufactured, brought together, and endued with vital warmth.

Night waned upon this talk, and even the witching hour had gone by before we retired to rest. When I placed my head on my pillow, I did not sleep, nor could I be said to think. My imagination, unbidden, possessed and guided me, gifting the

► What goal does Shelley have for her story?

► What subject of conversation between Byron and Percy Shelley sparks the author's imagination?

► What does Shelley imagine when she tries to sleep?

9. **galvanism.** Galvanism uses electric currents to cause movement in dead muscles.

successive images that arose in my mind with a vividness far beyond the usual bounds of <u>reverie</u>. I saw—with shut eyes, but acute mental vision—I saw the pale student of unhallowed arts kneeling beside the thing he had put together. I saw the hideous phantasm of a man stretched out, and then, on the working of some powerful engine, show signs of life, and stir with an uneasy, half-vital motion. Frightful must it be, for supremely frightful would be the effect of any human endeavor to mock the stupendous mechanism of the Creator of the world. His success would terrify the artist; he would rush away from his odious handiwork, horror-stricken. He would hope that, left to itself, the slight spark of life which he had communicated would fade, that this thing which had received such imperfect animation would subside into dead matter, and he might sleep in the belief that the silence of the grave would quench forever the transient existence of the hideous corpse which he had looked upon as the cradle of life. He sleeps; but he is awakened; he opens his eyes; behold, the horrid thing stands at his bedside, opening his curtains, and looking on him with yellow, watery, but speculative eyes.

I opened mine in terror. The idea so possessed my mind that a thrill of fear ran through me, and I wished to exchange the ghastly image of my fancy for the realities around. I see them still: the very room, the dark parquet, the closed shutters with the moonlight struggling through, and the sense I had that the glassy lake and white high Alps were beyond. I could not so easily get rid of my hideous phantom; still it haunted me. I must try to think of something else. I recurred to my ghost story—my tiresome unlucky ghost story! O! if I could only contrive one which would frighten my reader as I myself had been frightened that night!

Swift as light and as cheering was the idea that broke in upon me. "I have found it! What terrified me will terrify others; and I need only describe the specter which had haunted my midnight pillow." On the morrow I announced that I had *thought of a story*. I began that day with the words "It was on a dreary night of November," making only a transcript of the grim terrors of my waking dream.

At first I thought but of a few pages, of a short tale, but Shelley urged me to develop the idea at greater length. I certainly did not owe the suggestion of one incident, nor

◄ *For what is Percy Shelley responsible?*

Words For Everyday Use

rev • er • ie (rev´ər ē) *n.*, dreaming

scarcely of one train of feeling, to my husband, and yet but for his incitement, it would never have taken the form in which it was presented to the world. From this declaration I must except the preface. As far as I can recollect, it was entirely written by him.

▶ *What does Shelley call her novel? How does she feel about her work?*

And now, once again, I bid my hideous <u>progeny</u> go forth and prosper. I have an affection for it, for it was the offspring of happy days, when death and grief were but words which found no true echo in my heart. Its several pages speak of many a walk, many a drive, and many a conversation, when I was not alone; and my companion was one who, in this world, I shall never see more. But this is for myself: my readers have nothing to do with these associations.

I will add but one word as to the alterations I have made. They are principally those of style. I have changed no portion of the story nor introduced any new ideas or circumstances. I have mended the language where it was so bald as to interfere with the interest of the narrative; and these changes occur almost exclusively in the beginning of the first volume. Throughout they are entirely confined to such parts as are mere <u>adjuncts</u> to the story, leaving the core and substance of it untouched.

Words For Everyday Use	prog • e • ny (präj´ə nē) *n.,* offspring ad • junct (a´ junkt´) *n.,* a thing added to something else, but not essential to it

Letter 1

St. Petersburgh,[1] Dec. 11th, 17—

You will rejoice to hear that no disaster has accompanied the <u>commencement</u> of an <u>enterprise</u> which you have regarded with such evil forebodings. I arrived here yesterday, and my first task is to assure my dear sister of my welfare and increasing confidence in the success of my undertaking.

I am already far north of London, and as I walk in the streets of Petersburgh, I feel a cold northern breeze play upon my cheeks, which braces my nerves, and fills me with delight. Do you understand this feeling? This breeze, which has traveled from the regions towards which I am advancing, gives me a foretaste of those icy climes. Inspirited[2] by this wind of promise, my daydreams become more fervent and vivid. I try in vain to be persuaded that the pole is the seat of frost and desolation; it ever presents itself to my imagination as the region of beauty and delight. There, Margaret, the sun is forever visible, its broad disc just skirting the horizon and diffusing a perpetual splendor. There—for with your leave, my sister, I will put some trust in preceding navigators—there snow and frost are banished; and, sailing over a calm sea, we may be wafted to a land surpassing in wonders and in beauty every region hitherto discovered on the habitable globe. Its productions and features may be without example, as the phenomena of the heavenly bodies undoubtedly are in those undiscovered solitudes. What may not be expected in a country of eternal light? I may there discover the wondrous power which attracts the needle[3] and may regulate a thousand celestial observations that require only this voyage to render their seeming <u>eccentricities</u> consistent forever. I shall <u>satiate</u> my <u>ardent</u> curiosity with the sight of a part of the world never before visited, and may tread a land never before imprinted

◄ *From where does the narrator write? How does he feel about being in this place? Why does he feel this way?*

◄ *Why is the narrator embarking on this journey? What does he hope to accomplish?*

---

1. **St. Petersburgh.** City in Russia on the Gulf of Finland, at times called Petrograd or Leningrad
2. **Inspirited.** Filled with spirit or vigor
3. **power which attracts the needle.** Refers to the magnetic force that affects the needle of a compass

Words For Everyday Use	
com • mence • ment (kə mens′mənt) *n.*, beginning	deviation from what is ordinary or customary; oddity
en • ter • prise (ent′ər prīz) *n.*, bold or dangerous undertaking or project	**sa • ti • ate** (sā′shē āt′) *vt.*, satisfy or gratify completely
ec • cen • tric • i • ty (ek′sen tris′ə tē) *n.*,	**ar • dent** (ärd′′nt) *adj.*, intensely enthusiastic;

by the foot of man. These are my <u>enticements</u>, and they are sufficient to conquer all fear of danger or death and to induce me to commence this laborious voyage with the joy a child feels when he embarks in a little boat, with his holiday mates, on an expedition of discovery up his native river. But supposing all these conjectures to be false, you cannot contest the <u>inestimable</u> benefit which I shall confer on all mankind, to the last generation, by discovering a passage near the pole to those countries, to reach which at present so many months are requisite; or by ascertaining the secret of the magnet, which, if at all possible, can only be effected by an undertaking such as mine.

These reflections have dispelled the agitation with which I began my letter, and I feel my heart glow with an enthusiasm which elevates me to heaven, for nothing contributes so much to tranquilize the mind as a steady purpose—a point on which the soul may fix its intellectual eye. This expedition has been the favorite dream of my early years. I have read with ardor the accounts of the various voyages which have been made in the prospect of arriving at the North Pacific Ocean through the seas which surround the pole. You may remember that a history of all the voyages made for purposes of discovery composed the whole of our good Uncle Thomas's library. My education was neglected, yet I was passionately fond of reading. These volumes were my study day and night, and my familiarity with them increased that regret which I had felt, as a child, on learning that my father's dying <u>injunction</u> had forbidden my uncle to allow me to embark in a seafaring life.

These visions faded when I <u>perused</u>, for the first time, those poets whose effusions entranced my soul, and lifted it to heaven. I also became a poet and for one year lived in a Paradise of my own creation; I imagined that I also might obtain a niche in the temple where the names of Homer and Shakespeare are consecrated.[4] You are well acquainted with my failure, and how heavily I bore the disappointment. But just at that time I inherited the fortune of my cousin, and my thoughts were turned into the channel of their earlier bent.

---

4. **temple . . . consecrated.** The narrator had aspirations to be a renowned writer like Shakespeare or Homer.

► What calms the narrator? What does he mean by "intellectual eye"?

► What is the narrator forbidden to do by his father's dying wish?

► To what did the narrator turn his energy? What hope did he have for his efforts? What happened to this dream?

Words For Everyday Use

en • tice • ment (en tīs´mənt) n., allurement; temptation

in • es • ti •ma • ble (in es´tə mə bəl) adj., too great or valuable to be measured; invaluable

in • junc • tion (in juŋk´shən) n., command

pe • ruse (pə ro͞oz´) vt., read carefully; examine

Six years have passed since I resolved on my present undertaking. I can, even now, remember the hour from which I dedicated myself to this great enterprise. I commenced by <u>inuring</u> my body to hardship. I accompanied the whale-fishers on several expeditions to the North Sea; I voluntarily endured cold, famine, thirst, and want of sleep; I often worked harder than the common sailors during the day and devoted my nights to the study of mathematics, the theory of medicine, and those branches of physical science from which a naval adventurer might derive the greatest practical advantage. Twice I actually hired myself as an under-mate in a Greenland whaler, and acquitted myself to admiration. I must own I felt a little proud when my captain offered me the second dignity[5] in the vessel and entreated me to remain with the greatest <u>earnestness</u>, so valuable did he consider my services.

And now, dear Margaret, do I not deserve to accomplish some great purpose? My life might have been passed in ease and luxury, but I preferred glory to every enticement that wealth placed in my path. Oh, that some encouraging voice would answer in the affirmative! My courage and my resolution are firm; but my hopes <u>fluctuate</u> and my spirits are often depressed. I am about to proceed on a long and difficult voyage, the emergencies of which will demand all my fortitude: I am required not only to raise the spirits of others, but sometimes to sustain my own, when theirs are failing.

◄ *What does the narrator seek in his life?*

This is the most favorable period for traveling in Russia. They fly quickly over the snow in their sledges; the motion is pleasant, and, in my opinion, far more agreeable than that of an English stagecoach. The cold is not excessive, if you are wrapped in furs—a dress which I have already adopted, for there is a great difference between walking the deck and remaining seated motionless for hours, when no exercise prevents the blood from actually freezing in your veins. I have no ambition to lose my life on the post-road between St. Petersburgh and Archangel.[6]

◄ *What differences does the narrator note between England and Russia? In what ways has he adapted to his current surroundings?*

I shall depart for the latter town in a fortnight or three weeks; and my intention is to hire a ship there, which can easily be done by paying the insurance for the owner, and to

---

5. **second dignity.** Second highest rank
6. **Archangel.** Seaport in northwestern Russia

Words
For
Everyday
Use

in • ure (in yo͞or´) *vt.*, make accustomed to
ear • nest • ness (ʉr´nist nəs) *n.*, seriousness
fluc • tu • ate (fluk´cho͞o āt´) *vi.*, rise and fall

engage as many sailors as I think necessary among those who are accustomed to the whale-fishing. I do not intend to sail until the month of June; and when shall I return? Ah, dear sister, how can I answer this question? If I succeed, many, many months, perhaps years, will pass before you and I may meet. If I fail, you will see me again soon, or never.

Farewell, my dear, excellent Margaret. Heaven shower down blessings on you, and save me, that I may again and again testify my gratitude for all your love and kindness.

Your affectionate brother,
R. Walton.

Letter 2

To Mrs. Saville, England.

Archangel, 28th March, 17—

How slowly the time passes here, encompassed as I am by frost and snow! Yet a second step is taken towards my enterprise. I have hired a vessel and am occupied in collecting my sailors; those whom I have already engaged appear to be men on whom I can depend and are certainly possessed of <u>dauntless</u> courage.

But I have one want which I have never yet been able to satisfy, and the absence of the object of which I now feel as a most severe evil. I have no friend, Margaret: when I am glowing with the enthusiasm of success, there will be none to participate my joy; if I am <u>assailed</u> by disappointment, no one will endeavor to sustain me in dejection. I shall commit my thoughts to paper, it is true; but that is a poor medium for the communication of feeling. I desire the company of a man who could sympathize with me, whose eyes would reply to mine. You may deem me romantic, my dear sister, but I bitterly feel the want of a friend. I have no one near me, gentle yet courageous, possessed of a cultivated as well as of a <u>capacious</u> mind, whose tastes are like my own, to approve or amend my plans. How would such a friend repair the faults of your poor brother! I am too ardent in execution, and too impatient of difficulties. But it is a still greater evil to me that I am self-educated: for the first fourteen years of my life I ran wild on a common and read nothing but our Uncle Thomas's books of voyages. At that age I became acquainted with the celebrated poets of our own country; but it was only when it had ceased to be in my power to derive its most important benefits from such a conviction that I perceived the necessity of becoming acquainted with more languages than that of my native country. Now I am twenty-eight and am in reality more illiterate than many schoolboys of fifteen. It is true that I have thought more and that my daydreams are more extended and magnificent, but they want (as the painters call it) *keeping;* and I greatly need a friend who would have sense enough not to despise me as romantic, and affection enough for me to endeavor to regulate my mind.

◄ *Who is missing in the narrator's life? What would Walton expect from such a person?*

Words For Everyday Use	**daunt • less** (dônt´lis) *adj.,* fearless
	as • sail (ə sāl´) *vt.,* attack; assault
	ca • pa • cious (kə pā´shəs) *adj.,* able to contain or hold much

Well, these are useless complaints; I shall certainly find no friend on the wide ocean, nor even here in Archangel, among merchants and seamen. Yet some feelings, <u>unallied</u> to the dross[1] of human nature, beat even in these rugged bosoms. My lieutenant, for instance, is a man of wonderful courage and enterprise; he is madly desirous of glory, or rather, to word my phrase more characteristically, of advancement in his profession. He is an Englishman, and in the midst of national and professional prejudices, unsoftened by cultivation, retains some of the noblest <u>endowments</u> of humanity. I first became acquainted with him on board a whale vessel; finding that he was unemployed in this city, I easily engaged him to assist in my enterprise.

▶ What qualities does Walton note in his lieutenant?

The master[2] is a person of an excellent disposition and is remarkable in the ship for his gentleness and the mildness of his discipline. This circumstance, added to his well-known <u>integrity</u> and dauntless courage, made me very desirous to engage him. A youth passed in solitude, my best years spent under your gentle and feminine fosterage, has so refined the groundwork of my character that I cannot overcome an intense distaste to the usual brutality exercised on board ship: I have never believed it to be necessary, and when I heard of a mariner equally noted for his kindliness of heart and the respect and obedience paid to him by his crew, I felt myself peculiarly fortunate in being able to secure his services. I heard of him first in rather a romantic manner, from a lady who owes to him the happiness of her life. This, briefly, is his story. Some years ago he loved a young Russian lady of moderate fortune, and having amassed a considerable sum in prize-money, the father of the girl consented to the match. He saw his mistress once before the destined ceremony; but she was bathed in tears, and throwing herself at his feet, entreated him to spare her, confessing at the same time that she loved another, but that he was poor, and that her father would never consent to the union. My generous friend reassured the <u>suppliant</u>, and on being informed of the name of her lover, instantly abandoned his pursuit. He had already bought a farm with his money, on which he had designed to pass the remainder of his life; but he bestowed the whole on

▶ For what reason does Walton choose the master of the ship? In what way does his sister's influence show in this choice?

▶ What actions in the history of the master does Walton find admirable?

---

1. **dross.** Something that is trivial or inferior
2. **master.** Person licensed to command a merchant ship

Words For Everyday Use

un • al • lied (un´ə līd´) *adj.*, not united

en • dow • ment (en dou´mənt) *n.*, gift of nature; inherent ability

in • teg • ri • ty (in teg´rə tē) *n.*, uprightness, honesty, and sincerity

sup • pli • ant (sup´lē ənt) *n.*, petitioner; person who makes a request

his rival, together with the remains of his prize-money to purchase stock, and then himself solicited the young woman's father to consent to her marriage with her lover. But the old man decidedly refused, thinking himself bound in honor to my friend, who, when he found the father <u>inexorable</u>, quitted his country, nor returned until he heard that his former mistress was married according to her inclinations. "What a noble fellow!" you will exclaim. He is so; but then he is wholly uneducated: he is as silent as a Turk, and a kind of ignorant carelessness attends him, which, while it renders his conduct the more astonishing, detracts from the interest and sympathy which otherwise he would command.

◀ What does Walton find lacking in the master? In what way does this lack affect Walton's opinion of the man?

Yet do not suppose, because I complain a little, or because I can conceive a consolation for my toils which I may never know, that I am wavering in my resolutions. Those are as fixed as fate; and my voyage is only now delayed until the weather shall permit my embarkation. The winter has been dreadfully severe, but the spring promises well, and it is considered as a remarkably early season, so that perhaps I may sail sooner than I expected. I shall do nothing <u>rashly</u>: you know me sufficiently to confide in my <u>prudence</u> and considerateness whenever the safety of others is committed to my care.

I cannot describe to you my sensations on the near prospect of undertaking. It is impossible to communicate to you a conception of the trembling sensation, half pleasurable and half fearful, with which I am preparing to depart. I am going to unexplored regions, to "the land of mist and snow," but I shall kill no albatross; therefore do not be alarmed for my safety or if I should come back to you as worn and woeful as the "Ancient Mariner."[3] You will smile at my allusion, but I will disclose a secret. I have often attributed my attachment to, my passionate enthusiasm for, the dangerous mysteries of ocean to that production of the most imaginative of modern poets. There is something at work in my soul which I do not understand. I am practically industrious—painstaking, a workman to execute with perseverance and labor—but

◀ What mixed feelings does Walton have as he prepares to depart?

◀ What does Walton mean when he says he will "kill no albatross"?

---

3. **kill no albatross . . . "Ancient Mariner."** In "The Rime of the Ancient Mariner," a poem by Samuel Taylor Coleridge, the ancient mariner kills an albatross, a large, web-footed sea bird, thus bringing a curse on the ship and his crew. The phrase "an albatross around one's neck" means a distressing burden or sense of guilt.

Words For Everyday Use

in • ex • or • a • ble (in eks´ə rə bəl) *adj.*, unrelenting
rash • ly (rash´lē) *adv.*, recklessly; hastily
pru • dence (prōōd´'ns) *n.*, cautiousness; discretion

besides this there is a love for the marvelous, a belief in the marvelous, intertwined in all my projects, which hurries me out of the common pathways of men, even to the wild sea and unvisited regions I am about to explore.

► Explain whether Walton is optimistic about the outcome of his venture.

But to return to dearer considerations. Shall I meet you again, after having <u>traversed</u> immense seas, and returned by the most southern cape of Africa or America? I dare not expect such success, yet I cannot bear to look on the reverse of the picture. Continue for the present to write to me by every opportunity: I may receive your letters on some occasions when I need them most to support my spirits. I love you very tenderly. Remember me with affection, should you never hear from me again.

Your affectionate brother,
Robert Walton.

Words
For
Everyday
Use

tra • verse (trə vʉrs´) *vt.*, cross

Letter 3

To Mrs. Saville, England.

July 7th, 17—

My dear Sister,—I write a few lines in haste, to say that I am safe and well advanced on my voyage. This letter will reach England by a merchantman now on its homeward voyage from Archangel; more fortunate than I, who may not see my native land, perhaps, for many years. I am, however, in good spirits: my men are bold and apparently firm of purpose, nor do the floating sheets of ice that continually pass us, indicating the dangers of the region towards which we are advancing, appear to dismay them. We have already reached a very high latitude;[1] but it is the height of summer, and although not so warm as in England, the southern gales, which blow us speedily towards those shores which I so <u>ardently</u> desire to attain, breathe a degree of renovating warmth which I had not expected.

No incidents have hitherto befallen us that would make a figure in a letter. One or two stiff gales, and the springing of a leak, are accidents which experienced navigators scarcely remember to record, and I shall be well content if nothing worse happen to us during our voyage.

Adieu,[2] my dear Margaret. Be assured that for my own sake, as well as yours, I will not rashly encounter danger. I will be cool, persevering, and prudent.

But success *shall* crown my endeavors. Wherefore[3] not? Thus far I have gone, tracing a secure way over the pathless seas, the very stars themselves being witnesses and testimonies of my triumph. Why not still proceed over the untamed yet obedient element? What can stop the determined heart and resolved will of man?

My swelling heart involuntarily pours itself out thus. But I must finish. Heaven bless my beloved sister!

R.W.

How does Walton feel about his journey so far? What does he see as the positive and negative aspects of the situation?

---

1. **latitude.** Distance from the equator
2. **Adieu.** Farewell
3. **Wherefore.** Why

Words For Everyday Use

ar • dent • ly (ärd´ 'nt lē) *adv.*, passionately; eagerly

Letter 4

To Mrs. Saville, England.

August 5th, 17—

So strange an accident has happened to us that I cannot forbear recording it, although it is very probable that you will see me before these papers can come into your possession.

► In what dangerous situation do Walton and his crew find themselves on July 31?

Last Monday (July 31st), we were nearly surrounded by ice, which closed in the ship on all sides, scarcely leaving her the sea-room in which she floated. Our situation was somewhat dangerous, especially as we were compassed round by a very thick fog. We accordingly lay to,[1] hoping that some change would take place in the atmosphere and weather.

About two o'clock the mist cleared away, and we beheld, stretched out in every direction, vast and irregular plains of ice, which seemed to have no end. Some of my comrades groaned, and my own mind began to grow watchful with anxious thoughts, when a strange sight suddenly attracted our attention and diverted our solicitude from our own situation. We perceived a low carriage, fixed on a sledge and drawn by dogs, pass on towards the north, at the distance of half a mile; a being which had the shape of a man, but apparently of gigantic stature, sat in the sledge and guided the dogs. We watched the rapid progress of the traveler with our telescopes until he was lost among the distant inequalities of the ice.

► What do Walton and his comrades see? Why is this figure strange?

This appearance excited our unqualified wonder. We were, as we believed, many hundred miles from any land; but this apparition seemed to denote that it was not, in reality, so distant as we had supposed. Shut in, however, by ice, it was impossible to follow his track, which we had observed with the greatest attention.

► What sound occurs two hours after the strange sight? What might this occurrence mean for the figure Walton saw?

About two hours after this occurrence we heard the ground sea, and before night the ice broke and freed our ship. We, however, lay to until the morning, fearing to encounter in the dark those large loose masses which float about after the breaking up of the ice. I profited of this time to rest for a few hours.

---

1. **lay to.** Kept the ship at anchor

Words For Everyday Use

so • lic • i • tude (sə lis´ə tōōd) *n.*, excessive care or concern

ap • pa • ri • tion (ap´ə rish´ən) *n.*, anything that appears unexpectedly or in an extraordinary way

de • note (dē nōt´) *vt.*, indicate

In the morning, however, as soon as it was light, I went upon the deck and found all the sailors busy on one side of the vessel, apparently talking to someone in the sea. It was, in fact, a sledge, like that we had seen before, which had drifted towards us in the night on a large fragment of ice. Only one dog remained alive; but there was a human being within it whom the sailors were persuading to enter the vessel. He was not, as the other traveler seemed to be, a savage inhabitant of some undiscovered island, but a European. When I appeared on deck the master said, "Here is our captain, and he will not allow you to perish on the open sea."

On perceiving me, the stranger addressed me in English, although with a foreign accent. "Before I come on board your vessel," said he, "will you have the kindness to inform me whither² you are bound?"

You may conceive my astonishment on hearing such a question addressed to me from a man on the brink of destruction and to whom I should have supposed that my vessel would have been a resource which he would not have exchanged for the most precious wealth the earth can afford. I replied, however, that we were on a voyage of discovery towards the northern pole.

Upon hearing this he appeared satisfied and consented to come on board. Good God! Margaret, if you had seen the man who thus <u>capitulated</u> for his safety, your surprise would have been boundless. His limbs were nearly frozen, and his body dreadfully <u>emaciated</u> by fatigue and suffering. I never saw a man in so wretched a condition. We attempted to carry him into the cabin, but as soon as he had quitted the fresh air he fainted. We accordingly brought him back to the deck and restored him to <u>animation</u> by rubbing him with brandy and forcing him to swallow a small quantity. As soon as he showed signs of life we wrapped him up in blankets and placed him near the chimney of the kitchen stove. By slow degrees he recovered and ate a little soup, which restored him wonderfully.

Two days passed in this manner before he was able to speak and I often feared that his sufferings had deprived him of understanding. When he had in some measure recovered, I

◄ In what way does the man being persuaded to enter the ship differ from the figure seen the night before?

◄ What does the traveler ask? Why is this question strange?

---

2. **whither.** Where

Words For Everyday Use	**ca • pit • u • late** (kə pich′ yōō lāt′) *vi.,* give up; stop resisting
	e • ma • ci • ate (ē mā′shē āt′) *vt.,* cause to become abnormally thin, as by starvation
	an • i • ma • tion (an′i mā′shən) *n.,* life; liveliness

► Why does Walton find the stranger's eyes interesting?

removed him to my own cabin and attended on him as much as my duty would permit. I never saw a more interesting creature: his eyes have generally an expression of wildness, and even madness, but there are moments when, if anyone performs an act of kindness towards him or does him the most <u>trifling</u> service, his whole <u>countenance</u> is lighted up, as it were, with a beam of <u>benevolence</u> and sweetness that I never saw equaled. But he is generally <u>melancholy</u> and despairing, and sometimes he gnashes his teeth, as if impatient of the weight of woes that oppresses him.

When my guest was a little recovered I had great trouble to keep off the men, who wished to ask him a thousand questions; but I would not allow him to be tormented by their idle curiosity, in a state of body and mind whose restoration evidently depended upon entire repose. Once, however, the lieutenant asked why he had come so far upon the ice in so strange a vehicle.

► Why had the stranger been traveling in such an odd manner?

His countenance instantly assumed an aspect of the deepest gloom, and he replied, "To seek one who fled from me."

"And did the man whom you pursued travel in the same fashion?"

"Yes."

"Then I fancy we have seen him, for the day before we picked you up we saw some dogs drawing a sledge, with a man in it, across the ice."

This aroused the stranger's attention, and he asked a multitude of questions concerning the route which the demon, as he called him, had pursued. Soon after, when he was alone with me, he said, "I have, doubtless, excited your curiosity, as well as that of these good people; but you are too considerate to make inquiries."

"Certainly; it would indeed be very <u>impertinent</u> and inhuman in me to trouble you with any inquisitiveness of mine."

"And yet you rescued me from a strange and perilous situation; you have benevolently restored me to life."

► What might have happened to the other figure? Why is Walton unable to say for sure?

Soon after this he inquired if I thought that the breaking up of the ice had destroyed the other sledge. I replied that I could not answer with any degree of certainty, for the ice had not broken until near midnight, and the traveler might have arrived at a place of safety before that time; but of this I could not judge.

Words For Everyday Use

tri • fling (trī′fliŋ) *adj.*, trivial; of little value or importance
coun • te • nance (koun′tə nəns) *n.*, face
be • nev • o • lence (bə nev′ə ləns) *n.*, kindness

mel • an • chol • y (mel′ən käl′ē) *adj.*, sad and depressed; gloomy
im • per • ti • nent (im pʉrt′'n ənt) *adj.*, disrespectful; insolent

From this time a new spirit of life animated the decaying frame of the stranger. He <u>manifested</u> the greatest eagerness to be upon deck to watch for the sledge which had before appeared; but I have persuaded him to remain in the cabin, for he is far too weak to sustain the rawness of the atmosphere. I have promised that someone should watch for him and give him instant notice if any new object should appear in sight.

Such is my journal of what relates to this strange occurrence up to the present day. The stranger has gradually improved in health but is very silent and appears uneasy when anyone except myself enters his cabin. Yet his manners are so <u>conciliating</u> and gentle that the sailors are all interested in him, although they have had very little communication with him. For my own part, I begin to love him as a brother, and his constant and deep grief fills me with sympathy and compassion. He must have been a noble creature in his better days, being even now in wreck so attractive and amiable.

I said in one of my letters, my dear Margaret, that I should find no friend on the wide ocean; yet I have found a man who, before his spirit had been broken by misery, I should have been happy to have possessed as the brother of my heart.

I shall continue my journal concerning the stranger at intervals, should I have any fresh incidents to record.

◄ In what way does the stranger fill the one thing Walton is lacking?

August 13, 17—

My affection for my guest increases every day. He excites at once my admiration and my pity to an astonishing degree. How can I see so noble a creature destroyed by misery without feeling the most <u>poignant</u> grief? He is so gentle, yet so wise; his mind is so cultivated, and when he speaks, although his words are <u>culled</u> with the choicest art, yet they flow with rapidity and unparalleled eloquence.

He is now much recovered from his illness and is continually on deck, apparently watching for the sledge that preceded his own. Yet, although unhappy, he is not so utterly occupied by his own misery but that he interests himself deeply in the projects of others. He has frequently conversed with me on mine, which I have communicated to him without disguise. He entered attentively into all my arguments in favor of my

---

Words For Everyday Use

man • i • fest (man´ə fest´) vt., show plainly
con • cil • i • at • ing (kən sil´ē āt´iŋ) adj., soothing; placating

poign • ant (poin´yənt) adj., sharply painful; evoking pity; emotionally touching
cull (kul) vt., select

► What is Walton willing to sacrifice to achieve his goals? How does the stranger react to Walton's assertions?

eventual success and into every minute detail of the measures I had taken to secure it. I was easily led by the sympathy which he <u>evinced</u> to use the language of my heart, to give utterance to the burning ardor of my soul, and to say, with all the fervor that warmed me, how gladly I would sacrifice my fortune, my existence, my every hope, to the furtherance of my enterprise. One man's life or death were but a small price to pay for the acquirement of the knowledge which I sought, for the dominion I should acquire and transmit over the elemental foes of our race. As I spoke, a dark gloom spread over my listener's countenance. At first I perceived that he tried to suppress his emotion; he placed his hands before his eyes, and my voice quivered and failed me as I beheld tears trickle fast from between his fingers; a groan burst from his heaving breast. I paused; at length he spoke, in broken accents: "Unhappy man! Do you share my madness? Have you drank also of the intoxicating draught? Hear me; let me reveal my tale, and you will dash the cup from your lips!"

Such words, you may imagine, strongly excited my curiosity; but the <u>paroxysm</u> of grief that had seized the stranger overcame his weakened powers, and many hours of repose and tranquil conversation were necessary to restore his composure.

Having conquered the violence of his feelings, he appeared to despise himself for being the slave of passion; and <u>quelling</u> the dark tyranny of despair, he led me again to converse concerning myself personally. He asked me the history of my earlier years. The tale was quickly told, but it awakened various trains of reflection. I spoke of my desire of finding a friend, of my thirst for a more intimate sympathy with a fellow mind than had ever fallen to my lot, and expressed my conviction that a man could boast of little happiness who did not enjoy this blessing.

► Why does the stranger think he is fit to judge friendship? What difference does the stranger note between Walton and himself?

"I agree with you," replied the stranger; "we are unfashioned creatures, but half made up, if one wiser, better, dearer than ourselves—such a friend ought to be—do not lend his aid to perfectionate our weak and faulty natures. I once had a friend, the most noble of human creatures, and am entitled, therefore, to judge respecting friendship. You have hope, and the world before you, and have no cause for despair. But I—I have lost everything, and cannot begin life anew."

Words For Everyday Use	e • vince (ē vins´) vt., indicate; show plainly
	par • ox • ysm (par´əks iz´əm) n., sudden convulsion or outburst
	quell (kwel) vt., subdue; put an end to

As he said this his countenance became expressive of a calm, settled grief that touched me to the heart. But he was silent and presently retired to his cabin.

Even broken in spirit as he is, no one can feel more deeply than he does the beauties of nature. The starry sky, the sea, and every sight afforded by these wonderful regions seem still to have the power of elevating his soul from earth. Such a man has a double existence: he may suffer misery and be overwhelmed by disappointments, yet, when he has retired into himself, he will be like a celestial spirit that has a halo around him, within whose circle no grief or folly ventures.

◀ What effect, according to Walton, does nature have on the stranger?

Will you smile at the enthusiasm I express concerning this divine wanderer? You would not if you saw him. You have been tutored and refined by books and retirement from the world, and you are therefore somewhat <u>fastidious</u>; but this only renders you the more fit to appreciate the extraordinary merits of this wonderful man. Sometimes I have endeavored to discover what quality it is which he possesses that elevates him so immeasurably above any other person I ever knew. I believe it to be an <u>intuitive</u> discernment, a quick but never-failing power of judgment, a penetration into the causes of things, unequaled for clearness and precision; add to this a facility of expression, and a voice whose varied intonations are soul-subduing music.

◀ What quality does Walton feel makes the stranger exceptional?

August 19, 17—

Yesterday the stranger said to me, "You may easily perceive, Captain Walton, that I have suffered great and unparalleled misfortunes. I had determined at one time that the memory of these evils should die with me, but you have won me to alter my determination. You seek for knowledge and wisdom, as I once did; and I ardently hope that the gratification of your wishes may not be a serpent to sting you, as mine has been. I do not know that the relation of my disasters will be useful to you; yet, when I reflect that you are pursuing the same course, exposing yourself to the same dangers which have <u>rendered</u> me what I am, I imagine that you may deduce an apt moral from my tale, one that may direct you if you succeed in your undertaking, and console you in case of failure. Prepare to hear of occurrences which are usually deemed marvelous. Were we among the tamer scenes of nature I

◀ Why does the stranger tell Walton his tale?

Words For Everyday Use

fas • tid • i • ous (fas tid´ē əs) *adj.*, hard to please; oversensitive

in • tu • i • tive (in tōō´i tiv) *adj.*, having to do with perceptions or knowledge that are not based on conscious reasoning

ren • der (ren´dər) *vt.*, cause to be or become; make

► What effect does the stranger think the setting will have on Walton's ability to believe his story?

might fear to encounter your unbelief, perhaps your ridicule; but many things will appear possible in these wild and mysterious regions which would provoke the laughter of those unacquainted with the ever-varied powers of nature; nor can I doubt but that my tale conveys in its series internal evidence of the truth of the events of which it is composed."

You may easily imagine that I was much gratified by the offered communication, yet I could not endure that he should renew his grief by a recital of his misfortunes. I felt the greatest eagerness to hear the promised narrative, partly from curiosity and partly from a strong desire to <u>ameliorate</u> his fate, if it were in my power. I expressed these feelings in my answer.

► For what does the stranger wait?

"I thank you," he replied, "for your sympathy, but it is useless; my fate is nearly fulfilled. I wait but for one event, and then I shall repose in peace. I understand your feeling," continued he, perceiving that I wished to interrupt him; "but you are mistaken, my friend, if thus you will allow me to name you; nothing can alter my destiny; listen to my history, and you will perceive how <u>irrevocably</u> it is determined."

He then told me that he would commence his narrative the next day when I should be at leisure. This promise drew from me the warmest thanks. I have resolved every night, when I am not imperatively occupied by my duties, to record, as nearly as possible in his own words, what he has related during the day. If I should be engaged, I will at least make notes. This manuscript will doubtless afford you the greatest pleasure; but to me, who know him and who hear it from his own lips—with what interest and sympathy shall I read it in some future day! Even now, as I commence my task, his full-toned voice swells in my ears; his <u>lustrous</u> eyes dwell on me with all their melancholy sweetness; I see his thin hand raised in animation, while the lineaments of his face are <u>irradiated</u> by the soul within. Strange and harrowing must be his story, frightful the storm which embraced the gallant vessel on its course and wrecked it—thus!

Words For Everyday Use

a • mel • io • rate (ə mēl´yə rāt) vt., improve; make better

ir • rev • o • ca • bly (ir rev´ə kə blē) adv., unalterably

lus • trous (lus´trəs) adj., bright; shining

ir • ra • di • ate (ir rā´dē āt) vt., illuminate; light up; make bright

Responding to the Selection

Walton waits eagerly to hear the stranger's tale. What do you think the stranger will say? In what way do you think his tale will serve as a warning to Walton?

Reviewing the Selection

Recalling and Interpreting

1. **R:** According to the preface and the author's introduction, under what circumstances was *Frankenstein* written?

2. **I:** Percy Shelley wrote the preface to the first edition (1818) while Mary Shelley wrote her own introduction to the 1831 edition. In what way do these two introductory works differ in subject and style?

3. **R:** To whom does the narrator write? From where does he write? What is the purpose of his voyage?

4. **I:** What are the narrator's main goals? Based on his first letter, what qualities do you note in the narrator?

5. **R:** What is one thing Walton says he is missing? Who fills this need for him?

6. **I:** In what way does the stranger differ from the various members of the crew Walton has described?

7. **R:** What strange sight does the crew see one day? What question does the stranger they pick up the following day ask? What is the stranger's goal?

8. **I:** In what way is the stranger's goal similar to Walton's goal? Why is the stranger upset when he hears what Walton is willing to do to reach his goal?

Synthesizing

9. What ideas did you have about *Frankenstein* when you began reading? In what way do the letters at the beginning of the story relate to these ideas?

10. Describe the role of contemporary scientific ideas in the writing of *Frankenstein*.

Understanding Literature (QUESTIONS FOR DISCUSSION)

1. Frame Tale, Epistolary Novel, and Theme. A **frame tale** is a story that itself provides a vehicle for the telling of other stories. An **epistolary novel** is a work of imaginative prose that tells a story through letters. The letters at the beginning of *Frankenstein* act as a frame to the story told by the stranger Walton's crew rescues. A **theme** is a central idea in a literary work. What themes are introduced in this epistolary frame?

2. Setting. The **setting** of a literary work is the time and place in which it occurs, together with all the details used to create a sense of a particular time and place. Describe the setting of the story thus far. What effect does this setting have on Walton? on the stranger?

3. Allusion. An **allusion** is a rhetorical technique in which reference is made to a person, event, object, or work from history or literature. In Letter 2, Walton alludes to Samuel Taylor Coleridge's "The Rime of the Ancient Mariner." What does this allusion suggest about Walton's plan?

Chapter 1

I am by birth a Genevese[1] and my family is one of the most distinguished of that republic. My ancestors had been for many years counselors and syndics,[2] and my father had filled several public situations with honor and reputation. He was respected by all who knew him for his integrity and <u>indefatigable</u> attention to public business. He passed his younger days perpetually occupied by the affairs of his country; a variety of circumstances had prevented his marrying early, nor was it until the decline of life that he became a husband and the father of a family.

◀ Describe the narrator's family background.

As the circumstances of his marriage illustrate his character, I cannot refrain from relating them. One of his most intimate friends was a merchant who, from a flourishing state, fell, through numerous mischances, into poverty. This man, whose name was Beaufort, was of a proud and unbending <u>disposition</u>, and could not bear to live in poverty and <u>oblivion</u> in the same country where he had formerly been distinguished for his rank and magnificence. Having paid his debts, therefore, in the most honorable manner, he retreated with his daughter to the town of Lucerne,[3] where he lived unknown and in wretchedness. My father loved Beaufort with the truest friendship and was deeply grieved by his retreat in these unfortunate circumstances. He bitterly deplored the false pride which led his friend to a conduct so little worthy of the affection that united them. He lost no time in endeavoring to seek him out, with the hope of persuading him to begin the world again through his credit and assistance.

◀ What kind of man is Beaufort? Why does the narrator's father seek out Beaufort?

Beaufort had taken effectual measures to conceal himself, and it was ten months before my father discovered his abode. Overjoyed at this discovery, he hastened to the house, which was situated in a mean street, near the Reuss. But when he entered, misery and despair alone welcomed him. Beaufort had saved but a very small sum of money from the wreck of his fortunes, but it was sufficient to provide him

---

1. **Genevese.** Of ancestry from Geneva, Switzerland
2. **syndics.** Government officials
3. **Lucerne.** Capital of a canton, or state, of the same name in central Switzerland

Words For Everyday Use	**in • de • fat • i • ga • ble** (in′di fat′i gə bəl) *adj.,* untiring **dis • po • si • tion** (dis′pə zish′ən) *n.,* nature or temperament; customary frame of mind **ob • liv • i • on** (ə bliv′ē ən) *n.,* condition of being forgotten or overlooked

with sustenance for some months, and in the meantime he hoped to procure some respectable employment in a merchant's house. The interval was, consequently, spent in inaction; his grief only became more deep and <u>rankling</u> when he had leisure for reflection, and at length it took so fast hold of his mind that at the end of three months he lay on a bed of sickness, incapable of any exertion.

► How does Caroline, Beaufort's daughter, react to their situation?

His daughter attended him with the greatest tenderness, but she saw with despair that their little fund was rapidly decreasing and that there was no other prospect of support. But Caroline Beaufort possessed a mind of an uncommon mold, and her courage rose to support her in her adversity. She procured plain work; she plaited straw and by various means contrived to earn a <u>pittance</u> scarcely sufficient to support life.

► What happens to Caroline when Beaufort dies?

Several months passed in this manner. Her father grew worse; her time was more entirely occupied in attending him; her means of subsistence decreased; and in the tenth month her father died in her arms, leaving her an orphan and a beggar. This last blow overcame her, and she knelt by Beaufort's coffin weeping bitterly, when my father entered the chamber. He came like a protecting spirit to the poor girl, who committed herself to his care; and after the interment of his friend, he conducted her to Geneva, and placed her under the protection of a relation. Two years after this event Caroline became his wife.

► On what does the narrator's father base his love for the narrator's mother?

There was a considerable difference between the ages of my parents, but this circumstance seemed to unite them only closer in bonds of devoted affection. There was a sense of justice in my father's upright mind which rendered it necessary that he should approve highly to love strongly. Perhaps during former years he had suffered from the late-discovered unworthiness of one beloved and so was disposed to set a greater value on tried worth. There was a show of gratitude and worship in his attachment to my mother, differing wholly from the <u>doting</u> fondness of age, for it was inspired by reverence for her virtues and a desire to be the means of, in some degree, recompensing her for the sorrows she had endured, but which gave inexpressible grace to his behavior to her. Everything was made to yield to her wishes and her convenience. He strove to shelter her, as a fair exotic is sheltered by the gardener, from every rougher wind and to surround

Words For Everyday Use	**ran • kling** (raŋ´kliŋ) *adj.,* causing anger or resentment
	pit • tance (pit´´ns) *n.,* small amount; barely sufficient sum of money
	dot • ing (dōt´iŋ) *adj.,* foolishly or excessively fond

her with all that could tend to excite pleasurable emotion in her soft and benevolent mind. Her health, and even the tranquility of her hitherto constant spirit, had been shaken by what she had gone through. During the two years that had elapsed previous to their marriage my father had gradually relinquished all his public functions; and immediately after their union they sought the pleasant climate of Italy, and the change of scene and interest attendant on a tour through that land of wonders, as a restorative for her weakened frame.

From Italy they visited Germany and France. I, their eldest child, was born at Naples,[4] and as an infant accompanied them in their rambles. I remained for several years their only child. Much as they were attached to each other, they seemed to draw inexhaustible stores of affection from a very mine of love to bestow them upon me. My mother's tender caresses and my father's smile of benevolent pleasure while regarding me are my first recollections. I was their plaything and their idol, and something better—their child, the innocent and helpless creature bestowed on them by heaven, whom to bring up to good, and whose future lot it was in their hands to direct to happiness fulfilled their duties towards me. With this deep consciousness of what they owed towards the being to which they had given life, added to the active spirit of tenderness that animated both, it may be imagined that while during every hour of my infant life I received a lesson of patience, of charity, and of self-control, I was so guided by a silken cord that all seemed but one train of enjoyment to me.

◀ What are the first things the narrator remembers? In what way do his parents view their child? What attitude do they have toward the being to whom they have given life?

For a long time I was their only care. My mother had much desired to have a daughter, but I continued their single offspring. When I was about five years old, while making an excursion beyond the frontiers of Italy, they passed a week on the shores of the Lake of Como. Their benevolent disposition often made them enter the cottages of the poor. This, to my mother, was more than a duty; it was a necessity, a passion—remembering what she had suffered, and how she had been relieved—for her to act in her turn the guardian angel to the afflicted. During one of their walks a poor cot in the foldings of a vale attracted their notice as being singularly <u>disconsolate</u>,

◀ Why do the narrator's parents, especially his mother, often enter the cottages of the poor?

---

4. **Naples.** City in southern Italy

Words For Everyday Use   **dis • con • so • late** (dis kän′sə lit) *adj.,* dejected; inconsolable

while the number of half-clothed children gathered about it spoke of <u>penury</u> in its worst shape. One day, when my father had gone by himself to Milan,[5] my mother, accompanied by me, visited this abode. She found a peasant and his wife, hard working, bent down by care and labor, distributing a scanty meal to five hungry babes. Among these there was one which attracted my mother far above all the rest. She appeared of a different stock. The four others were dark-eyed, hardy little vagrants; this child was thin, and very fair. Her hair was the brightest living gold, and despite the poverty of her clothing, seemed to set a crown of distinction on her head. Her brow was clear and ample, her blue eyes cloudless, and her lips and the molding of her face so expressive of sensibility and sweetness that none could behold her without looking on her as of a distinct species, a being heaven-sent, and bearing a celestial stamp[6] in all her features.

The peasant woman, perceiving that my mother fixed eyes of wondering admiration on this lovely girl, eagerly communicated her history. She was not her child, but the daughter of a Milanese nobleman. Her mother was a German and had died on giving her birth. The infant had been placed with these good people to nurse: they were better off then. They had not been long married, and their eldest child was but just born. The father of their charge was one of those Italians nursed in the memory of the antique glory of Italy—one among the *schiavi ognor frementi*,[7] who exerted himself to obtain the liberty of his country. He became the victim of weakness. Whether he had died or still lingered in the dungeons of Austria, was not known. His property was confiscated; his child became an orphan and a beggar. She continued with her foster parents and bloomed in their rude abode, fairer than a garden rose among dark-leaved brambles.

When my father returned from Milan, he found playing with me in the hall of our villa a child fairer than pictured cherub—a creature who seemed to shed radiance from her looks and whose form and motions were lighter than the chamois of the hills. The apparition was soon explained. With his permission my mother <u>prevailed</u> on her rustic

▶ How does the child who attracts attention differ from the other four children?

▶ What happened to this child's parents?

---

5. **Milan.** City in northwestern Italy
6. **celestial stamp.** Sign of blessings from the heavens
7. ***schiavi ognor frementi.*** Slaves who trembled under Austrian rule

Words For Everyday Use

pen • u • ry (pen′yo͞o rē) *n.*, poverty; destitution
pre • vail (prē vāl′) *vi.*, persuade; induce

guardians to yield their charge to her. They were fond of the sweet orphan. Her presence had seemed a blessing to them, but it would be unfair to her to keep her in poverty and want when Providence[8] afforded her such powerful protection. They consulted their village priest, and the result was that Elizabeth Lavenza became the inmate of my parents' house—my more than sister—the beautiful and adored companion of all my occupations and my pleasures.

Everyone loved Elizabeth. The passionate and almost <u>reverential</u> attachment with which all regarded her became, while I shared it, my pride and my delight. On the evening previous to her being brought to my home, my mother had said playfully, "I have a pretty present for my Victor—tomorrow he shall have it." And when, on the morrow, she presented Elizabeth to me as her promised gift, I, with childish seriousness, interpreted her words literally, and looked upon Elizabeth as mine—mine to protect, love, and cherish. All praises bestowed on her I received as made to a possession of my own. We called each other familiarly by the name of cousin. No word, no expression could body forth the kind of relation in which she stood to me—my more than sister, since till death she was to be mine only.

◀ *What "present" does Victor's mother give him? In what way does he interpret his mother's words?*

---

8. **Providence.** God as the guiding power of the universe

Words For Everyday Use

rev • er • en • tial (rev´ə ren´shəl) *adj.,* showing or caused by deep respect, love, or awe

Chapter 2

We were brought up together; there was not quite a year difference in our ages. I need not say that we were strangers to any species of disunion or dispute. Harmony was the soul of our companionship, and the diversity and contrast that subsisted in our characters drew us nearer together. Elizabeth was of a calmer and more concentrated disposition; but, with all my ardor, I was capable of a more intense application, and was more deeply smitten with a thirst for knowledge. She busied herself with following the aerial creations of the poets; and in the majestic and wondrous scenes which surrounded our Swiss home—the sublime shapes of the mountains, the changes of the seasons, tempest and calm, the silence of winter, and the life and turbulence of our Alpine summers—she found ample scope for admiration and delight. While my companion <u>contemplated</u> with a serious and satisfied spirit the magnificent appearances of things, I delighted in investigating their causes. The world was to me a secret which I desired to <u>divine</u>. Curiosity, earnest research to learn the hidden laws of nature, gladness akin to rapture, as they were unfolded to me, are among the earliest sensations I can remember.

On the birth of a second son, my junior by seven years, my parents gave up entirely their wandering life and fixed themselves in their native country. We possessed a house in Geneva, and a *campagne*[1] on Belrive, the eastern shore of the lake, at the distance of rather more than a league[2] from the city. We resided principally in the latter, and the lives of my parents were passed in considerable seclusion. It was my temper to avoid a crowd and to attach myself <u>fervently</u> to a few. I was indifferent, therefore, to my schoolfellows in general; but I united myself in the bonds of the closest friendship to one among them. Henry Clerval was the son of a merchant of Geneva. He was a boy of singular talent and fancy. He loved enterprise, hardship, and even danger for its own sake. He was deeply read in books of chivalry and romance. He composed heroic songs and began to write

▶ *What different interests do Elizabeth and Victor pursue?*

▶ *Who is Victor's closest friend? What interests does Victor's friend have?*

---

1. *campagne.* Country estate
2. **league.** Unit of measurement equal to about three miles

Words For Everyday Use

con • tem • plate (kän´ tem plāt´) *vt.,* study carefully

di • vine (də vīn´) *vt.,* find out by intuition

fer • vent • ly (fur´vənt lē) *adv.,* passionately; earnestly

many a tale of enchantment and knightly adventure. He tried to make us act plays and to enter into masquerades, in which the characters were drawn from the heroes of Roncesvalles, of the Round Table of King Arthur, and the chivalrous train who shed their blood to redeem the holy sepulchre from the hands of the infidels.[3]

No human being could have passed a happier childhood than myself. My parents were possessed by the very spirit of kindness and <u>indulgence</u>. We felt that they were not the tyrants to rule our lot according to their <u>caprice</u>, but the agents and creators of all the many delights which we enjoyed. When I mingled with other families, I distinctly discerned how peculiarly fortunate my lot was, and gratitude assisted the development of filial love.

◄ *What opinion does Victor have of his family life in comparison to that of others?*

My temper was sometimes violent, and my passions <u>vehement</u>; but by some law in my temperature they were turned not towards childish pursuits but to an eager desire to learn, and not to learn all things <u>indiscriminately</u>. I confess that neither the structure of languages, nor the code of governments, nor the politics of various states, possessed attractions for me. It was the secrets of heaven and earth that I desired to learn; and whether it was the outward substance of things or the inner spirit of nature and the mysterious soul of man that occupied me, still my inquiries were directed to the metaphysical,[4] or, in its highest sense, the physical secrets of the world.

◄ *About what subject is Victor passionate? To what questions does he seek answers?*

Meanwhile Clerval occupied himself, so to speak, with the moral relations of things. The busy stage of life, the virtues of heroes, and the actions of men were his theme; and his hope and his dream was to become one among those whose names are recorded in story as the gallant and adventurous benefactors of our species. The saintly soul of Elizabeth shone like a shrine-dedicated lamp in our peaceful home. Her sympathy was ours; her smile, her soft voice, the sweet glance of her celestial eyes, were ever there to bless and animate us. She was the living spirit of love to soften and attract; I might have

◄ *Describe Elizabeth's disposition. What effect does she have on Victor?*

---

3. **heroes of Roncesvalles . . . hands of the infidels.** Refers to those who fought in the Battle of Roncesvalles, as recounted in the heroic epic *The Song of Roland;* the legendary knights of King Arthur; and the many Crusaders who fought to return the holy lands to Christian control.
4. **metaphysical.** Supernatural; reality beyond the perception of the senses

Words For Everyday Use		
in • dul • gence (in dul´jəns) *n.,* leniency; act of giving in to the wishes of another		**ve • he • ment** (vē´ə mənt) *adj.,* characterized by intense feelings; forceful
ca • price (kə prēs´) *n.,* whim; sudden, impulsive change of mind or emotion		**in • dis • crim • i • nate • ly** (in´di skrim´i nit lē) *adv.,* randomly; without making sound choices

become sullen in my study, rough through the ardor of my nature, but that she was there to subdue me to a semblance of her own gentleness. And Clerval—could aught ill entrench on the noble spirit of Clerval? Yet he might not have been so perfectly humane, so thoughtful in his generosity, so full of kindness and tenderness amidst his passion for adventurous exploit, had she not unfolded to him the real loveliness of beneficence, and made the doing good the end and aim of his soaring ambition.

I feel exquisite pleasure in dwelling on the recollections of childhood, before misfortune had tainted my mind and changed its bright visions of extensive usefulness into gloomy and narrow reflections upon self. Besides, drawing the picture of early days, I also record those events which led, by insensible steps, to my after tale of misery, for when I would account to myself for the birth of that passion which afterwards ruled my destiny I find it arise, like a mountain river, from <u>ignoble</u> and almost forgotten sources; but, swelling as it proceeded, it became the torrent which, in its course, has swept away all my hopes and joys.

▶ *Why is Victor's childhood relevant to his "tale of misery"?*

Natural philosophy is the genius that has regulated my fate; I desire, therefore, in this narration, to state those facts which led to my predilection for that science. When I was thirteen years of age we all went on a party of pleasure to the baths near Thonon; the <u>inclemency</u> of the weather obliged us to remain a day confined to the inn. In this house I chanced to find a volume of the works of Cornelius Agrippa.[5] I opened it with <u>apathy</u>; the theory which he attempts to demonstrate and the wonderful facts which he relates soon changed this feeling into enthusiasm. A new light seemed to dawn upon my mind, and, bounding with joy, I communicated my discovery to my father. My father looked carelessly at the title page of my book, and said, "Ah! Cornelius Agrippa! My dear Victor, do not waste your time upon this; it is sad trash."

▶ *Why doesn't his father's comment dissuade Victor from reading Agrippa?*

If, instead of this remark, my father had taken the pains to explain to me that the principles of Agrippa had been entirely exploded and that a modern system of science had been introduced, which possessed much greater powers than

---

5. **Cornelius Agrippa.** German writer (1486–1535) on occult subjects whose best known work, *De Occulte Philosophia,* presents the argument that magic is a perfect science

---

Words For Everyday Use

ig • no • ble (ig nō′ bəl) *adj.,* not noble; common; base

in • clem • en • cy (in klem′ən sē) *n.,* storminess or severity

ap • a • thy (ap′ə thē) *n.,* lack of interest or emotion

the ancient, because the powers of the latter were <u>chimerical</u>, while those of the former were real and practical, under such circumstances I should certainly have thrown Agrippa aside and have contented my imagination, warmed as it was, by returning with greater ardor to my former studies. It is even possible that the train of my ideas would never have received the fatal impulse that led to my ruin. But the cursory glance my father had taken of my volume by no means assured me that he was acquainted with its contents, and I continued to read with the greatest <u>avidity</u>.

When I returned home, my first care was to procure the whole works of this author, and afterwards of Paracelsus and Albertus Magnus.[6] I read and studied the wild fancies of these writers with delight; they appeared to me treasures known to few beside myself. I have described myself as always having been <u>imbued</u> with a fervent longing to penetrate the secrets of nature. In spite of the intense labor and wonderful discoveries of modern philosophers, I always came from my studies discontented and unsatisfied. Sir Isaac Newton[7] is said to have avowed that he felt like a child picking up shells beside the great and unexplored ocean of truth. Those of his successors in each branch of natural philosophy with whom I was acquainted appeared even to my boy's apprehensions as tyros[8] engaged in the same pursuit.

◄ *How does Victor feel when he comes from his studies? Why does he feel this way?*

The untaught peasant beheld the elements around him, and was acquainted with their practical uses. The most learned philosopher knew little more. He had partially unveiled the face of Nature, but her immortal lineaments were still a wonder and a mystery. He might dissect, anatomize, and give names; but, not to speak of a final cause, causes in their secondary and tertiary grades were utterly unknown to him. I had gazed upon the fortifications and impediments that seemed to keep human beings from entering the citadel of nature, and rashly and ignorantly I had <u>repined</u>.

---

6. **Paracelsus and Albertus Magnus.** Paracelsus (1493–1541), a Swiss physician and alchemist, made many important discoveries in chemistry and pharmaceutics. Albertus Magnus (*c.* 1200–1280), a German theologian, philosopher, and scientist, was legendary as a magician and helped to introduce the ideas of Aristotle to medieval Europe.

7. **Sir Isaac Newton.** English physicist and mathematician (1642–1727), who invented forms of calculus and developed the idea of universal gravitation

8. **tyros.** Beginners; amateurs

Words For Everyday Use		
chi • mer • i • cal (kī mer´i kəl) *adj.*, imaginary; unreal		**im • bue** (im byoo´) *vt.*, permeate or inspire
a • vid • i • ty (ə vid´ə tē) *n.*, eagerness; enthusiasm		**re • pine** (ri pīn´) *vi.*, complain; fret

But here were books, and here were men who had penetrated deeper and knew more. I took their word for all that they averred, and I became their disciple. It may appear strange that such should arise in the eighteenth century; but while I followed the routine of education in the schools of Geneva, I was, to a great degree, self-taught with regard to my favorite studies. My father was not scientific, and I was left to struggle with a child's blindness, added to a student's thirst for knowledge. Under the guidance of my new preceptors, I entered with the greatest diligence into the search of the philosopher's stone and the elixir of life;[9] but the latter soon obtained my undivided attention. Wealth was an inferior object, but what glory would attend the discovery if I could banish disease from the human frame and render man invulnerable to any but a violent death!

► Why is Victor's father of no help to Victor in his studies? What does Victor seek with "the greatest diligence"? What is Victor's motivation in his search?

Nor were these my only visions. The raising of ghosts or devils was a promise liberally accorded by my favorite authors, the fulfillment of which I most eagerly sought; and if my incantations[10] were always unsuccessful, I attributed the failure rather to my own inexperience and mistake than to a want of skill or <u>fidelity</u> in my instructors. And thus for a time I was occupied by exploded systems, mingling, like an unadept, a thousand contradictory theories, and floundering desperately in a very <u>slough</u> of <u>multifarious</u> knowledge, guided by an ardent imagination and childish reasoning, till an accident again changed the current of my ideas.

► What accident "changed the current" of Victor's ideas?

When I was about fifteen years old we had retired to our house near Belrive, when we witnessed a most violent and terrible thunderstorm. It advanced from behind the mountains of Jura,[11] and the thunder burst at once with frightful loudness from various quarters of the heavens. I remained, while the storm lasted, watching its progress with curiosity and delight. As I stood at the door, on a sudden I beheld a stream of fire issue from an old and beautiful oak which stood about twenty yards from our house; and so soon as the dazzling light vanished, the oak had disappeared, and nothing

9. **philosopher's stone . . . life.** Alchemists believed that the philosopher's stone was a substance that would turn other metals into silver or gold; the elixir of life was a substance alchemists believed would grant everlasting life.
10. **incantations.** Magical chants or formulas used to cast spells
11. **mountains of Jura.** Mountain range on the border of Switzerland and France

Words For Everyday Use	fi • del • i • ty (fə del´ə tē) *n.*, loyalty; devotion to duty
	slough (slōō) *n.*, bog or swamp
	mul • ti • far • i • ous (mul´tə far´ē əs) *adj.*, diverse; having many kinds of parts

remained but a blasted stump. When we visited it the next morning, we found the tree shattered in a singular manner. It was not splintered by the shock, but entirely reduced to thin ribands of wood. I never beheld anything so utterly destroyed.

Before this I was not unacquainted with the more obvious laws of electricity. On this occasion a man of great research in natural philosophy was with us, and, excited by this catastrophe, he entered on the explanation of a theory which he had formed on the subject of electricity and galvanism,[12] which was at once new and astonishing to me. All that he said threw greatly into the shade Cornelius Agrippa, Albertus Magnus, and Paracelsus, the lords of my imagination; but by some fatality the overthrow of these men disinclined me to pursue my accustomed studies. It seemed to me as if nothing would or could ever be known. All that had so long engaged my attention suddenly grew <u>despicable</u>. By one of those caprices of the mind, which we are perhaps most subject to in early youth, I at once gave up my former occupations, set down natural history and all its <u>progeny</u> as a deformed and abortive creation, and entertained the greatest disdain for a would-be science, which could never even step within the threshold of real knowledge. In this mood of mind I betook myself to the mathematics and the branches of study <u>appertaining</u> to that science, as being built upon secure foundations, and so worthy of my consideration.

Thus strangely are our souls constructed, and by such slight ligaments are we bound to prosperity or ruin. When I look back, it seems to me as if this almost miraculous change of inclination and will was the immediate suggestion of the guardian angel of my life—the last effort made by the spirit of preservation to avert the storm that was even then hanging in the stars, and ready to envelope me. Her victory was announced by an unusual tranquility and gladness of soul, which followed the relinquishing of my ancient and latterly tormenting studies. It was thus that I was to be taught to associate evil with their prosecution, happiness with their disregard.

It was a strong effort of the spirit of good, but it was ineffectual. Destiny was too potent, and her immutable laws had decreed my utter and terrible destruction.

◄ *What explanation is prompted by this accident?*

◄ *What new course of studies does Victor undertake? Why does he dismiss his former studies?*

◄ *What does Victor think of his change of course? Explain whether Victor believes the choices he has made have led to his misery.*

12. **galvanism.** Use of electrical current to stimulate nerves and muscles

Words For Everyday Use	**des • pi • ca • ble** (des´pi kə bəl) *adj.*, deserving to be despised; contemptible
	prog • e • ny (präj´ə nē) *n.*, offspring
	ap • per • tain (ap´ər tān´) *vt.*, relate; have to do with; pertain

Chapter 3

When I had attained the age of seventeen my parents resolved that I should become a student at the university of Ingolstadt.[1] I had hitherto attended the schools of Geneva, but my father thought it necessary, for the completion of my education, that I should be made acquainted with other customs than those of my native country. My departure was therefore fixed at an early date, but before the day resolved upon could arrive, the first misfortune of my life occurred—an omen, as it were, of my future misery.

Elizabeth had caught the scarlet fever;[2] her illness was severe, and she was in the greatest danger. During her illness, many arguments had been urged to persuade my mother to refrain from attending upon her. She had, at first, yielded to our <u>entreaties</u>, but when she heard that the life of her favorite was menaced, she could no longer control her anxiety. She attended her sick bed; her watchful attentions triumphed over the <u>malignity</u> of the distemper—Elizabeth was saved, but the consequences of this imprudence were fatal to her preserver. On the third day my mother sickened; her fever was accompanied by the most alarming symptoms, and the looks of her medical attendants <u>prognosticated</u> the worst event. On her death-bed the <u>fortitude</u> and benignity of this best of women did not desert her. She joined the hands of Elizabeth and myself: "My children," she said, "my firmest hopes of future happiness were placed on the prospect of your union. This expectation will now be the consolation of your father. Elizabeth, my love, you must supply my place to my younger children. Alas! I regret that I am taken from you; and, happy and beloved as I have been, is it not hard to quit you all? But these are not thoughts befitting me; I will endeavor to resign myself cheerfully to death and will indulge a hope of meeting you in another world."

She died calmly, and her countenance expressed affection even in death. I need not describe the feelings of those whose dearest ties are rent by that most <u>irreparable</u> evil, the

---

> ▶ What delays Victor's departure for the university? What does he, in hindsight, call this event?

> ▶ Under what circumstances does Victor's mother die? What is her dying wish?

---

1. **Ingolstadt.** City in southwest Germany; a university was founded there in 1472.
2. **scarlet fever.** Disease characterized by inflammation and a red rash

---

Words For Everyday Use

en • treat • y (en trēt´ē) *n.*, earnest request; plea
ma • lig • ni • ty (mə lig´nə tē) *n.*, quality of being very harmful or dangerous
prog • nos • ti • cate (präg näs´ti kāt) *vt.*, foretell or predict; indicate beforehand
for • ti • tude (fôrt´ə to͞od´) *n.*, strength to bear misfortune or pain calmly
ir • rep • a • ra • ble (ir rep´ə rə bəl) *adj.*, not able to be repaired, mended, or remedied

void that presents itself to the soul, and the despair that is exhibited on the countenance. It is so long before the mind can persuade itself that she whom we saw every day and whose very existence appeared a part of our own can have departed forever—that the brightness of beloved eye can have been extinguished and the sound of a voice so familiar and dear to the ear can be hushed, never more to be heard. These are the reflections of the first days; but when the lapse of time proves the reality of the evil, then the actual bitterness of grief commences. Yet from whom has not that rude hand rent away some dear connection? And why should I describe a sorrow which all have felt, and must feel? The time at length arrives when grief is rather an indulgence than a necessity; and the smile that plays upon the lips, although it may be deemed a sacrilege, is not banished. My mother was dead, but we had still duties which we ought to perform; we must continue our course with the rest and learn to think ourselves fortunate whilst one remains whom the spoiler has not seized.

My departure for Ingolstadt, which had been <u>deferred</u> by these events, was now again determined upon. I obtained from my father a respite of some weeks. It appeared to me sacrilege so soon to leave the repose, akin to death, of the house of mourning, and to rush into the thick of life. I was new to sorrow, but it did not the less alarm me. I was unwilling to quit the sight of those that remained to me, and above all, I desired to see my sweet Elizabeth in some degree consoled.

She indeed veiled her grief and strove to act the comforter to us all. She looked steadily on life and assumed its duties with courage and <u>zeal</u>. She devoted herself to those whom she had been taught to call her uncle and cousins. Never was she so enchanting as at this time, when she recalled the sunshine of her smiles and spent them upon us. She forgot even her own regret in her endeavors to make us forget.

◀ *How does Elizabeth respond to her own and the family's grief?*

The day of my departure at length arrived. Clerval spent the last evening with us. He had endeavored to persuade his father to permit him to accompany me and to become my fellow student, but in vain. His father was a narrow-minded trader and saw idleness and ruin in the aspirations and ambition of his son. Henry deeply felt the misfortune of being debarred from a liberal education. He said little, but when he

◀ *Who would like to accompany Victor? Why is he unable to do so?*

Words For Everyday Use

de • fer (dē fu̇r´) *vt.*, postpone or delay

zeal (zēl) *n.*, enthusiastic devotion in pursuit of an ideal

spoke I read in his kindling[3] eye and in his animated glance a restrained but firm resolve not to be chained to the miserable details of commerce.

We sat late. We could not tear ourselves away from each other nor persuade ourselves to say the word "Farewell!" It was said, and we retired under the pretense of seeking repose, each fancying that the other was deceived; but when at morning's dawn I descended to the carriage which was to convey me away, they were all there—my father again to bless me, Clerval to press my hand once more, my Elizabeth to renew her entreaties that I would write often and to bestow the last feminine attentions on her playmate and friend.

▶ What major change does Victor note in his life upon leaving for the university?

I threw myself into the chaise[4] that was to convey me away and indulged in the most melancholy reflections. I, who had ever been surrounded by amiable companions, continually engaged in endeavoring to bestow mutual pleasure—I was now alone. In the university whither I was going, I must form my own friends and be my own protector. My life had hitherto been remarkably secluded and domestic, and this had given me <u>invincible</u> <u>repugnance</u> to new countenances. I loved my brothers, Elizabeth, and Clerval; these were "old familiar faces," but I believed myself totally unfitted for the company of strangers. Such were my reflections as I commenced my journey; but as I proceeded, my spirits and hopes rose. I ardently desired the acquisition of knowledge. I had often, when at home, thought it hard to remain during my youth cooped up in one place and had longed to enter the world and take my station among other human beings. Now my desires were complied with, and it would, indeed, have been folly to repent.

▶ Why do Victor's spirits rise?

I had sufficient leisure for these and many other reflections during my journey to Ingolstadt, which was long and fatiguing. At length the high white steeple of the town met my eyes. I alighted, and was conducted to my solitary apartment to spend the evening as I pleased.

The next morning I delivered my letters of introduction[5] and paid a visit to some of the principal professors. Chance—

▶ Who or what does Victor claim has influence over him as soon as he leaves his father's house?

3. **kindling.** Flaming; burning
4. **chaise.** Two-wheeled carriage
5. **letters of introduction.** Former custom under which written introductions were exchanged when a person moved to a new area

Words For Everyday Use	**in • vin • ci • ble** (in vin′sə bəl) *adj.*, unconquerable
	re • pug • nance (ri pug′nəns) *n.*, extreme dislike or distaste

or rather the evil influence, the Angel of Destruction, which asserted <u>omnipotent</u> sway over me from the moment I turned my reluctant steps from my father's door—led me first to M. Krempe, professor of natural philosophy. He was an <u>uncouth</u> man, but deeply imbued in the secrets of his science. He asked me several questions concerning my progress in the different branches of science appertaining to natural philosophy.[6] I replied carelessly, and, partly in contempt, mentioned the names of my alchemists as the principal authors I had studied. The professor stared. "Have you," he said, "really spent your time in studying such nonsense?"

I replied in the affirmative. "Every minute," continued M. Krempe with warmth, "every instant that you have wasted on those books is utterly and entirely lost. You have burdened your memory with exploded systems and useless names. Good God! in what desert land have you lived, where no one was kind enough to inform you that these fancies which you have so greedily imbibed are a thousand years old, and as musty as they are ancient? I little expected, in this enlightened and scientific age, to find a disciple of Albertus Magnus and Paracelsus. My dear sir, you must begin your studies entirely anew."

◄ *How does Professor Krempe react to Victor's past studies?*

So saying, he stepped aside and wrote down a list of several books treating of natural philosophy which he desired me to <u>procure</u>, and dismissed me after mentioning that in the beginning of the following week he intended to commence a course of lectures upon natural philosophy in its general relations, and that M. Waldman, fellow professor, would lecture upon chemistry the alternate days that he omitted.

I returned home not disappointed, for I have said that I had long considered those authors useless whom the professor <u>reprobated</u>; but I returned, not at all the more inclined to recur to these studies in any shape. M. Krempe was a little squat man with a gruff voice and a repulsive countenance; the teacher, therefore, did not prepossess me in favor of his pursuits. In rather a too philosophical and connected a strain, perhaps, I have given an account of the conclusions I had come to concerning them in my early years. As a child I had not been content with the results promised by the modern professors of natural science. With a confusion of

◄ *Why is Victor disinclined to listen to Professor Krempe?*

6. **natural philosophy.** Natural, or physical, science

ideas only to be accounted for by my extreme youth and my want of a guide on such matters, I had retrod the steps of knowledge along the paths of time and exchanged the discoveries of recent inquirers for the dreams of forgotten alchemists. Besides, I had a contempt for the uses of modern natural philosophy. It was very different when the masters of the science sought immortality and power; such views, although <u>futile</u>, were grand; but now the scene was changed. The ambition of the inquirer seemed to limit itself to the <u>annihilation</u> of those visions on which my interest in science was chiefly founded. I was required to exchange chimeras[7] of boundless grandeur for realities of little worth.

Such were my reflections during the first two or three days of my residence at Ingolstadt, which were chiefly spent in becoming acquainted with the localities, and the principal residents in my new abode. But as the ensuing week commenced, I thought of the information which M. Krempe had given me concerning the lectures. And although I could not consent to go and hear that little conceited fellow deliver sentences out of a pulpit, I recollected what he had said of M. Waldman, whom I had never seen, as he had hitherto been out of town.

▶ In what ways does Professor Waldman differ from Professor Krempe?

Partly from curiosity and partly from idleness, I went into the lecturing room, which M. Waldman entered shortly after. This professor was very unlike his colleague. He appeared about fifty years of age, but with an aspect expressive of the greatest benevolence; a few grey hairs covered his temples, but those at the back of his head were nearly black. His person was short, but remarkably erect; and his voice the sweetest I had ever heard. He began his lecture by a <u>recapitulation</u> of the history of chemistry, and the various improvements made by different men of learning, pronouncing with fervor the names of the most distinguished discoverers. He then took a cursory view of the present state of the science and explained many of its elementary terms. After having made a few preparatory experiments, he concluded with a <u>panegyric</u> upon modern chemistry, the terms of which I shall never forget:

▶ What message about modern chemistry does Victor remember?

"The ancient teachers of this science," said he, "promised impossibilities and performed nothing. The modern masters promise very little; they know that metals cannot be transmuted and that the elixir of life is a chimera. But these

---

7. **chimeras.** Creations of the imagination; impossible and foolish fancies

| Words For Everyday Use | **fu • tile** (fy$\overline{oo}$t´ 'l) *adj.,* ineffective; unimportant
an • ni • hi • la • tion (ə nī´ə lā´shən) *n.,* destruction; nullification
re • ca • pit • u • la • tion (rē´kə pich´ə | lā´shən) *n.,* summary or brief restatement
pan • e • gyr • ic (pan´ə jir´ik) *n.,* formal speech or writing in praise of a person or event; tribute |

philosophers, whose hands seem only made to dabble in dirt, and their eyes to pore over the microscope or crucible,[8] have indeed performed miracles. They penetrate into the recesses of nature and show how she works in her hiding places. They ascend into the heavens; they have discovered how the blood circulates, and the nature of the air we breathe. They have acquired new and almost unlimited powers; they can command the thunders of heaven, mimic the earthquake, and even mock the invisible world with its own shadows."

Such were the professor's words—rather let me say such the words of fate—<u>enounced</u> to destroy me. As he went on, I felt as if my soul were grappling with a <u>palpable</u> enemy; one by one the various keys were touched which formed the mechanism of my being; chord after chord was sounded, and soon my mind was filled with one thought, one conception, one purpose. So much has been done, exclaimed the soul of Frankenstein—more, far more, will I achieve; treading in the steps already marked, I will pioneer a new way, explore unknown powers, and unfold to the world the deepest mysteries of creation.

◄ *What one thought and purpose fills Victor Frankenstein after the lecture?*

I closed not my eyes that night. My internal being was in a state of insurrection and turmoil; I felt that order would thence arise, but I had no power to produce it. By degrees after the morning's dawn, sleep came. I awoke, and my yesternight's thoughts were as a dream. There only remained a resolution to return to my ancient studies and to devote myself to a science for which I believed myself to possess a natural talent. On the same day I paid M. Waldman a visit. His manners in private were even more mild and attractive than in public, for there was a certain dignity in his <u>mien</u> during his lecture, which in his own house was replaced by the greatest <u>affability</u> and kindness. I gave him pretty nearly the same account of my former pursuits as I had given to his fellow professor. He heard with attention the little narration concerning my studies and smiled at the names of Cornelius Agrippa and Paracelsus, but without the contempt that M. Krempe had exhibited. He said that "These were men to whose indefatigable zeal modern philosophers were indebted for most of the foundations of their knowledge. They had left to us, as an easier task, to give new names, and arrange

◄ *Describe the difference between the reactions of Professor Waldman and Professor Krempe to Frankenstein's course of study.*

---

8. **crucible.** Vessel used for melting substances with high heat

| Words For Everyday Use | e • nounce (ē nouns´) *vt.*, enunciate; announce or proclaim | mien (mēn) *n.*, bearing; way of carrying oneself |
| | pal • pa • ble (pal´pə bəl) *adj.*, easily perceived by the senses | af • fa • bil • i • ty (af´ə bil´ə tē) *n.*, gentleness; friendly and pleasant manner |

in connected classifications, the facts which they in a great degree had been the instruments of bringing to light. The labors of men of genius, however <u>erroneously</u> directed, scarcely ever fail in ultimately turning to the solid advantage of mankind." I listened to his statement, which was delivered without any presumption or affectation, and then added that his lecture had removed my prejudices against modern chemists; I expressed myself in measured terms, with the modesty and <u>deference</u> due from a youth to his instructor, without letting escape (inexperience in life would have made me ashamed) any of the enthusiasm which stimulated my intended labors. I requested his advice concerning the books I ought to procure.

▶ What advice does Professor Waldman give Frankenstein?

"I am happy," said M. Waldman, "to have gained a disciple; and if your application equals your ability, I have no doubt of your success. Chemistry is that branch of natural philosophy in which the greatest improvements have been and may be made; it is on that account that I have made it my peculiar study; but at the same time, I have not neglected the other branches of science. A man would make but a very sorry chemist if he attended to that department of human knowledge alone. If your wish is to become really a man of science, and not merely a <u>petty</u> experimentalist, I should advise you to apply to every branch of natural philosophy, including mathematics."

He then took me into his laboratory and explained to me the uses of his various machines, instructing me as to what I ought to procure and promising me the use of his own when I should have advanced far enough in the science not to derange their mechanism. He also gave me the list of books which I had requested, and I took my leave.

▶ Why was this day memorable to Frankenstein?

Thus ended a day memorable to me; it decided my future destiny.

Words For Everyday Use

er • ro • ne • ous • ly (ər rō´nē əs lē) *adv.*, mistakenly; wrongly
def • er • ence (def´ər əns) *n.*, respect
pet • ty (pet´ē) *adj.*, unimportant; small-scale

Chapter 4

From this day natural philosophy, and particularly chemistry, in the most comprehensive sense of the term, became nearly my sole occupation. I read with ardor those works, so full of genius and discrimination, which modern inquirers have written on these subjects. I attended the lectures and cultivated the acquaintance of the men of science of the university, and I found even in M. Krempe a great deal of sound sense and real information, combined, it is true, with a repulsive physiognomy and manners, but not on that account the less valuable. In M. Waldman I found a true friend. His gentleness was never tinged by dogmatism[1] and his instructions were given with an air of frankness and good nature that banished every idea of <u>pedantry</u>. In a thousand ways he smoothed for me the path of knowledge and made the most <u>abstruse</u> inquiries clear and <u>facile</u> to my apprehension. My application was at first fluctuating and uncertain; it gained strength as I proceeded and soon became so ardent and eager that the stars often disappeared in the light of morning whilst I was yet engaged in my laboratory.

As I applied so closely, it may be easily conceived that my progress was rapid. My ardor was indeed the astonishment of the students, and my proficiency that of the masters. Professor Krempe often asked me, with a sly smile, how Cornelius Agrippa went on, whilst M. Waldman expressed the most heartfelt <u>exultation</u> in my progress. Two years passed in this manner, during which I paid no visit to Geneva, but was engaged, heart and soul, in the pursuit of some discoveries which I hoped to make. None but those who have experienced them can conceive of the enticements of science. In other studies you go as far as others have gone before you, and there is nothing more to know; but in a scientific pursuit there is continual food for discovery and wonder. A mind of moderate capacity which closely pursues one study must <u>infallibly</u> arrive at great proficiency in that study; and I, who continually sought the attainment of one object of pursuit and was solely wrapped up in this, improved so rapidly that

◀ *What detail demonstrates the degree to which Frankenstein attends to his studies?*

◀ *Why doesn't Frankenstein return to Geneva during the first two years of his study?*

◀ *In what way, according to Frankenstein, does science differ from other courses of study?*

---

1. **dogmatism.** Unwarranted or arrogant assertion, usually without reference to evidence

► What achieve-
ment does
Frankenstein reach at
the end of two
years? Why does he
plan to return home?
Why does he change
his mind?

► What phenome-
non attracts
Frankenstein's
attention? What
question does he
seek to answer?

► What does
Frankenstein study to
find the answers to
his question?

at the end of two years I made some discoveries in the improvement of some chemical instruments which procured me great esteem and admiration at the university. When I had arrived at this point and had become as well acquainted with the theory and practice of natural philosophy as depended on the lessons of any of the professors at Ingolstadt, my residence there being no longer conducive to my improvement, I thought of returning to my friends and my native town, when an incident happened that protracted my stay.

One of the phenomena which had peculiarly attracted my attention was the structure of the human frame, and, indeed, any animal endued with life. Whence, I often asked myself, did the principle of life proceed? It was a bold question, and one which has ever been considered as a mystery; yet with how many things are we upon the brink of becoming acquainted, if cowardice or carelessness did not restrain our inquiries. I revolved these circumstances in my mind and determined thenceforth to apply myself more particularly to those branches of natural philosophy which relate to physiology.[2] Unless I had been animated by an almost supernatural enthusiasm, my application to this study would have been irksome and almost intolerable. To examine the causes of life, we must first have recourse to death. I became acquainted with the science of anatomy, but this was not sufficient; I must also observe the natural decay and corruption of the human body. In my education my father had taken the greatest precautions that my mind should be impressed with no supernatural horrors. I do not ever remember to have trembled at a tale of superstition or to have feared the apparition of a spirit. Darkness had no effect upon my fancy, and a churchyard was to me merely the receptacle of bodies deprived of life, which, from being the seat of beauty and strength, had become food for the worm. Now I was led to examine the cause and progress of this decay and forced to spend days and nights in vaults and charnel houses.[3] My attention was fixed upon every object the most insupportable to the delicacy of the human feelings. I saw how the fine form of man was degraded and wasted; I beheld the corruption

---

2. **physiology.** Branch of biology that deals with the functions and activities of living things
3. **charnel houses.** Buildings where bones or bodies are deposited

---

| Words For Everyday Use | con • du • cive (kən do͞o′siv) *adj.*, tending or leading to |
| | pro • tract (prō trakt′) *vt.*, draw out; lengthen |

of death succeed to the blooming cheek of life; I saw how the worm inherited the wonders of the eye and brain. I paused, examining and analyzing all the minutiae[4] of causation, as exemplified in the change from life to death, and death to life, until from the midst of this darkness a sudden light broke in upon me—a light so brilliant and wondrous, yet so simple, that while I became dizzy with the immensity of the prospect which it illustrated, I was surprised that among so many men of genius who had directed their inquiries towards the same science, that I alone should be reserved to discover so astonishing a secret.

Remember, I am not recording the vision of a madman. The sun does not more certainly shine in the heavens than that which I now affirm is true. Some miracle might have produced it, yet the stages of the discovery were distinct and probable. After days and nights of incredible labor and fatigue, I succeeded in discovering the cause of generation and life; nay, more, I became myself capable of bestowing animation upon lifeless matter.

◄ *After many days and nights of labor, what does Frankenstein discover?*

The astonishment which I had at first experienced on this discovery soon gave place to delight and rapture. After so much time spent in painful labor, to arrive at once at the summit of my desires was the most gratifying <u>consummation</u> of my toils. But this discovery was so great and overwhelming that all the steps by which I had been progressively led to it were obliterated, and I beheld only the result. What had been the study and desire of the wisest men since the creation of the world was now within my grasp. Not that, like a magic scene, it all opened upon me at once: the information I had obtained was of a nature rather to direct my endeavors so soon as I should point them towards the object of my search than to exhibit that object already accomplished. I was like the Arabian who had been buried with the dead and found a passage to life aided only by one glimmering and seemingly ineffectual light.[5]

◄ *What emotions does Frankenstein experience upon his discovery?*

◄ *To what does Frankenstein compare his search?*

I see by your eagerness, and the wonder and hope which your eyes express, my friend, that you expect to be informed

◄ *What does Walton want to learn from Frankenstein? Why won't Frankenstein share this information with Walton?*

---

4. **minutiae.** Minute or minor details
5. **Arabian . . . light.** In a story from *The Thousand and One Nights,* Sinbad is buried alive with the corpse of his wife. He escapes by following a distant light which turns out to be a small passage.

| Words For Everyday Use | con • sum • ma • tion (kän′sə mā′shən) *n.,* completion; fulfillment |

of the secret with which I am acquainted; that cannot be; listen patiently until the end of my story, and you will easily perceive why I am reserved upon that subject. I will not lead you on, unguarded and ardent as I then was, to your destruction and infallible misery. Learn from me, if not by my precepts, at least by my example, how dangerous is the acquirement of knowledge and how much happier that man is who believes his native town to be the world, than he who aspires to become greater than his nature will allow.

▶ What difficulties does Frankenstein face despite his discovery?

When I found so astonishing a power placed within my hands, I hesitated a long time concerning the manner in which I should employ it. Although I possessed the capacity of bestowing animation, yet to prepare a frame for the reception of it, with all its <u>intricacies</u> of fibers, muscles, and veins, still remained a work of inconceivable difficulty and labor. I doubted at first whether I should attempt the creation of a being like myself, or one of simpler organization; but my imagination was too much <u>exalted</u> by my first success to permit me to doubt of my ability to give life to an animal as complex and wonderful as man. The materials at present within my command hardly appeared adequate to so arduous an undertaking, but I doubted not that I should ultimately succeed. I prepared myself for a multitude of reverses; my operations might be incessantly baffled, and at last my work be imperfect, yet when I considered the improvement which every day takes place in science and mechanics, I was encouraged to hope my present attempts would at least lay the foundations of future success. Nor could I consider the magnitude and complexity of my plan as any argument of its impracticability. It was with these feelings that I began the creation of a human being. As the minuteness of the parts formed a great hindrance to my speed, I resolved, contrary to my first intention, to make the being of a gigantic stature, that is to say, about eight feet in height, and proportionably large. After having formed this determination and having spent some months in successfully collecting and arranging my materials, I began.

▶ Why does Frankenstein decide to forego starting on a simpler organism?

▶ Why does Frankenstein create a gigantic creature?

No one can conceive the variety of feelings which bore me onwards, like a hurricane, in the first enthusiasm of success. Life and death appeared to me ideal bounds, which I should first break through, and pour a torrent of light into our dark

Words For Everyday Use	**in • tri • ca • cy** (in´tri kə sē) *n.,* complexity **ex • alt** (eg zôlt´) *vt.,* fill with pride or joy

world. A new species would bless me as its creator and source; many happy and excellent natures would owe their being to me. No father could claim the gratitude of his child so completely as I should deserve theirs. Pursuing these reflections, I thought that if I could bestow animation upon lifeless matter, I might in process of time (although I now found it impossible) renew life where death had apparently devoted the body to corruption.

These thoughts supported my spirits, while I pursued my undertaking with <u>unremitting</u> ardor. My cheek had grown pale with study, and my person had become emaciated with confinement. Sometimes, on the very brink of certainty, I failed; yet still I clung to the hope which the next day or the next hour might realize. One secret which I alone possessed was the hope to which I had dedicated myself; and the moon gazed on my midnight labors, while, with unrelaxed and breathless eagerness, I pursued nature to her hiding-places. Who shall conceive the horrors of my secret toil as I dabbled among the unhallowed damps of the grave or tortured the living animal to animate the lifeless clay? My limbs now tremble, and my eyes swim with the remembrance; but then a resistless and almost frantic impulse urged me forward; I seemed to have lost all soul or sensation but for this one pursuit. It was indeed but a passing trance, that only made me feel with renewed <u>acuteness</u> so soon as, the unnatural stimulus ceasing to operate, I had returned to my old habits. I collected bones from charnel houses and disturbed, with <u>profane</u> fingers, the tremendous secrets of the human frame. In a solitary chamber, or rather cell, at the top of the house, and separated from all the other apartments by a gallery and staircase, I kept my workshop of filthy creation; my eyeballs were starting from their sockets in attending to the details of my employment. The dissecting room and the slaughter-house furnished many of my materials; and often did my human nature turn with loathing from my occupation, whilst, still urged on by an eagerness which perpetually increased, I brought my work near to a conclusion.

The summer months passed while I was thus engaged, heart and soul, in one pursuit. It was a most beautiful season; never did the fields bestow a more plentiful harvest, or the vines yield a more luxuriant vintage, but my eyes were

◀ *What does Frankenstein expect to happen upon the success of his venture?*

◀ *How does Frankenstein now react to his past actions? What impact did his experiments have on him at the time?*

◀ *What two things does Frankenstein neglect while absorbed in his studies?*

Words For Everyday Use	**un • re • mit • ting** (un ri mit´iŋ) *adj.*, not stopping or relaxing; incessant **a • cute • ness** (ə kyo͞ot´nis) *n.*, shrewdness; severity **pro • fane** (prō fān´) *adj.*, not consecrated; secular

insensible to the charms of nature. And the same feelings which made me neglect the scenes around me caused me also to forget those friends who were so many miles absent, and whom I had not seen for so long a time. I knew my silence disquieted them, and I well remembered the words of my father: "I know that while you are pleased with yourself you will think of us with affection, and we shall hear regularly from you. You must pardon me if I regard any interruption in your correspondence as a proof that your other duties are equally neglected."

I knew well therefore what would be my father's feelings, but I could not tear my thoughts from my employment, <u>loathsome</u> in itself, but which had taken an irresistible hold of my imagination. I wished, as it were, to procrastinate all that related to my feelings of affection until the great object, which swallowed up every habit of my nature, should be completed.

I then thought that my father would be unjust if he <u>ascribed</u> my neglect to vice or faultiness on my part, but I am now convinced that he was justified in conceiving that I should not be altogether free from blame. A human being in perfection ought always to preserve a calm and peaceful mind and never to allow passion or a <u>transitory</u> desire to disturb his tranquility. I do not think that the pursuit of knowledge is an exception to this rule. If the study to which you apply yourself has a tendency to weaken your affections and to destroy your taste for those simple pleasures in which no alloy can possibly mix, then that study is certainly unlawful, that is to say, not befitting the human mind. If this rule were always observed; if no man allowed any pursuit whatsoever to interfere with the tranquility of his domestic affections, Greece had not been enslaved, Caesar would have spared his country, America would have been discovered more gradually, and the empires of Mexico and Peru had not been destroyed.[6]

But I forget that I am moralizing in the most interesting part of my tale, and your looks remind me to proceed.

My father made no reproach in his letters and only took notice of my silence by inquiring into my occupations more particularly than before. Winter, spring, and summer passed away during my labors; but I did not watch the blossom or

▶ According to Frankenstein, what should a perfect person do? What does he claim should not be an exception to this rule?

▶ What events in history would have been altered if Frankenstein's rule had been followed?

---

6. **Greece . . . destroyed.** Refers to several historical occurrences in which overzealous attentions led to the oppression or destruction of various peoples

Words For Everyday Use	**loath • some** (lōth´səm) *adj.*, disgusting; detestable **as • cribe** (ə skrīb´) *vt.*, attribute **tran • si • to • ry** (tran´sə tôr´ē) *adj.*, temporary; not permanent

the expanding leaves—sights which before always yielded me supreme delight—so deeply was I engrossed in my occupation. The leaves of that year had withered before my work drew near to a close, and now every day showed me more plainly how well I had succeeded. But my enthusiasm was checked by my anxiety, and I appeared rather like one doomed by slavery to toil in the mines, or any other unwholesome trade, than an artist occupied by his favorite employment. Every night I was oppressed by a slow fever, and I became nervous to a most painful degree; the fall of a leaf startled me, and I shunned my fellow creatures as if I had been guilty of a crime. Sometimes I grew alarmed at the wreck I perceived that I had become; the energy of my purpose alone sustained me: my labors would soon end, and I believed that exercise and amusement would then drive away incipient disease; and I promised myself both of these when my creation should be complete.

◀ *What checks Frankenstein's enthusiasm? What effect has Frankenstein's work had on him?*

Chapter 5

▶ Describe the time and place in which the creature comes to life.

▶ Explain whether the creature's appearance matches Frankenstein's expectations.

▶ What change does Frankenstein experience upon succeeding in his dream? What does he do?

▶ About what does Frankenstein dream?

It was on a dreary night of November that I beheld the accomplishment of my toils. With an anxiety that almost amounted to agony, I collected the instruments of life around me, that I might infuse a spark of being into the lifeless thing that lay at my feet. It was already one in the morning; the rain pattered dismally against the panes, and my candle was nearly burnt out, when, by the glimmer of the half-extinguished light, I saw the dull yellow eye of the creature open; it breathed hard, and a <u>convulsive</u> motion <u>agitated</u> its limbs.

How can I describe my emotions at this catastrophe, or how delineate the wretch whom with such infinite pains and care I had endeavored to form? His limbs were in proportion, and I had selected his features as beautiful. Beautiful! Great God! His yellow skin scarcely covered the work of muscles and arteries beneath; his hair was of a lustrous black, and flowing; his teeth of a pearly whiteness; but these luxuriances only formed a more horrid contrast with his watery eyes, that seemed almost of the same color as the dun-white sockets in which they were set, his shrivelled complexion and straight black lips.

The different accidents of life are not so changeable as the feelings of human nature. I had worked hard for nearly two years, for the sole purpose of <u>infusing</u> life into an inanimate body. For this I had deprived myself of rest and health. I had desired it with an ardor that far exceeded moderation; but now that I had finished, the beauty of the dream vanished, and breathless horror and disgust filled my heart. Unable to endure the aspect of the being I had created, I rushed out of the room and continued a long time traversing my bedchamber, unable to compose my mind to sleep. At length <u>lassitude</u> succeeded to the tumult I had before endured, and I threw myself on the bed in my clothes, endeavoring to seek a few moments of forgetfulness. But it was in vain; I slept, indeed, but I was disturbed by the wildest dreams. I thought I saw Elizabeth, in the bloom of health, walking in the streets of Ingolstadt. Delighted and surprised, I embraced her, but as I imprinted the first kiss on her lips, they became livid with the hue of death; her features appeared to change, and I

Words For Everyday Use

con • vul • sive (kən vul′siv) *adj.*, having the nature of involuntary spasms

ag • i • tate (aj′ i tāt′) *vt.*, move violently

in • fuse (in fyōōz′) *vt.*, put into; fill

las • si • tude (las′ i tōōd′) *n.*, listlessness; weariness

thought that I held the corpse of my dead mother in my arms; a shroud enveloped her form, and I saw the grave-worms crawling in the folds of the flannel. I started from my sleep with horror; a cold dew covered my forehead, my teeth chattered, and every limb became convulsed; when, by the dim and yellow light of the moon, as it forced its way through the window shutters, I beheld the wretch—the miserable monster whom I had created. He held up the curtain of the bed and his eyes, if eyes they may be called, were fixed on me. His jaws opened, and he muttered some <u>inarticulate</u> sounds, while a grin wrinkled his cheeks. He might have spoken, but I did not hear; one hand was stretched out, seemingly to detain me, but I escaped and rushed downstairs. I took refuge in the courtyard belonging to the house which I inhabited; where I remained during the rest of the night, walking up and down in the greatest agitation, listening attentively, catching and fearing each sound as if it were to announce the approach of the demoniacal corpse to which I had so miserably given life.

Oh! no mortal could support the horror of that countenance. A mummy again endued with animation[1] could not be so hideous as that wretch. I had gazed on him while unfinished; he was ugly then, but when those muscles and joints were rendered capable of motion, it became a thing such as even Dante[2] could not have conceived.

I passed the night wretchedly. Sometimes my pulse beat so quickly and hardly that I felt the palpitation of every artery; at others, I nearly sank to the ground through languor and extreme weakness. Mingled with this horror, I felt the bitterness of disappointment; dreams that had been my food and pleasant rest for so long a space were now become a hell to me; and the change was so rapid, the overthrow so complete!

Morning, dismal and wet, at length dawned, and discovered[3] to my sleepless and aching eyes the church of Ingolstadt, white steeple and clock, which indicated the sixth hour. The porter opened the gates of the court, which had that night been my asylum, and I issued into the streets, pacing

◄ What could not be more hideous than the creature? Why does Frankenstein find the creature suddenly so hideous?

◄ What does Frankenstein do in the morning? Why doesn't he return home?

---

1. **mummy . . . animation.** Body prepared for burial again brought back to life
2. **Dante.** Dante Aligheri (1265–1321) was an Italian poet who wrote *The Divine Comedy,* a long verse in which he travels through several circles of Hell.
3. **discovered.** Revealed

Words
For
Everyday
Use

in • ar • tic • u • late (in´ är tik´yo͞o lit) *adj.,* unable to be understood

them with quick steps, as if I sought to avoid the wretch whom I feared every turning of the street would present to my view. I did not dare return to the apartment which I inhabited, but felt <u>impelled</u> to hurry on, although drenched by the rain which poured from a black and comfortless sky.

I continued walking in this manner for some time, endeavoring, by bodily exercise, to ease the load that weighed upon my mind. I traversed the streets without any clear conception of where I was or what I was doing. My heart <u>palpitated</u> in the sickness of fear, and I hurried on with irregular steps, not daring to look about me:

▶ To whom is Frankenstein's condition compared?

> "Like one who, on a lonely road,
> Doth walk in fear and dread,
> And, having once turned round, walks on,
> And turns no more his head;
> Because he knows a frightful fiend
> Doth close behind him tread."
>
> —Coleridge's "Ancient Mariner"

Continuing thus, I came at length opposite to the inn at which the various diligences and carriages usually stopped. Here I paused, I knew not why; but I remained some minutes with my eyes fixed on a coach that was coming towards me from the other end of the street. As it drew nearer I observed that it was the Swiss diligence: it stopped just where I was standing, and on the door being opened, I perceived Henry Clerval, who, on seeing me, instantly sprung out. "My dear Frankenstein," exclaimed he, "how glad I am to see you! how fortunate that you should be here at the very moment of my alighting!"

▶ Who breaks Frankenstein out of his horrified stupefaction? What emotions does he feel for the first time in many months upon seeing this person?

Nothing could equal my delight on seeing Clerval; his presence brought back to my thoughts my father, Elizabeth, and all those scenes of home so dear to my recollection. I grasped his hand, and in a moment forgot my horror and misfortune; I felt suddenly, and for the first time during many months, calm and serene joy. I welcomed my friend, therefore, in the most <u>cordial</u> manner, and we walked towards my college. Clerval continued talking for some time about our mutual friends and his own good fortune in being permitted to come to Ingolstadt. "You may easily believe,"

Words For Everyday Use	im • pel (im pel´) *vt.,* force; urge
	pal • pi • tate (pal´pə tāt´) *vi.,* beat rapidly or flutter
	cor • dial (kôr´jəl) *adj.,* warm and friendly; hearty

said he, "how great was the difficulty to persuade my father that all necessary knowledge was not comprised in the noble art of bookkeeping; and, indeed, I believe I left him incredulous to the last, for his constant answer to my unwearied entreaties was the same as that of the Dutch schoolmaster in the *Vicar of Wakefield:* 'I have ten thousand florins a year without Greek, I eat heartily without Greek.'[4] But his affection for me at length overcame his dislike of learning, and he has permitted me to undertake a voyage of discovery to the land of knowledge."

"It gives me the greatest delight to see you; but tell me how you left my father, brothers, and Elizabeth."

"Very well, and very happy, only a little uneasy that they hear from you so seldom. By the by, I mean to lecture you a little upon their account myself. But, my dear Frankenstein," continued he, stopping short and gazing full in my face, "I did not before remark how very ill you appear; so thin and pale; you look as if you had been watching for several nights."

"You have guessed right; I have lately been so deeply engaged in one occupation that I have not allowed myself sufficient rest, as you see; but I hope, I sincerely hope, that all these employments are now at an end and that I am at length free."

I trembled excessively; I could not endure to think of, and far less to allude to, the occurrences of the preceding night. I walked with a quick pace, and we soon arrived at my college. I then reflected, and the thought made me shiver, that the creature whom I had left in my apartment might still be there, alive, and walking about. I dreaded to behold this monster, but I feared still more that Henry should see him. Entreating him, therefore, to remain a few minutes at the bottom of the stairs, I darted up towards my own room. My hand was already on the lock of the door before I recollected myself. I then paused, and a cold shivering came over me. I threw the door forcibly open, as children are accustomed to do when they expect a specter to stand in waiting for them on the other side; but nothing appeared. I stepped fearfully

◄ Why doesn't Frankenstein allow Henry to enter his apartment immediately?

---

4. **Dutch schoolmaster . . . without Greek.** Reference is to Oliver Goldsmith's *The Vicar of Wakefield*, in which the schoolmaster referred to is the principal of the University of Louvain.

Words For Everyday Use

en • treat (en trēt´) *vt.*, implore

► How does Frankenstein feel upon seeing the empty room?

► What does Clerval first make of Frankenstein's mood? What does he notice in Frankenstein's eyes?

► What happens to Frankenstein?

in: the apartment was empty, and my bedroom was also freed from its hideous guest. I could hardly believe that so great a good fortune could have befallen me, but when I became assured that my enemy had indeed fled, I clapped my hands for joy, and ran down to Clerval.

We ascended into my room, and the servant presently brought breakfast; but I was unable to contain myself. It was not joy only that possessed me; I felt my flesh tingle with excess of sensitiveness, and my pulse beat rapidly. I was unable to remain for a single instant in the same place; I jumped over the chairs, clapped my hands, and laughed aloud. Clerval at first attributed my unusual spirits to joy on his arrival, but when he observed me more attentively, he saw a wildness in my eyes for which he could not account, and my loud, unrestrained, heartless laughter frightened and astonished him.

"My dear Victor," cried he, "what, for God's sake, is the matter? Do not laugh in that manner. How ill you are! What is the cause of all this?"

"Do not ask me," cried I, putting my hands before my eyes, for I thought I saw the dreaded specter glide into the room; "*he* can tell. Oh, save me! save me!" I imagined that the monster seized me; I struggled furiously and fell down in a fit.

Poor Clerval! What must have been his feelings? A meeting, which he anticipated with such joy, so strangely turned to bitterness. But I was not the witness of his grief, for I was lifeless and did not recover my senses for a long, long time.

This was the commencement of a nervous fever, which confined me for several months. During all that time Henry was my only nurse. I afterwards learned that, knowing my father's advanced age and unfitness for so long a journey, and how wretched my sickness would make Elizabeth, he spared them this grief by concealing the extent of my disorder. He knew that I could not have a more kind and attentive nurse than himself; and, firm in the hope he felt of my recovery, he did not doubt that, instead of doing harm, he performed the kindest action that he could towards them.

But I was in reality very ill, and surely nothing but the <u>unbounded</u> and unremitting attentions of my friend could have restored me to life. The form of the monster on whom I had bestowed existence was forever before my eyes, and I

Words For Everyday Use

un • bound • ed (un bounʹdid) *adj.*, unlimited

raved incessantly concerning him. Doubtless my words surprised Henry; he at first believed them to be the wanderings of my disturbed imagination, but the <u>pertinacity</u> with which I continually recurred to the same subject persuaded him that my disorder indeed owed its origin to some uncommon and terrible event.

By very slow degrees, and with frequent relapses that alarmed and grieved my friend, I recovered. I remember the first time I became capable of observing outward objects with any kind of pleasure, I perceived that the fallen leaves had disappeared and that the young buds were shooting forth from the trees that shaded my window. It was a divine spring, and the season contributed greatly to my <u>convalescence</u>. I felt also sentiments of joy and affection revive in my bosom; my gloom disappeared, and in a short time I became as cheerful as before I was attacked by the fatal passion.

"Dearest Clerval," exclaimed I, "how kind, how very good you are to me. This whole winter, instead of being spent in study, as you promised yourself, has been consumed in my sick room. How shall I ever repay you? I feel the greatest remorse for the disappointment of which I have been the occasion, but you will forgive me."

"You will repay me entirely if you do not discompose yourself, but get well as fast as you can; and since you appear in such good spirits, I may speak to you on one subject, may I not?"

I trembled. One subject! what could it be? Could he allude to an object on whom I dared not even think?

◀ What subject does Frankenstein fear Clerval is going to bring up? What suggestions does Clerval make instead?

"Compose yourself," said Clerval, who observed my change of color, "I will not mention it, if it agitates you; but your father and cousin would be very happy if they received a letter from you in your own handwriting. They hardly know how ill you have been and are uneasy at your long silence."

"Is that all, my dear Henry? How could you suppose that my first thoughts would not fly towards those dear, dear friends whom I love, and who are so deserving of my love?"

"If this is your present temper, my friend, you will perhaps be glad to see a letter that has been lying here some days for you; it is from your cousin, I believe."

Words For Everyday Use	**per • ti • nac • i • ty** (pur´tə nas´ə tē) *n.*, stubborn persistence
	con • va • les • cence (kän´və les´əns) *n.*, recovery after illness

Chapter 6

Clerval then put the following letter into my hands. It was from my own Elizabeth:

My dearest Cousin,

You have been ill, very ill, and even the constant letters of dear kind Henry are not sufficient to reassure me on your account. You are forbidden to write—to hold a pen; yet one word from you, dear Victor, is necessary to calm our apprehensions. For a long time I have thought that each post would bring this line, and my persuasions have restrained my uncle from undertaking a journey to Ingolstadt. I have prevented his encountering the inconveniences and perhaps dangers of so long a journey, yet how often have I regretted not being able to perform it myself! I figure to myself that the task of attending on your sick bed has devolved on some <u>mercenary</u> old nurse, who could never guess your wishes nor minister to them with the care and affection of your poor cousin. Yet that is over now: Clerval writes that indeed you are getting better. I eagerly hope that you will confirm this intelligence soon in your own handwriting.

Get well—and return to us. You will find a happy, cheerful home and friends who love you dearly. Your father's health is vigorous, and he asks but to see you, but to be assured that you are well; not a care will ever cloud his benevolent countenance. How pleased you would be to remark the improvement of our Ernest! He is now sixteen, and full of activity and spirit. He is desirous to be a true Swiss, and to enter into foreign service, but we cannot part with him, at least until his elder brother return to us. My uncle is not pleased with the idea of a military career in a distant country, but Ernest never had your powers of application. He looks upon study as an <u>odious</u> fetter; his time is spent in the open air, climbing the hills or rowing on the lake. I fear that he will become an idler unless we yield the point and permit him to enter on the profession which he has selected.

▶ *What does Elizabeth urge Victor to do?*

▶ *What does Ernest aspire to be? In what way does he differ from his older brother?*

Words
For
Everyday
Use

mer • ce • nar • y (mur´se ner ē) *adj.,* motivated by desire for money; greedy

o • di • ous (ō´dē əs) *adj.,* disgusting; deserving hatred

Little alteration, except the growth of our dear children, has taken place since you left us. The blue lake and snow-clad mountains—they never change; and I think our placid home and our contented hearts are regulated by the same <u>immutable</u> laws. My trifling occupations take up my time and amuse me, and I am rewarded for any exertions by seeing none but happy, kind faces around me. Since you left us, but one change has taken place in our little household. Do you remember on what occasion Justine Moritz entered our family? Probably you do not; I will relate her history, therefore, in a few words. Madame Moritz, her mother, was a widow with four children, of whom Justine was the third. This girl had always been the favorite of her father, but through a strange <u>perversity</u>, her mother could not endure her, and after the death of M. Moritz, treated her very ill. My aunt observed this, and when Justine was twelve years of age, prevailed on her mother to allow her to live at our house. The republican[1] institutions of our country have produced simpler and happier manners than those which prevail in the great monarchies that surround it. Hence there is less distinction between the several classes of its inhabitants; and the lower orders, being neither so poor nor so despised, their manners are more refined and moral. A servant in Geneva does not mean the same thing as a servant in France and England. Justine, thus received in our family, learned the duties of a servant, a condition which, in our fortunate country, does not include the idea of ignorance, and a sacrifice of the dignity of a human being.

Justine, you may remember, was a great favorite of yours; and I recollect you once remarked that if you were in an ill humor, one glance from Justine could <u>dissipate</u> it, for the same reason that Ariosto gives concerning the beauty of Angelica[2]—she looked so frank-hearted and happy. My aunt conceived a great attachment for her, by which she was induced to give

◀ Who is Justine Moritz?

◀ What opinion does Elizabeth hold of the class systems of England and France in comparison to Switzerland?

◀ Why has Justine had a positive effect on Victor's moods?

---

1. **republican.** Based on equality of all people
2. **Ariosto . . . Angelica.** In Ludovico Ariosto's epic *Orlando Furioso,* many knights including Orlando pursue Angelica, but she marries Medora, a poor man.

Words For Everyday Use

im • mu • ta • ble (im myo͞ot´ə bəl) *adj.,* unchangeable
per • ver • si • ty (pər vur´sə tē) *n.,* contrariness
dis • si • pate (dis´ə pāt´) *vt.,* make disappear; drive away

her an education superior to that which she had at first intended. This benefit was fully repaid; Justine was the most grateful little creature in the world: I do not mean that she made any professions; I never heard one pass her lips, but you could see by her eyes that she almost adored her protectress. Although her disposition was gay and in many respects inconsiderate, yet she paid the greatest attention to every gesture of my aunt. She thought her the model of all excellence, and endeavored to imitate her phraseology and manners, so that even now she often reminds me of her.

▶ *What trials does Justine face?*

When my dearest aunt died everyone was too much occupied in their own grief to notice poor Justine, who had attended her during her illness with the most anxious affection. Poor Justine was very ill, but other trials were reserved for her.

One by one, her brothers and sister died; and her mother, with the exception of her neglected daughter, was left childless. The conscience of the woman was troubled; she began to think that the deaths of her favorites was a judgment from heaven to chastise her <u>partiality</u>. She was a Roman Catholic, and I believe her confessor[3] confirmed the idea which she had conceived. Accordingly, a few months after your departure for Ingolstadt, Justine was called home by her repentant mother. Poor girl! She wept when she quitted our house; she was much altered since the death of my aunt; grief had given softness and a winning mildness to her manners which had before been remarkable for vivacity. Nor was her residence at her mother's house of a nature to restore her gaiety. The poor woman was very <u>vacillating</u> in her repentance. She sometimes begged Justine to forgive her unkindness, but much oftener accused her of having caused the deaths of her brothers and sister. Perpetual fretting at length threw Madame Moritz into a decline, which at first increased her irritability, but she is now at peace forever. She died on the first approach of cold weather, at the beginning of this last winter. Justine has returned to us, and I assure you I love her

---

3. **confessor.** Priest authorized to hear confessions

Words For Everyday Use

par • ti • al • i • ty (pär´shē al´ə tē) *n.,* tendency to favor unfairly; bias

vac • il • lat • ing (vas´ə lāt´iŋ) *adj.,* wavering

tenderly. She is very clever and gentle and extremely pretty; as I mentioned before, her mien and her expressions continually remind me of my dear aunt.

I must say also a few words to you, my dear cousin, of little darling William. I wish you could see him; he is very tall for his age, with sweet laughing blue eyes, dark eyelashes, and curling hair. When he smiles, two little dimples appear on each cheek, which are rosy with health. He has already had one or two little *wives*, but Louisa Biron is his favorite, a pretty little girl five years of age.

◀ About whom else does Elizabeth write? What is this person like?

Now, dear Victor, I dare say you wish to be <u>indulged</u> in a little gossip concerning the good people of Geneva. The pretty Miss Mansfield has already received the congratulatory visits on her approaching marriage with a young Englishman, John Melbourne, Esq. Her ugly sister, Manon, married M. Duvillard, the rich banker, last autumn. Your favorite schoolfellow, Louis Manoir, has suffered several misfortunes since the departure of Clerval from Geneva. But he has already recovered his spirits, and is reported to be on the point of marrying a very lively, pretty Frenchwoman, Madame Tavernier. She is a widow, and much older than Manoir; but she is very much admired and a favorite with everybody.

I have written myself into better spirits, dear cousin; but my anxiety returns upon me as I conclude. Write, dearest Victor—one line—one word will be a blessing to us. Ten thousand thanks to Henry for his kindness, his affection, and his many letters; we are sincerely grateful. Adieu! My cousin, take care of yourself, and, I entreat you, write!

Elizabeth Lavenza

"Dear, dear Elizabeth!" I exclaimed when I had read her letter. "I will write instantly, and relieve them from the anxiety they must feel." I wrote, and this exertion greatly fatigued me; but my convalescence had commenced, and proceeded regularly. In another fortnight[4] I was able to leave my chamber.

---

4. **fortnight.** Two weeks

Words For Everyday Use

in • dulge (in dulj´) *vt.*, satisfy (a desire); gratify

▶ What does Frankenstein do upon his recovery? What change has occurred in him?

One of my first duties on my recovery was to introduce Clerval to the several professors of the university. In doing this, I underwent a kind of rough usage, ill befitting the wounds that my mind had sustained. Ever since the fatal night, the end of my labors, and the beginning of my misfortunes, I had conceived a violent <u>antipathy</u> even to the name of natural philosophy. When I was otherwise quite restored to health, the sight of a chemical instrument would renew all the agony of my nervous symptoms. Henry saw this, and had removed all my apparatus from my view. He had also changed my apartment, for he perceived that I had acquired a dislike for the room which had previously been my laboratory. But these cares of Clerval were made of no avail when I visited the professors. M. Waldman inflicted torture when he praised, with kindness and warmth, the astonishing progress I had made in the sciences. He soon perceived that I disliked the subject, but not guessing the real cause, he attributed my feelings to modesty and changed the subject from my improvement to the science itself, with a desire, as I evidently saw, of drawing me out. What could I do? He meant to please, and he tormented me. I felt as if he had placed carefully, one by one, in my view those instruments which were to be afterwards used in putting me to a slow and cruel death. I <u>writhed</u> under his words yet dared not exhibit the pain I felt. Clerval, whose eyes and feelings were always quick in discerning the sensations of others, declined the subject, alleging, in excuse, his total ignorance; and the conversation took a more general turn. I thanked my friend from my heart, but I did not speak. I saw plainly that he was surprised, but he never attempted to draw my secret from me; and although I loved him with a mixture of affection and reverence that knew no bounds, yet I could never persuade myself to confide to him that event which was so often present to my recollection but which I feared the detail to another would only impress more deeply.

▶ Why do Professor Waldman's words torture Frankenstein?

M. Krempe was not equally <u>docile</u>; and in my condition at that time, of almost insupportable sensitiveness, his harsh blunt encomiums[5] gave me even more pain than the benevolent <u>approbation</u> of M. Waldman. "D—n the fellow!" cried

▶ Does the conversation with Professor Krempe have the same effect on Frankenstein as the conversation with Professor Waldman did? Explain.

---

5. **encomiums.** Formal expressions of praise

Words For Everyday Use	
an • tip • a • thy (an tip´ə thē) *n.*, aversion; strong dislike	**doc • ile** (däs´əl) *adj.*, easy to manage; submissive
writhe (rīth) *vi.*, twist, contort, squirm	**ap • pro • ba • tion** (ap´rə bā´shən) *n.*, commendation; official approval

he. "Why, M. Clerval, I assure you he has outstripped us all. Ay, stare if you please; but it is nevertheless true. A youngster who, but a few years ago, believed in Cornelius Agrippa as firmly as in the Gospel, has now set himself at the head of the university; and if he is not soon pulled down, we shall all be out of countenance. Ay, ay," continued he, observing my face expressive of suffering, "M. Frankenstein is modest, an excellent quality in a young man. Young men should be <u>diffident</u> of themselves, you know, M. Clerval; I was myself when young, but that wears out in a very short time."

M. Krempe had now commenced a eulogy on himself, which happily turned the conversation from a subject that was so annoying to me.

Clerval had never sympathized in my tastes for natural science, and his literary pursuits differed wholly from those which had occupied me. He came to the university with the design of making himself complete master of the Oriental languages, as thus he should open a field for the plan of life he had marked out for himself. Resolved to pursue no inglorious career, he turned his eyes toward the East, as affording scope for his spirit of enterprise. The Persian, Arabic, and Sanskrit languages engaged his attention, and I was easily induced to enter on the same studies. Idleness had ever been irksome to me, and now that I wished to fly from reflection, and hated my former studies, I felt great relief in being the fellow pupil with my friend, and found not only instruction but consolation in the works of the Orientalists. I did not, like him, attempt a critical knowledge of their dialects, for I did not contemplate making any other use of them than temporary amusement. I read merely to understand their meaning, and they well repaid my labors. Their melancholy is soothing, and their joy elevating, to a degree I never experienced in studying the authors of any other country. When you read their writings, life appears to consist in a warm sun and a garden of roses, in the smiles and frowns of a fair enemy, and the fire that consumes your own heart. How different from the manly and heroical poetry of Greece and Rome!

◄ *What studies does Clerval pursue? What are his goals?*

Summer passed away in these occupations, and my return to Geneva was fixed for the latter end of autumn; but being delayed by several accidents, winter and snow arrived, the roads were deemed impassable, and my journey was

◄ *Why is Frankenstein's return to Geneva delayed? For how long is it delayed?*

Words For Everyday Use   **dif • fi • dent** (dif´ə dənt) *adj.*, shy

retarded until the ensuing spring. I felt this delay very bitterly, for I longed to see my native town and my beloved friends. My return had only been delayed so long from an unwillingness to leave Clerval in a strange place before he had become acquainted with any of its inhabitants. The winter, however, was spent cheerfully, and although the spring was uncommonly late, when it came its beauty compensated for its <u>dilatoriness</u>.

The month of May had already commenced, and I expected the letter daily which was to fix the date of my departure, when Henry proposed a pedestrian[6] tour in the environs of Ingolstadt, that I might bid a personal farewell to the country I had so long inhabited. I <u>acceded</u> with pleasure to this proposition: I was fond of exercise, and Clerval had always been my favorite companion in the rambles of this nature that I had taken among the scenes of my native country.

We passed a fortnight in these <u>perambulations</u>; my health and spirits had long been restored, and they gained additional strength from the <u>salubrious</u> air I breathed, the natural incidents of our progress, and the conversation of my friend. Study had before secluded me from the intercourse of my fellow creatures, and rendered me unsocial, but Clerval called forth the better feelings of my heart; he again taught me to love the aspect of nature and the cheerful faces of children. Excellent friend! how sincerely did you love me and endeavor to elevate my mind until it was on a level with your own! A selfish pursuit had cramped and narrowed me until your gentleness and affection warmed and opened my senses; I became the same happy creature who, a few years ago, loved and beloved by all, had no sorrow or care. When happy, inanimate nature had the power of bestowing on me the most delightful sensations. A serene sky and verdant[7] fields filled me with ecstasy. The present season was indeed divine; the flowers of spring bloomed in the hedges, while those of summer were already in bud. I was undisturbed by thoughts which during the preceding year had pressed upon me, notwithstanding my endeavors to throw them off, with an invincible burden.

▶ *What joys had Frankenstein forgotten during his studies?*

---

6. **pedestrian.** Walking; on foot
7. **verdant.** Green with vegetation

Words For Everyday Use	**dil • a • to • ri • ness** (dilʹə tôrʹē nəs) *n.,* delay **ac • cede** (ak sēdʹ) *vi.,* consent; agree to	**per • am • bu • la • tion** (pər amʹ byōō lāʹ shən) *n.,* walk **sa • lu • bri • ous** (sə lōōʹbrē əs) *adj.,* healthful; wholesome

Henry rejoiced in my gaiety and sincerely sympathized in my feelings; he exerted himself to amuse me, while he expressed the sensations that filled his soul. The resources of his mind on this occasion were truly astonishing; his conversation was full of imagination, and very often, in imitation of the Persian and Arabic writers, he invented tales of wonderful fancy and passion. At other times he repeated my favorite poems or drew me out into arguments, which he supported with great <u>ingenuity</u>.

We returned to our college on a Sunday afternoon; the peasants were dancing, and every one we met appeared gay and happy. My own spirits were high, and I bounded along with feelings of unbridled joy and hilarity.

◀ *In what mood does Frankenstein return to his college?*

Words For Everyday Use

in • ge • nu • i • ty (in´jə nōō´ə tē) *n.*, cleverness; originality and skill

Responding to the Selection

Victor Frankenstein does not want anyone, even his good friend Clerval, to know what he has created. How do you think Clerval would react if Frankenstein were to tell him about his work? if Clerval saw the creature? Write your responses to these questions or roleplay with a partner a discussion between Frankenstein and Clerval in which Frankenstein discloses his secret.

Reviewing the Selection

Recalling and Interpreting

1. **R:** What information about his family does Frankenstein present at the beginning of his tale? How do Frankenstein's parents feel about creating a new life in the form of a child? What responsibilities do they believe they have to this child?

2. **I:** Why do you think Frankenstein begins with this information about his family? What does this information reveal about him as a character?

3. **R:** Describe the circumstances under which Elizabeth came to be part of the Frankenstein family. As what does Victor view her? What characteristics does she display in chapters 1 through 6?

4. **I:** If Elizabeth represents the ideal woman of the period, what are the qualities of this ideal woman?

5. **R:** What field of study interests Frankenstein? What course of study does he devise on his own? What event causes him to change his focus? What reactions to his previous study does he receive from his father and from Professors Krempe and Waldman?

6. **I:** In what way do the reactions of his father and professors affect Frankenstein's studies? Explain whether Frankenstein takes responsibility for the results of his studies and experiments.

7. **R:** What secret does Frankenstein learn? Describe the creature that he creates. What reaction toward his creation does Frankenstein have? What physical and emotional effects does Frankenstein's work have on him?

8. **I:** On what is Frankenstein's reaction to the monster based? What problems might arise from Frankenstein's method of dealing with the creature? Compare and contrast Frankenstein's feelings toward the creature he has created to the feelings of Frankenstein's parents to creating a life in their child, Victor.

Synthesizing

9. In her introduction, Shelley writes, "I bid my hideous progeny go forth and prosper." Compare Mary Shelley's reaction to her creation to Victor Frankenstein's reaction to his creation. Are both works "hideous progeny"? Explain.

10. As scientific knowledge and technology expand, questions about the dangers of such endeavors as creating and altering life continue to arise. What do you think Frankenstein would think about current issues involving genetic engineering and cloning?

Understanding Literature (QUESTIONS FOR DISCUSSION)

1. Science Fiction. Science fiction is highly imaginative fiction containing fantastic elements based on scientific principles, discoveries, or laws. Explain why Mary Shelley's *Frankenstein* is considered an early precursor of modern science fiction.

2. Narrator. A **narrator** is one who tells a story. The narrator shifts between the letters that begin the story and the tale that begins in chapter 1. Identify the narrator in each section. Who is the audience of each narrator? What is the purpose of each narrator?

3. Simile and Allusion. A **simile** is a comparison using *like* or *as*. An **allusion** is a rhetorical technique in which reference is made to a person, event, object, or work from history or literature. To what does Frankenstein compare his endeavors? The simile he uses alludes to a story from *The Thousand and One Nights*. Why do you think he makes this allusion?

Chapter 7

On my return, I found the following letter from my father:

My dear Victor,

You have probably waited impatiently for a letter to fix the date of your return to us, and I was at first tempted to write only a few lines, merely mentioning the day on which I should expect you. But that would be a cruel kindness, and I dare not do it. What would be your surprise, my son, when you expected a happy and glad welcome, to behold, on the contrary, tears and wretchedness? And how, Victor, can I relate our misfortune? Absence cannot have rendered you <u>callous</u> to our joys and griefs, and how shall I inflict pain on my long-absent son? I wish to prepare you for the woe-ful news, but I know it is impossible; even now your eye skims over the page, to seek the words which are to convey to you the horrible tidings.

William is dead! That sweet child, whose smiles delighted and warmed my heart, who was so gentle, yet so gay! Victor, he is murdered!

I will not attempt to console you, but will simply relate the circumstances of the transaction.

Last Thursday (May 7th) I, my niece, and your two brothers went to walk in Plainpalais. The evening was warm and serene, and we prolonged our walk farther than usual. It was already dusk before we thought of returning, and then we discovered that William and Ernest, who had gone on before, were not to be found. We accordingly rested on a seat until they should return. Presently Ernest came and inquired if we had seen his brother; he said that he had been playing with him, that William had run away to hide himself, and that he vainly sought for him, and afterwards waited for him a long time, but that he did not return.

This account rather alarmed us, and we continued to search for him until night fell, when Elizabeth conjectured that he might have returned to the house. He was not there. We returned again, with torches, for I could

> ► What bad news does Frankenstein receive upon his return?

Words For Everyday Use

cal • lous (kal´əs) *adj.,* unfeeling

not rest when I thought that my sweet boy had lost himself and was exposed to all the damps and dews of night; Elizabeth also suffered extreme anguish. About five in the morning I discovered my lovely boy, whom the night before I had seen blooming and active in health, stretched on the grass livid and motionless; the print of the murderer's finger was on his neck.

◄ Who discovered William? What has happened to William?

He was conveyed home, and the anguish that was visible in my countenance betrayed the secret to Elizabeth. She was very earnest to see the corpse. At first I attempted to prevent her, but she persisted, and entering the room where it lay, hastily examined the neck of the victim, and clasping her hands, exclaimed, "O God! I have murdered my darling child!"

She fainted, and was restored with extreme difficulty. When she again lived, it was only to weep and sigh. She told me that that same evening William had teased her to let him wear a very valuable miniature[1] that she possessed of your mother. This picture is gone and was doubtless the temptation which urged the murderer to the deed. We have no trace of him at present, although our exertions to discover him are unremitted; but they will not restore my beloved William!

◄ Why does Elizabeth feel responsible for William's death?

Come, dearest Victor; you alone can console Elizabeth. She weeps continually, and accuses herself unjustly as the cause of his death; her words pierce my heart. We are all unhappy, but will not that be an additional motive for you, my son, to return and be our comforter? Your dear mother! Alas, Victor! I now say, Thank God she did not live to witness the cruel, miserable death of her youngest darling!

Come, Victor; not brooding thoughts of vengeance against the assassin, but with feelings of peace and gentleness, that will heal, instead of festering, the wounds of our minds. Enter the house of mourning, my friend, but with kindness and affection for those who love you, and not with hatred for your enemies.

Your affectionate and afflicted father,
Alphonse Frankenstein

Geneva, May 12th, 17—

---

1. **miniature.** Small portrait

Words For Everyday Use	**venge • ance** (ven´jəns) *n.*, revenge

Clerval, who had watched my countenance as I read this letter, was surprised to observe the despair that succeeded to the joy I at first expressed on receiving news from my friends. I threw the letter on the table and covered my face with my hands.

"My dear Frankenstein," exclaimed Henry, when he perceived me weep with bitterness, "are you always to be unhappy? My dear friend, what has happened?"

I motioned to him to take up the letter, while I walked up and down the room in the extremest agitation. Tears also gushed from the eyes of Clerval, as he read the account of my misfortune.

"I can offer you no consolation, my friend," said he; "your disaster is irreparable. What do you intend to do?"

"To go instantly to Geneva; come with me, Henry, to order the horses."

► What words of sympathy does Clerval offer?

During our walk Clerval endeavored to say a few words of consolation; he could only express his heartfelt sympathy. "Poor William!" said he, "Dear lovely child, he now sleeps with his angel mother! Who that had seen him bright and joyous in his young beauty but must weep over his untimely loss! To die so miserably, to feel the murderer's grasp! How much more a murderer, that could destroy such radiant innocence! Poor little fellow! One only consolation have we; his friends mourn and weep, but he is at rest. The pang is over, his sufferings are at an end forever. A sod covers his gentle form, and he knows no pain. He can no longer be a subject for pity; we must reserve that for his miserable survivors."

Clerval spoke thus as we hurried through the streets; the words impressed themselves on my mind, and I remembered them afterwards in solitude. But now, as soon as the horses arrived, I hurried into a cabriolet,[2] and bade farewell to my friend.

► How does Frankenstein feel during his journey home?

My journey was very melancholy. At first I wished to hurry on, for I longed to console and sympathize with my loved and sorrowing friends; but when I drew near my native town, I slackened my progress. I could hardly sustain the multitude of feelings that crowded into my mind. I passed through scenes familiar to my youth but which I had not seen for nearly six years. How altered everything might be during that time! One sudden and desolating change had taken place; but a thousand little circumstances might have by degrees worked other alterations, which, although they were done more tranquilly, might not be the less decisive. Fear overcame

---

2. **cabriolet.** Light, two-wheeled carriage

me; I dared not advance, dreading a thousand nameless evils that made me tremble, although I was unable to define them.

I remained two days at Lausanne[3] in this painful state of mind. I contemplated the lake; the waters were placid, all around was calm, and the snowy mountains, "the palaces of nature," were not changed. By degrees the calm and heavenly scene restored me, and I continued my journey towards Geneva.

The road ran by the side of the lake, which became narrower as I approached my native town. I discovered more distinctly the black sides of Jura and the bright summit of Mont Blanc.[4] I wept like a child. "Dear mountains! My own beautiful lake! how do you welcome your wanderer? Your summits are clear; the sky and lake are blue and placid. Is this to prognosticate peace or to mock at my unhappiness?"

I fear, my friend, that I shall render myself tedious by dwelling on these preliminary circumstances, but they were days of comparative happiness, and I think of them with pleasure. My country, my beloved country! Who but a native can tell the delight I took in again beholding thy streams, thy mountains, and, more than all, thy lovely lake!

Yet, as I drew nearer home, grief and fear again overcame me. Night also closed around, and when I could hardly see the dark mountains, I felt still more gloomily. The picture appeared a vast and dim scene of evil, and I foresaw obscurely that I was destined to become the most wretched of human beings. Alas! I prophesied truly, and failed only in one single circumstance, that in all the misery I imagined and dreaded, I did not conceive the hundredth part of the anguish I was destined to endure.

It was completely dark when I arrived in the environs of Geneva; the gates of the town were already shut, and I was obliged to pass the night at Secheron, a village at the distance of half a league from the city. The sky was serene, and as I was unable to rest, I resolved to visit the spot where my poor William had been murdered. As I could not pass through the town, I was obliged to cross the lake in a boat to arrive at Plainpalais. During this short voyage I saw the lightnings playing on the summit of Mont Blanc in the most beautiful figures. The storm appeared to approach rapidly; and, on landing, I ascended a low hill, that I might observe its progress. It advanced; the heavens were clouded, and I soon felt the rain coming slowly in large drops, but its violence quickly increased.

◄ How does nature influence Frankenstein's inner feelings?

◄ What does Frankenstein foresee about his future? What does he not realize?

◄ Why does Frankenstein cross the lake in a boat? What does he see during his passage?

---

3. **Lausanne.** City in western Switzerland
4. **Mont Blanc.** Mountain in eastern France near the Italian border; highest point in the Alps

I quitted my seat and walked on, although the darkness and storm increased every minute and the thunder burst with a terrific crash over my head. It was echoed from Salêve, the Juras, and the Alps of Savoy;[5] vivid flashes of lightning dazzled my eyes, illuminating the lake, making it appear like a vast sheet of fire; then for an instant everything seemed of a pitchy darkness, until the eye recovered itself from the preceding flash. The storm, as is often the case in Switzerland, appeared at once in various parts of the heavens. The most violent storm hung exactly north of the town, over that part of the lake which lies between the promontory of Belrive and the village of Copêt. Another storm enlightened Jura with faint flashes, and another darkened and sometimes disclosed the Môle, a peaked mountain to the east of the lake.

▶ What effect does the storm have on Frankenstein's emotions? As what does he see the storm?

▶ Who is illuminated by the lightning? What thought makes Frankenstein shudder?

While I watched the tempest, so beautiful yet terrific, I wandered on with a hasty step. This noble war in the sky elevated my spirits; I clasped my hands and exclaimed aloud, "William, dear angel! This is thy funeral, this thy dirge!" As I said these words, I perceived in the gloom a figure which stole from behind a clump of trees near me; I stood fixed, gazing intently; I could not be mistaken. A flash of lightning illuminated the object and discovered its shape plainly to me; its gigantic stature, and the deformity of its aspect, more hideous than belongs to humanity, instantly informed me that it was the wretch, the filthy demon to whom I had given life. What did he there? Could he be (I shuddered at the conception) the murderer of my brother? No sooner did that idea cross my imagination, than I became convinced of its truth; my teeth chattered, and I was forced to lean against a tree for support. The figure passed me quickly, and I lost it in the gloom. Nothing in human shape could have destroyed that fair child. *He* was the murderer! I could not doubt it. The mere presence of the idea was an irresistible proof of the fact. I thought of pursuing the devil, but it would have been in vain, for another flash discovered him to me hanging among the rocks of the nearly perpendicular ascent of Mont Salêve, a hill that bounds Plainpalais on the south. He soon reached the summit and disappeared.

▶ What does Frankenstein consider the fact that proves his theory about the murder?

I remained motionless. The thunder ceased, but the rain still continued, and the scene was enveloped in an impenetrable darkness. I revolved in my mind the events which I had until now sought to forget: the whole train of my progress towards the creation, the appearance of the work of my own hands alive at my bedside, its departure. Two years had now nearly elapsed since the night on which he first

▶ What thoughts does the sight of the creature prompt in Frankenstein? What does he think the creature is?

---

5. **Salêve . . . Savoy.** Refers to various mountains around Geneva

received life, and was this his first crime? Alas! I had turned loose into the world a depraved wretch whose delight was in carnage and misery; had he not murdered my brother?

No one can conceive the anguish I suffered during the remainder of the night, which I spent, cold and wet, in the open air. But I did not feel the inconvenience of the weather; my imagination was busy in scenes of evil and despair. I considered the being whom I had cast among mankind and endowed with the will and power to effect purposes of horror, such as the deed which he had now done, nearly in the light of my own vampire, my own spirit let loose from the grave and forced to destroy all that was dear to me.

◄ With what has Frankenstein endowed his creation?

Day dawned, and I directed my steps towards the town. The gates were open, and I hastened to my father's house. My first thought was to discover what I knew of the murderer and cause instant pursuit to be made. But I paused when I reflected on the story that I had to tell. A being whom I myself had formed, and endued with life, had met me at midnight among the <u>precipices</u> of an inaccessible mountain. I remembered also the nervous fever with which I had been seized just at the time that I dated my creation, and which would give an air of delirium to a tale otherwise so utterly improbable. I well knew that if any other had communicated such a relation to me, I should have looked upon it as the ravings of insanity. Besides, the strange nature of the animal would elude all pursuit, even if I were so far credited as to persuade my relatives to commence it. And then of what use would be pursuit? Who could arrest a creature capable of scaling the overhanging sides of Mont Salêve? These reflections determined me, and I resolved to remain silent.

◄ Why doesn't Frankenstein reveal what he knows of the murderer?

It was about five in the morning when I entered my father's house. I told the servants not to disturb the family and went into the library to attend their usual hour of rising.

Six years had elapsed, passed as a dream but for one <u>indelible</u> trace, and I stood in the same place where I had last embraced my father before my departure for Ingolstadt. Beloved and <u>venerable</u> parent! He still remained to me. I gazed on the picture of my mother which stood over the mantelpiece. It was a historical subject, painted at my father's desire, and represented Caroline Beaufort in an agony of despair, kneeling by the coffin of her dead father.

Words For Everyday Use	prec • i • pice (pres´i pis) *n.,* steep cliff
	in • del • i • ble (in del´ə bəl) *adj.,* permanent; lasting
	ven • er • a • ble (ven´ər ə bəl) *adj.,* worthy of respect by reason of age, dignity, character, or position

Her garb was rustic and her cheek pale, but there was an air of dignity and beauty that hardly permitted the sentiment of pity. Below this picture was a miniature of William, and my tears flowed when I looked upon it. While I was thus engaged, Ernest entered; he had heard me arrive and hastened to welcome me. He expressed a sorrowful delight to see me: "Welcome, my dearest Victor," said he. "Ah! I wish you had come three months ago, and then you would have found us all joyous and delighted. You come to us now to share a misery which nothing can <u>alleviate</u>; yet your presence will, I hope, revive our father, who seems sinking under his misfortune; and your persuasions will induce poor Elizabeth to cease her vain and tormenting self-accusations. Poor William! he was our darling and our pride!"

▶ What emotion steals over Frankenstein? What does he now realize?

Tears, unrestrained, fell from my brother's eyes; a sense of mortal agony crept over my frame. Before, I had only imagined the wretchedness of my desolated home; the reality came on me as a new and a not less terrible disaster. I tried to calm Ernest; I inquired more minutely concerning my father and her I named my cousin.

"She most of all," said Ernest, "requires consolation; she accused herself of having caused the death of my brother, and that made her very wretched. But since the murderer has been discovered—"

▶ What news does Ernest give Frankenstein? Why is Frankenstein surprised to hear this news?

"The murderer discovered! Good God! How can that be? who could attempt to pursue him? It is impossible; one might as well try to overtake the winds or confine a mountain stream with a straw. I saw him too; he was free last night!"

"I do not know what you mean," replied my brother in accents of wonder, "but to us the discovery we have made completes our misery. No one would believe it at first; and even now Elizabeth will not be convinced, notwithstanding all the evidence. Indeed, who would credit that Justine Moritz, who was so amiable and fond of all the family, could suddenly become capable of so frightful, so appalling a crime?"

▶ Who is accused of the murder?

"Justine Moritz! Poor, poor girl, is she the accused? But it is wrongfully; every one knows that; no one believes it, surely, Ernest?"

"No one did at first, but several circumstances came out that have almost forced conviction upon us; and her own behavior has been so confused as to add to the evidence of

▶ What circumstances encourage belief in the guilt of the suspected murderer?

Words For Everyday Use	al • le • vi • ate (ə lē′vē āt′) vt., lighten or relieve; reduce or decrease

facts a weight that, I fear, leaves no hope for doubt. But she will be tried today, and you will then hear all."

He related that, the morning on which the murder of poor William had been discovered, Justine had been taken ill and confined to her bed for several days. During this interval, one of the servants, happening to examine the apparel she had worn on the night of the murder, had discovered in her pocket the picture of my mother, which had been judged to be the temptation of the murderer. The servant instantly showed it to one of the others, who, without saying a word to any of the family, went to a magistrate;[6] and, upon their deposition, Justine was apprehended. On being charged with the fact, the poor girl confirmed the suspicion in a great measure by her extreme confusion of manner.

This was a strange tale, but it did not shake my faith, and I replied earnestly, "You are all mistaken; I know the murderer. Justine, poor, good Justine, is innocent."

At that instant my father entered. I saw unhappiness deeply impressed on his countenance, but he endeavored to welcome me cheerfully, and after we had exchanged our mournful greeting, would have introduced some other topic than that of our disaster, had not Ernest exclaimed, "Good God, Papa! Victor says that he knows who was the murderer of poor William."

"We do also, unfortunately," replied my father; "for indeed I had rather have been forever ignorant than have discovered so much <u>depravity</u> and ingratitude in one I valued so highly."

◀ Why does the identity of the suspected murderer make the situation more difficult for Frankenstein's father?

"My dear father, you are mistaken; Justine is innocent."

"If she is, God forbid that she should suffer as guilty. She is to be tried today, and I hope, I sincerely hope, that she will be acquitted."

This speech calmed me. I was firmly convinced in my own mind that Justine, and indeed every human being, was guiltless of this murder. I had no fear, therefore, that any circumstantial evidence could be brought forward strong enough to convict her. My tale was not one to announce publicly; its astounding horror would be looked upon as madness by the vulgar. Did anyone indeed exist, except I, the creator, who

◀ Why is Frankenstein convinced that Justine will be found innocent? What will he do to aid her cause?

6. **magistrate.** Civil officer who can administer the law

Words For Everyday Use

de • prav • i • ty (dē prav´ə tē) *n.*, corruption; wickedness

would believe, unless his senses convinced him, in the existence of the living monument of presumption and rash ignorance which I had let loose upon the world?

We were soon joined by Elizabeth. Time had altered her since I last beheld her; it had endowed her with loveliness surpassing the beauty of her childish years. There was the same candor, the same vivacity, but it was allied to an expression more full of sensibility and intellect. She welcomed me with the greatest affection. "Your arrival, my dear cousin," said she, "fills me with hope. You perhaps will find some means to justify my poor guiltless Justine. Alas! who is safe, if she be convicted of crime? I rely on her innocence as certainly as I do upon my own. Our misfortune is doubly hard to us; we have not only lost that lovely darling boy, but this poor girl, whom I sincerely love, is to be torn away by even a worse fate. If she is condemned, I never shall know joy more. But she will not, I am sure she will not; and then I shall be happy again, even after the sad death of my little William."

▶ Why is the family's unhappiness double?

"She is innocent, my Elizabeth," said I, "and that shall be proved; fear nothing, but let your spirits be cheered by the assurance of her acquittal."

"How kind and generous you are! Everyone else believes in her guilt, and that made me wretched, for I knew that it was impossible, and to see everyone else prejudiced in so deadly a manner rendered me hopeless and despairing." She wept.

"Dearest niece," said my father, "dry your tears. If she is, as you believe, innocent, rely on the justice of our laws, and the activity with which I shall prevent the slightest shadow of partiality."

Chapter 8

We passed a few sad hours until eleven o'clock, when the trial was to commence. My father and the rest of the family being obliged to attend as witnesses, I accompanied them to the court. During the whole of this wretched mockery of justice I suffered living torture. It was to be decided whether the result of my curiosity and lawless devices would cause the death of two of my fellow beings: one a smiling babe full of innocence and joy, the other far more dreadfully murdered, with every aggravation of <u>infamy</u> that could make the murder memorable in horror. Justine also was a girl of merit and possessed qualities which promised to render her life happy; now all was to be <u>obliterated</u> in an ignominious grave, and I the cause! A thousand times rather would I have confessed myself guilty of the crime ascribed to Justine, but I was absent when it was committed, and such a declaration would have been considered as the ravings of a madman and would not have <u>exculpated</u> her who suffered through me.

◀ Why does Frankenstein feel that he should be tried for the two murders?

The appearance of Justine was calm. She was dressed in mourning, and her countenance, always engaging, was rendered, by the solemnity of her feelings, exquisitely beautiful. Yet she appeared confident in innocence and did not tremble, although gazed on and <u>execrated</u> by thousands, for all the kindness which her beauty might otherwise have excited was obliterated in the minds of the spectators by the imagination of the enormity she was supposed to have committed. She was tranquil, yet her tranquility was evidently constrained; and as her confusion had before been <u>adduced</u> as a proof of her guilt, she worked up her mind to an appearance of courage. When she entered the court she threw her eyes round it and quickly discovered where we were seated. A tear seemed to dim her eye when she saw us, but she quickly recovered herself, and a look of sorrowful affection seemed to attest her utter guiltlessness.

The trial began, and, after the advocate against her had stated the charge, several witnesses were called. Several strange facts combined against her, which might have staggered anyone who had not such proof of her innocence as I had. She had been out the whole of the night on which the

◀ What strange facts suggest Justine's guilt?

Words For Everyday Use	in • fa • my (in´fə mē) *n.*, disgrace, dishonor; bad reputation	guiltless
	ob • lit • er • ate (ə blit´ər āt´) *vt.*, blot out; destroy	ex • e • crate (ek´si krāt´) *vt.*, curse; denounce
	ex • cul • pate (əks kul´pāt´) *vt.*, prove	ad • duce (ə doos´) *vt.*, give as a reason; cite as an example

murder had been committed and towards morning had been perceived by a market-woman not far from the spot where the body of the murdered child had been afterwards found. The woman asked her what she did there, but she looked very strangely and only returned a confused and <u>unintelligible</u> answer. She returned to the house about eight o'clock; and when one inquired where she had passed the night, she replied that she had been looking for the child, and demanded earnestly if anything had been heard concerning him. When shown the body, she fell into violent hysterics and kept her bed for several days. The picture was then produced which the servant had found in her pocket; and when Elizabeth, in a faltering voice, proved that it was the same which, an hour before the child had been missed, she had placed round his neck, a murmur of horror and indignation filled the court.

Justine was called on for her defense. As the trial had proceeded, her countenance had altered. Surprise, horror, and misery were strongly expressed. Sometimes she struggled with her tears, but when she was desired to plead, she collected her powers and spoke in an audible although variable voice.

► What plea does Justine enter? What does she hope will save her from being found guilty?

"God knows," she said, "how entirely I am innocent. But I do not pretend that my protestations should acquit me; I rest my innocence on a plain and simple explanation of the facts which have been adduced against me, and I hope the character I have always borne will incline my judges to a favorable interpretation where any circumstance appears doubtful or suspicious."

► What explanation does Justine give of her actions on the night of the murder?

She then related that, by the permission of Elizabeth, she had passed the evening of the night on which the murder had been committed at the house of an aunt at Chene, a village situated at about a league from Geneva. On her return, at about nine o'clock, she met a man who asked her if she had seen anything of the child who was lost. She was alarmed by this account and passed several hours in looking for him, when the gates of Geneva were shut, and she was forced to remain several hours of the night in a barn belonging to a cottage, being unwilling to call up the inhabitants, to whom she was well known. Most of the night she spent here watching; towards morning she believed that she slept for a few minutes; some steps disturbed her, and she awoke.

Words
For
Everyday
Use

un • in • tel • li • gi • ble (un in tel´i jə bəl) *adj.,* incomprehensible; that cannot be understood

It was dawn, and she quitted her asylum, that she might again endeavor to find my brother. If she had gone near the spot where his body lay, it was without her knowledge. That she had been bewildered when questioned by the market-woman was not surprising, since she had passed a sleepless night and the fate of poor William was yet uncertain. Concerning the picture she could give no account.

◀ What piece of evidence is she unable to explain?

"I know," continued the unhappy victim, "how heavily and fatally this one circumstance weighs against me, but I have no power of explaining it; and when I have expressed my utter ignorance, I am only left to conjecture concerning the probabilities by which it might have been placed in my pocket. But here also I am checked. I believe that I have no enemy on earth, and none surely would have been so wicked as to destroy me <u>wantonly</u>. Did the murderer place it there? I know of no opportunity afforded him for so doing; or, if I had, why should he have stolen the jewel, to part with it again so soon?

"I commit my cause to the justice of my judges, yet I see no room for hope. I beg permission to have a few witnesses examined concerning my character, and if their testimony shall not overweigh my supposed guilt, I must be condemned, although I would pledge my salvation on my innocence."[1]

Several witnesses were called, who had known her for many years, and they spoke well of her; but fear and hatred of the crime of which they supposed her guilty rendered them <u>timorous</u>, and unwilling to come forward. Elizabeth saw even this last resource, her excellent dispositions and <u>irreproachable</u> conduct, about to fail the accused, when, although violently agitated, she desired permission to address the court.

◀ Why does Elizabeth testify on behalf of Justine?

"I am," said she, "the cousin of the unhappy child who was murdered, or rather his sister, for I was educated by and have lived with his parents ever since and even long before his birth. It may therefore be judged indecent in me to come forward on this occasion, but when I see a fellow creature about to perish through the cowardice of her pretended friends, I wish to be allowed to speak, that I may say what I know of her character. I am well acquainted with the accused.

---

1. **pledge . . . innocence.** She is so complete in her innocence she would swear her eternal life on it.

Words For Everyday Use

wan • ton • ly (wän′ tən lē) *adv.*, deliberately; recklessly

tim • or • ous (tim′ ər əs) *adj.*, timid; full of fear

ir • re • proach • a • ble (ir′ri prō′chə bəl) *adj.*, blameless; faultless

I have lived in the same house with her, at one time for five and at another for nearly two years. During all that period she appeared to me the most amiable and benevolent of human creatures. She nursed Madame Frankenstein, my aunt, in her last illness, with the greatest affection and care, and afterwards attended her own mother during a tedious illness, in a manner that excited the admiration of all who knew her, after which she again lived in my uncle's house, where she was beloved by all the family. She was warmly attached to the child who is now dead and acted towards him like a most affectionate mother. For my own part, I do not hesitate to say, that, notwithstanding all the evidence produced against her, I believe and rely on her perfect innocence. She had no temptation for such an action; as to the bauble[2] on which the chief proof rests, if she had earnestly desired it, I should have willingly given it to her, so much do I esteem and value her."

A murmur of approbation followed Elizabeth's simple and powerful appeal, but it was excited by her generous interference, and not in favor of poor Justine, on whom the public indignation was turned with renewed violence, charging her with the blackest ingratitude. She herself wept as Elizabeth spoke, but she did not answer. My own agitation and anguish was extreme during the whole trial. I believed in her innocence; I knew it. Could the demon, who had (I did not for a minute doubt) murdered my brother also in his hellish sport have betrayed the innocent to death and <u>ignominy</u>? I could not sustain the horror of my situation, and when I perceived that the popular voice and the countenances of the judges had already condemned my unhappy victim, I rushed out of the court in agony. The tortures of the accused did not equal mine; she was sustained by innocence, but the fangs of remorse tore my bosom and would not forego their hold.

I passed a night of unmingled wretchedness. In the morning I went to the court; my lips and throat were parched. I dared not ask the fatal question, but I was known, and the officer guessed the cause of my visit. The ballots had been thrown; they were all black, and Justine was condemned.

I cannot pretend to describe what I then felt. I had before experienced sensations of horror, and I have endeavored to

> ► In what way does Frankenstein feel his tortures compare to Justine's?

> ► What is the verdict? What information surprises Frankenstein?

2. **bauble.** Showy but useless thing; trinket

Words
For
Everyday
Use

ig • no • min • y (ig´nə min´ē) *n.*, disgrace; dishonor

bestow upon them adequate expressions, but words cannot convey an idea of the heart-sickening despair that I then endured. The person to whom I addressed myself added that Justine had already confessed her guilt. "That evidence," he observed, "was hardly required in so glaring a case, but I am glad of it; and, indeed, none of our judges like to condemn a criminal upon circumstantial evidence, be it ever so decisive."

This was strange and unexpected intelligence; what could it mean? Had my eyes deceived me? And was I really as mad as the whole world would believe me to be if I disclosed the object of my suspicions? I hastened to return home, and Elizabeth eagerly demanded the result.

"My cousin," replied I, "it is decided as you may have expected; all judges had rather that ten innocent should suffer, than that one guilty should escape. But she has confessed."

This was a dire blow to poor Elizabeth, who had relied with firmness upon Justine's innocence. "Alas!" said she, "How shall I ever again believe in human goodness? Justine, whom I loved and esteemed as my sister, how could she put on those smiles of innocence only to betray? Her mild eyes seemed incapable of any severity or <u>guile</u>, and yet she has committed a murder."

◀ *What additional blow does Elizabeth receive?*

Soon after we heard that the poor victim had expressed a desire to see my cousin. My father wished her not to go but said that he left it to her own judgment and feelings to decide. "Yes," said Elizabeth, "I will go, although she is guilty; and you, Victor, shall accompany me; I cannot go alone." The idea of this visit was torture to me, yet I could not refuse.

We entered the gloomy prison chamber and beheld Justine sitting on some straw at the farther end; her hands were manacled, and her head rested on her knees. She rose on seeing us enter, and when we were left alone with her, she threw herself at the feet of Elizabeth, weeping bitterly. My cousin wept also.

"Oh, Justine!" said she, "why did you rob me of my last consolation? I relied on your innocence, and although I was then very wretched, I was not so miserable as I am now."

"And do you also believe that I am so very, very wicked? Do you also join with my enemies to crush me, to condemn me as a murderer?" Her voice was suffocated with sobs.

"Rise, my poor girl," said Elizabeth, "why do you kneel, if you are innocent? I am not one of your enemies; I believed

Words
For
Everyday
Use

guile (gīl) *n.*, slyness and cunning

you guiltless, notwithstanding every evidence, until I heard that you had yourself declared your guilt. That report, you say, is false; and be assured, dear Justine, that nothing can shake my confidence in you for a moment, but your own confession."

► Why did Justine confess?

"I did confess, but I confessed a lie. I confessed, that I might obtain <u>absolution</u>; but now that falsehood lies heavier at my heart than all my other sins. The God of heaven forgive me! Ever since I was condemned, my confessor has <u>besieged</u> me; he threatened and menaced, until I almost began to think that I was the monster that he said I was. He threatened excommunication[3] and hell fire in my last moments, if I continued <u>obdurate</u>. Dear lady, I had none to support me; all looked on me as a wretch doomed to ignominy and <u>perdition</u>. What could I do? In an evil hour I subscribed to a lie; and now only am I truly miserable."

She paused, weeping, and then continued, "I thought with horror, my sweet lady, that you should believe your Justine, whom your blessed aunt had so highly honored and whom you loved, was a creature capable of a crime which none but the devil himself could have perpetrated. Dear William! Dearest blessed child! I soon shall see you again in heaven, where we shall all be happy; and that consoles me, going as I am to suffer ignominy and death."

"Oh, Justine! Forgive me for having for one moment distrusted you. Why did you confess? But, do not mourn, dear girl. Do not fear. I will proclaim, I will prove your innocence. I will melt the stony hearts of your enemies by my tears and prayers. You shall not die! You, my playfellow, my companion, my sister, perish on the scaffold![4] No! no! I never could survive so horrible a misfortune."

Justine shook her head mournfully. "I do not fear to die," she said; "that pang is past. I leave a sad and bitter world; and if you remember me, and think of me as of one unjustly condemned, I am <u>resigned</u> to the fate awaiting me. Learn from me, dear lady, to submit in patience to the will of Heaven!"

► How does Frankenstein act while visiting Justine in prison?

During this conversation I had retired to a corner of the prison room, where I could conceal the horrid anguish that possessed me. Despair! Who dared talk of that? The poor

---

3. **excommunication.** Exclusion from the church
4. **scaffold.** Raised platform for the public execution of condemned criminals

---

Words For Everyday Use

ab • so • lu • tion (ab′sə loo′shən) n., formal freeing from guilt; remission from sin
be • siege (bē sēj′) vt., harass or beset with questions
ob • du • rate (äb′door it) adj., inflexible; hardened and unrepenting
per • di • tion (pər dish′ən) n., loss of the soul; damnation
re • signed (ri zīnd′) adj., yielding and uncomplaining

victim, who on the morrow was to pass the awful boundary between life and death, felt not, as I did, such deep and bitter agony. I gnashed my teeth, and ground them together, uttering a groan that came from my inmost soul. Justine started. When she saw who it was, she approached me, and said, "Dear sir, you are kind to visit me; you, I hope, do not believe that I am guilty?"

I could not answer. "No, Justine," said Elizabeth; "he is more convinced of your innocence than I was, for even when he heard that you had confessed, he did not credit it."

"I truly thank him. In these last moments I feel the sincerest gratitude towards those who think of me with kindness. How sweet is the affection of others to such a wretch as I am! It removes more than half my misfortune, and I feel as if I could die in peace now that my innocence is acknowledged by you, dear lady, and your cousin."

Thus the poor sufferer tried to comfort others and herself. She indeed gained the resignation she desired. But I, the true murderer, felt the never-dying worm alive in my bosom, which allowed of no hope or consolation. Elizabeth also wept and was unhappy, but hers also was the misery of innocence, which, like a cloud that passes over the fair moon, for a while hides but cannot tarnish its brightness. Anguish and despair had penetrated into the core of my heart; I bore a hell within me which nothing could extinguish. We stayed several hours with Justine, and it was with great difficulty that Elizabeth could tear herself away. "I wish," cried she, "that I were to die with you; I cannot live in this world of misery."

Justine assumed an air of cheerfulness, while she with difficulty repressed her bitter tears. She embraced Elizabeth, and said, in a voice of half-suppressed emotion, "Farewell, sweet lady, dearest Elizabeth, my beloved and only friend; may heaven, in its bounty, bless and preserve you; may this be the last misfortune that you will ever suffer! Live, and be happy, and make others so."

And on the morrow Justine died. Elizabeth's heart-rending eloquence failed to move the judges from their settled conviction in the criminality of the saintly sufferer. My passionate and indignant appeals were lost upon them. And when I received their cold answers and heard the harsh, unfeeling reasoning of these men, my purposed avowal died away on

◀ *What is Justine's sentence? Is Frankenstein able to save her?*

Words For Everyday Use	**el • o • quence** (el´ə kwəns) *n.,* graceful and persuasive speech **in • dig • nant** (in dig´nənt) *adj.,* feeling or expressing anger or scorn

► For what does Frankenstein feel responsible? What does he expect will happen?

my lips. Thus I might proclaim myself a madman, but not revoke the sentence passed upon my wretched victim. She perished on the scaffold as a murderess!

From the tortures of my own heart, I turned to contemplate the deep and voiceless grief of my Elizabeth. This also was my doing! And my father's woe, and the desolation of that late so smiling home—all was the work of my thrice-accursed hands! Ye weep, unhappy ones, but these are not your last tears! Again shall you raise the funeral wail, and the sound of your lamentations shall again and again be heard! Frankenstein, your son, your kinsman, your early, much-loved friend; he who would spend each vital drop of blood for your sakes, who has no thought nor sense of joy except as it is mirrored also in your dear countenances, who would fill the air with blessings and spend his life in serving you— he bids you weep, to shed countless tears; happy beyond his hopes, if thus <u>inexorable</u> fate be satisfied, and if the destruction pause before the peace of the grave have succeeded to your sad torments!

Thus spoke my prophetic soul, as, torn by remorse, horror, and despair, I beheld those I loved spend vain sorrow upon the graves of William and Justine, the first hapless victims to my <u>unhallowed</u> arts.

Words For Everyday Use

in • ex • o • ra • ble (in eksˊə rə bəl) *adj.,* unalterable
un • hal • lowed (un halˊ ōd) *adj.,* unholy; evil

Chapter 9

Nothing is more painful to the human mind than, after the feelings have been worked up by a quick succession of events, the dead calmness of inaction and certainty which follows and <u>deprives</u> the soul both of hope and fear. Justine died, she rested, and I was alive. The blood flowed freely in my veins, but a weight of despair and remorse pressed on my heart which nothing could remove. Sleep fled from my eyes; I wandered like an evil spirit, for I had committed deeds of mischief beyond description horrible, and more, much more (I persuaded myself) was yet behind. Yet my heart overflowed with kindness and the love of virtue. I had begun life with benevolent intentions and thirsted for the moment when I should put them in practice and make myself useful to my fellow beings. Now all was blasted; instead of that <u>serenity</u> of conscience which allowed me to look back upon the past with self-satisfaction, and from thence to gather promise of new hopes, I was seized by remorse and the sense of guilt, which hurried me away to a hell of intense tortures such as no language can describe.

◀ What happens to Frankenstein after Justine's death? What had he begun life prepared to do? How does he feel upon examining his past?

This state of mind preyed upon my health, which had perhaps never entirely recovered from the first shock it had sustained. I shunned the face of man; all sound of joy or <u>complacency</u> was torture to me; solitude was my only consolation—deep, dark, deathlike solitude.

My father observed with pain the alteration perceptible in my disposition and habits and endeavored by arguments deduced from the feelings of his serene conscience and guiltless life to inspire me with fortitude and awaken in me the courage to dispel the dark cloud which brooded over me. "Do you think, Victor," said he, "that I do not suffer also? No one could love a child more than I loved your brother" (tears came into his eyes as he spoke); "but is it not a duty to the survivors that we should refrain from augmenting[1] their unhappiness by an appearance of immoderate grief? It is also a duty owed to yourself, for excessive sorrow prevents improvement or enjoyment, or even the discharge of daily usefulness, without which no man is fit for society."

◀ What does Frankenstein's father suggest about Frankenstein's grief? What doesn't the father understand about his son's suffering?

---

1. **refrain from augmenting.** Prevent the increase of

Words For Everyday Use	**de • prive** (dē prīv´) *vt.*, take something away from forcibly; keep from having, using, or enjoying
	se • ren • i • ty (sə ren´ə tē) *n.*, calmness; tranquility
	com • pla • cen • cy (kəm plā´sən sē) *n.*, quiet satisfaction

This advice, although good, was totally inapplicable to my case; I should have been the first to hide my grief and console my friends if remorse had not mingled its bitterness, and terror its alarm, with my other sensations. Now I could only answer my father with a look of despair and endeavor to hide myself from his view.

About this time we retired to our house at Belrive. This change was particularly agreeable to me. The shutting of the gates regularly at ten o'clock, and the impossibility of remaining on the lake after that hour had rendered our residence within the walls of Geneva very irksome to me. I was now free. Often, after the rest of the family had retired for the night, I took the boat and passed many hours upon the water. Sometimes, with my sails set, I was carried by the wind; and sometimes, after rowing into the middle of the lake, I left the boat to pursue its own course and gave way to my own miserable reflections. I was often tempted, when all was at peace around me, and I the only unquiet thing that wandered restless in a scene so beautiful and heavenly—if I except some bat, or the frogs, whose harsh and interrupted croaking was heard only when I approached the shore— often, I say, I was tempted to plunge into the silent lake, that the waters might close over me and my calamities forever. But I was restrained, when I thought of the heroic and suffering Elizabeth, whom I tenderly loved, and whose existence was bound up in mine. I thought also of my father and surviving brother; should I by my base desertion leave them exposed and unprotected to the malice of the fiend whom I had let loose among them?

At these moments I wept bitterly and wished that peace would revisit my mind only that I might afford them consolation and happiness. But that could not be. Remorse extinguished every hope. I had been the author of unalterable evils, and I lived in daily fear, lest the monster whom I had created should <u>perpetrate</u> some new wickedness. I had an obscure feeling that all was not over, and that he would still commit some signal crime, which by its enormity should almost efface the recollection of the past. There was always scope for fear, so long as anything I loved remained behind. My <u>abhorrence</u> of this fiend cannot be conceived. When I thought of him I gnashed my teeth, my eyes became inflamed,

> ► What does Frankenstein often consider doing? Why doesn't he follow this temptation?

> ► What does Frankenstein fear?

> ► When Frankenstein thinks of the creature he created, what happens?

Words For Everyday Use	**per • pe • trate** (pʉr´pə trāt´) *vt.*, commit; perform something evil **ab • hor • rence** (ab hôr´əns) *n.*, hatred; aversion

and I ardently wished to extinguish that life which I had so thoughtlessly bestowed. When I reflected on his crimes and malice, my hatred and revenge burst all bounds of moderation. I would have made a pilgrimage to the highest peak of the Andes, could I when there have <u>precipitated</u> him to their base. I wished to see him again, that I might wreak the utmost extent of abhorrence on his head and avenge the deaths of William and Justine.

Our house was the house of mourning. My father's health was deeply shaken by the horror of the recent events. Elizabeth was sad and desponding; she no longer took delight in her ordinary occupations; all pleasure seemed to her sacrilege toward the dead; eternal woe and tears she then thought was the just tribute she should pay to innocence so blasted and destroyed. She was no longer that happy creature who in earlier youth wandered with me on the banks of the lake and talked with ecstasy of our future prospects. The first of those sorrows which are sent to wean us from the earth had visited her, and its dimming influence quenched her dearest smiles.

◀ In what ways has Elizabeth changed?

"When I reflect, my dear cousin," said she, "on the miserable death of Justine Moritz, I no longer see the world and its works as they before appeared to me. Before, I looked upon the accounts of vice and injustice that I read in books or heard from others as tales of ancient days or imaginary evils; at least they were remote and more familiar to reason than to the imagination; but now misery has come home, and men appear to me as monsters thirsting for each other's blood. Yet I am certainly unjust. Everybody believed that poor girl to be guilty, and if she could have committed the crime for which she suffered, assuredly she would have been the most depraved of human creatures. For the sake of a few jewels, to have murdered the son of her benefactor and friend, a child whom she had nursed from its birth, and appeared to love as if it had been her own! I could not consent to the death of any human being, but certainly I should have thought such a creature unfit to remain in the society of men. But she was innocent. I know, I feel she was innocent; you are of the same opinion, and that confirms me. Alas! Victor, when falsehood can look so like the truth, who can assure themselves of certain happiness? I feel if I were walking on the edge of a precipice, towards which thousands

Words For Everyday Use

pre • cip • i • tate (prē sip′ə tāt′) *vt.*, throw headlong; hurl downward

are crowding, and endeavoring to plunge me into the <u>abyss</u>. William and Justine were assassinated, and the murderer escapes; he walks about the world free, and perhaps respected. But even if I were condemned to suffer on the scaffold for the same crimes, I would not change places with such a wretch."

I listened to this discourse with the extremest agony. I, not in deed, but in effect, was the true murderer. Elizabeth read my anguish in my countenance, and kindly taking my hand, said, "My dearest friend, you must calm yourself. These events have affected me, God knows how deeply; but I am not so wretched as you are. There is an expression of despair, and sometimes of revenge, in your countenance that makes me tremble. Dear Victor, banish these dark passions. Remember the friends around you, who center all their hopes in you. Have we lost the power of rendering you happy? Ah! While we love, while we are true to each other, here in this land of peace and beauty, your native country, we may reap every tranquil blessing—what can disturb our peace?"

And could not such words from her whom I fondly prized before every other gift of fortune <u>suffice</u> to chase away the fiend that lurked in my heart? Even as she spoke I drew near to her, as if in terror, lest at that very moment the destroyer had been near to rob me of her.

Thus not the tenderness of friendship, nor the beauty of earth, nor of heaven, could redeem my soul from woe; the very accents of love were ineffectual. I was encompassed by a cloud which no beneficial influence could penetrate. The wounded deer dragging its fainting limbs to some untrodden brake,[2] there to gaze upon the arrow which had pierced it, and to die, was but a type of me.

Sometimes I could cope with the sullen despair that overwhelmed me, but sometimes the whirlwind passions of my soul drove me to seek, by bodily exercise and by change of place, some relief from my intolerable sensations. It was during an access of this kind that I suddenly left my home, and bending my steps towards the near Alpine valleys, sought in the magnificence, the eternity of such scenes, to forget myself and my <u>ephemeral</u>, because human, sorrows. My wanderings were directed towards the valley of Chamounix.[3]

▶ *Why does Elizabeth's declaration cause Frankenstein anguish?*

▶ *In what way does Frankenstein seek escape or relief from his despair?*

---

2. **brake.** Clump of brush; thicket
3. **Chamounix.** Also Chamonix, a valley in eastern France, north of Mont Blanc

Words For Everyday Use	**a • byss** (ə bis´) *n.*, deep chasm
	suf • fice (sə fīs´) *vi.*, be enough; be sufficient
	e • phem • er • al (e fem´ər əl) *adj.*, short-lived; fleeting

I had visited it frequently during my boyhood. Six years had passed since then: *I* was a wreck, but nought had changed in those savage and enduring scenes.

I performed the first part of my journey on horseback. I afterwards hired a mule, as the more sure-footed and least liable to receive injury on these rugged roads. The weather was fine; it was about the middle of the month of August, nearly two months after the death of Justine, that miserable epoch from which I dated all my woe. The weight upon my spirit was sensibly lightened as I plunged yet deeper in the ravine of Arve.[4] The immense mountains and precipices that overhung me on every side, the sound of the river raging among the rocks, and the dashing of the waterfalls around spoke of a power mighty as Omnipotence—and I ceased to fear or to bend before any being less almighty than that which had created and ruled the elements, here displayed in their most terrific guise. Still, as I ascended higher, the valley assumed a more magnificent and astonishing character. Ruined castles hanging on the precipices of piny mountains, the impetuous Arve, and cottages every here and there peeping forth from among the trees, formed a scene of singular beauty. But it was augmented and rendered <u>sublime</u> by the mighty Alps, whose white and shining pyramids and domes towered above all, as belonging to another earth, the habitations of another race of beings.

What force does Frankenstein experience as he climbs into the mountains? What effect does this experience have on him?

I passed the bridge of Pelissier, where the ravine, which the river forms, opened before me, and I began to ascend the mountain that overhangs it. Soon after, I entered the valley of Chamounix. This valley is more wonderful and sublime, but not so beautiful and picturesque, as that of Servox,[5] through which I had just passed. The high and snowy mountains were its immediate boundaries, but I saw no more ruined castles and fertile fields. Immense glaciers approached the road; I heard the rumbling thunder of the falling avalanche and marked the smoke of its passage. Mont Blanc, the supreme and magnificent Mont Blanc, raised itself from the surrounding *aiguilles*,[6] and its tremendous dome overlooked the valley.

---

4. **Arve.** River valley in the Alps
5. **Servox.** Valley in the Alps
6. ***aiguilles.*** Peaks

Words For Everyday Use

sub • lime (sə blīm´) *adj.,* majestic; awe-inspiring

► What fluctuating emotions does Victor feel during this trip?

A tingling long-lost sense of pleasure often came across me during this journey. Some turn in the road, some new object suddenly perceived and recognized, reminded me of days gone by, and were associated with the light-hearted gaiety of boyhood. The very winds whispered in soothing accents, and maternal Nature bade me weep no more. Then again the kindly influence ceased to act—I found myself <u>fettered</u> again to grief and indulging in all the misery of reflection. Then I spurred on my animal, striving so to forget the world, my fears, and more than all, myself—or, in a more desperate fashion, I alighted and threw myself on the grass, weighed down by horror and despair.

At length I arrived at the village of Chamounix. Exhaustion succeeded to the extreme fatigue both of body and of mind which I had endured. For a short space of time I remained at the window, watching the pallid lightnings that played above Mont Blanc and listening to the rushing of the Arve, which pursued its noisy way beneath. The same lulling sounds acted as a lullaby to my too keen sensations; when I placed my head upon my pillow, sleep crept over me; I felt it as it came, and blessed the giver of oblivion.

Words
For
Everyday
Use

fet • ter (fet´ər) vt., confine; restrain

Chapter 10

I spent the following day roaming through the valley. I stood beside the sources of the Arveiron, which take their rise in a glacier, that with slow pace is advancing down from the summit of the hills to barricade the valley. The abrupt sides of vast mountains were before me; the icy wall of the glacier overhung me; a few shattered pines were scattered around; and the solemn silence of this glorious presence-chamber of imperial Nature was broken only by the brawling waves or the fall of some vast fragment, the thunder sound of the avalanche or the cracking, <u>reverberated</u> along the mountains, of the accumulated ice, which, by the silent working of immutable laws, was ever and anon rent and torn, if it had been but a plaything in their hands. These sublime and magnificent scenes afforded me the greatest consolation that I was capable of receiving. They elevated me from all littleness of feeling, and although they did not remove my grief, they subdued and tranquilized it. In some degree, also, they diverted my mind from the thoughts over which it had brooded for the last month. I retired to rest at night; my slumbers, as it were, waited on and <u>ministered</u> to by the assemblance of grand shapes which I had contemplated during the day. They congregated round me; the unstained snowy mountaintop, the glittering pinnacle, the pine woods, and ragged bare ravine, the eagle, soaring amidst the clouds— they all gathered round me, and bade me be at peace.

◀ *From what does Frankenstein receive some consolation?*

Where had they fled when the next morning I awoke? All of soul-inspiring fled with sleep, and dark melancholy clouded every thought. The rain was pouring in torrents, and thick mists hid the summits of the mountains, so that I even saw not the faces of those mighty friends. Still I would penetrate their misty veil and seek them in their cloudy retreats. What were rain and storm to me? My mule was brought to the door, and I resolved to ascend to the summit of Montanvert.[1] I remembered the effect that the view of the tremendous and ever-moving glacier had produced upon my mind when I first saw it. It had then filled me with a sublime ecstasy that gave wings to the soul and allowed it to soar

---

1. **Montanvert.** Mountain peak in the Alps

Words For Everyday Use

re • ver • ber • ate (ri vʉr´bə rāt´) *vt.*, echo or resound
min • is • ter (min´is tər) *vi.*, give help; attend to needs

from the obscure world to light and joy. The sight of the awful and majestic in nature had indeed always the effect of solemnizing my mind and causing me to forget the passing cares of life. I determined to go without a guide, for I was well acquainted with the path, and the presence of another would destroy the solitary grandeur of the scene.

The ascent is precipitous, but the path is cut into continual and short windings, which enable you to surmount the perpendicularity of the mountain. It is a scene terrifically desolate. In a thousand spots the traces of the winter avalanche may be perceived, where trees lie broken and strewed on the ground, some entirely destroyed, others bent, leaning upon the jutting rocks of the mountain or transversely upon other trees. The path, as you ascend higher, is intersected by ravines of snow, down which stones continually roll from above; one of them is particularly dangerous, as the slightest sound, such as even speaking in a loud voice, produces a concussion of air sufficient to draw destruction upon the head of the speaker. The pines are not tall or luxuriant, but they are <u>somber</u> and add an air of severity to the scene. I looked on the valley beneath; vast mists were rising from the rivers which ran through it and curling in thick wreaths around the opposite mountains, whose summits were hid in the uniform clouds, while rain poured from the dark sky and added to the melancholy impression I received from the objects around me. Alas! why does man boast of sensibilities superior to those apparent in the brute; it only renders them more necessary beings. If our impulses were confined to hunger, thirst, and desire, we might be nearly free; but now we are moved by every wind that blows and a chance word or scene that that word may convey to us.

► What is the mood of this scene?

► What does this stanza reflect about Frankenstein's feelings about change and free will?

"We rest; a dream has power to poison sleep.
    We rise; one wandering thought pollutes the day.
We feel, conceive, or reason; laugh or weep,
    Embrace fond woe, or cast our cares away;
It is the same: for, be it joy or sorrow,
    The path of its departure still is free.
Man's yesterday may ne'er be like his morrow;
    Nought may endure but mutability!"[2]

2. "We rest . . . mutability!" From Percy Shelley's poem "Mutability"

Words For Everyday Use	**som • ber** (säm′bər) *adj.*, dark and gloomy

It was nearly noon when I arrived at the top of the ascent. For some time I sat upon the rock that overlooks the sea of ice. A mist covered both that and the surrounding mountains. Presently a breeze dissipated the cloud, and I descended upon the glacier. The surface is very uneven, rising like the waves of a troubled sea, descending low, and interspersed by rifts that sink deep. The field of ice is almost a league in width, but I spent nearly two hours in crossing it. The opposite mountain is a bare perpendicular rock. From the side where I now stood Montanvert was exactly opposite, at the distance of a league; and above it rose Mont Blanc, in awful majesty. I remained in a recess of the rock, gazing on this wonderful and stupendous scene. The sea, or rather the vast river of ice, wound among its dependent mountains, whose aerial summits hung over its recesses. Their icy and glittering peaks shone in the sunlight over the clouds. My heart, which was before sorrowful, now swelled with something like joy; I exclaimed, "Wandering spirits, if indeed ye wander, and do not rest in your narrow beds, allow me this faint happiness, or take me, as your companion, away from the joys of life."

As I said this I suddenly beheld the figure of a man, at some distance, advancing towards me with superhuman speed. He bounded over the <u>crevices</u> in the ice, among which I had walked with caution; his stature, also, as he approached, seemed to exceed that of man. I was troubled; a mist came over my eyes, and I felt a faintness seize me; but I was quickly restored by the cold gale of the mountains. I perceived, as the shape came nearer (sight tremendous and abhorred!) that it was the wretch whom I had created. I trembled with rage and horror, resolving to wait his approach and then close with him in mortal combat. He approached; his countenance bespoke bitter anguish, combined with disdain and malignity, while its unearthly ugliness rendered it almost too horrible for human eyes. But I scarcely observed this; rage and hatred had at first deprived me of utterance, and I recovered only to overwhelm him with words expressive of furious detestation and contempt.

"Devil," I exclaimed, "do you dare approach me? and do not you fear the fierce vengeance of my arm wreaked on your miserable head? Begone, vile insect! Or rather, stay, that I may trample you to dust! And, oh! That I could, with the

◄ Who does Frankenstein meet on the ice field? What details allow him to determine who it is even from a distance?

◄ What emotions mark the face of the creature?

Words
For
Everyday
Use

crev • ice (krevʹis) n., narrow opening caused by a crack

► How does the creature react to Frankenstein's greeting? What choice does he give Frankenstein?

extinction of your miserable existence, restore those victims whom you have so <u>diabolically</u> murdered!"

"I expected this reception," said the demon. "All men hate the wretched; how, then, must I be hated, who am miserable beyond all living things! Yet you, my creator, detest and spurn me, thy creature, to whom thou art bound by ties only <u>dissoluble</u> by the annihilation of one of us. You purpose to kill me. How dare you sport thus with life? Do your duty towards me, and I will do mine towards you and the rest of mankind. If you will comply with my conditions, I will leave them and you at peace; but if you refuse, I will glut the maw[3] of death, until it be satiated with the blood of your remaining friends."

"Abhorred monster! Fiend that thou art! The tortures of hell are too mild a vengeance for thy crimes. Wretched devil! You reproach me with your creation; come on, then, that I may extinguish the spark which I so negligently bestowed."

My rage was without bounds; I sprang on him, impelled by all the feelings which can arm one being against the existence of another.

► Of what does the creature remind Frankenstein? What does the creature ask of Frankenstein?

He easily eluded me, and said, "Be calm! I entreat you to hear me, before you give vent to your hatred on my devoted head. Have I not suffered enough that you seek to increase my misery? Life, although it may only be an accumulation of anguish, is dear to me, and I will defend it. Remember, thou hast made me more powerful than thyself; my height is superior to thine, my joints more supple. But I will not be tempted to set myself in opposition to thee. I am thy creature, and I will be even mild and docile to my natural lord and king if thou wilt also perform thy part, the which thou owest me. Oh, Frankenstein, be not <u>equitable</u> to every other and trample upon me alone, to whom thy justice, and even thy clemency and affection, is most due. Remember that I am thy creature; I ought to be thy Adam,[4] but I am rather the fallen angel, whom thou drivest from joy for no misdeed. Everywhere I see bliss, from which I alone am irrevocably excluded. I was benevolent and good; misery made me a fiend. Make me happy, and I shall again be virtuous."

► What does the creature say was his natural disposition? Why has it changed?

3. **maw.** Throat, jaw, or stomach; anything that devours
4. **Adam.** Beloved first creation; Frankenstein should see his creation as God looked upon Adam.

Words For Everyday Use	**di • a • bol i • cal • ly** (dī´ə bäl´ik lē) *adv.*, wickedly; fiendishly **dis • sol • u • ble** (di säl´yo͞o bəl) *adj.*, capable of being dissolved or broken up	**eq • ui • ta • ble** (ek´wit ə bəl) *adj.*, characterized by equity; fair; just

"Begone! I will not hear you. There can be no community between you and me; we are enemies. Begone, or let us try our strength in a fight, in which one must fall."

"How can I move thee? Will no entreaties cause thee to turn a favorable eye upon thy creature, who implores thy goodness and compassion? Believe me, Frankenstein, I was benevolent; my soul glowed with love and humanity, but am I not alone, miserably alone? You, my creator, abhor me; what hope can I gather from your fellow creatures, who owe me nothing? They spurn and hate me. The desert mountains and dreary glaciers are my refuge. I have wandered here many days; the caves of ice, which I only do not fear, are a dwelling to me, and the only one which man does not grudge. These bleak skies I hail, for they are kinder to me than your fellow beings. If the multitude of mankind knew of my existence, they would do as you do, and arm themselves for my destruction. Shall I not then hate them who abhor me? I will keep no terms with my enemies. I am miserable, and they shall share my wretchedness. Yet it is in your power to recompense me, and deliver them from an evil which it only remains for you to make so great, that not only you and your family, but thousands of others, shall be swallowed up in the whirlwinds of its rage. Let your compassion be moved, and do not <u>disdain</u> me. Listen to my tale; when you have heard that, abandon or <u>commiserate</u> me, as you shall judge that I deserve. But hear me. The guilty are allowed, by human laws, bloody as they are, to speak in their own defense before they are condemned. Listen to me, Frankenstein. You accuse me of murder, and yet you would, with a satisfied conscience, destroy your own creature. Oh, praise the eternal justice of man! Yet I ask you not to spare me; listen to me, and then, if you can, and if you will, destroy the work of your hands."

"Why do you call to my remembrance," I rejoined, "circumstances of which I shudder to reflect, that I have been the miserable origin and author? Cursed be the day, abhorred devil, in which you first saw light! Cursed (although I curse myself) be the hands that formed you! You have made me wretched beyond expression. You have left me no power to consider whether I am just to you or not. Begone! Relieve me from the sight of your detested form."

◀ What does Frankenstein have the power to do? What does the creature want Frankenstein to do before judging him?

◀ What irony about Frankenstein's intentions does the creature point out?

Words For Everyday Use

dis • dain (dis dān´) vt., treat as unworthy; reject with scorn
com • mis • er • ate (kə miz´ər āt´) vt., feel or show sorrow or pity

"Thus I relieve thee, my creator," he said, and placed his hated hands before my eyes, which I flung from me with violence; "thus I take from thee a sight which you abhor. Still thou canst listen to me and grant me thy compassion. By the virtues that I once possessed, I demand this from you. Hear my tale; it is long and strange, and the temperature of this place is not fitting to your fine sensations; come to the hut upon the mountain. The sun is yet high in the heavens; before it descends to hide itself behind yon snowy precipices, and illuminate another world, you will have heard my story, and can decide. On you it rests whether I quit forever the neighborhood of man and lead a harmless life, or become the <u>scourge</u> of your fellow creatures and the author of your own speedy ruin."

▶ Why does Frankenstein agree to hear the creature's tale? What does he understand for the first time?

As he said this he led the way across the ice; I followed. My heart was full, I did not answer him, but, as I proceeded, I weighed the various arguments that he had used, and determined at least to listen to his tale. I was partly urged by curiosity, and compassion confirmed my resolution. I had hitherto supposed him to be the murderer of my brother, and I eagerly sought a confirmation or denial of this opinion. For the first time, also, I felt what the duties of a creator towards his creature were, and that I ought to render him happy before I complained of his wickedness. These motives urged me to comply with his demand. We crossed the ice, therefore, and ascended the opposite rock. The air was cold, and the rain again began to descend; we entered the hut, the fiend with an air of exultation, I with a heavy heart and depressed spirits. But I consented to listen, and, seating myself by the fire which my odious companion had lighted, he thus began his tale.

Words For Everyday Use	**scourge** (skurj) *n.*, cause of serious trouble or affliction

Chapter 11

"It is with considerable difficulty that I remember the original era of being; all the events of that period appear confused and indistinct. A strange multiplicity of sensations seized me, and I saw, felt, heard, and smelt, at the same time; and it was, indeed, a long time before I learned to distinguish between the operations of my various senses. By degrees, I remember, a stronger light pressed upon my nerves, so that I was obliged to shut my eyes. Darkness then came over me, and troubled me, but hardly had I felt this when, by opening my eyes, as I now suppose, the light poured in upon me again. I walked and, I believe, descended, but I presently found a great alteration in my sensations. Before, dark and opaque bodies had surrounded me, impervious to my touch or sight; but I now found that I could wander on at liberty, with no obstacles which I could not either <u>surmount</u> or avoid. The light became more and more oppressive to me, and the heat wearying me as I walked, I sought a place where I could receive shade. This was the forest near Ingolstadt; and here I lay by the side of a brook resting from my fatigue, until I felt tormented by hunger and thirst. This roused me from my nearly <u>dormant</u> state, and I ate some berries which I found hanging on the trees or lying on the ground. I slaked my thirst at the brook, and then lying down, was overcome by sleep.

"It was dark when I awoke; I felt cold also, and half frightened, as it were instinctively, finding myself so desolate. Before I had quitted your apartment, on a sensation of cold, I had covered myself with some clothes, but these were insufficient to secure me from the dews of night. I was a poor, helpless, miserable wretch; I knew, and could distinguish, nothing; but feeling pain invade me on all sides, I sat down and wept.

"Soon a gentle light stole over the heavens and gave me a sensation of pleasure. I started up and beheld a radiant form rise from among the trees. I gazed with a kind of wonder. It moved slowly, but it enlightened my path, and I again went out in search of berries. I was still cold when under one of

◄ *What are the first things the creature remembers? What needs guide his actions?*

Words For Everyday Use	**sur • mount** (sər mount´) *vt.,* overcome **dor • mant** (dôr´mənt) *adj.,* alive but not moving; sleeping

▶ *How does the creature warm himself?*

▶ *What happens when the creature tries to express himself?*

▶ *How does the creature again warm himself?*

▶ *What does the creature learn through this experience?*

the trees I found a huge cloak, with which I covered myself, and sat down upon the ground. No distinct ideas occupied my mind; all was confused. I felt light, and hunger, and thirst, and darkness; innumerable sounds rang in my ears, and on all sides various scents saluted me; the only object that I could distinguish was the bright moon, and I fixed my eyes on that with pleasure.

"Several changes of day and night passed, and the orb of night had greatly lessened, when I began to distinguish my sensations from each other. I gradually saw plainly the clear stream that supplied me with drink and the trees that shaded me with their foliage. I was delighted when I first discovered that a pleasant sound, which often saluted my ears, proceeded from the throats of the little winged animals who had often intercepted the light from my eyes. I began also to observe, with greater accuracy, the forms that surrounded me and to perceive the boundaries of the radiant roof of light which canopied me. Sometimes I tried to imitate the pleasant songs of the birds but was unable. Sometimes I wished to express my sensations in my own mode, but the uncouth and inarticulate sounds which broke from me frightened me into silence again.

"The moon had disappeared from the night, and again, with a lessened form, showed itself, while I still remained in the forest. My sensations had by this time become distinct, and my mind received every day additional ideas. My eyes became accustomed to the light and to perceive objects in their right forms; I distinguished the insect from the herb, and by degrees, one herb from another. I found that the sparrow uttered none but harsh notes, whilst those of the blackbird and thrush were sweet and enticing.

"One day, when I was oppressed by cold, I found a fire which had been left by some wandering beggars, and was overcome with delight at the warmth I experienced from it. In my joy I thrust my hand into the live embers, but quickly drew it out again with a cry of pain. How strange, I thought, that the same cause should produce such opposite effects! I examined the materials of the fire, and to my joy found it to be composed of wood. I quickly collected some branches, but they were wet and would not burn. I was pained at this and sat still watching the operation of the fire. The wet wood which I had placed near the heat dried and itself became inflamed. I reflected on this, and by touching the various branches, I discovered the cause, and busied myself in collecting a great quantity of wood, that I might dry it and have a plentiful supply of fire. When night came on, and brought sleep with it, I was in the greatest fear lest my fire should be extinguished. I covered it carefully with dry wood and leaves and placed wet branches upon it; and then, spreading my cloak, I lay on the ground, and sank into sleep.

"It was morning when I awoke, and my first care was to visit the fire. I uncovered it, and a gentle breeze quickly fanned it into a flame. I observed this also and contrived a fan of branches, which roused the embers when they were nearly extinguished. When night came again I found, with pleasure, that the fire gave light as well as heat and that the discovery of this element was useful to me in my food, for I found some of the offals[1] that the travelers had left had been roasted, and tasted much more <u>savory</u> than the berries I gathered from the trees. I tried, therefore, to dress my food in the same manner, placing it on the live embers. I found that the berries were spoiled by this operation, and the nuts and roots much improved.

"Food, however, became scarce, and I often spent the whole day searching in vain for a few acorns to <u>assuage</u> the pangs of hunger. When I found this, I resolved to quit the place that I had hitherto inhabited, to seek for one where the few wants I experienced would be more easily satisfied. In this emigration I exceedingly lamented the loss of the fire which I had obtained through accident and knew not how to reproduce it. I gave several hours to the serious consideration of this difficulty, but I was obliged to <u>relinquish</u> all attempt to supply it, and, wrapping myself up in my cloak, I struck across the wood towards the setting sun. I passed three days in these rambles and at length discovered the open country. A great fall of snow had taken place the night before, and the fields were of one uniform white; the appearance was disconsolate, and I found my feet chilled by the cold damp substance that covered the ground.

"It was about seven in the morning, and I longed to obtain food and shelter; at length I perceived a small hut, on a rising ground, which had doubtless been built for the convenience of some shepherd. This was a new sight to me, and I examined the structure with great curiosity. Finding the door open, I entered. An old man sat in it, near a fire, over which he was

◄ How does the old man react when the creature enters his hut?

---

1. **offals.** Waste

Words For Everyday Use

sa • vor • y (sā´vər ē) *adj.*, appetizing
as • suage (ə swāj´) *vt.*, lessen; allay
re • lin • quish (ri liŋ´kwish) *vt.*, give up; abandon

preparing his breakfast. He turned on hearing a noise and, perceiving me, shrieked loudly, and, quitting the hut, ran across the fields with a speed of which his debilitated form hardly appeared capable. His appearance, different from any I had ever before seen, and his flight somewhat surprised me. But I was enchanted by the appearance of the hut; here the snow and rain could not penetrate; the ground was dry; and it presented to me then as <u>exquisite</u> and divine a retreat as Pandemonium[2] appeared to the demons of hell after their sufferings in the lake of fire.[3] I greedily devoured the remnants of the shepherd's breakfast, which consisted of bread, cheese, milk, and wine; the latter, however, I did not like. Then, overcome by fatigue, I lay down among some straw and fell asleep.

"It was noon when I awoke, and, <u>allured</u> by the warmth of the sun, which shone brightly on the white ground, I determined to recommence my travels; and, depositing the remains of the peasant's breakfast in a wallet I found, I proceeded across the fields for several hours, until at sunset I arrived at a village. How miraculous did this appear! The huts, the neater cottages, and stately houses engaged my admiration by turns. The vegetables in the gardens, the milk and cheese that I saw placed at the windows of some of the cottages, allured my appetite. One of the best of these I entered, but I had hardly placed my foot within the door before the children shrieked, and one of the women fainted. The whole village was roused; some fled, some attacked me, until, grievously bruised by stones and many other kinds of missile weapons, I escaped to the open country and fearfully took refuge in a low <u>hovel</u>, quite bare, and making a wretched appearance after the palaces I had beheld in the village. This hovel, however, joined a cottage of a neat and pleasant appearance, but after my late dearly bought experience, I dared not enter it. My place of refuge was constructed of wood, but so low that I could with difficulty sit upright in it. No wood, however, was placed on the earth, which formed the floor, but it was dry; and although the wind entered it by innumerable chinks, I found it an agreeable <u>asylum</u> from the snow and rain.

> ► What do the villagers do when the creature tries to enter a cottage? Where does the creature find refuge?

---

2. **Pandemonium.** Hell
3. **lake of fire.** Place of eternal torment for the devil and his demons (Revelation 20)

Words For Everyday Use

ex • qui • site (eks´kwi zit) *adj.*, beautiful and of highest quality

al • lure (ə loor´) *vt.*, tempt, attract, entice

hov • el (huv´əl) *n.*, hut; miserable dwelling

a • sy • lum (ə sī´ləm) *n.*, refuge; place where one is safe

"Here, then, I retreated and lay down happy to have found a shelter, however miserable, from the <u>inclemency</u> of the season, and still more from the <u>barbarity</u> of man.

"As soon as morning dawned I crept from my kennel, that I might view the adjacent cottage and discover if I could remain in the habitation I had found. It was situated against the back of the cottage and surrounded on the sides which were exposed by a pig sty and a clear pool of water. One part was open, and by that I had crept in; but now I covered every crevice by which I might be perceived with stones and wood, yet in such a manner that I might move them on occasion to pass out; all the light I enjoyed came through the sty, and that was sufficient for me.

"Having thus arranged my dwelling and carpeted it with clean straw, I retired, for I saw the figure of a man at a distance, and I remembered too well my treatment the night before to trust myself in his power. I had first, however, provided for my sustenance for that day by a loaf of coarse bread, which I <u>purloined</u>, and a cup with which I could drink more conveniently than from my hand of the pure water which flowed by my retreat. The floor was a little raised, so that it was kept perfectly dry, and by its vicinity to the chimney of the cottage it was tolerably warm.

◄ *Why does the creature hide from the man? What does the creature do to make himself comfortable?*

"Being thus provided, I resolved to reside in this hovel until something should occur which might alter my determination. It was indeed a paradise compared to the bleak forest, my former residence, the rain-dropping branches, and dank earth. I ate my breakfast with pleasure and was about to remove a plank to procure myself a little water when I heard a step, and looking through a small chink, I beheld a young creature, with a pail on her head, passing before my hovel. The girl was young and of gentle demeanor, unlike what I have since found cottagers and farmhouse servants to be. Yet she was meanly dressed, a coarse blue petticoat and a linen jacket being her only garb; her fair hair was plaited but not adorned: she looked patient yet sad. I lost sight of her, and in about a quarter of an hour she returned bearing the pail, which was now partly filled with milk. As she walked along, seemingly <u>incommoded</u> by the burden, a young man met her, whose countenance expressed a deeper despondence. Uttering a few sounds with an air of melancholy, he took the

◄ *What does the creature notice about the cottagers?*

Words For Everyday Use	**in • clem • en • cy** (in klem´ən sē) *n.*, storminess; severity
	bar • bar • i • ty (bär ber´ə tē) *n.*, cruel behavior; inhumanity
	pur • loin (pər loin´) *vt.*, steal
	in • com • mode (in´kə mōd´) *vt.*, bother; inconvenience

pail from her head and bore it to the cottage himself. She followed, and they disappeared. Presently I saw the young man again, with some tools in his hand, cross the field behind the cottage; and the girl was also busied, sometimes in the house, and sometimes in the yard.

"On examining my dwelling, I found that one of the windows of the cottage had formerly occupied a part of it, but the panes had been filled up with wood. In one of these was a small and almost <u>imperceptible</u> chink through which the eye could just penetrate. Through this crevice a small room was visible, whitewashed and clean but very bare of furniture. In one corner, near a small fire, sat an old man, leaning his head on his hands in a disconsolate attitude. The young girl was occupied in arranging the cottage; but presently she took something out of a drawer, which employed her hands, and she sat down beside the old man, who, taking up an instrument, began to play, and to produce sounds sweeter than the voice of the thrush or the nightingale. It was a lovely sight, even to me, poor wretch who had never beheld aught beautiful before. The silver hair and benevolent countenance of the aged cottager won my reverence, while the gentle manners of the girl enticed my love. He played a sweet mournful air which I perceived drew tears from the eyes of his amiable companion, of which the old man took no notice, until she sobbed audibly; he then pronounced a few sounds, and the fair creature, leaving her work, knelt at his feet. He raised her and smiled with such kindness and affection that I felt sensations of a peculiar and over-powering nature; they were a mixture of pain and pleasure, such as I had never before experienced, either from hunger or cold, warmth or food; and I withdrew from the window, unable to bear these emotions.

"Soon after this the young man returned, bearing on his shoulders a load of wood. The girl met him at the door, helped to relieve him of his burden, and, taking some of the fuel into the cottage, placed it on the fire; then she and the youth went apart into a nook of the cottage, and he showed her a large loaf and a piece of cheese. She seemed pleased, and went into the garden for some roots and plants, which she placed in water, and then upon the fire. She afterwards continued her work, whilst the young man went into the

► *While looking in the window, what does the creature see? Why does he withdraw from the window?*

Words For Everyday Use

im • per • cep • ti • ble (im´pər sep´tə bəl) *adj.*, not easily perceived or seen

garden and appeared busily employed in digging and pulling up roots. After he had been employed thus about an hour, the young woman joined him and they entered the cottage together.

"The old man had, in the meantime, been <u>pensive</u>, but on the appearance of his companions he assumed a more cheerful air, and they sat down to eat. The meal was quickly dispatched. The young woman was again occupied in arranging the cottage; the old man walked before the cottage in the sun for a few minutes, leaning on the arm of the youth. Nothing could exceed in beauty the contrast between these two excellent creatures. One was old, with silver hairs and a countenance beaming with benevolence and love; the younger was slight and graceful in his figure, and his features were molded with the finest symmetry, yet his eyes and attitude expressed the utmost sadness and despondency. The old man returned to the cottage, and the youth, with tools different from those he had used in the morning, directed his steps across the fields.

"Night quickly shut in, but to my extreme wonder, I found that the cottagers had a means of prolonging light by the use of tapers,[4] and was delighted to find that the setting of the sun did not put an end to the pleasure I experienced in watching my human neighbors. In the evening, the young girl and her companion were employed in various occupations which I did not understand; and the old man again took up the instrument which produced the divine sounds that had enchanted me in the morning. So soon as he had finished, the youth began, not to play, but to utter sounds that were monotonous, and neither resembling the harmony of the old man's instrument nor the songs of the birds; I since found that he read aloud, but at that time I knew nothing of the science of words or letters.

"The family, after having been thus occupied for a short time, extinguished their lights, and retired, as I conjectured, to rest."

◄ *As night settles, what surprises the creature? Why does this discovery please him?*

---

4. **tapers.** Candles

Words For Everyday Use

pen • sive (pen′siv) *adj.*, thinking deeply or seriously

Responding to the Selection

Based on Frankenstein's account of his creation and on the beginning of the creature's own story, are you sympathetic toward Frankenstein? toward the creature? Do you think Frankenstein's treatment of the creature is justified? Explain your responses.

Reviewing the Selection

Recalling and Interpreting

1. **R:** Of whose death is Frankenstein informed upon returning from his trip? Describe the circumstances of this death. Who is accused as the murderer? What evidence links this person to the murder? What happens to the accused person?

2. **I:** Frankenstein blames himself for two deaths because he created the creature who committed the murder. Explain whether you think Frankenstein is responsible for either death. Do you think his creation should be held accountable for the deaths of these two people? Why, or why not?

3. **R:** Frankenstein claims to know who the real murderer is, yet he will not reveal the culprit. What reasons does he give for not divulging this information?

4. **I:** Do you think Frankenstein is honest about his reasons for remaining quiet about the murderer's identity? What other reasons might he have for remaining quiet?

5. **R:** With what intentions does Frankenstein say he began to create this life? How does he now feel upon looking back on his attempt to create life? What caused his ideas to change?

6. **I:** Compare and contrast the changes in disposition or in moral character that occur in Frankenstein and in his creation.

7. **R:** What things does Frankenstein's creation learn in the beginning of his life as described in chapter 11? Describe the experiences he has with the people he encounters in chapter 11.

8. **I:** In what ways do the creature's experiences mirror those of any human from birth? In what ways do his experiences differ? What does he learn from the way people treat him?

Synthesizing

9. Remember that Walton is listening to Frankenstein's tale. What reaction do you think Walton has to the story at this point? Describe the settings in which Frankenstein and the creature choose to tell their stories. Why might both narrators decide to tell their stories in such places?

10. The concept of the noble savage—the idea that primitive human beings are naturally good and that any evil they develop is a result of the corrupting force of civilization—was extremely popular in Europe from the sixteenth century to the nineteenth century. Explain whether the monster embodies this concept.

Understanding Literature (QUESTIONS FOR DISCUSSION)

1. Romanticism. Romanticism was a literary and artistic movement of the eighteenth and nineteenth centuries that placed value on emotion or imagination over reason, the individual over society, nature and wildness over human works, the country over the town, common people over aristocrats, and freedom over control or authority. Explain whether Shelley's novel reflects or rejects Romantic ideals.

2. Imagery. The images—words or phrases that name something that can be seen, heard, touched, tasted, or smelled—in a literary work are referred to, collectively, as the work's **imagery.** Find two passages that include nature imagery in chapters 7–11. Identify the images and explain the purpose of each passage.

3. Theme and Dramatic Irony. A **theme** is a central idea in a literary work. *Frankenstein* explores the combination of good and evil in people and the way we view these forces and the roles of justice and injustice in the world. Elizabeth says, "Before [Justine's execution], I looked upon the accounts of vice and injustice that I read in books or heard from others as tales of ancient days or imaginary evils . . . but now misery has come home, and men appear to me as monsters thirsting for each other's blood." What view of human nature does Elizabeth have? Does she believe people are primarily good or primarily evil? Explain. **Irony** is a difference between appearance and reality; **dramatic irony** occurs when something is known by the reader or audience but unknown to the characters. Why is the last part of Elizabeth's statement ironic?

Chapter 12

▶ What is most striking to the creature about the cottagers? Why doesn't he join them?

"I lay on my straw, but I could not sleep. I thought of the occurrences of the day. What chiefly struck me was the gentle manners of these people, and I longed to join them, but dared not. I remembered too well the treatment I had suffered the night before from the barbarous villagers, and resolved, whatever course of conduct I might hereafter think it right to pursue, that for the present I would remain quietly in my hovel, watching and endeavoring to discover the motives which influenced their actions.

"The cottagers arose the next morning before the sun. The young woman arranged the cottage and prepared the food, and the youth departed after the first meal.

"This day was passed in the same routine as that which preceded it. The young man was constantly employed out of doors, and the girl in various <u>laborious</u> occupations within. The old man, whom I soon perceived to be blind, employed his leisure hours on his instrument or in contemplation. Nothing could exceed the love and respect which the younger cottagers exhibited towards their venerable companion. They performed towards him every little office of affection and duty with gentleness, and he rewarded them by his benevolent smiles.

▶ What emotions do the younger cottagers have for the old man? In what way do these people show their feelings for one another?

▶ How does the creature know that the cottagers are not always happy? Why is he surprised by this discovery?

"They were not entirely happy. The young man and his companion often went apart and appeared to weep. I saw no cause for their unhappiness, but I was deeply affected by it. If such lovely creatures were miserable, it was less strange that I, an imperfect and solitary being, should be wretched. Yet why were these gentle beings unhappy? They possessed a delightful house (for such it was in my eyes) and every luxury; they had a fire to warm them when chill and delicious viands[1] when hungry; they were dressed in excellent clothes; and, still more, they enjoyed one another's company and speech, interchanging each day looks of affection and kindness. What did their tears imply? Did they really express pain? I was at first unable to solve these questions, but perpetual attention and time explained to me many appearances which were at first <u>enigmatic</u>.

---

1. **viands.** Food

Words For Everyday Use	**la • bo • ri • ous** (lə bôr′ē əs) *adj.*, involving or calling for much hard work; difficult
	en • ig • mat • ic (en′ig mat′ik) *adj.*, perplexing; baffling

"A considerable period elapsed before I discovered one of the causes of the uneasiness of this amiable family: it was poverty, and they suffered that evil in a very distressing degree. Their nourishment consisted entirely of the vegetables of their garden and the milk of one cow, which gave very little during the winter, when its masters could scarcely procure food to support it. They often, I believe, suffered the pangs of hunger very poignantly, especially the two younger cottagers, for several times they placed food before the old man when they reserved none for themselves.

◀ What is the source of the cottagers' distress? Why is this problem more difficult for the younger cottagers?

"This trait of kindness moved me sensibly. I had been accustomed, during the night, to steal a part of their store for my own consumption, but when I found that in doing this I inflicted pain on the cottagers, I <u>abstained</u> and satisfied myself with berries, nuts, and roots, which I gathered from a neighboring wood.

◀ Why does the creature start seeking berries, nuts, and roots to eat?

"I discovered also another means through which I was enabled to assist their labors. I found that the youth spent a great part of each day in collecting wood for the family fire, and, during the night, I often took his tools, the use of which I quickly discovered, and brought home firing sufficient for the consumption of several days.

◀ What does the creature do to assist the cottagers?

"I remember, the first time that I did this, the young woman, when she opened the door in the morning, appeared greatly astonished on seeing a great pile of wood on the outside. She uttered some words in a loud voice, and the youth joined her, who also expressed surprise. I observed, with pleasure, that he did not go to the forest that day, but spent it in repairing the cottage and cultivating the garden.

"By degrees I made a discovery of still greater moment. I found that these people possessed a method of communicating their experience and feelings to one another by articulate sounds. I perceived that the words they spoke sometimes produced pleasure or pain, smiles or sadness, in the minds and countenances of the hearers. This was indeed a godlike science, and I ardently desired to become acquainted with it. But I was baffled in every attempt I made for this purpose. Their pronunciation was quick, and the words they uttered, not having any apparent connection with visible objects, I was unable to discover any clue by which I could unravel the mystery of their reference. By great application, however,

◀ What important discovery does the creature make?

Words For Everyday Use

ab • stain (əb stān´) *vi.*, voluntarily do without

► *What words does the creature learn?*

and after having remained during the space of several revolutions of the moon in my hovel, I discovered the names that were given to some of the most familiar objects of discourse; I learned and applied the words, 'fire,' 'milk,' 'bread,' and 'wood.' I learned also the names of the cottagers themselves. The youth and his companion had each of them several names, but the old man had only one, which was 'father.' The girl was called 'sister,' or 'Agatha;' and the youth 'Felix,' 'brother,' or 'son.' I cannot describe the delight I felt when I learned the ideas appropriated to each of these sounds and was able to pronounce them. I distinguished several other words without being able as yet to understand or apply them, such as 'good,' 'dearest,' 'unhappy.'

"I spent the winter in this manner. The gentle manners and beauty of the cottagers greatly endeared them to me; when they were unhappy, I felt depressed; when they rejoiced, I sympathized in their joys. I saw few human beings beside them, and if any other happened to enter the cottage, their harsh manners and rude gait only enhanced to me the superior accomplishments of my friends. The old man, I could perceive, often endeavored to encourage his children, as sometimes I found that he called them, to cast off their melancholy. He would talk in a cheerful accent, with an expression of goodness that bestowed pleasure even upon me. Agatha listened with respect, her eyes sometimes filled with tears, which she endeavored to wipe away unperceived; but I generally found that her countenance and tone were more cheerful after having listened to the <u>exhortations</u> of

► *Who is the saddest of the group?*

her father. It was not thus with Felix. He was always the saddest of the group, and, even to my unpracticed senses, he appeared to have suffered more deeply than his friends. But if his countenance was more sorrowful, his voice was more cheerful than that of his sister, especially when he addressed the old man.

"I could mention innumerable instances, which, although slight, marked the dispositions of these amiable cottagers. In the midst of poverty and want, Felix carried with pleasure to his sister the first little white flower that peeped out from beneath the snowy ground. Early in the morning, before she had risen, he cleared away the snow that obstructed her path to the milkhouse, drew water from the well, and brought the

Words For Everyday Use	**ex • hor • ta • tion** (eǵzôr tāʹshən) *n.,* urging plea

wood from the out-house, where, to his perpetual astonishment, he found his store always replenished by an invisible hand. In the day, I believe, he worked sometimes for a neighboring farmer, because he often went forth and did not return until dinner, yet brought no wood with him. At other times he worked in the garden, but as there was little to do in the frosty season, he read to the old man and Agatha.

◄ What does Felix do during the frosty season?

"This reading had puzzled me extremely at first, but by degrees I discovered that he uttered many of the same sounds when he read as when he talked. I conjectured, therefore, that he found on the paper signs for speech which he understood, and I ardently longed to comprehend these also; but how was that possible when I did not even understand the sounds for which they stood as signs? I improved, however, sensibly in this science, but not sufficiently to follow up any kind of conversation, although I applied my whole mind to the endeavor, for I easily perceived that, although I eagerly longed to discover myself to the cottagers, I ought not to make the attempt until I had first become master of their language, which knowledge might enable me to make them overlook the deformity of my figure, for with this also the contrast perpetually presented to my eyes had made me acquainted.

◄ What conclusion does the creature make regarding Felix's activity?

◄ Why does the creature think it is important to learn the language of the cottagers?

"I had admired the perfect forms of my cottagers—their grace, beauty, and delicate complexions; but how was I terrified when I viewed myself in a transparent pool! At first I started back, unable to believe that it was indeed I who was reflected in the mirror; and when I became fully convinced that I was in reality the monster that I am, I was filled with the bitterest sensations of <u>despondence</u> and <u>mortification</u>. Alas! I did not yet entirely know the fatal effects of this miserable deformity.

◄ How does the creature react when he sees his own reflection?

"As the sun became warmer and the light of day longer, the snow vanished, and I beheld the bare trees and the black earth. From this time Felix was more employed, and the heart-moving indications of impending famine disappeared. Their food, as I afterwards found, was coarse, but it was wholesome; and they procured a sufficiency of it. Several new kinds of plants sprung up in the garden, which they dressed; and these signs of comfort increased daily as the season advanced.

Words For Everyday Use

de • spond • ence (di spän′dəns) n., dejection; lack of hope
mor • ti • fi • ca • tion (môr′tə fi kā′shən) n., humiliation; loss of self-respect

"The old man, leaning on his son, walked each day at noon, when it did not rain, as I found it was called when the heavens poured forth its waters. This frequently took place, but a high wind quickly dried the earth, and the season became far more pleasant than it had been.

"My mode of life in my hovel was uniform. During the morning I attended the motions of the cottagers, and when they were dispersed in various occupations, I slept: the remainder of the day was spent in observing my friends. When they had retired to rest, if there was any moon or the night was star-light, I went into the woods and collected my own food and fuel for the cottage. When I returned, as often as it was necessary, I cleared their path of the snow and performed those offices that I had seen done by Felix. I afterwards found that these labors, performed by an invisible hand, greatly astonished them; and once or twice I heard them, on these occasions, utter the words 'good spirit,' 'wonderful'; but I did not then understand the signification of these terms.

"My thoughts now became more active, and I longed to discover the motives and feelings of these lovely creatures; I was inquisitive to know why Felix appeared so miserable and Agatha so sad. I thought (foolish wretch!) that it might be in my power to restore happiness to these deserving people. When I slept or was absent, the forms of the venerable blind father, the gentle Agatha, and the excellent Felix flitted before me, I looked upon them as superior beings who would be the arbiters of my future destiny. I formed in my imagination a thousand pictures of presenting myself to them, and their reception of me. I imagined that they would be disgusted, until, by my gentle demeanor and conciliating words, I should first win their favor, and afterwards their love.

"These thoughts exhilarated me and led me to apply with fresh ardor to the acquiring the art of language. My organs were indeed harsh, but supple; and although my voice was very unlike the soft music of their tones, yet I pronounced such words as I understood with tolerable ease. It was as the ass and the lap-dog; yet surely the gentle ass whose intentions were affectionate, although his manners were rude, deserved better treatment than blows and execration.

▶ What thoughts do the cottagers have about the creature based solely on his actions?

▶ What thoughts exhilarate the creature? What do these thoughts prompt him to do?

| Words For Everyday Use | **ar • bi • ter** (är′ bət ər) *n.*, judge |
| | **ex • e • cra • tion** (ek′si krā′shən) *n.*, cursing |

"The pleasant showers and genial warmth of spring greatly altered the aspect of the earth. Men who before this change seemed to have been hid in caves dispersed themselves, and were employed in various arts of cultivation. The birds sang in more cheerful notes, and the leaves began to bud forth on the trees. Happy, happy earth! Fit habitation for gods, which, so short a time before, was bleak, damp, and unwholesome. My spirits were elevated by the enchanting appearance of nature; the past was blotted from my memory, the present was tranquil, and the future gilded by bright rays of hope and anticipations of joy."

◄ *What effect does the coming of spring have on the creature?*

Chapter 13

"I now hasten to the more moving part of my story. I shall relate events that impressed me with feelings which, from what I had been, have made me what I am.

"Spring advanced rapidly; the weather became fine and the skies cloudless. It surprised me that what before was desert and gloomy should now bloom with the most beautiful flowers and verdure. My senses were gratified and refreshed by a thousand scents of delight and a thousand sights of beauty.

"It was on one of these days, when my cottagers periodically rested from labor—the old man played on his guitar, and the children listened to him—that I observed the countenance of Felix was melancholy beyond expression; he sighed frequently, and once his father paused in his music, and I conjectured by his manner that he inquired the cause of his son's sorrow. Felix replied in a cheerful accent, and the old man was recommencing his music when someone tapped at the door.

"It was a lady on horseback, accompanied by a countryman as a guide. The lady was dressed in a dark suit and covered with a thick black veil. Agatha asked a question, to which the stranger only replied by pronouncing, in a sweet accent, the name of Felix. Her voice was musical, but unlike that of either of my friends. On hearing this word, Felix came up hastily to the lady, who, when she saw him, threw up her veil, and I beheld a countenance of angelic beauty and expression. Her hair of a shining raven black, and curiously braided; her eyes were dark, but gentle, although animated; her features of a regular proportion, and her complexion wondrously fair, each cheek tinged with a lovely pink.

"Felix seemed <u>ravished</u> with delight when he saw her, every trait of sorrow vanished from his face, and it instantly expressed a degree of ecstatic joy, of which I could hardly have believed it capable; his eyes sparkled as his cheek flushed with pleasure; and at that moment I thought him as beautiful as the stranger. She appeared affected by different feelings; wiping a few tears from her lovely eyes, she held out her hand to Felix, who kissed it <u>rapturously</u>, and called her, as well as I could distinguish, his sweet Arabian. She did not

▶ What happens to end Felix's depression?

Words For Everyday Use	rav • ish (rav´ish) vt., transport with joy rap • tur • ous • ly (rap´chər əs lē) adv., with ecstasy; as if carried away with love or joy

appear to understand him, but smiled. He assisted her to dismount, and dismissing her guide, conducted her into the cottage. Some conversation took place between him and his father, and the young stranger knelt at the old man's feet and would have kissed his hand, but he raised her, and embraced her affectionately.

"I soon perceived that, although the stranger uttered articulate sounds and appeared to have a language of her own, she was neither understood by nor herself understood the cottagers. They made many signs which I did not comprehend, but I saw that her presence diffused gladness through the cottage, dispelling their sorrow as the sun dissipates the morning mists. Felix seemed peculiarly happy and with smiles of delight welcomed his Arabian. Agatha, the ever-gentle Agatha, kissed the hands of the lovely stranger, and pointing to her brother, made signs which appeared to me to mean that he had been sorrowful until she came. Some hours passed thus, while they, by their countenances, expressed joy, the cause of which I did not comprehend. Presently I found, by the frequent recurrence of some sound which the stranger repeated after them, that she was endeavoring to learn their language; and the idea instantly occurred to me that I should make use of the same instructions to the same end. The stranger learned about twenty words at the first lesson; most of them, indeed, were those which I had before understood, but I profited by the others.

◀ What does the creature realize about the newcomer's language?

◀ In what way does the newcomer's arrival help the creature?

"As night came on Agatha and the Arabian retired early. When they separated, Felix kissed the hand of the stranger, and said, 'Good night, sweet Safie.' He sat up much longer, conversing with his father, and, by the frequent repetition of her name I conjectured that their lovely guest was the subject of their conversation. I ardently desired to understand them, and bent every faculty towards that purpose, but found it utterly impossible.

"The next morning Felix went out to his work, and, after the usual occupations of Agatha were finished, the Arabian sat at the feet of the old man, and, taking his guitar, played some airs so entrancingly beautiful that they at once drew tears of sorrow and delight from my eyes. She sang, and her voice flowed in a rich <u>cadence</u>, swelling or dying away, like a nightingale of the woods.

Words
For
Everyday
Use

ca • dence (kād´'ns) *n.*, inflection; rhythmic flow of sound

"When she had finished, she gave the guitar to Agatha, who at first declined it. She played a simple air, and her voice accompanied it in sweet accents, but unlike the wondrous strain of the stranger. The old man appeared enraptured and said some words which Agatha endeavored to explain to Safie, and by which he appeared to wish to express that she bestowed on him the greatest delight by her music.

"The days now passed as peacefully as before, with the sole alteration that joy had taken the place of sadness in the countenances of my friends. Safie was always gay and happy; she and I improved rapidly in the knowledge of language, so that in two months I began to comprehend most of the words uttered by my protectors.

▶ How long does it take the creature to become proficient in the cottagers' language?

"In the meanwhile also the black ground was covered with herbage, and the green banks interspersed with innumerable flowers, sweet to the scent and the eyes, stars of pale radiance among the moonlight woods; the sun became warmer, the nights clear and balmy; and my nocturnal rambles were an extreme pleasure to me, although they were considerably shortened by the late setting and early rising of the sun, for I never ventured abroad during daylight, fearful of meeting with the same treatment I had formerly endured in the first village which I entered.

"My days were spent in close attention, that I might more speedily master the language; and I may boast that I improved more rapidly than the Arabian, who understood very little, and conversed in broken accents, whilst I comprehended and could imitate almost every word that was spoken.

▶ What does the creature learn along with the spoken language of the cottagers?

"While I improved in speech, I also learned the science of letters as it was taught to the stranger, and this opened before me a wide field for wonder and delight.

"The book from which Felix instructed Safie was Volney's *Ruins of Empires*.[1] I should not have understood the purport of this book had not Felix, in reading it, given very minute explanations. He had chosen this work, he said, because the declamatory style was framed in imitation of the eastern authors. Through this work I obtained a cursory knowledge of history and a view of the several empires at present existing

▶ What historical events does the creature learn of? How does he feel about these events?

---

1. **Volney's *Ruins of Empires*.** Essay about the philosophy of history by the Comte de Volney, Constantin-François Chaseboeuf (1757–1820)

Words For Everyday Use

balm • y (bäm´ē) *adj.*, mild and pleasant

de • clam • a • to • ry (dē klam´ə tôr´ē) *adj.*, marked by artificial eloquence

cur • so • ry (kʉr´sə rē) *adj.*, superficial

in the world; it gave me an insight into the manners, governments, and religions of the different nations of the earth. I heard of the slothful Asiatics, of the stupendous genius and mental activity of the Grecians, of the wars and wonderful virtue of the early Romans—of their subsequent degenerating—of the decline of that mighty empire, of chivalry, Christianity, and kings. I heard of the discovery of the American hemisphere and wept with Safie over the hapless fate of its original inhabitants.

"These wonderful narrations inspired me with strange feelings. Was man, indeed, at once so powerful, so virtuous and magnificent, yet so vicious and base? He appeared at one time a mere <u>scion</u> of the evil principle and at another as all that can be conceived of noble and godlike. To be a great and virtuous man appeared the highest honor that can befall a sensitive being; to be base and vicious, as many on record have been, appeared the lowest degradation, a condition more <u>abject</u> than that of the blind mole or harmless worm. For a long time I could not conceive how one man could go forth to murder his fellow, or even why there were laws and governments; but when I heard details of vice and bloodshed, my wonder ceased, and I turned away with disgust and loathing.

◄ *Why is the creature puzzled by what he has learned?*

"Every conversation of the cottagers now opened new wonders to me. While I listened to the instructions which Felix bestowed upon the Arabian, the strange system of human society was explained to me. I heard of the division of property, of immense wealth and <u>squalid</u> poverty, of rank, descent, and noble blood.

"The words induced me to turn towards myself. I learned that the possessions most esteemed by your fellow creatures were high and unsullied descent united with riches. A man might be respected with only one of these advantages, but without either he was considered, except in very rare instances, as a vagabond and a slave, doomed to waste his powers for the profits of the chosen few! And what was I? Of my creation and creator I was absolutely ignorant, but I knew that I possessed no money, no friends, no kind of property. I was, besides, endued with a figure hideously deformed and loathsome; I was not even of the same nature as man. I was more agile than they and could subsist upon coarser diet; I bore the extremes of heat and cold with less injury to

◄ *What does the creature learn about what humans esteem in each other? In what way does this knowledge apply to the creature's condition? What does the creature think he may be?*

Words For Everyday Use	sci • on (sī´ən) *n.*, shoot or bud
	ab • ject (ab´jekt´) *adj.*, miserable, wretched
	squal • id (skwäl´id) *adj.*, wretched; miserable

my frame; my stature far exceeded theirs. When I looked around I saw and heard of none like me. Was I then a monster, a blot upon the earth, from which all men fled and whom all men disowned?

"I cannot describe to you the agony that these reflections inflicted upon me; I tried to dispel them, but sorrow only increased with knowledge. Oh, that I had forever remained in my native wood, nor known nor felt beyond the sensations of hunger, thirst, and heat!

▶ To what does the creature compare knowledge? What does he learn is the only end to his suffering?

"Of what a strange nature is knowledge! It clings to the mind when it has once seized on it like a lichen on the rock. I wished sometimes to shake off all thought and feeling, but I learned that there was but one means to overcome the sensation of pain, and that was death—a state which I feared yet did not understand. I admired virtue and good feelings and loved the gentle manners and amiable qualities of my cottagers, but I was shut out from intercourse with them, except through means which I obtained by stealth, when I was unseen and unknown, and which rather increased than satisfied the desire I had of becoming one among my fellows. The gentle words of Agatha and the animated smiles of the charming Arabian were not for me. The mild exhortations of the old man and the lively conversation of the loved Felix were not for me. Miserable, unhappy wretch!

▶ What does the creature learn about relationships? Why does this knowledge add to his misery?

"Other lessons were impressed upon me even more deeply. I heard of the difference of sexes, and the birth and growth of children, how the father doted on the smiles of the infant, and the lively <u>sallies</u> of the older child, how all the life and cares of the mother were wrapped up in the precious charge, how the mind of youth expanded and gained knowledge, of brother, sister, and all the various relationships which bind one human being to another in mutual bonds.

"But where were my friends and relations? No father had watched my infant days, no mother had blessed me with smiles and caresses; or if they had, all my past life was now a blot, a blind vacancy in which I distinguished nothing. From my earliest remembrance I had been as I then was in height and proportion. I had never yet seen a being resembling me or who claimed any intercourse with me. What was I? The question again recurred, to be answered only with groans.

Words
For
Everyday
Use

sal • ly (sal´ē) n., sudden start into activity

"I will soon explain to what these feelings tended, but allow me now to return to the cottagers, whose story excited in me such various feelings of indignation, delight, and wonder, but which all terminated in additional love and reverence for my protectors (for so I loved, in an innocent, half painful self-deceit, to call them)."

◄ *Why does the creature call the cottagers his "protectors"?*

Chapter 14

"Some time elapsed before I learned the history of my friends. It was one which could not fail to impress itself deeply on my mind, unfolding as it did a number of circumstances, each interesting and wonderful to one so utterly inexperienced as I was.

▶ *What was the life of the cottagers like before they came to the cottage?*

"The name of the old man was De Lacey. He was descended from a good family in France, where he had lived for many years in affluence, respected by his superiors and beloved by his equals. His son was bred in the service of his country, and Agatha had ranked with ladies of the highest distinction. A few months before my arrival they had lived in a large and luxurious city called Paris, surrounded by friends and possessed of every enjoyment which virtue, refinement of intellect, or taste, accompanied by a moderate fortune, could afford.

▶ *What connection does Safie have to the De Lacey family?*

"The father of Safie had been the cause of their ruin. He was a Turkish merchant and had inhabited Paris for many years, when, for some reason which I could not learn, he became obnoxious to the government. He was seized and cast into prison the very day that Safie arrived from Constantinople[1] to join him. He was tried and condemned to death. The injustice of his sentence was very <u>flagrant</u>; all Paris was indignant; and it was judged that his religion and wealth rather than the crime alleged against him had been the cause of his condemnation.

"Felix had accidentally been present at the trial; his horror and indignation were uncontrollable when he heard the decision of the court. He made, at that moment, a solemn vow to deliver him and then looked around for the means. After many <u>fruitless</u> attempts to gain admittance to the prison, he found a strongly grated window in an unguarded part of the building which lighted the dungeon of the unfortunate Muhammadan,[2] who, loaded with chains, waited in despair the execution of the barbarous sentence. Felix visited the grate at night and made known to the prisoner his

---

1. **Constantinople.** Seaport in Turkey, formerly Byzantium, now Istanbul
2. **Muhammadan.** Muslim

Words For Everyday Use	fla • grant (flā´grənt) *adj.,* outrageous fruit • less (frōōt´ lis) *adj.,* unsuccessful; futile

intentions in his favor. The Turk, amazed and delighted, endeavored to kindle the zeal of his deliverer by promises of reward and wealth. Felix rejected his offers with contempt, yet when he saw the lovely Safie, who was allowed to visit her father and who by her gestures expressed her lively gratitude, the youth could not help owning to his own mind that the captive possessed a treasure which would fully reward his toil and hazard.

◄ What promises does the Turk make to Felix? What does Felix want instead?

"The Turk quickly perceived the impression that his daughter had made on the heart of Felix and endeavored to secure him more entirely in his interests by the promise of her hand in marriage so soon as he should be conveyed to a place of safety. Felix was too delicate to accept this offer, yet he looked forward to the probability of the event as to the consummation of his happiness.

"During the ensuing days, while the preparations were going forward for the escape of the merchant, the zeal of Felix was warmed by several letters that he received from this lovely girl, who found means to express her thoughts in the language of her lover by the aid of an old man, a servant of her father who understood French. She thanked him in the most ardent terms for his intended services towards her parent, and at the same time deeply deplored her own fate.

"I have copies of these letters, for I found means, during my residence in the hovel, to procure the implements of writing; and the letters were often in the hands of Felix or Agatha. Before I depart I will give them to you; they will prove the truth of my tale; but at present, as the sun is already far declined, I shall only have time to repeat the substance of them to you.

◄ How did the creature learn some of his information about the cottagers?

"Safie related that her mother was a Christian Arab, seized and made a slave by the Turks; recommended by her beauty, she had won the heart of the father of Safie, who married her. The young girl spoke in high and enthusiastic terms of her mother, who, born in freedom, spurned the bondage to which she was now reduced. She instructed her daughter in the tenets[3] of her religion and taught her to aspire to higher powers of intellect and an independence of spirit forbidden to the female followers of Muhammad. This lady died, but her lessons were indelibly impressed on the mind of Safie,

◄ What lessons does Safie learn from her mother? In what way do these lessons contribute to her desire to stay with Felix?

---

3. **tenets.** Principle doctrines

Words For Everyday Use

spurn (spurn) *vt.*, reject with contempt

who sickened at the prospect of again returning to Asia and being immured within the walls of a harem, allowed only to occupy herself with infantile amusements, ill suited to the temper of her soul, now accustomed to grand ideas and a noble <u>emulation</u> for virtue. The prospect of marrying a Christian and remaining in a country where women were allowed to take a rank in society was enchanting to her.

"The day for the execution of the Turk was fixed, but, on the night previous to it he quitted his prison and before morning was distant many leagues from Paris. Felix had procured passports in the name of his father, sister, and himself. He had previously communicated his plan to the former, who aided the deceit by quitting his house, under the pretense of a journey and concealed himself, with his daughter, in an obscure part of Paris.

"Felix conducted the fugitives through France to Lyons and across Mont Cenis to Leghorn,[4] where the merchant had decided to wait a favorable opportunity of passing into some part of the Turkish dominions.[5]

"Safie resolved to remain with her father until the moment of his departure, before which time the Turk renewed his promise that she should be united to his deliverer; and Felix remained with them in expectation of that event; and in the meantime he enjoyed the society of the Arabian, who exhibited towards him the simplest and tenderest affection. They conversed with one another through the means of an interpreter, and sometimes with the interpretation of looks; and Safie sang to him the divine airs of her native country.

▶ What plan does the Turk seem to endorse? What does he actually intend to do? Why does he conceal his plan?

"The Turk allowed this intimacy to take place and encouraged the hopes of the youthful lovers, while in his heart he had formed far other plans. He loathed the idea that his daughter should be united to a Christian, but he feared the resentment of Felix if he should appear luke-warm, for he knew that he was still in the power of his deliverer, if he should choose to betray him to the Italian state which they inhabited. He revolved a thousand plans by which he should be enabled to prolong the deceit until it might be no longer

---

4. **Mont Cenis to Leghorn.** Mountain in the Alps to a seaport in Tuscany in western Italy
5. **Turkish dominions.** Lands ruled by Turkey

Words For Everyday Use

em • u • la • tion (em′yo͞o lā′shən) *n.*, desire to equal or surpass

necessary, and secretly to take his daughter with him when he departed. His plans were <u>facilitated</u> by the news which arrived from Paris.

"The government of France were greatly enraged at the escape of their victim and spared no pains to detect and punish his deliverer. The plot of Felix was quickly discovered, and De Lacey and Agatha were thrown into prison. The news reached Felix and roused him from his dream of pleasure. His blind and aged father and his gentle sister lay in a <u>noisome</u> dungeon while he enjoyed the free air and the society of her whom he loved. This idea was torture to him. He quickly arranged with the Turk that if the latter should find a favorable opportunity for escape before Felix could return to Italy, Safie should remain as a boarder at a convent at Leghorn; and then, quitting the lovely Arabian, he hastened to Paris, and delivered himself up to the vengeance of the law, hoping to free De Lacey and Agatha by this proceeding.

◄ What happens when Felix's role in the Turk's escape is discovered?

◄ What plan does Felix make with the Turk? Why does he go to Paris? What is the result of his efforts?

"He did not succeed. They remained confined for five months before the trial took place, the result of which deprived them of their fortune and condemned them to a perpetual exile from their native country.

"They found a miserable asylum in the cottage in Germany where I discovered them. Felix soon learned that the treacherous Turk, for whom he and his family endured such unheard-of oppression, on discovering that his deliverer was thus reduced to poverty and ruin, became a traitor to good feeling and honor and had quitted Italy with his daughter, insultingly sending Felix a pittance of money to aid him, as he said, in some plan of future maintenance.

◄ How does the Turk react when he hears about Felix's change in fortunes?

"Such were the events that preyed on the heart of Felix, and rendered him, when I first saw him, the most miserable of his family. He could have endured poverty, and while this distress had been the meed[6] of his virtue, he gloried in it; but the ingratitude of the Turk and the loss of his beloved Safie were misfortunes more bitter and irreparable. The arrival of the Arabian now infused new life into his soul.

"When the news reached Leghorn that Felix was deprived of his wealth and rank, the merchant commanded his daughter to think no more of her lover, but to prepare to return to her native country. The generous nature of Safie

6. **meed.** Reward, recompense

Words For Everyday Use	**fa • cil • i • tate** (fə sil´ə tāt´) *vt.*, make easy or easier **noi • some** (noi´səm) *adj.*, foul smelling and unhealthy

was outraged by this command; she attempted to <u>expostu-late</u> with her father, but he left her angrily, reiterating his tyrannical mandate.

"A few days after, the Turk entered his daughter's apartment and told her hastily that he had reason to believe that his residence at Leghorn had been divulged and that he should speedily be delivered up to the French government; he had consequently hired a vessel to convey him to Constantinople, for which city he should sail in a few hours. He intended to leave his daughter under the care of a confidential servant, to follow at her leisure with the greater part of his property, which had not yet arrived at Leghorn.

"When alone, Safie resolved in her own mind the plan of conduct that it would become her to pursue in this emergency. A residence in Turkey was abhorrent to her; her religion and her feelings were alike <u>averse</u> to it. By some papers of her father which fell into her hands she heard of the exile of her lover and learnt the name of the spot where he then resided. She hesitated some time, but at length she formed her determination. Taking with her some jewels that belonged to her and a sum of money, she quitted Italy with an attendant, a native of Leghorn, but who understood the common language of Turkey, and departed for Germany.

"She arrived in safety at a town about twenty leagues from the cottage of De Lacey, when her attendant fell dangerously ill. Safie nursed her with the most devoted affection, but the poor girl died, and the Arabian was left alone, unacquainted with the language of the country, and utterly ignorant of the customs of the world. She fell, however, into good hands. The Italian had mentioned the name of the spot for which they were bound and, after her death the woman of the house in which they had lived took care that Safie should arrive in safety at the cottage of her lover."

▶ How does Safie learn where Felix is?

▶ What difficulties does Safie face in her quest to find Felix?

| Words For Everyday Use | ex • pos • tu • late (eks päs´chə lāt´) *vi.*, reason with earnestly |
| | a • verse (ə vʉrs´) *adj.*, opposed |

Chapter 15

"Such was the history of my beloved cottagers. It impressed me deeply. I learned, from the views of social life which it developed, to admire their virtues and to <u>deprecate</u> the vices of mankind.

"As yet I looked upon crime as a distant evil, benevolence and generosity were ever present before me, <u>inciting</u> within me a desire to become an actor in the busy scene where so many admirable qualities were called forth and displayed. But in giving an account of the progress of my intellect, I must not omit a circumstance which occurred in the beginning of the month of August of the same year.

◄ What view of crime and evil does the creature have at this point?

"One night during my accustomed visit to the neighboring wood where I collected my own food and brought home firing for my protectors, I found on the ground a leathern portmanteau[1] containing several articles of dress and some books. I eagerly seized the prize and returned with it to my hovel. Fortunately the books were written in the language the elements of which I had acquired at the cottage; they consisted of *Paradise Lost,* a volume of Plutarch's *Lives,* and the *Sorrows of Werter.*[2] The possession of these treasures gave me extreme delight; I now continually studied and exercised my mind upon these histories, whilst my friends were employed in their ordinary occupations.

◄ What event aids the progress of the creature's intellectual endeavors?

"I can hardly describe to you the effect of these books. They produced in me an infinity of new images and feelings that sometimes raised me to ecstasy, but more frequently sank me into the lowest dejection. In the *Sorrows of Werter,* besides the interest of its simple and affecting story, so many opinions are <u>canvassed</u> and so many lights thrown upon what had hitherto been to me obscure subjects that I found in it a never-ending source of speculation and astonishment. The gentle and domestic manners it described, combined

---

1. **leathern portmanteau.** Leather traveling case
2. *Paradise Lost . . . Sorrows of Werter.* Refers to three works: John Milton's *Paradise Lost,* an epic poem about the fall of humans from grace; Plutarch's biographies of Greek and Roman heroes; and Johann Wolfgang von Goethe's *The Sorrows of Young Werter,* a novel about a sensitive artist in love with a woman engaged to another man.

Words For Everyday Use

dep • re • cate (dep′rə kāt) *vt.,* feel and express disapproval of
in • cite (in sīt′) *vt.,* urge; stir up
can • vas (kan′vəs) *vt.,* examine or discuss in detail

with lofty sentiments and feelings, which had for their object something out of self, accorded well with my experience among my protectors and with the wants which were forever alive in my own bosom. But I thought Werter himself a more divine being than I had ever beheld or imagined; his character contained no pretension, but it sank deep. The <u>disquisitions</u> upon death and suicide were calculated to fill me with wonder. I did not pretend to enter into the merits of the case, yet I inclined towards the opinions of the hero, whose extinction I wept, without precisely understanding it.

▶ In what way does the creature relate to the literature that he reads?

"As I read, however, I applied much personally to my own feelings and condition. I found myself similar yet at the same time strangely unlike to the beings concerning whom I read and to whose conversation I was a listener. I sympathized with and partly understood them, but I was unformed in mind; I was dependent on none and related to none. 'The path of my departure was free', and there was none to lament my annihilation. My person was hideous and my stature gigantic. What did this mean? Who was I? What was I? Whence did I come? What was my destination? These questions continually recurred, but I was unable to solve them.

"The volume of Plutarch's *Lives* which I possessed contained the histories of the first founders of the ancient republics. This book had a far different effect upon me from the *Sorrows of Werter*. I learned from Werter's imaginations <u>despondency</u> and gloom, but Plutarch taught me high thoughts; he elevated me above the wretched sphere of my own reflections, to admire and love the heroes of past ages. Many things I read surpassed my understanding and experience. I had a very confused knowledge of kingdoms, wide extents of country, mighty rivers, and boundless seas. But I was perfectly unacquainted with towns and large assemblages of men. The cottage of my protectors had been the only school in which I had studied human nature, but this book developed new and mightier scenes of action. I read of men concerned in public affairs, governing or massacring their species. I felt the greatest ardor for virtue rise within me, and abhorrence for vice, as far as I understood the signification of those terms, relative as they were, as I applied them, to pleasure and pain alone. Induced by these feelings,

| Words For Everyday Use | dis • qui • si • tion (dis´kwi zish´ən) *n.*, formal discussion |
| | de • spond • en • cy (di spän´dən sē) *n.*, dejection; loss of courage or hope |

I was of course led to admire peaceable lawgivers, Numa, Solon, and Lycurgus, in preference to Romulus and Theseus.[3] The patriarchal lives of my protectors caused these impressions to take a firm hold on my mind; perhaps, if my first introduction to humanity had been made by a young soldier, burning for glory and slaughter, I should have been imbued with different sensations.

◀ Why do the characters of the cottages have such a profound effect on the creature?

"But *Paradise Lost* excited different and far deeper emotions. I read it, as I had read the other volumes which had fallen into my hands, as a true history. It moved every feeling of wonder and awe that the picture of an omnipotent God warring with his creatures was capable of exciting. I often referred the several situations, as their similarity struck me, to my own. Like Adam, I was apparently united by no link to any other being in existence; but his state was far different from mine in every other respect. He had come forth from the hands of God a perfect creature, happy and prosperous, guarded by the especial care of his Creator; he was allowed to converse with and acquire knowledge from beings of a superior nature, but I was wretched, helpless, and alone. Many times I considered Satan as the fitter emblem of my condition, for often, like him, when I viewed the bliss of my protectors, the bitter <u>gall</u> of envy rose within me.

◀ What comparisons to his own life does the creature make while reading Paradise Lost?

"Another circumstance strengthened and confirmed these feelings. Soon after my arrival in the hovel I discovered some papers in the pocket of the dress which I had taken from your laboratory. At first I had neglected them, but now that I was able to decipher the characters in which they were written, I began to study them with <u>diligence</u>. It was your journal of the four months that preceded my creation. You minutely described in these papers every step you took in the progress of your work; this history was mingled with accounts of domestic occurrences. You doubtless recollect these papers. Here they are. Everything is related in them which bears reference to my accursed origin; the whole detail of that series of disgusting circumstances which produced it is set in view; the minutest description of my odious and loathsome person is given, in language which painted your own horrors and

◀ Now that the creature can read, what is he able to use? What does he learn from this source?

---

3. **Numa . . . Theseus.** Numa was the second king of Rome; Solon and Lycurgus were Athenian government officials; according to legend, Romulus was one of the founders of Rome; and Theseus is an Athenian hero.

Words For Everyday Use

gall (gôl) *n.,* something that is distasteful

dil • i • gence (dil´ə jəns) *n.,* constant, careful effort; perseverance

▶ How does the creature feel about himself after learning of his origin and his creator's attitude toward him? What questions does he pose to Frankenstein? To what does he contrast his situation?

rendered mine indelible. I sickened as I read. 'Hateful day when I received life!' I exclaimed in agony. 'Accursed creator! Why did you form a monster so hideous that even *you* turned from me in disgust? God, in pity, made man beautiful and alluring, after his own image; but my form is a filthy type of yours, more horrid even from the very resemblance. Satan had his companions, fellow-devils, to admire and encourage him, but I am solitary and abhorred.'

"These were the reflections of my hours of despondency and solitude; but when I contemplated the virtues of the cottagers, their amiable and benevolent dispositions, I persuaded myself that when they should become acquainted with my admiration of their virtues they would compassionate[4] me, and overlook my personal deformity. Could they turn from their door one, however monstrous, who solicited their compassion and friendship? I resolved, at least not to despair, but in every way to fit myself for an interview with them which would decide my fate. I postponed this attempt for some months longer, for the importance attached to its success inspired me with a dread lest I should fail. Besides, I found that my understanding improved so much with every day's experience that I was unwilling to commence this undertaking until a few more months should have added to my sagacity.

▶ Why does the creature put off trying to contact his protectors?

"Several changes, in the meantime, took place in the cottage. The presence of Safie diffused happiness among its inhabitants, and I also found that a greater degree of plenty reigned there. Felix and Agatha spent more time in amusement and conversation, and were assisted in their labors by servants. They did not appear rich, but they were contented and happy; their feelings were serene and peaceful, while mine became every day more tumultuous. Increase of knowledge only discovered to me more clearly what a wretched outcast I was. I cherished hope, it is true, but it vanished when I beheld my person reflected in water, or my shadow in the moonshine, even as that frail image and that inconstant shade.

▶ What things cause the creature's hope to fade?

"I endeavored to crush these fears, and to fortify myself for the trial which in a few months I resolved to undergo; and sometimes I allowed my thoughts, unchecked by reason,

---

4. **compassionate.** Pity

Words
For
Everyday
Use

sa • gac • i • ty (sə gas´ə tē) *n.,* shrewdness; wisdom and good judgment

tu • mul • tu • ous (tōō mul´chōō əs) *adj.,* wild and noisy; greatly agitated

to ramble in the fields of Paradise, and dared to fancy amiable and lovely creatures sympathizing with my feelings and cheering my gloom; their angelic countenances breathed smiles of consolation. But it was all a dream; no Eve[5] soothed my sorrows nor shared my thoughts; I was alone. I remembered Adam's supplication to his Creator.[6] But where was mine? He had abandoned me, and in the bitterness of my heart I cursed him.

◀ What does the creature allow himself to imagine? In what way does his reality differ from his dreams?

"Autumn passed thus. I saw, with surprise and grief, the leaves decay and fall, and nature again assume the <u>barren</u> and bleak appearance it had worn when I first beheld the woods and the lovely moon. Yet I did not heed the bleakness of the weather; I was better fitted by my conformation for the endurance of cold than heat. But my chief delights were the sight of the flowers, the birds, and all the gay apparel of summer; when those deserted me, I turned with more attention towards the cottagers. Their happiness was not decreased by the absence of summer. They loved, and sympathized with one another; and their joys, depending on each other, were not interrupted by the casualties that took place around them. The more I saw of them, the greater became my desire to claim their protection and kindness; my heart <u>yearned</u> to be known and loved by these amiable creatures; to see their sweet looks directed towards me with affection was the utmost limit of my ambition. I dared not think that they would turn them from me with disdain and horror. The poor that stopped at their door were never driven away. I asked, it is true, for greater treasures than a little food or rest: I required kindness and sympathy; but I did not believe myself utterly unworthy of it.

◀ Why doesn't the change in season affect the creature? What aspect of the change does affect him?

◀ What aspects give the creature hope that his overtures to the cottagers will be successful?

"The winter advanced, and an entire revolution of the seasons had taken place since I awoke into life. My attention at this time was solely directed towards my plan of introducing myself into the cottage of my protectors. I revolved many projects, but that on which I finally fixed was to enter the dwelling when the blind old man should be alone. I had sagacity enough to discover that the unnatural hideousness of my person was the chief object of horror with those who had formerly beheld me. My voice, although harsh, had

◀ Who does the creature plan to approach first? Why?

---

5. **Eve.** First woman, companion to Adam
6. **Adam's . . . Creator.** Adam asks God for a human companion.

| Words For Everyday Use | **bar • ren** (bar´ən) *adj.,* dull; unproductive
yearn (yʉrn) *vi.,* be filled with longing |

nothing terrible in it; I thought, therefore, that if in the absence of his children I could gain the good will and mediation of the old De Lacey, I might by his means be tolerated by my younger protectors.

"One day, when the sun shone on the red leaves that strewed the ground and diffused cheerfulness, although it denied warmth, Safie, Agatha, and Felix departed on a long country walk, and the old man, at his own desire, was left alone in the cottage. When his children had departed, he took up his guitar and played several mournful but sweet airs, more sweet and mournful than I had ever heard him play before. At first his countenance was illuminated with pleasure, but as he continued, thoughtfulness and sadness succeeded; at length, laying aside the instrument, he sat absorbed in reflection.

"My heart beat quick; this was the hour and moment of trial which would decide my hopes or realize my fears. The servants were gone to a neighboring fair. All was silent in and around the cottage; it was an excellent opportunity; yet, when I proceeded to execute my plan, my limbs failed me and I sank to the ground. Again I rose, and exerting all the firmness of which I was master, removed the planks which I had placed before my hovel to conceal my retreat. The fresh air revived me and, with renewed determination I approached the door of their cottage.

"I knocked. 'Who is there?' said the old man. 'Come in.'

"I entered. 'Pardon this intrusion,' said I; 'I am a traveler in want of a little rest; you would greatly oblige me if you would allow me to remain a few minutes before the fire.'

"'Enter,' said De Lacey; 'and I will try to relieve your wants; but, unfortunately, my children are from home, and as I am blind, I am afraid I shall find it difficult to procure food for you.'

"'Do not trouble yourself, my kind host; I have food; it is warmth and rest only that I need.'

"I sat down, and a silence ensued. I knew that every minute was precious to me, yet I remained irresolute in what manner to commence the interview, when the old man addressed me. "'By your language, stranger, I suppose you are my countryman; are you French?'

> ► How does De Lacey first greet the creature?

me • di • a • tion (mē´dē ā´shən) n., diplomatic intervention to settle differences

o • blige (ə blīj´) vt., make indebted for a favor or kindness done

ir • res • o • lute (ir rez´ə lōōt´) adj., wavering in decision or purpose

"'No; but I was educated by a French family and understand that language only. I am now going to claim the protection of some friends, whom I sincerely love, and of whose favor I have some hopes.'

"'Are they Germans?'

"'No, they are French. But let us change the subject. I am an unfortunate and deserted creature; I look around and I have no relation or friend upon earth. These amiable people to whom I go have never seen me and know little of me. I am full of fears, for if I fail there, I am an outcast in the world forever.'

◄ What fears does the creature express to De Lacey?

"'Do not despair. To be friendless is indeed to be unfortunate, but the hearts of men, when unprejudiced by any obvious self-interest, are full of brotherly love and charity. Rely, therefore, on your hopes; and if these friends are good and amiable, do not despair.'

"'They are kind—they are the most excellent creatures in the world; but, unfortunately, they are prejudiced against me. I have good dispositions; my life has been hitherto harmless and in some degree beneficial; but a fatal prejudice clouds their eyes, and where they ought to see a feeling and kind friend, they behold only a detestable monster.'

◄ What does the creature say about the friends he is seeking? Why is he concerned? What do the friends see?

"'That is indeed unfortunate; but if you are really blameless, cannot you undeceive them?'

"'I am about to undertake that task; and it is on that account that I feel so many overwhelming terrors. I tenderly love these friends; I have, unknown to them, been for many months in the habits of daily kindness towards them; but they believe that I wish to injure them, and it is that prejudice which I wish to overcome.'

"'Where do these friends reside?'

"'Near this spot.'

"The old man paused and then continued, 'If you will unreservedly <u>confide</u> to me the particulars of your tale, I perhaps may be of use in undeceiving them. I am blind and cannot judge of your countenance, but there is something in your words which persuades me that you are sincere. I am poor and an exile, but it will afford me true pleasure to be in any way serviceable to a human creature.'

◄ How does De Lacey react to the creature's story?

"'Excellent man! I thank you and accept your generous offer. You raise me from the dust by this kindness; and I trust

Words For Everyday Use

con • fide (kən fīd´) *vt.*, entrust to someone; tell confidentially

that, by your aid, I shall not be driven from the society and sympathy of your fellow creatures.'

"'Heaven forbid! Even if you were really criminal, for that can only drive you to desperation, and not <u>instigate</u> you to virtue. I also am unfortunate; I and my family have been condemned, although innocent: judge, therefore, if I do not feel for your misfortunes.'

"'How can I thank you, my best and only benefactor? From your lips first have I heard the voice of kindness directed towards me; I shall be forever grateful; and your present humanity assures me of success with those friends whom I am on the point of meeting.'

"'May I know the names and residence of those friends?'

"I paused. This, I thought, was the moment of decision, which was to rob me of or bestow happiness on me forever. I struggled vainly for firmness sufficient to answer him, but the effort destroyed all my remaining strength; I sank on the chair and sobbed aloud. At that moment I heard the steps of my younger protectors. I had not a moment to lose, but seizing the hand of the old man, I cried, 'Now is the time! Save and protect me! You and your family are the friends whom I seek. Do not you desert me in the hour of trial!'

"'Great God!' exclaimed the old man, 'Who are you?'

"At that instant the cottage door was opened, and Felix, Safie, and Agatha entered. Who can describe their horror and <u>consternation</u> on beholding me? Agatha fainted, and Safie, unable to attend to her friend, rushed out of the cottage. Felix darted forward, and with supernatural force tore me from his father, to whose knees I clung, in a transport of fury, he dashed me to the ground and struck me violently with a stick. I could have torn him limb from limb, as a lion rends the antelope. But my heart sank within me as with bitter sickness, and I refrained. I saw him on the point of repeating his blow, when, overcome by pain and anguish, I quitted the cottage and in the general tumult escaped unperceived to my hovel."

▶ Why is the creature spurred to sudden action? What does he do?

▶ How do the returning cottagers react when they see the creature? What does Felix do? Why doesn't the creature retaliate?

| Words For Everyday Use | **in • sti • gate** (inˊstə gātˊ) *vt.*, urge on or spur to some action |
| | **con • ster • na • tion** (känˊstər nāˊshən) *n.*, great fear or shock that makes one feel confused |

Chapter 16

"Cursed, cursed creator! Why did I live? Why, in that instant, did I not extinguish the spark of existence which you had so wantonly bestowed? I know not; despair had not yet taken possession of me; my feelings were those of rage and revenge. I could with pleasure have destroyed the cottage and its inhabitants and have glutted myself with their shrieks and misery.

◀ What emotions take control of the creature?

"When night came I quitted my retreat and wandered in the wood; and now, no longer restrained by the fear of discovery, I gave vent to my anguish in fearful howlings. I was like a wild beast that had broken the toils,[1] destroying the objects that obstructed me and ranging through the wood with a staglike swiftness. Oh! What a miserable night I passed! The cold stars shone in mockery, and the bare trees waved their branches above me; now and then the sweet voice of a bird burst forth amidst the universal stillness. All, save I, were at rest or in enjoyment; I, like the arch-fiend, bore a hell within me, and finding myself unsympathized with, wished to tear up the trees, spread <u>havoc</u> and destruction around me, and then to have sat down and enjoyed the ruin.

◀ To what does the creature compare himself? What does he spend the night doing?

"But this was a luxury of sensation that could not endure; I became fatigued with excess of bodily exertion and sank on the damp grass in the sick <u>impotence</u> of despair. There was none among the <u>myriads</u> of men that existed who would pity or assist me; and should I feel kindness towards my enemies? No; from that moment I declared everlasting war against the species, and more than all, against him who had formed me and sent me forth to this insupportable misery.

◀ What will the creature spend the rest of his life doing?

"The sun rose; I heard the voices of men and knew that it was impossible to return to my retreat during that day. Accordingly I hid myself in some thick underwood, determining to devote the ensuing hours to reflection on my situation.

"The pleasant sunshine and the pure air of day restored me to some degree of tranquility; and when I considered what had passed at the cottage, I could not help believing that I had been too hasty in my conclusions. I had certainly

---

1. **toils.** Snares, traps

Words For Everyday Use	**hav • oc** (hav´ek) *n.*, great destruction and devastation
	im • po • tence (im´pə təns) *n.*, weakness; powerlessness
	myr • i • ad (mir´ē əd) *n.*, indefinitely large number

▶ Why does the creature think the plan went awry? Does he have any hope to make amends?

acted <u>imprudently</u>. It was apparent that my conversation had interested the father in my behalf, and I was a fool in having exposed my person to the horror of his children. I ought to have familiarized the old De Lacey to me, and by degrees to have discovered myself to the rest of his family, when they should have been prepared for my approach. But I did not believe my errors to be irretrievable, and after much consideration I resolved to return to the cottage, seek the old man, and by my representations win him to my party.

"These thoughts calmed me, and in the afternoon I sank into a profound sleep; but the fever of my blood did not allow me to be visited by peaceful dreams. The horrible scene of the preceding day was forever acting before my eyes; the females were flying and the enraged Felix tearing me from his father's feet. I awoke exhausted, and finding that it was already night, I crept forth from my hiding place, and went in search of food.

▶ For what does the creature wait? What worries him?

"When my hunger was <u>appeased</u>, I directed my steps towards the well-known path that conducted to the cottage. All there was at peace. I crept into my hovel and remained in silent expectation of the accustomed hour when the family arose. That hour passed, the sun mounted high in the heavens, but the cottagers did not appear. I trembled violently, apprehending some dreadful misfortune. The inside of the cottage was dark, and I heard no motion; I cannot describe the agony of this suspense.

"Presently two countrymen passed by, but pausing near the cottage, they entered into conversation, using violent <u>gesticulations</u>; but I did not understand what they said, as they spoke the language of the country, which differed from that of my protectors. Soon after, however, Felix approached with another man; I was surprised, as I knew that he had not quitted the cottage that morning, and waited anxiously to discover, from his discourse, the meaning of these unusual appearances.

▶ What does the creature realize Felix intends to do?

"'Do you consider,' said his companion to him, 'that you will be obliged to pay three months' rent, and to lose the produce of your garden? I do not wish to take any unfair advantage, and I beg therefore that you will take some days to consider of your determination.'

Words For Everyday Use	im • pru • dent • ly (im proo͞od″′nt lē) adv., without thought to the consequences
	ap • pease (ə pēz′) vt., satisfy
	ges • tic • u • la • tion (jes tik′yoo͞o lā′shən) n., energetic gesture

"'It is utterly useless,' replied Felix; 'we can never again inhabit your cottage. The life of my father is in the greatest danger, owing to the dreadful circumstance that I have related. My wife and my sister will never recover their horror. I entreat you not to reason with me any more. Take possession of your tenement and let me fly from this place.'

"Felix trembled violently as he said this. He and his companion entered the cottage, in which they remained for a few minutes, and then departed. I never saw any of the family of De Lacey more.

"I continued for the remainder of the day in my hovel in a state of utter and stupid despair. My protectors had departed and had broken the only link that held me to the world. For the first time the feelings of revenge and hatred filled my bosom, and I did not strive to control them, but allowing myself to be borne away by the stream, I bent my mind towards injury and death. When I thought of my friends, of the mild voice of De Lacey, the gentle eyes of Agatha, and the exquisite beauty of the Arabian, these thoughts vanished and a gush of tears somewhat soothed me. But again, when I reflected that they had spurned and deserted me, anger returned, a rage of anger, and unable to injure anything human, I turned my fury towards inanimate objects. As night advanced I placed a variety of combustibles around the cottage, and after having destroyed every vestige of cultivation in the garden, I waited with forced impatience until the moon had sunk to commence my operations.

◄ How do the creature's thoughts about the cottagers change?

"As the night advanced, a fierce wind arose from the woods and quickly dispersed the clouds that had loitered in the heavens; the blast tore along like a mighty avalanche and produced a kind of insanity in my spirits that burst all bounds of reason and reflection. I lighted the dry branch of a tree, and danced with fury around the devoted cottage, my eyes still fixed on the western horizon, the edge of which the moon nearly touched. A part of its orb was at length hid, and I waved my brand; it sank, and with a loud scream I fired the straw, and heath, and bushes, which I had collected. The wind fanned the fire, and the cottage was quickly enveloped by the flames, which clung to it and licked it with their forked and destroying tongues.

◄ The creature had formerly discovered and used fire. In what way does the use of fire here differ from his use of fire in the past?

Words For Everyday Use	spurn (spurn) *vt.*, refuse or reject
	in • an • i • mate (in an´ə mit) *adj.*, not endowed with life
	ves • tige (ves´tij) *n.*, trace, bit

▶ Who is the only possible source of aid to the creature?

▶ How does the creature feel toward Frankenstein? Why does the creature seek Frankenstein despite these feelings?

"As soon as I was convinced that no assistance could save any part of the habitation, I quitted the scene and sought for refuge in the woods.

"And now, with the world before me, whither should I bend my steps? I resolved to fly far from the scene of my misfortunes; but to me, hated and despised, every country must be equally horrible. At length the thought of you crossed my mind. I learned from your papers that you were my father, my creator; and to whom could I apply with more fitness than to him who had given me life? Among the lessons that Felix had bestowed upon Safie, geography had not been omitted; I had learned from these the relative situations of the different countries of the earth. You had mentioned Geneva as the name of your native town, and towards this place I resolved to proceed.

"But how was I to direct myself? I knew that I must travel in a southwesterly direction to reach my destination, but the sun was my only guide. I did not know the names of the towns that I was to pass through, nor could I ask information from a single human being; but I did not despair. From you only could I hope for <u>succor</u>, although towards you I felt no sentiment but that of hatred. Unfeeling, heartless creator! You had endowed me with perceptions and passions and then cast me abroad an object for the scorn and horror of mankind. But on you only had I any claim for pity and <u>redress</u>, and from you I determined to seek that justice which I vainly attempted to gain from any other being that wore the human form.

"My travels were long and the sufferings I endured intense. It was late in autumn when I quitted the district where I had so long resided. I traveled only at night, fearful of encountering the visage of a human being. Nature decayed around me, and the sun became heatless; rain and snow poured around me; mighty rivers were frozen; the surface of the earth was hard, and chill, and bare, and I found no shelter. Oh, earth! How often did I <u>imprecate</u> curses on the cause of my being! The mildness of my nature had fled, and all within me was turned to gall and bitterness. The nearer I approached to your habitation, the more deeply did I feel the spirit of revenge enkindled in my heart. Snow fell, and the waters were hardened, but I rested not. A few incidents now and

Words For Everyday Use	
	suc • cor (suk´ər) *n.*, aid, help, or relief
	re • dress (rē´dres´) *n.*, compensation for wrong done
	im • pre • cate (im´pri kāt´) *vt.*, invoke

then directed me, and I possessed a map of the country; but I often wandered wide from my path. The agony of my feelings allowed me no respite; no incident occurred from which my rage and misery could not extract its food; but a circumstance that happened when I arrived on the confines of Switzerland, when the sun had recovered its warmth and the earth again began to look green, confirmed in an especial manner the bitterness and horror of my feelings.

"I generally rested during the day and traveled only when I was secured by night from the view of man. One morning, however, finding that my path lay through a deep wood, I ventured to continue my journey after the sun had risen; the day, which was one of the first of spring, cheered even me by the loveliness of its sunshine and the balminess of the air. I felt emotions of gentleness and pleasure, that had long appeared dead, revive within me. Half surprised by the novelty of these sensations, I allowed myself to be borne away by them, and forgetting my solitude and deformity, dared to be happy. Soft tears again bedewed my cheeks, and I even raised my humid eyes with thankfulness towards the blessed sun which bestowed such joy upon me.

◀ What emotions are reawakened in the creature by the balmy weather?

"I continued to wind among the paths of the wood, until I came to its boundary, which was skirted by a deep and rapid river, into which many of the trees bent their branches, now budding with the fresh spring. Here I paused, not exactly knowing what path to pursue, when I heard the sound of voices, that induced me to conceal myself under the shade of a cypress.[2] I was scarcely hid when a young girl came running towards the spot where I was concealed, laughing, as if she ran from someone in sport. She continued her course along the precipitous sides of the river, when suddenly her foot slipped, and she fell into the rapid stream. I rushed from my hiding-place and with extreme labor from the force of the current, saved her and dragged her to shore. She was senseless, and I endeavored by every means in my power to restore animation, when I was suddenly interrupted by the approach of a rustic,[3] who was probably the person from whom she had playfully fled. On seeing me, he darted towards me, and tearing the girl from my arms, hastened towards the deeper parts of the wood. I followed speedily, I hardly knew why; but when the man saw me draw near, he aimed a gun, which he carried, at my body, and fired. I sank to the ground, and my injurer, with increased swiftness, escaped into the wood.

◀ What happens to the young girl the creature sees from his concealment? What does he do in response?

◀ How does the young man react to seeing the creature with the young girl? What does he do to the creature?

---

2. **cypress.** Type of conifer tree
3. **rustic.** Simple, country person

"This was then the reward of my benevolence! I had saved a human being from destruction, and as a recompense I now writhed under the miserable pain of a wound which shattered the flesh and bone. The feelings of kindness and gentleness which I had entertained but a few moments before gave place to hellish rage and gnashing of teeth. Inflamed by pain, I vowed eternal hatred and vengeance to all mankind. But the agony of my wound overcame me; my pulses paused, and I fainted.

"For some weeks I led a miserable life in the woods, endeavoring to cure the wound which I had received. The ball had entered my shoulder, and I knew not whether it had remained there or passed through; at any rate I had no means of extracting it. My sufferings were augmented also by the oppressive sense of the injustice and ingratitude of their infliction. My daily vows rose for revenge—a deep and deadly revenge, such as would alone compensate for the outrages and anguish I had endured.

"After some weeks my wound healed, and I continued my journey. The labors I endured were no longer to be alleviated by the bright sun or gentle breezes of spring; all joy was but a mockery which insulted my desolate state and made me feel more painfully that I was not made for the enjoyment of pleasure.

"But my toils now drew near a close, and in two months from this time I reached the environs of Geneva.

"It was evening when I arrived, and I retired to a hiding-place among the fields that surround it to meditate in what manner I should apply to you. I was oppressed by fatigue and hunger and far too unhappy to enjoy the gentle breezes of evening or the prospect of the sun setting behind the stupendous mountains of Jura.

"At this time a slight sleep relieved me from the pain of reflection, which was disturbed by the approach of a beautiful child, who came running into the recess I had chosen, with all the sportiveness of infancy. Suddenly, as I gazed on him, an idea seized me that this little creature was unprejudiced and had lived too short a time to have imbibed a horror of deformity. If, therefore, I could seize him and educate him as my companion and friend, I should not be so desolate in this peopled earth.

► *What adds to the creature's physical sufferings?*

► *What idea occurs to the creature upon seeing the young child?*

Words For Everyday Use	**im • bibe** (im bīb´) *vt.,* take into mind and keep

"Urged by this impulse, I seized on the boy as he passed and drew him towards me. As soon as he beheld my form, he placed his hands before his eyes and uttered a shrill scream; I drew his hand forcibly from his face and said, 'Child, what is the meaning of this? I do not intend to hurt you; listen to me.'

"He struggled violently. 'Let me go,' he cried; 'monster! Ugly wretch! You wish to eat me, and tear me to pieces. You are an ogre. Let me go, or I will tell my papa.'

"'Boy, you will never see your father again; you must come with me.'

"'Hideous monster! let me go. My papa is a syndic[4]—he is M. Frankenstein—he will punish you. You dare not keep me.'

"'Frankenstein! you belong then to my enemy—to him towards whom I have sworn eternal revenge; you shall be my first victim.'

"The child still struggled and loaded me with <u>epithets</u> which carried despair to my heart; I grasped his throat to silence him, and in a moment he lay dead at my feet.

"I gazed on my victim, and my heart swelled with exultation and hellish triumph; clapping my hands, I exclaimed, 'I, too can create desolation; my enemy is not invulnerable; this death will carry despair to him, and a thousand other miseries shall torment and destroy him.'

"As I fixed my eyes on the child, I saw something glittering on his breast. I took it; it was a portrait of a most lovely woman. In spite of malignity, it softened and attracted me. For a few moments I gazed with delight on her dark eyes, fringed by deep lashes, and her lovely lips; but presently my rage returned; I remembered that I was forever deprived of the delights that such beautiful creatures could bestow and that she whose resemblance I contemplated would, in regarding me, have changed that air of divine benignity to one expressive of disgust and affright.

"Can you wonder that such thoughts transported me with rage? I only wonder that at that moment, instead of venting my sensations in exclamations and agony, I did not rush among mankind and perish in the attempt to destroy them.

"While I was overcome by these feelings, I left the spot where I had committed the murder, and seeking a more

How does the child react when he sees the monster?

What does the child reveal that interests the creature? How does this information seal the child's fate?

What effect does the portrait have on the creature?

---

4. **syndic.** Magistrate; judge

Words For Everyday Use

ep • i • thet (ep´ə thət´) *n.*, disparaging word or phrase

secluded hiding-place, I entered a barn which had appeared to me to be empty. A woman was sleeping on some straw; she was young, not indeed so beautiful as her whose portrait I held, but of an agreeable aspect and blooming in the loveliness of youth and health. Here, I thought, is one of those whose joy-imparting smiles are bestowed on all but me. And then I bent over her and whispered, 'Awake, fairest, thy lover is near—he who would give his life but to obtain one look of affection from thine eyes; my beloved, awake!'

"The sleeper stirred; a thrill of terror ran through me. Should she indeed awake, and see me, and curse me, and <u>denounce</u> the murderer? Thus would she assuredly act if her darkened eyes opened and she beheld me. The thought was madness; it stirred the fiend within me—not I, but she, shall suffer; the murder I have committed because I am forever robbed of all that she could give me, she shall atone. The crime had its source in her; be hers the punishment! Thanks to the lessons of Felix and the <u>sanguinary</u> laws of man, I had learned now to work mischief. I bent over her and placed the portrait securely in one of the folds of her dress. She moved again, and I fled.

"For some days I haunted the spot where these scenes had taken place, sometimes wishing to see you, sometimes resolved to quit the world and its miseries forever. At length I wandered towards these mountains, and have ranged through their immense recesses, consumed by a burning passion which you alone can gratify. We may not part until you have promised to comply with my <u>requisition</u>. I am alone, and miserable; man will not associate with me; but one as deformed and horrible as myself would not deny herself to me. My companion must be of the same species and have the same defects. This being you must create."

▶ Who does the creature find in the barn? Why does he think she should suffer?

▶ What does the creature demand of Frankenstein?

Words For Everyday Use	de • nounce (dē nouns´) vt., condemn; criticize
	san • gui • na • ry (saŋ´gwi ner´ē) adj., accompanied by or eager for bloodshed
	req • ui • si • tion (rek´wə zish´ən) n., formal request

Chapter 17

The being finished speaking and fixed his looks upon me in expectation of a reply. But I was bewildered, perplexed, and unable to arrange my ideas sufficiently to understand the full extent of his proposition. He continued:

"You must create a female for me with whom I can live in the interchange of those sympathies necessary for my being. This you alone can do, and I demand it of you as a right which you must not refuse to concede."

The latter part of his tale had kindled anew in me the anger that had died away while he narrated his peaceful life among the cottagers, and as he said this I could no longer suppress the rage that burned within me.

"I do refuse it," I replied; "and no torture shall ever <u>extort</u> a consent from me. You may render me the most miserable of men, but you shall never make me <u>base</u> in my own eyes. Shall I create another like yourself, whose joint wickedness might desolate the world. Begone! I have answered you; you may torture me, but I will never consent."

"You are in the wrong," replied the fiend; "and, instead of threatening, I am content to reason with you. I am malicious because I am miserable. Am I not shunned and hated by all mankind? You, my creator, would tear me to pieces and triumph; remember that, and tell me why I should pity man more than he pities me? You would not call it murder if you could precipitate me into one of those ice-rifts and destroy my frame, the work of your own hands. Shall I respect man when he condemns me? Let him live with me in the interchange of kindness, and instead of injury I would bestow every benefit upon him with tears of gratitude at his acceptance. But that cannot be; the human senses are insurmountable barriers to our union. Yet mine shall not be the submission of abject slavery. I will revenge my injuries; if I cannot inspire love, I will cause fear, and chiefly towards you my arch-enemy, because my creator, do I swear inextinguishable hatred. Have a care; I will work at your destruction, nor finish until I desolate your heart, so that you shall curse the hour of your birth."

◄ *What further explanation does the creature give of his needs?*

◄ *What emotions does the creature arouse in Frankenstein?*

◄ *How does the creature excuse his actions? Why is he unable to respect man, especially Frankenstein?*

Words For Everyday Use	**ex • tort** (eks tôrt´) *vt.*, get from somebody through threats or violence; extract
	base (bās) *adj.*, contemptible; inferior

A fiendish rage animated him as he said this; his face was wrinkled into contortions too horrible for human eyes to behold; but presently he calmed himself and proceeded,

"I intended to reason. This passion is detrimental to me, for you do not reflect that you are the cause of its excess. If any being felt emotions of benevolence towards me, I should return them a hundred and a hundred fold; for that one creature's sake, I would make peace with the whole kind! But I now indulge in dreams of bliss that cannot be realized. What I ask of is reasonable and moderate; I demand a creature of another sex, but as hideous as myself; the gratification is small, but it is all that I can receive, and it shall content me. It is true, we shall be monsters, cut off from all the world; but on that account we shall be more attached to one another. Our lives will not be happy, but they will be harmless and free from the misery I now feel. Oh! My creator, make me happy; let me feel gratitude towards you for one benefit! Let me see that I excite the sympathy of some existing thing; do not deny me my request!"

► Why do Frankenstein's feelings waver?

I was moved. I shuddered when I thought of the possible consequences of my consent, but I felt that there was some justice in his argument. His tale and the feelings he now expressed proved him to be a creature of fine sensations, and did I not as his maker owe him all the portion of happiness that it was in my power to bestow? He saw my change of feeling and continued,

► What promise does the creature make to Frankenstein?

"If you consent, neither you nor any other human being shall ever see us again; I will go to the vast wilds of South America. My food is not that of man; I do not destroy the lamb and the kid[1] to glut my appetite; acorns and berries afford me sufficient nourishment. My companion will be of the same nature as myself and will be content with the same fare. We shall make our bed of dried leaves; the sun will shine on us as on man and will ripen our food. The picture I present to you is peaceful and human, and you must feel that you could deny it only in the wantonness of power and cruelty. Pitiless as you have been towards me, I now see compassion in your eyes; let me seize the favorable moment, and persuade you to promise what I so ardently desire."

► What problem does Frankenstein detect in this plan?

"You propose," replied I, "to fly from the habitations of man, to dwell in those wilds where the beasts of the field will be your only companions. How can you, who long for the

---

1. **kid.** Young goat

love and sympathy of man, <u>persevere</u> in this exile? You will return and again seek their kindness, and you will meet with their detestation; your evil passions will be renewed, and you will then have a companion to aid you in the task of destruction. This may not be: cease to argue the point, for I cannot consent."

"How inconstant are your feelings! But a moment ago you were moved by my representations, and why do you again harden yourself to my complaints? I swear to you, by the earth which I inhabit, and by you that made me, that with the companion you bestow I will quit the neighborhood of man and dwell as it may chance in the most savage of places. My evil passions will have fled, for I shall meet with sympathy! My life will flow quietly away, and in my dying moments I shall not curse my maker."

His words had a strange effect upon me. I compassionated him and sometimes felt a wish to console him, but when I looked upon him, when I saw the filthy mass that moved and talked, my heart sickened and my feelings were altered to those of horror and hatred. I tried to stifle these sensations; I thought that as I could not sympathize with him, I had no right to withhold from him the small portion of happiness which was yet in my power to bestow.

◀ *What emotions does Frankenstein feel toward the creature? What changes these feelings to those of disgust?*

"You swear," I said, "to be harmless; but have you not already shown a degree of malice that should reasonably make me distrust you? May not even this be a <u>feint</u> that will increase your triumph by affording a wider scope for your revenge?"

"How is this? I must not be trifled with, and I demand an answer. If I have no ties and no affections, hatred and vice must be my portion; the love of another will destroy the cause of my crimes, and I shall become a thing of whose existence everyone will be ignorant. My vices are the children of a forced solitude that I abhor, and my virtues will necessarily arise when I live in communion with an equal. I shall feel the affections of a sensitive being and become linked to the chain of existence and events from which I am now excluded."

◀ *In what way does the creature try to dispel Frankenstein's fears about his character?*

I paused some time to reflect on all he had related, and the various arguments which he had employed. I thought of the promise of virtues which he had displayed on the opening of his existence and the subsequent <u>blight</u> of all kindly feeling by the loathing and scorn which his protectors had

Words For Everyday Use	**per • se • vere** (pur´sə vir´) *vi.*, continue in some course of action despite difficulty; be persistent **feint** (fānt) *n.*, sham; false show **blight** (blīt) *n.*, that which destroys growth, causes devastation

manifested towards him. His power and threats were not omitted in my calculations; a creature who could exist in the ice caves of the glaciers, and hide himself from pursuit among the ridges of inaccessible precipices was a being possessing faculties it would be vain to cope with. After a long pause of reflection I concluded that the justice due both to him and my fellow creatures demanded of me that I should comply with his request. Turning to him, therefore, I said,

► What answer does Frankenstein finally give?

"I consent to your demand, on your solemn oath to quit Europe forever and every other place in the neighborhood of man, as soon as I shall deliver into your hands a female who will accompany you in your exile."

"I swear," he cried, "by the sun, and by the blue sky of heaven, and by the fire of love that burns my heart, that if you grant my prayer, while they exist you shall never behold me again. Depart to your home and commence your labors; I shall watch their progress with unutterable anxiety; and fear not but that when you are ready I shall appear."

Saying this, he suddenly quitted me, fearful, perhaps, of any change in my sentiments. I saw him descend the mountain with greater speed than the flight of an eagle, and quickly lost among the <u>undulations</u> of the sea of ice.

His tale had occupied the whole day, and the sun was upon the verge of the horizon when he departed. I knew that I ought to hasten my descent towards the valley, as I should soon be encompassed in darkness; but my heart was heavy, and my steps slow. The labor of winding among the little paths of the mountain and fixing my feet firmly as I advanced perplexed me, occupied as I was by the emotions which the occurrences of the day had produced. Night was far advanced when I came to the halfway resting-place, and seated myself beside the fountain. The stars shone at intervals as the clouds passed from over them; the dark pines rose before me, and every here and there a broken tree lay on the ground; it was a scene of wonderful solemnity and stirred strange thoughts within me. I wept bitterly, and clasping my hands in agony, I exclaimed, "Oh! Stars and clouds and winds, ye are all about to mock me; if ye really pity me, crush sensation and memory; let me become as nought; but if not, depart, depart, leave me in darkness."

► What does Frankenstein say nature does to him? What does he ask nature to do?

Words For Everyday Use

un • du • la • tion (un´dyo͞o lā´shən) *n.*, wavy motion

These were wild and miserable thoughts, but I cannot describe to you how the eternal twinkling of the stars weighed upon me and how I listened to every blast of wind as if it were a dull ugly siroc[2] on its way to consume me.

Morning dawned before I arrived at the village of Chamounix; I took no rest, but returned immediately to Geneva. Even in my own heart I could give no expression to my sensations—they weighed on me with a mountain's weight and their excess destroyed my agony beneath them. Thus I returned home, and entering the house, presented myself to the family. My <u>haggard</u> and wild appearance awoke intense alarm, but I answered no question, scarcely did I speak. I felt as if I were placed under a ban—as if I had no right to claim their sympathies—as if never more might I enjoy companionship with them. Yet even thus I loved them to adoration; and to save them, I resolved to dedicate myself to my most abhorred task. The prospect of such an occupation made every other circumstance of existence pass before me like a dream, and that thought only had to me the reality of life.

◄ *Upon returning home, how does Frankenstein feel toward his family?*

---

2. **siroc.** Sirocco, a hot, oppressive wind that blows from North Africa across the Mediterranean

Words For Everyday Use

hag • gard (hag´ərd) *adj.,* having a wild, worn look, caused by sleeplessness or grief

Responding to the Selection

The monster often says that he was driven to violence. Do you believe him? Do you think the creature could have chosen to act differently? Explain your responses.

Reviewing the Selection

Recalling and Interpreting

1. **R:** What about the cottagers does the creature find most striking? What actions demonstrate this aspect of their characters? What emotion does the creature find puzzling in the cottagers? What kind actions does the creature perform for the cottagers?

2. **I:** In what way do the cottagers differ from the people the creature has met so far? Explain whether the creature's assessment of the cottagers and his comparison of them to other people is logical. Why is the creature puzzled by the cottagers' tears? Why does the creature want to help the cottagers?

3. **R:** In what way does the arrival of Safie help the creature? What does he learn from Felix's lessons? What books does the creature read on his own?

4. **I:** Compare and contrast the subject of the creature's lessons to his own experience.

5. **R:** Describe the circumstances under which Felix and Safie met. In what way were these events related to the cottagers' current living conditions?

6. **I:** What does the creature learn about humans from this story?

7. **R:** How does De Lacey react when he hears the monster's plight? How do his children react when they return and see the monster? What does the monster do when he sees the girl fall in the river? What happens when he is discovered with the girl? What hope does the monster have when he sees the child? Why is this hope dashed?

8. **I:** What role does appearance play in the monster's plight? What do these incidents suggest about human nature?

Synthesizing

9. The monster in this novel is often mistakenly referred to as Frankenstein. This common error suggests an interesting issue—is Victor Frankenstein in fact a monster? Explain whether you think Frankenstein or his creation is more monstrous.

10. The monster describes the effect that several literary works had on him and how they related to his own experience. Choose a book that you have read recently and imagine how the monster would react to it. Write a brief description of his reaction and explain why he would be so affected.

Understanding Literature (QUESTIONS FOR DISCUSSION)

1. Biographical Criticism. Biographical criticism attempts to account for elements of literary works by relating them to events in the lives of their authors. Shelley's mother died days after Shelley was born. Only one of Shelley's children grew to adulthood. In what way might these events from Shelley's life have influenced *Frankenstein*?

2. Character. A **character** is a person who figures in the action of a literary work. A *protagonist,* or main character, is the central figure in the literary work. An *antagonist* is a character who is pitted against a protagonist. A *one-dimensional character* is one who exhibits a single dominant quality, or character trait. A *three-dimensional, full,* or *rounded character* is one who exhibits the complexity of traits associated with actual human beings. Who is the protagonist in *Frankenstein*? Who is the antagonist? Is the monster a one-dimensional or a three-dimensional character? Explain your response.

Chapter 18

▶ Why doesn't Frankenstein begin on the second being immediately?

Day after day, week after week, passed away on my return to Geneva; and I could not collect the courage to recommence my work. I feared the vengeance of the disappointed fiend, yet I was unable to overcome my repugnance to the task which was enjoined me. I found that I could not compose a female without again devoting several months to profound study and laborious disquisition. I had heard of some discoveries having been made by an English philosopher, the knowledge of which was material to my success, and I sometimes thought of obtaining my father's consent to visit England for this purpose; but I clung to every <u>pretense</u> of delay, and shrunk from taking the first step in an undertaking whose immediate necessity began to appear less absolute

▶ What change has Frankenstein experienced?

to me. A change indeed had taken place in me; my health, which had hitherto declined, was now much restored; and my spirits, when unchecked by the memory of my unhappy promise, rose proportionably. My father saw this change with pleasure, and he turned his thoughts towards the best method of eradicating the remains of my melancholy, which every now and then would return by fits, and with a devouring blackness overcast the approaching sunshine. At these moments I took refuge in the most perfect solitude. I passed whole days on the lake alone in a little boat, watching the clouds and listening to the rippling of the waves, silent and listless. But the fresh air and bright sun seldom failed to restore me to some degree of composure, and on my return I met the salutations of my friends with a readier smile and a more cheerful heart.

It was after my return from one of these rambles that my father, calling me aside, thus addressed me,

"I am happy to remark, my dear son, that you have resumed your former pleasures and seem to be returning to yourself. And yet you are still unhappy and still avoid our society. For some time I was lost in conjecture as to the cause of this, but yesterday an idea struck me, and if it is well founded, I conjure you to avow it. Reserve on such a point would be not only useless, but draw down treble misery on us all."

Words For Everyday Use	pre • tense (prē tens´) n., false reason; unsupported claim

I trembled violently at this <u>exordium</u>, and my father continued, "I confess, my son, that I have always looked forward to your marriage with our dear Elizabeth as the tie of our domestic comfort and the stay of my declining years. You were attached to each other from your earliest infancy; you studied together, and appeared, in dispositions and tastes, entirely suited to one another. But so blind is the experience of man that what I conceived to be the best assistants to my plan may have entirely destroyed it. You, perhaps, regard her as your sister, without any wish that she might become your wife. Nay, you may have met with another whom you may love; and considering yourself as bound in honor to Elizabeth, this struggle may occasion the poignant misery which you appear to feel."

◄ What does Frankenstein's father fear is the cause of his son's melancholy?

"My dear father, reassure yourself. I love my cousin tenderly and sincerely. I never saw any woman who excited, as Elizabeth does, my warmest admiration and affection. My future hopes and prospects are entirely bound up in the expectation of our union."

"The expression of your sentiments on this subject, my dear Victor, gives me more pleasure than I have for some time experienced. If you feel thus, we shall assuredly be happy, however present events may cast a gloom over us. But it is this gloom which appears to have taken so strong a hold of your mind that I wish to dissipate. Tell me, therefore, whether you object to an immediate solemnization of the marriage. We have been unfortunate, and recent events have drawn us from that everyday tranquility befitting my years and infirmities. You are younger; yet I do not suppose, possessed as you are of a competent fortune, that an early marriage would at all interfere with any future plans of honor and utility that you may have formed. Do not suppose, however, that I wish to dictate happiness to you or that a delay on your part would cause me any serious uneasiness. Interpret my words with candor and answer me, I conjure you, with confidence and sincerity."

◄ What plan does Frankenstein's father suggest to diminish the gloom the family has experienced?

I listened to my father in silence, and remained for some time incapable of offering any reply. I revolved rapidly in my mind a multitude of thoughts and endeavored to arrive at some conclusion. Alas! To me the idea of an immediate union with my Elizabeth was one of horror and dismay. I was

◄ Why is Frankenstein horrified by his father's suggestion?

Words
For
Everyday
Use

ex • or • di • um (eg zôr´dē əm) *n.*, opening part of a statement

bound by a solemn promise which I had not yet fulfilled and dared not break, or if I did, what <u>manifold</u> miseries might not impend over me and my devoted family! Could I enter into a festival with this deadly weight yet hanging round my neck and bowing me to the ground? I must perform my engagement and let the monster depart with his mate before I allowed myself to enjoy the delight of an union from which I expected peace.

I remembered also the necessity imposed upon me of either journeying to England or entering into a long correspondence with those philosophers of that country, whose knowledge and discoveries were of indispensable use to me in my present undertaking. The latter method of obtaining the desired intelligence was <u>dilatory</u> and unsatisfactory; besides, I had an insurmountable aversion to the idea of engaging myself in my loathsome task in my father's house while in habits of familiar intercourse with those I loved. I knew that a thousand fearful accidents might occur, the slightest of which would disclose a tale to thrill all connected with me with horror. I was aware also that I should often lose all self-command, all capacity of hiding the harrowing sensations that would possess me during the progress of my unearthly occupation. I must absent myself from all I loved while thus employed. Once commenced, it would quickly be achieved, and I might be restored to my family in peace and happiness. My promise fulfilled, the monster would depart forever. Or (so my fond fancy imaged) some accident might meanwhile occur to destroy him, and put an end to my slavery forever.

These feelings dictated my answer to my father. I expressed a wish to visit England, but concealing the true reasons of this request, I clothed my desires under a guise which excited no suspicion, while I urged my desire with an earnestness that easily induced my father to comply. After so long a period of an absorbing melancholy that resembled madness in its intensity and effects, he was glad to find that I was capable of taking pleasure in the idea of such a journey, and he hoped that change of scene and varied amusement would, before my return, have restored me entirely to myself.

The duration of my absence was left to my own choice; a few months, or at most a year, was the period contemplated. One paternal kind precaution he had taken to ensure my

> ▶ Why does Frankenstein choose not to complete his work from his home?

> ▶ Why is Frankenstein's father pleased by his son's plan?

| Words For Everyday Use | man • i • fold (man´ə fōld´) *adj.*, many and varied |
| | dil • a • to • ry (dil´ə tôr´ē) *adj.*, slow or late; intending to cause delay |

having a companion. Without previously communicating with me, he had, in concert with Elizabeth, arranged that Clerval should join me at Strasburgh.[1] This interfered with the solitude I coveted for the prosecution of my task; yet at the commencement of my journey the presence of my friend could in no way be an impediment, and truly I rejoiced that thus I should be saved many hours of lonely, maddening reflection. Nay, Henry might stand between me and the intrusion of my foe. If I were alone, would he not at times force his abhorred presence on me to remind me of my task or to contemplate its progress?

◀ Who will join Frankenstein on his journey? How does Frankenstein feel about having a companion?

To England, therefore, I was bound, and it was understood that my union with Elizabeth should take place immediately on my return. My father's age rendered him extremely averse to delay. For myself, there was one reward I promised myself from my detested toils—one consolation for my unparalleled sufferings; it was the prospect of that day when, enfranchised from my miserable slavery, I might claim Elizabeth and forget the past in my union with her.

◀ What one reward does Frankenstein hope one day to receive?

I now made arrangements for my journey, but one feeling haunted me which filled me with fear and agitation. During my absence I should leave my friends unconscious of the existence of their enemy and unprotected from his attacks, exasperated as he might be by my departure. But he had promised to follow me wherever I might go, and would he not accompany me to England? This imagination was dreadful in itself, but soothing inasmuch as it supposed the safety of my friends. I was agonized with the idea of the possibility that the reverse of this might happen. But through the whole period during which I was the slave of my creature I allowed myself to be governed by the impulses of the moment; and my present sensations strongly intimated that the fiend would follow me and exempt my family from the danger of his machinations.

◀ What fears does Frankenstein have upon leaving his family? What thought allays his fears?

It was in the latter end of September that I again quitted my native country. My journey had been my own suggestion, and Elizabeth, therefore, acquiesced, but she was filled with disquiet at the idea of my suffering, away from her, the inroads of misery and grief. It had been her care which provided me

---

1. **Strasburgh.** Also Strasbourg, city in northeastern France on the Rhine

| Words For Everyday Use | **en • fran • chise** (en fran´chīz´) *vt.*, free |
| | **ac • qui • esce** (ak´wē əs´) *vi.*, agree without protest but without enthusiasm |

a companion in Clerval—and yet a man is blind to a thousand minute circumstances which call forth a woman's <u>sedulous</u> attention. She longed to bid me hasten my return; a thousand conflicting emotions rendered her mute as she bade me a tearful, silent farewell.

I threw myself into the carriage that was to convey me away, hardly knowing whither I was going, and careless of what was passing around. I remembered only, and it was with a bitter anguish that I reflected on it, to order that my chemical instruments should be packed to go with me. Filled with dreary imaginations, I passed through many beautiful and majestic scenes, but my eyes were fixed and unobserving. I could only think of the bourne[2] of my travels and the work which was to occupy me whilst they endured.

After some days spent in listless <u>indolence</u>, during which I traversed many leagues, I arrived at Strasburgh, where I waited two days for Clerval. He came. Alas, how great was the contrast between us! He was alive to every new scene, joyful when he saw the beauties of the setting sun, and more happy when he beheld it rise, and recommence a new day. He pointed out to me the shifting colors of the landscape and the appearances of the sky. "This is what it is to live," he cried, "now I enjoy existence! But you, Frankenstein, wherefore are you desponding and sorrowful!" In truth, I was occupied by gloomy thoughts and neither saw the descent of the evening star nor the golden sunrise reflected in the Rhine. And you, my friend, would be far more amused with the journal of Clerval, who observed the scenery with an eye of feeling and delight, than in listening to my reflections. I, a miserable wretch, haunted by a curse that shut up every avenue to enjoyment.

We had agreed to descend the Rhine in a boat from Strasburgh to Rotterdam,[3] whence we might take shipping for London. During this voyage we passed many willowy islands and saw several beautiful towns. We stayed a day at Manheim, and on the fifth from our departure from Strasburgh, arrived at Mayence.[4] The course of the Rhine below Mayence becomes

► Why is Frankenstein unable to enjoy the beauty of the land he travels through?

► How does Clerval's attitude toward the journey differ from that of Frankenstein?

---

2. **bourne.** Goal, objective
3. **Rotterdam.** Seaport on the Rhine delta, in southwestern Netherlands
4. **Manheim . . . Mayence.** Manheim, or Mannheim, and Mayence, or Mainz, are both cities on the Rhine.

Words For Everyday Use

sed • u • lous (sej´o͞o ləs) adj., persistent
in • do • lence (in´də ləns) n., idleness, laziness

much more picturesque. The river descends rapidly and winds between hills, not high, but steep, and of beautiful forms. We saw many ruined castles standing on the edges of precipices, surrounded by black woods, high and inaccessible. This part of the Rhine, indeed, presents a singularly <u>variegated</u> landscape. In one spot you view rugged hills, ruined castles overlooking tremendous precipices, with the dark Rhine rushing beneath; and on the sudden turn of a promontory, flourishing vineyards with green sloping banks and a meandering river and populous towns occupy the scene.

We traveled at the time of the vintage[5] and heard the song of the laborers, as we glided down the stream. Even I, depressed in mind, and my spirits continually agitated by gloomy feelings, even I was pleased. I lay at the bottom of the boat, and as I gazed on the cloudless blue sky, I seemed to drink in a tranquility to which I had long been a stranger. And if these were my sensations, who can describe those of Henry? He felt as if he had been transported to fairyland and enjoyed a happiness seldom tasted by man. "I have seen," he said, "the most beautiful scenes of my own country; I have visited the lakes of Lucerne and Uri, where the snowy mountains descend almost perpendicularly to the water, casting black and impenetrable shades, which would cause a gloomy and mournful appearance were it not for the most verdant islands that relieve the eye by their gay appearance; I have seen this lake agitated by a tempest, when the wind tore up whirlwinds of water and gave you an idea of what the waterspout must be on the great ocean; and the waves dash with fury the base of the mountain, where the priest and his mistress were overwhelmed by an avalanche and where their dying voices are still said to be heard amid the pauses of the nightly wind; I have seen the mountains of La Valais, and the Pays de Vaud;[6] but this country, Victor, pleases me more than all those wonders. The mountains of Switzerland are more majestic and strange, but there is a charm in the banks of this divine river that I never before saw equaled. Look at that castle which overhangs yon precipice; and that also on the island, almost concealed amongst the foliage of those lovely trees; and now that group of laborers coming from

---

5. **vintage.** Season of gathering grapes or making wine
6. **La Valais, and the Pays de Vaud.** Cantons, or states, of Switzerland

var • i • e • gat • ed (ver´ ē ə gāt´id) *adj.,* varied; diversified

► Why is Clerval so drawn to this countryside?

among their vines; and that village half hid in the recess of the mountain. Oh, surely the spirit that inhabits and guards this place has a soul more in harmony with man than those who pile the glacier or retire to the inaccessible peaks of the mountains of our own country."

Clerval! Beloved friend! Even now it delights me to record your words and to dwell on the praise of which you are so <u>eminently</u> deserving. He was a being formed in the "very poetry of nature." His wild and enthusiastic imagination was chastened by the sensibility of his heart. His soul overflowed with ardent affections, and his friendship was of that devoted and wondrous nature that the worldly-minded teach us to look for only in the imagination. But even human sympathies were not sufficient to satisfy his eager mind. The scenery of external nature, which others regard only with admiration, he loved with ardor:

► What effect does nature have on Clerval?

"The sounding cataract
Haunted *him* like a passion: the tall rock,
The mountain, and the deep and gloomy wood,
Their colors and their forms, were then to him
An appetite; a feeling, and a love,
That had no need of a remoter charm,
By thought supplied, or any interest
Unborrow'd from the eye."
—Wordsworth's "Tintern Abbey."[7]

► What happens to Clerval?

And where does he now exist? Is this gentle and lovely being lost forever? Has this mind, so <u>replete</u> with ideas, imaginations fanciful and magnificent, which formed a world, whose existence depended on the life of its creator— has the mind perished? Does it now only exist in my memory? No, it is not thus; your form so divinely wrought, and beaming with beauty, has decayed, but your spirit still visits and consoles your unhappy friend.

Pardon this gush of sorrow; these ineffectual words are but a slight tribute to the unexampled worth of Henry, but they soothe my heart, overflowing with the anguish which his remembrance creates. I will proceed with my tale.

---

7. **Wordsworth's "Tintern Abbey."** Shelley has changed *me* to *him* in lines 76- 83 of "Lines composed a few miles above Tintern Abbey" by William Wordsworth (1770–1850).

Words For Everyday Use	
	em • i • nent • ly (em´ə nənt lē) *adv.*, outstandingly; remarkably
	re • plete (ri plēt´) *adj.*, well-filled

Beyond Cologne[8] we descended to the plains of Holland; and we resolved to post the remainder of our way, for the wind was contrary[9] and the stream of the river was too gentle to aid us.

Our journey here lost the interest arising from beautiful scenery, but we arrived in a few days at Rotterdam, whence we proceeded by sea to England. It was on a clear morning, in the latter days of October, that I first saw the white cliffs of Britain. The banks of the Thames[10] presented a new scene; they were flat, but fertile, and almost every town was marked by the remembrance of some story. We saw Tilbury Fort and remembered the Spanish Armada, Gravesend, Woolwich, and Greenwich, places which I had heard of even in my country.

At length we saw the numerous steeples of London, St. Paul's[11] towering above all, and the Tower[12] famed in English history.

---

8. **Cologne.** City on the Rhine in western Germany
9. **wind was contrary.** Wind would not propel their boat in the correct direction
10. **St.Paul's** Of St. Paul's Cathedral
11. **Tower.** Tower of London

Chapter 19

London was our present point of rest; we determined to remain several months in this wonderful and celebrated city. Clerval desired the intercourse[1] of the men of genius and talent who flourished at this time, but this was with me a secondary object; I was principally occupied with the means of obtaining the information necessary for the completion of my promise and quickly availed myself of the letters of introduction that I had brought with me, addressed to the most distinguished natural philosophers.

If this journey had taken place during my days of study and happiness, it would have afforded me inexpressible pleasure. But a blight had come over my existence, and I only visited these people for the sake of the information they might give me on the subject in which my interest was so terribly profound. Company was irksome to me; when alone, I could fill my mind with the sights of heaven and earth; the voice of Henry soothed me, and I could thus cheat myself into a transitory peace. But busy, uninteresting joyous faces brought back despair to my heart. I saw an insurmountable barrier placed between me and my fellow men; this barrier was sealed with the blood of William and Justine, and to reflect on the events connected with those names filled my soul with <u>anguish</u>.

► Why does Frankenstein despair at the joyous faces he sees?

But in Clerval I saw the image of my former self; he was inquisitive, and anxious to gain experience and instruction. The difference of manners which he observed was to him an inexhaustible source of instruction and amusement. He was also pursuing an object he had long had in view. His design was to visit India, in the belief that he had in his knowledge of its various languages, and in the views he had taken of its society, the means of materially assisting the progress of European colonization and trade.[2] In Britain only could he further the execution of his plan. He was forever busy, and the only check to his enjoyments was my sorrowful and

► What similarities does Frankenstein see in himself and in Clerval? What goal does Clerval have?

---

1. **intercourse.** Communication; exchange of ideas
2. **India . . . colonization and trade.** The British colonized India in the nineteenth century and ruled it until 1947. During this time, many British people aspired to bring British custom, trade, and religion to the Indian people.

Words For Everyday Use	**an • guish** (aŋ´gwish) *n.*, great suffering; distress

dejected mind. I tried to conceal this as much as possible, that I might not <u>debar</u> him from the pleasures natural to one who was entering on a new scene of life, undisturbed by any care or bitter recollection. I often refused to accompany him, <u>alleging</u> another engagement, that I might remain alone. I now also began to collect the materials necessary for my new creation, and this was to me like the torture of single drops of water continually falling on the head. Every thought that was devoted to it was an extreme anguish, and every word that I spoke in allusion to it caused my lips to quiver, and my heart to palpitate.

◄ How does Frankenstein feel about beginning his work?

After passing some months in London, we received a letter from a person in Scotland who had formerly been our visitor at Geneva. He mentioned the beauties of his native country and asked us if those were not sufficient allurements to induce us to prolong our journey as far north as Perth,[3] where he resided. Clerval eagerly desired to accept this invitation, and I, although I abhorred society, wished to view again mountains and streams, and all the wondrous works with which Nature adorns her chosen dwelling-places.

We had arrived in England at the beginning of October, and it was now February. We accordingly determined to commence our journey towards the north at the expiration of another month. In this expedition we did not intend to follow the great road to Edinburgh, but to visit Windsor, Oxford, Matlock, and the Cumberland lakes,[4] resolving to arrive at the completion of this tour about the end of July. I packed up my chemical instruments and the materials I had collected, resolving to finish my labors in some obscure nook in the northern highlands of Scotland.

◄ Why does Frankenstein pack up his instruments? What will become of his project?

We quitted London on the 27th of March and remained a few days at Windsor, rambling in its beautiful forest. This was a new scene to us mountaineers; the majestic oaks, the quantity of game, and the herds of stately deer, were all novelties to us.

From thence we proceeded to Oxford. As we entered this city our minds were filled with the remembrance of the events that had been transacted there more than a century

---

3. **Perth.** City in central Scotland
4. **Windsor . . . Cumberland lakes.** All places in England

Words For Everyday Use	**de • bar** (dē bär´) vt., keep a person from some right or privilege; exclude
	al • lege (ə lej´) vt., declare; offer as an excuse

and a half before. It was here that Charles I[5] had collected his forces. This city had remained faithful to him, after the whole nation had <u>forsaken</u> his cause to join the standard of Parliament and liberty. The memory of that unfortunate king and his companions, the amiable Falkland, the insolent Goring,[6] his queen, and son, gave a peculiar interest to every part of the city which they might be supposed to have inhabited. The spirit of elder days found a dwelling here, and we delighted to trace its footsteps. If these feelings had not found an imaginary <u>gratification</u>, the appearance of the city had yet in itself sufficient beauty to obtain our admiration. The colleges are ancient and picturesque; the streets are almost magnificent; and the lovely Isis,[7] which flows beside it through meadows of exquisite verdure, is spread forth into a placid expanse of waters, which reflects its majestic assemblage of towers, and spires, and domes, embosomed among aged trees.

> What effect would this scene have had on Frankenstein in the past? Why doesn't it have this effect on him now?

I enjoyed this scene, and yet my enjoyment was embittered both by the memory of the past and the anticipation of the future. I was formed for peaceful happiness. During my youthful days discontent never visited my mind, and if I was ever overcome by <u>ennui</u>, the sight of what is beautiful in nature or the study of what is excellent and sublime in the productions of man could always interest my heart and communicate elasticity to my spirits. But I am a blasted tree; the bolt has entered my soul; and I felt then that I should survive to exhibit what I shall soon cease to be—a miserable spectacle of wrecked humanity, pitiable to others, and intolerable to myself.

> What does Frankenstein say he is? What does he mean by this statement?

We passed a considerable period at Oxford, rambling among its environs and endeavoring to identify every spot which might relate to the most animating epoch of English history. Our little voyages of discovery were often prolonged by the successive objects that presented themselves. We visited the tomb of the illustrious Hampden[8] and the field on

---

5. **Charles I.** King of England from 1625 to 1649; civil war began when he declared war on Parliamentarians in 1642. After his defeat, he sought refuge at Oxford.
6. **Falkland . . . Goring.** Refers to Lucius Cary, 2nd Viscount Falkner, a Royalist who opposed Charles I, and to George Goring, Earl of Norwich, also a Royalist
7. **Isis.** English name for the Thames River west of Oxford
8. **Hampden.** John Hampden (1594–1643) led the opposition to Charles I; Hampden was killed near Oxford

Words For Everyday Use	
for • sake (fôr sāk´) vt., abandon	
grat • i • fi • ca • tion (grat´i fi kā´shən) n., cause of satisfaction	
en • nui (än´wē´) n., boredom	

which that patriot fell. For a moment my soul was elevated from its debasing and miserable fears to contemplate the divine ideas of liberty and self-sacrifice of which these sights were the monuments and the remembrancers. For an instant I dared to shake off my chains and look around me with a free and lofty spirit, but the iron had eaten into my flesh, and I sank again, trembling and hopeless, into my miserable self.

We left Oxford with regret and proceeded to Matlock, which was our next place of rest. The country in the neighborhood of this village resembled, to a greater degree, the scenery of Switzerland; but everything is on a lower scale, and the green hills want the crown of distant white Alps which always attend on the piny mountains of my native country. We visited the wondrous cave and the little cabinets of natural history, where the curiosities are disposed in the same manner as in the collections at Servox and Chamounix. The latter name made me tremble when pronounced by Henry, and I hastened to quit Matlock, with which that terrible scene was thus associated.

From Derby, still journeying northward, we passed two months in Cumberland and Westmoreland. I could now almost fancy myself among the Swiss mountains. The little patches of snow which yet lingered on the northern sides of the mountains, the lakes, and the dashing of the rocky streams, were all familiar and dear sights to me. Here also we made some acquaintances, who almost contrived to cheat me into happiness. The delight of Clerval was proportionably greater than mine; his mind expanded in the company of men of talent, and he found in his own nature greater capacities and resources than he could have imagined himself to have possessed while he associated with his inferiors. "I could pass my life here," said he to me; "and among these mountains I should scarcely regret Switzerland and the Rhine."

◄ Does the trip have a positive effect on Frankenstein's mood? How does his happiness compare to Clerval's?

But he found that a traveler's life is one that includes much pain amidst its enjoyments. His feelings are forever on the stretch; and when he begins to sink into <u>repose</u>, he finds himself obliged to quit that on which he rests in pleasure for something new, which again engages his attention, and which also he forsakes for other novelties.

We had scarcely visited the various lakes of Cumberland and Westmoreland and <u>conceived</u> an affection for some of

Words For Everyday Use	**re • pose** (ri pōz) *n.*, rest **con • ceive** (kən sēv´) *vt.*, form or develop in the mind

▶ Why is Frankenstein happy to pursue their journey? Why does he worry when letters from Switzerland are late?

▶ Why does Frankenstein sometimes feel the need to follow Henry?

the inhabitants when the period of our appointment with our Scotch friend approached, and we left them to travel on. For my own part I was not sorry. I had now neglected my promise for some time, and I feared the effects of the demon's disappointment. He might remain in Switzerland and wreak his vengeance on my relatives. This idea pursued me and tormented me at every moment from which I might otherwise have snatched repose and peace. I waited for my letters with feverish impatience; if they were delayed I was miserable and overcome by a thousand fears; and when they arrived and I saw the superscription[9] of Elizabeth or my father, I hardly dared to read and ascertain my fate. Sometimes I thought that the fiend followed me and might <u>expedite</u> my <u>remissness</u> by murdering my companion. When these thoughts possessed me, I would not quit Henry for a moment, but followed him as his shadow, to protect him from the fancied rage of his destroyer. I felt as if I had committed some great crime, the consciousness of which haunted me. I was guiltless, but I had indeed drawn down a horrible curse upon my head, as mortal as that of crime.

I visited Edinburgh with <u>languid</u> eyes and mind; and yet that city might have interested the most unfortunate being. Clerval did not like it so well as Oxford, for the antiquity of the latter city was more pleasing to him. But the beauty and regularity of the new town of Edinburgh, its romantic castle and its environs, the most delightful in the world, Arthur's Seat, St. Bernard's Well, and the Pentland Hills[10] compensated him for the change and filled him with cheerfulness and admiration. But I was impatient to arrive at the termination of my journey.

We left Edinburgh in a week, passing through Coupar, St. Andrew's, and along the banks of the Tay,[11] to Perth, where our friend expected us. But I was in no mood to laugh and talk with strangers, or enter into their feelings or plans with the good humor expected from a guest; and accordingly I told Clerval that I wished to make the tour of Scotland alone. "Do you," said I, "enjoy yourself, and let this be our rendezvous. I may be absent a month or two; but do not interfere

---

9. **superscription.** Address on a letter
10. **Arthur's Seat . . . Pentland Hills.** Sights in Scotland
11. **Tay.** River in Scotland

Words For Everyday Use	ex • pe • dite (eks´pə dīt´) vt., speed up; facilitate
	re • miss • ness (ri mis´nəs) n., carelessness; negligence
	lan • guid (laŋ´gwid) adj., without vitality or spirit; dull

with my motions, I entreat you: leave me to peace and solitude for a short time; and when I return, I hope it will be with a lighter heart, more <u>congenial</u> to your own temper."

Henry wished to <u>dissuade</u> me, but seeing me bent on this plan, ceased to <u>remonstrate</u>. He entreated me to write often. "I had rather be with you," he said, "in your solitary rambles, than with these Scotch people, whom I do not know: hasten then, my dear friend, to return, that I may again feel myself somewhat at home, which I cannot do in your absence."

◄ *What plan do Frankenstein and Clerval agree to follow?*

Having parted from my friend, I determined to visit some remote spot of Scotland, and finish my work in solitude. I did not doubt but that the monster followed me and would discover himself me when I should have finished, that he might receive his companion.

With this resolution I traversed the northern highlands, and fixed on one of the remotest of the Orkneys[12] as the scene of my labors. It was a place fitted for such a work, being hardly more than a rock whose high sides were continually beaten upon by the waves. The soil was barren, scarcely affording pasture for a few miserable cows, and oatmeal for its inhabitants, which consisted of five persons, whose gaunt and scraggy limbs gave tokens of their miserable fare. Vegetables and bread, when they indulged in such luxuries, and even fresh water, was to be procured from the mainland, which was about five miles distant.

◄ *Where will Frankenstein complete his project?*

On the whole island there were but three miserable huts, and one of these was vacant when I arrived. This I hired. It contained but two rooms, and these exhibited all the <u>squalidness</u> of the most miserable penury. The thatch had fallen in, the walls were unplastered, and the door was off its hinges. I ordered it to be repaired, bought some furniture, and took possession, an incident which would doubtless have occasioned some surprise had not all the senses of the cottagers been benumbed by want and squalid poverty. As it was, I lived ungazed at and unmolested, hardly thanked for the pittance of food and clothes which I gave, so much does suffering blunt even the coarsest sensations of men.

◄ *Why don't the cottagers question Frankenstein's sudden appearance?*

In this retreat I devoted the morning to labor; but in the evening, when the weather permitted, I walked on the stony

---

12. **Orkneys.** Islands off the northern coast of Scotland

Words For Everyday Use	con • ge • ni • al (kən jēn´yəl) *adj.*, suited to one's needs or disposition; agreeable	re • mon • strate (ri man´strāt´) *vi.*, protest, object
	dis • suade (di swād´) *vt.*, turn away from by persuasion or advice	squal • id • ness (skwäl´id nəs) *n.*, wretchedness

beach of the sea to listen to the waves as they roared and dashed at my feet. It was a monotonous yet ever-changing scene. I thought of Switzerland; it was far different from this desolate and appalling landscape. Its hills are covered with vines, and its cottages are scattered thickly in the plains. Its fair lakes reflect a blue and gentle sky, and when troubled by the winds, their tumult is but as the play of a lively infant when compared to the roarings of the giant ocean.

In this manner I distributed my occupations when I first arrived, but as I proceeded in my labor, it became every day more horrible and irksome to me. Sometimes I could not <u>prevail</u> on myself to enter my laboratory for several days, and at other times I toiled day and night in order to complete my work. It was, indeed, a filthy process in which I was engaged. During my first experiment, a kind of enthusiastic frenzy had blinded me to the horror of my employment; my mind was intently fixed on the consummation of my labor, and my eyes were shut to the horror of my proceedings. But now I went to it in cold blood, and my heart often sickened at the work of my hands.

Thus situated, employed in the most detestable occupation, immersed in a solitude where nothing could for an instant call my attention from the actual scene in which I was engaged, my spirits became unequal; I grew restless and nervous. Every moment I feared to meet my persecutor. Sometimes I sat with my eyes fixed on the ground, fearing to raise them lest they should encounter the object which I so much dreaded to behold. I feared to wander from the sight of my fellow creatures lest when alone he should come to claim his companion.

In the meantime I worked on, and my labor was already considerably advanced. I looked towards its completion with a tremulous and eager hope, which I dared not trust myself to question but which was intermixed with obscure <u>forebodings</u> of evil, that made my heart sicken in my bosom.

▶ How does Frankenstein's approach to his current work differ from his approach to his first creation?

▶ What emotions are raised by the prospect of completing his work?

| Words For Everyday Use | **pre • vail** (prē vāl´) *vi.*, produce or achieve the desired effect
fore • bod • ing (fôr bōd´ iŋ) *n.*, prediction, especially of something bad |

Chapter 20

I sat one evening in my laboratory; the sun had set, and the moon was just rising from the sea; I had not sufficient light for my employment, and I remained idle, in a pause of consideration of whether I should leave my labor for the night, or hasten its conclusion by an unremitting attention to it. As I sat, a train of reflection occurred to me which led me to consider the effects of what I was now doing. Three years before, I was engaged in the same manner, and had created a fiend whose unparalleled barbarity had desolated my heart and filled it forever with the bitterest remorse. I was now about to form another being of whose dispositions I was alike ignorant; she might become ten thousand times more malignant than her mate and delight, for its own sake, in murder and wretchedness. He had sworn to quit the neighborhood of man and hide himself in deserts, but she had not; and she, who in all probability was to become a thinking and reasoning animal, might refuse to comply with a compact made before her creation. They might even hate each other; the creature who already lived loathed his own deformity, and might he not conceive a greater abhorrence for it when it came before his eyes in the female form? She also might turn with disgust from him to the superior beauty of man; she might quit him, and he be again alone, exasperated by the fresh <u>provocation</u> of being deserted by one of his own species.

◀ What concerns does Frankenstein have regarding his project?

Even if they were to leave Europe and inhabit the deserts of the new world, yet one of the first results of those sympathies for which the demon thirsted would be children, and a race of devils would be <u>propagated</u> upon the earth who might make the very existence of the species of man a condition <u>precarious</u> and full of terror. Had I right, for my own benefit, to inflict this curse upon everlasting generations? I had before been moved by the sophisms of the being I had created; I had been struck senseless by his fiendish threats; but now, for the first time, the wickedness of my promise burst upon me; I shuddered to think that future ages might curse me as their pest, whose selfishness had not hesitated to buy its own peace at the price, perhaps, of the existence of the whole human race.

◀ What additional danger might develop from Frankenstein's new creation?

◀ What does Frankenstein fear future ages will think of him? As what did he think he would be hailed by his first creation?

Words For Everyday Use	**prov • o • ca • tion** (präv´ə kā´shən) *n.,* something that excites a strong feeling, especially resentment or irritation
	prop • a • gate (präp´ə gāt´) *vt.,* reproduce
	pre • car • i • ous (prē ker´ē əs) *adj.,* uncertain; insecure

I trembled and my heart failed within me, when, on looking up, I saw by the light of the moon, the demon at the casement. A ghastly grin wrinkled his lips as he gazed on me, where I sat fulfilling the task which he had allotted to me. Yes, he had followed me in my travels; he had loitered in forests, hid himself in caves, or taken refuge in wide and desert heaths;[1] and he now came to mark my progress and claim the fulfillment of my promise.

▶ What expression does Frankenstein see on the monster's face? What does the creature see Frankenstein do?

As I looked on him, his countenance expressed the utmost extent of malice and <u>treachery</u>. I thought with a sensation of madness on my promise to create another like him, and trembling with passion, tore to pieces the thing on which I was engaged. The wretch saw me destroy the creature on whose future existence he depended for happiness, and with a howl of devilish despair and revenge, withdrew.

I left the room, and, locking the door, made a solemn vow in my own heart never to resume my labors; and then, with trembling steps, sought my own apartment. I was alone; none were near me to dissipate the gloom and relieve me from the sickening oppression of the most terrible reveries.

Several hours passed, and I remained near my window gazing on the sea; it was almost motionless, for the winds were hushed, and all nature reposed under the eye of the quiet moon. A few fishing vessels alone specked the water, and now and then the gentle breeze wafted the sound of voices as the fishermen called to one another. I felt the silence, although I was hardly conscious of its extreme <u>profundity</u>, until my ear was suddenly arrested by the paddling of oars near the shore, and a person landed close to my house.

▶ Who does Frankenstein fear has arrived?

In a few minutes after, I heard the creaking of my door, as if someone endeavored to open it softly. I trembled from head to foot; I felt a presentiment of who it was and wished to rouse one of the peasants who dwelt in a cottage not far from mine; but I was overcome by the sensation of helplessness, so often felt in frightful dreams, when you in vain endeavor to fly from an <u>impending</u> danger, and was rooted to the spot.

Presently I heard the sound of footsteps along the passage; the door opened, and the wretch whom I dreaded appeared.

---

1. **heaths.** Open wastelands

Words For Everyday Use	
treach • er • y (trech´ər ē) *n.*, betrayal of trust or faith; disloyalty
pro • fun • di • ty (prō fun´də tē) *n.*, great depth
im • pend • ing (im pend´iŋ) *adj.*, threatening; about to happen

Shutting the door, he approached me, and said, in a smothered voice, "You have destroyed the work which you began; what is it that you intend? Do you dare to break your promise? I have endured toil and misery: I left Switzerland with you; I crept along the shores of the Rhine, among its willow islands and over the summits of its hills. I have dwelt many months in the heaths of England and among the deserts of Scotland. I have endured <u>incalculable</u> fatigue, and cold, and hunger; do you dare destroy my hopes?"

◄ What troubles has the monster endured?

"Begone! I do break my promise; never will I create another like yourself, equal in deformity and wickedness."

"Slave, I before reasoned with you, but you have proved yourself unworthy of my <u>condescension</u>. Remember that I have power; you believe yourself miserable, but I can make you so wretched that the light of day will be hateful to you. You are my creator, but I am your master; obey!"

◄ According to the monster what relationship exists between him and Frankenstein?

"The hour of my irresolution is past, and the period of your power is arrived. Your threats cannot move me to do an act of wickedness; but they confirm me in a determination of not creating you a companion in vice. Shall I, in cool blood, set loose upon the earth a demon whose delight is in death and wretchedness? Begone! I am firm, and your words will only exasperate my rage."

The monster saw my determination in my face and gnashed his teeth in the impotence of anger. "Shall each man," cried he, "find a wife for his bosom, and each beast have his mate, and I be alone? I had feelings of affection, and they were requited by detestation and scorn. Man! You may hate; but beware! Your hours will pass in dread and misery, and soon the bolt will fall which must ravish from you your happiness forever. Are you to be happy while I grovel in the intensity of my wretchedness? You can blast my other passions, but revenge remains—revenge, henceforth dearer than light or food! I may die, but first you, my tyrant and tormentor, shall curse the sun that gazes on your misery. Beware, for I am fearless and therefore powerful. I will watch with the wiliness of a snake, that I may sting with its venom. Man, you shall repent of the injuries you inflict."

◄ Why might Frankenstein regret or come to regret his decision?

"Devil, cease; and do not poison the air with these sounds of malice. I have declared my resolution to you, and I am no coward to bend beneath words. Leave me; I am inexorable."

Words For Everyday Use	**in • cal • cu • la • ble** (in kal´kyo͞o lə bəl) *adj.,* too great to be calculated
	con • de • scen • sion (kan´di sen´shən) *n.,* patronizing manner or behavior

► When will the
monster be with
Frankenstein?

"It is well. I go; but remember, I shall be with you on your wedding night."

I started forward, and exclaimed, "Villain! Before you sign my death-warrant, be sure that you are yourself safe."

I would have seized him; but he <u>eluded</u> me, and quitted the house with <u>precipitation</u>. In a few moments I saw him in his boat, which shot across the waters with an arrowy swiftness and was soon lost amidst the waves.

All was again silent, but his words rung in my ears. I burned with rage to pursue the murderer of my peace and precipitate him into the ocean. I walked up and down my room hastily and <u>perturbed</u>, while my imagination conjured up a thousand images to torment and sting me. Why had I not followed him and closed with him in mortal strife? But I had suffered him to depart, and he had directed his course towards the mainland. I shuddered to think who might be the next victim sacrificed to his insatiate revenge. And then

► What does
Frankenstein think
the monster plans to
do? For whom is he
concerned?

I thought again of his words—"I will be with you on your wedding-night." That then was the period fixed for the fulfillment of my destiny. In that hour I should die and at once satisfy and extinguish his malice. The prospect did not move me to fear; yet when I thought of my beloved Elizabeth, of her tears and endless sorrow, when she should find her lover so barbarously snatched from her, tears, the first I had shed for many months, streamed from my eyes, and I resolved not to fall before my enemy without a bitter struggle.

The night passed away, and the sun rose from the ocean; my feelings became calmer, if it may be called calmness when the violence of rage sinks into the depths of despair. I left the house, the horrid scene of the last night's contention, and walked on the beach of the sea, which I almost regarded as an <u>insuperable</u> barrier between me and my fellow-creatures; nay, a wish that such should prove the fact stole across me. I desired that I might pass my life on that barren rock, wearily, it is true, but uninterrupted by any sudden shock of misery. If I returned, it was to be sacrificed or to see those whom I most loved die under the grasp of a demon whom I had myself created.

► Why doesn't
Frankenstein desire
to return home?

I walked about the isle like a restless specter, separated from all it loved and miserable in the separation. When it became noon, and the sun rose higher, I lay down on the

---

**Words
For
Everyday
Use**

e • lude (ē lōōd´) vt., avoid or escape
pre • cip • i • ta • tion (prē sip´ə tā´shən) n., rash haste

per • turb (pər turb´) vt., agitate, upset
in • su • per • a • ble (in sōō´pər ə bəl) adj., insurmountable

grass and was overpowered by a deep sleep. I had been awake the whole of the preceding night, my nerves were agitated, and my eyes inflamed by watching and misery. The sleep into which I now sank refreshed me; and when I awoke, I again felt as if I belonged to a race of human beings like myself, and I began to reflect upon what had passed with greater composure; yet still the words of the fiend rung in my ears like a death-knell; they appeared like a dream, yet distinct and oppressive as a reality.

◄ How does a good sleep change Frankenstein's perspective? What is sleep unable to erase?

The sun had far descended, and I still sat on the shore, satisfying my appetite, which had become ravenous, with an oaten cake, when I saw a fishing-boat land close to me, and one of the men brought me a packet; it contained letters from Geneva, and one from Clerval, entreating me to join him. He said that he was wearing away his time fruitlessly where he was, that letters from the friends he had formed in London desired his return to complete the negotiation they had entered into for his Indian enterprise. He could not any longer delay his departure; but as his journey to London might be followed, even sooner than he now conjectured, by his longer voyage, he entreated me to bestow as much of my society on him as I could spare. He besought me, therefore, to leave my solitary isle and to meet him at Perth, that we might proceed southwards together. This letter in a degree recalled me to life, and I determined to quit my island at the expiration of two days.

◄ Why does Frankenstein decide to leave the island?

Yet, before I departed, there was a task to perform, on which I shuddered to reflect; I must pack up my chemical instruments, and for that purpose I must enter the room which had been the scene of my odious work, and I must handle those utensils the sight of which was sickening to me. The next morning, at daybreak, I summoned sufficient courage, and unlocked the door of my laboratory. The remains of the half-finished creature, whom I had destroyed, lay scattered on the floor, and I almost felt as if I had mangled the living flesh of a human being. I paused to collect myself and then entered the chamber. With trembling hand I conveyed the instruments out of the room, but I reflected that I ought not to leave the relics of my work to excite the horror and suspicion of the peasants; and I accordingly put them into a basket, with a great quantity of stones, and, laying them up, determined to throw them into the sea that very night; and in the meantime I sat upon the beach, employed in cleaning and arranging my chemical apparatus.

◄ What does Frankenstein do before departing his cottage? Why does he take the remains of his project away?

Nothing could be more complete than the alteration that had taken place in my feelings since the night of the appearance of the demon. I had before regarded my promise with a gloomy despair as a thing that, with whatever consequences, must be fulfilled; but I now felt as if a film had been taken from before my eyes and that I for the first time saw clearly. The idea of renewing my labors did not for one instant occur to me; the threat I had heard weighed on my thoughts, but I did not reflect that a voluntary act of mine could avert it. I had resolved in my own mind that to create another like the fiend I had first made would be an act of the basest and most <u>atrocious</u> selfishness, and I banished from my mind every thought that could lead to a different conclusion.

Between two and three in the morning the moon rose; and I then, putting my basket aboard a little skiff, sailed out about four miles from the shore. The scene was perfectly solitary: a few boats were returning towards land, but I sailed away from them. I felt as if I was about the commission of a dreadful crime and avoided with shuddering anxiety any encounter with my fellow creatures. At one time the moon, which had before been clear, was suddenly overspread by a thick cloud, and I took advantage of the moment of darkness and cast my basket into the sea: I listened to the gurgling sound as it sank and then sailed away from the spot. The sky became clouded, but the air was pure, although chilled by the northeast breeze that was then rising. But it refreshed me and filled me with such agreeable sensations that I resolved to prolong my stay on the water, and fixing the rudder in a direct position, stretched myself at the bottom of the boat. Clouds hid the moon, everything was obscure, and I heard only the sound of the boat as its keel cut through the waves; the murmur lulled me, and in a short time I slept soundly.

I do not know how long I remained in this situation, but when I awoke I found that the sun had already mounted considerably. The wind was high, and the waves continually threatened the safety of my little skiff. I found that the wind was northeast, and must have driven me far from the coast from which I had <u>embarked</u>. I endeavored to change my course but quickly found that if I again made the attempt the boat would be instantly filled with water. Thus situated, my only resource was to drive before the wind. I confess that I felt a few sensations of terror. I had no compass with me

> What is Frankenstein going to do? Why does he avoid other people?

> In what situation does Frankenstein find himself when he wakes up?

| Words For Everyday Use | **a • tro • cious** (ə trō′shəs) *adj.*, appalling or dismaying; unpleasant and offensive |
| | **em • bark** (em bärk′) *vi.*, begin a journey |

and was so slenderly acquainted with the geography of this part of the world, that the sun was of little benefit to me. I might be driven into the wide Atlantic and feel all the tortures of starvation or be swallowed up in the immeasurable waters that roared and <u>buffeted</u> around me. I had already been out many hours and felt the torment of a burning thirst, a prelude to my other sufferings. I looked on the heavens, which were covered by clouds that flew before the wind, only to be replaced by others; I looked upon the sea; it was to be my grave. "Fiend," I exclaimed, "your task is already fulfilled!" I thought of Elizabeth, of my father, and of Clerval; all left behind, on whom the monster might satisfy his sanguinary and merciless passions. This idea plunged me into a revery so despairing and frightful that even now, when the scene is on the point of closing before me forever, I shudder to reflect on it.

◀ *What is Frankenstein's first thought when he realizes that he might die upon the sea?*

Some hours passed thus; but by degrees, as the sun declined towards the horizon, the wind died away into a gentle breeze and the sea became free from breakers. But these gave place to a heavy swell; I felt sick and hardly able to hold the rudder, when suddenly I saw a line of high land towards the south.

Almost <u>spent</u>, as I was, by fatigue, and the dreadful suspense I endured for several hours, this sudden certainty of life rushed like a flood of warm joy to my heart, and tears gushed from my eyes.

How mutable are our feelings, and how strange is that clinging love we have of life even in the excess of misery! I constructed another sail with a part of my dress and eagerly steered my course towards the land. It had a wild and rocky appearance, but as I approached nearer I easily perceived the traces of cultivation. I saw vessels near the shore and found myself suddenly transported back to the neighborhood of civilized man. I carefully traced the windings of the land and hailed a steeple which I at length saw issuing from behind a small <u>promontory</u>. As I was in a state of extreme debility, I resolved to sail directly towards the town, as a place where I could most easily procure nourishment. Fortunately I had money with me. As I turned the promontory I perceived a small neat town and a good harbor, which I entered, my heart bounding with joy at my unexpected escape.

◀ *How does Frankenstein feel upon viewing civilized land? What course does he set?*

Words For Everyday Use	**buf • fet** (buf´it) *vt.*, thrust about
	spent (spent) *adj.*, worn out; physically exhausted
	prom • on • to • ry (präm´ən tôr´ē) *n.*, headland; peak of land that juts into the water

▶ How is
Frankenstein
greeted?

As I was occupied in fixing the boat and arranging the sails, several people crowded towards the spot. They seemed much surprised at my appearance, but instead of offering me any assistance, whispered together with gestures that at any other time might have produced in me a slight sensation of alarm. As it was, I merely remarked that they spoke English, and I therefore addressed them in that language. "My good friends," said I, "will you be so kind as to tell me the name of this town and inform me where I am?"

"You will know that soon enough," replied a man with a hoarse voice. "Maybe you are come to a place that will not prove much to your taste, but you will not be consulted as to your quarters, promise you."

▶ Why does his
treatment by the
villagers surprise
Frankenstein? What
do the villagers think
of Frankenstein?

I was exceedingly surprised on receiving so rude an answer from a stranger, and I was also disconcerted on perceiving the frowning and angry countenances of his companions. "Why do you answer me so roughly?" I replied; "surely it is not the custom of Englishmen to receive strangers so <u>inhospitably</u>."

"I do not know," said the man, "what the custom of the English may be, but it is the custom of the Irish to hate villains."

While this strange dialogue continued, I perceived the crowd rapidly increase. Their faces expressed a mixture of curiosity and anger, which annoyed and in some degree alarmed me. I inquired the way to the inn, but no one replied. I then moved forward, and a murmuring sound arose from the crowd as they followed and surrounded me, when an ill-looking man approaching tapped me on the shoulder and said, "Come sir, you must follow me to Mr. Kirwin's, to give an account of yourself."

"Who is Mr. Kirwin? Why am I to give an account of myself? Is not this a free country?"

▶ Why must
Frankenstein speak
to Mr. Kirwin?

"Ay, sir, free enough for honest folks. Mr. Kirwin is a magistrate, and you are to give an account of the death of a gentleman who was found murdered here last night."

This answer startled me, but I presently recovered myself. I was innocent; that could easily be proved; accordingly I followed my conductor in silence, and was led to one of the best houses in the town. I was ready to sink from fatigue and hunger, but being surrounded by a crowd, I thought it <u>politic</u> to rouse all my strength, that no physical debility might be construed into apprehension or conscious guilt. Little did I

▶ Why does
Frankenstein try to
hide his exhaustion?
To what terrible
calamity do you
think he refers?

Words For Everyday Use	
in • hos • pi • ta • bly (in häs´pit ə blē) *adv.*, without kindness or friendliness toward guests
pol • i • tic (päl´ i tik´) *adj.*, prudent; shrewd

then expect the calamity that was in a few moments to overwhelm me, and extinguish in horror and despair all fear of ignominy or death.

I must pause here, for it requires all my fortitude to recall the memory of the frightful events which I am about to relate, in proper detail, to my recollection.

Chapter 21

I was soon introduced into the presence of the magistrate, an old benevolent man with calm and mild manners. He looked upon me, however, with some degree of severity, and then, turning towards my conductors, he asked who appeared as witnesses on this occasion.

About half a dozen men came forward; and one being selected by the magistrate, he deposed that he had been out fishing the night before with his son and brother-in-law, Daniel Nugent, when, about ten o'clock, they observed a strong northerly blast rising, and they accordingly put in for port. It was a very dark night, as the moon had not yet risen; they did not land at the harbor, but, as they had been accustomed, at a creek about two miles below. He walked on first, carrying a part of the fishing tackle, and his companions followed him at some distance. As he was proceeding along the sands, he struck his foot against something and fell at his length on the ground. His companions came up to assist him, and by the light of their lantern they found that he had fallen on the body of a man who was to all appearance dead. Their first <u>supposition</u> was that it was the corpse of some person who had been drowned and was thrown on shore by the waves, but on examination they found that the clothes were not wet, and even that the body was not then cold. They instantly carried it to the cottage of an old woman near the spot and endeavored, but in vain, to restore it to life. It appeared to be a handsome young man, about five and twenty years of age. He had apparently been strangled, for there was no sign of any violence, except the black mark of fingers on his neck.

The first part of this <u>deposition</u> did not in the least interest me, but when the mark of the fingers was mentioned I remembered the murder of my brother and felt myself extremely agitated; my limbs trembled, and a mist came over my eyes, which obliged me to lean on a chair for support. The magistrate observed me with a keen eye and of course drew an unfavorable <u>augury</u> from my manner.

The son confirmed his father's account, but when Daniel Nugent was called he swore positively that just before the fall

---

▶ *What had Daniel Nugent and his companions found? What did they assume at first about their find? What proved their assumption wrong?*

▶ *Which part of the story agitates Frankenstein? Why does this detail upset him? What might be construed from his reaction?*

▶ *Why is the boat used as evidence against Frankenstein?*

Words For Everyday Use	
sup • po • si • tion (sup´ə zish´ən) *n.*, assumption	
dep • o • si • tion (dep´ə zish´ən) *n.*, testimony	
au • gu • ry (ô´gyo͞o rē) *n.*, indication	

of his companion, he saw a boat, with a single man in it, at a short distance from the shore; and, as far as he could judge by the light of a few stars, it was the same boat in which I had just landed.

A woman deposed that she lived near the beach and was standing at the door of her cottage, waiting for the return of the fishermen, about an hour before she heard of the discovery of the body, when she saw a boat with only one man in it push off from that part of the shore where the corpse was afterwards found.

Another woman confirmed the account of the fishermen having brought the body into her house; it was not cold. They put it into a bed and rubbed it, and Daniel went to the town for an apothecary,[1] but life was quite gone.

Several other men were examined concerning my landing, and they agreed that, with the strong north wind that had arisen during the night, it was very probable that I had beaten about for many hours, and had been obliged to return nearly to the same spot from which I had departed. Besides, they observed that it appeared that I had brought the body from another place, and it was likely that, as I did not appear to know the shore, I might have put into the harbor ignorant of the distance of the town of—from the place where I had deposited the corpse.

◀ What theory is offered concerning Frankenstein's activities the night before?

Mr. Kirwin, on hearing this evidence, desired that I should be taken into the room where the body lay for interment, that it might be observed what effect the sight of it would produce upon me. This idea was probably suggested by the extreme agitation I had exhibited when the mode of the murder had been described. I was accordingly conducted, by the magistrate and several other persons, to the inn. I could not help being struck by the strange coincidences that had taken place during this eventful night; but, knowing that I had been conversing with several persons in the island I had inhabited about the time that the body had been found, I was perfectly tranquil as to the consequences of the affair.

◀ Why isn't Frankenstein concerned about the charges brought against him?

I entered the room where the corpse lay and was led up to the coffin. How can I describe my sensations on beholding it? I feel yet parched with horror, nor can I reflect on that terrible moment without shuddering and agony. The examination, the presence of the magistrate and witnesses, passed like a dream from my memory when I saw the lifeless form of Henry Clerval stretched before me. I gasped for breath, and throwing myself on the body, I exclaimed, "Have my

◀ Who is the murder victim? What does Frankenstein mean by his cries? What does Mr. Kirwin believe based on Frankenstein's comments?

---

1. **apothecary.** Pharmacist, and formerly a person who prescribed medicine

murderous <u>machinations</u> deprived you also, my dearest Henry, of life? Two I have already destroyed; other victims await their destiny; but you, Clerval, my friend, my benefactor—"

The human frame could no longer support the agonies that I endured, and I was carried out of the room in strong convulsions.

A fever succeeded to this. I lay for two months on the point of death; my ravings, as I afterwards heard, were frightful; I called myself the murderer of William, of Justine, and of Clerval. Sometimes I entreated my attendants to assist me in the destruction of the fiend by whom I was tormented; and at others I felt the fingers of the monster already grasping my neck, and screamed aloud with agony and terror. Fortunately, as I spoke my native language, Mr. Kirwin alone understood me; but my gestures and bitter cries were sufficient to affright the other witnesses.

Why did I not die? More miserable than man ever was before, why did I not sink into forgetfulness and rest? Death snatches away many blooming children, the only hopes of their doting parents; how many brides and youthful lovers have been one day in the bloom of health and hope, and the next a prey for worms and the decay of the tomb! Of what materials was I made that I could thus resist so many shocks, which, like the turning of the wheel, continually renewed the torture?

But I was doomed to live and in two months found myself as awaking from a dream, in a prison stretched on a wretched bed, surrounded by jailers, turnkeys, bolts, and all the miserable apparatus of a dungeon. It was morning, I remember, when I thus awoke to understanding; I had forgotten the particulars of what had happened and only felt as if some great misfortune had suddenly overwhelmed me; but when I looked around and saw the barred windows and the squalidness of the room in which I was, all flashed across my memory and I groaned bitterly.

This sound disturbed an old woman who was sleeping in a chair beside me. She was a hired nurse, the wife of one of the turnkeys, and her countenance expressed all those bad qualities which often characterize that class. The lines of her face were hard and rude, like that of persons accustomed to see without sympathizing in sights of misery. Her tone

▶ *What impact do Frankenstein's ravings have on his case?*

▶ *How does Frankenstein feel upon awaking from his fevered illness?*

▶ *How does Frankenstein's nurse treat him? What main characteristic does she demonstrate?*

Words
For
Everyday
Use

mach • i • na • tion (mak´ə nā´shən) *n.,* secret plot or scheme with evil intent

expressed her entire indifference; she addressed me in English, and the voice struck me as one that I had heard during my sufferings:—

"Are you better now, sir?" said she.

I replied in the same language, with a feeble voice, "I believe I am; but if it be all true, if indeed I did not dream, I am sorry that I am still alive to feel this misery and horror."

"For that matter," replied the old woman, "if you mean about the gentleman you murdered, I believe that it were better for you if you were dead, for I fancy it will go hard with you! However, that's none of my business; I am sent to nurse you and get you well; I do my duty with a safe conscience; it were well if everybody did the same."

I turned with loathing from the woman who could utter so unfeeling a speech to a person just saved, on the very edge of death; but I felt languid and unable to reflect on all that had passed. The whole series of my life appeared to me as a dream; I sometimes doubted if indeed it were all true, for it never presented itself to my mind with the force of reality.

How does Frankenstein feel about all that has happened to him?

As the images that floated before me became more distinct, I grew feverish; a darkness pressed around me; no one was near me who soothed me with the gentle voice of love; no dear hand supported me. The physician came and prescribed medicines, and the old woman prepared them for me; but utter carelessness was visible in the first, and the expression of brutality was strongly marked in the <u>visage</u> of the second. Who could be interested in the fate of a murderer but the hangman who would gain his fee?

Why are Frankenstein's caretakers disinterested in his fate?

These were my first reflections, but I soon learned that Mr. Kirwin had shown me extreme kindness. He had caused the best room in the prison to be prepared for me (wretched indeed was the best); and it was he who had provided a physician and a nurse. It is true, he seldom came to see me, for, although he ardently desired to relieve the sufferings of every human creature, he did not wish to be present at the agonies and miserable ravings of a murderer. He came, therefore, sometimes to see that I was not neglected but his visits were short and with long intervals.

In what way does Mr. Kirwin help Frankenstein? Why does he offer his aid from a distance?

One day, while I was gradually recovering, I was seated in a chair, my eyes half open and my cheeks <u>livid</u> like those in death. I was overcome by gloom and misery and often

Words For Everyday Use	**vis • age** (viz´ij) *n.,* face **liv • id** (liv´id) *adj.,* discolored like a bruise; grayish-blue

► Why does Frankenstein consider declaring himself guilty? Explain whether it be appropriate for him to do so.

reflected I had better seek death than desire to remain in a world which to me was replete with wretchedness. At one time I considered whether I should not declare myself guilty and suffer the penalty of the law, less innocent than poor Justine had been. Such were my thoughts when the door of my apartment was opened and Mr. Kirwin entered. His countenance expressed sympathy and compassion; he drew a chair close to mine, and addressed me in French,

"I fear that this place is very shocking to you; can I do anything to make you more comfortable?"

"I thank you, but all that you mention is nothing to me; on the whole earth there is no comfort which I am capable of receiving."

"I know that the sympathy of a stranger can be but of little relief to one borne down as you are by so strange a misfortune. But you will, I hope, soon quit this melancholy abode, for doubtless evidence can easily be brought to free you from the criminal charge."

► Why isn't Frankenstein comforted by Mr. Kirwin's assertion that he can be cleared of the charge?

"That is my least concern; I am, by a course of strange events, become the most miserable of mortals. Persecuted and tortured as I am and have been, can death be any evil to me?"

"Nothing indeed could be more unfortunate and agonizing than the strange chances that have lately occurred. You were thrown, by some surprising accident, on this shore renowned its hospitality, seized immediately, and charged with murder. The first sight that was presented to your eyes was the body of your friend, murdered in so unaccountable a manner and placed, as it were, by some fiend across your path."

► What has Mr. Kirwin learned about Frankenstein during his illness?

As Mr. Kirwin said this, notwithstanding the agitation I endured on this retrospect of my sufferings, I also felt considerable surprise at the knowledge he seemed to possess concerning me. I suppose some astonishment was exhibited in my countenance for Mr. Kirwin hastened to say,

"Immediately upon your being taken ill, all the papers that were on your person were brought me, and I examined them that I might discover some trace by which I could send to your relations an account of your misfortune and illness. I found several letters, and, among others, one which I discovered from its commencement to be from your father. I instantly wrote to Geneva; nearly two months have elapsed

Words For Everyday Use

re • nowned (ri nound´) *adj.,* famous

ret • ro • spect (re´ trə spekt´) *n.,* contemplation or survey of the past

since the departure of my letter. But you are ill; even now you tremble; you are unfit for agitation of any kind."

"This suspense is a thousand times worse than the most horrible event; tell me what new scene of death has been acted, and whose murder I am now to <u>lament</u>?"

"Your family is perfectly well," said Mr. Kirwin with gentleness; "and someone, a friend, is come to visit you."

I know not by what chain of thought the idea presented itself, but it instantly darted into my mind that the murderer had come to mock at my misery and taunt me with the death of Clerval, as a new incitement for me to comply with his hellish desires. I put my hand before my eyes and cried out in agony,

"Oh! take him away! I cannot see him; for God's sake do not let him enter!"

Mr. Kirwin regarded me with a troubled countenance. He could not help regarding my exclamation as a presumption of my guilt and said in rather a severe tone,

"I should have thought, young man, that the presence of your father would have been welcome instead of inspiring such violent repugnance."

"My father!" cried I, while every feature and every muscle was relaxed from anguish to pleasure: "Is my father indeed come? How kind, how very kind! But where is he, why does he not hasten to me?"

My change of manner surprised and pleased the magistrate; perhaps he thought that my former exclamation was a momentary return of delirium, and now he instantly resumed his former benevolence. He rose and quitted the room with my nurse, and in a moment my father entered it.

Nothing, at this moment, could have given me greater pleasure than the arrival of my father. I stretched out my hand to him and cried—

"Are you then safe—and Elizabeth—and Ernest?"

My father calmed me with assurances of their welfare and endeavored, by dwelling on these subjects so interesting to my heart, to raise my desponding spirits; but he soon felt that a prison cannot be the abode of cheerfulness. "What a place is this that you inhabit, my son!" said he, looking mournfully at the barred windows and wretched appearance of the room. "You traveled to seek happiness, but a fatality seems to pursue you. And poor Clerval—"

◀ What does Frankenstein fear has happened during his illness?

◀ Who does Frankenstein conceive has come to visit him?

◀ Why is Mr. Kirwin surprised and displeased by Frankenstein's response to the news of a visitor?

Words For Everyday Use

la • ment (lə ment´) *vi.*, feel or express deep sorrow; mourn

The name of my unfortunate and murdered friend was an agitation too great to be endured in my weak state; I shed tears.

"Alas! Yes, my father," replied I; "some destiny of the most horrible kind hangs over me, and I must live to fulfill it, or surely I should have died on the coffin of Henry."

We were not allowed to converse for any length of time, for the <u>precarious</u> state of my health rendered every precaution necessary that could ensure tranquility. Mr. Kirwin came in and insisted that my strength should not be exhausted by too much exertion. But the appearance of my father was to me like that of my good angel, and I gradually recovered my health.

As my sickness quitted me, I was absorbed by a gloomy and black melancholy that nothing could dissipate. The image of Clerval was forever before me, ghastly and murdered. More than once the agitation into which these reflections threw me made my friends dread a dangerous relapse. Alas! Why did they preserve so miserable and detested a life? It was surely that I might fulfill my destiny, which is now drawing to a close. Soon, oh! very soon, will death extinguish these throbbings and relieve me from the mighty weight of anguish that bears me to the dust; and, in executing the award of justice, I shall also sink to rest. Then the appearance of death was distant although the wish was ever present to my thoughts; and I often sat for hours motionless and speechless, wishing for some mighty revolution that might bury me and my destroyer in its ruins.

The season of the assizes[2] approached. I had already been three months in prison, and although I was still weak and in continual danger of a relapse, I was obliged to travel nearly a hundred miles to the county town where the court was held. Mr. Kirwin charged himself with every care of collecting witnesses and arranging my defense. I was spared the disgrace of appearing publicly as a criminal, as the case was not brought before the court that decides on life and death. The grand jury rejected the bill on its being proved that I was on the Orkney Islands at the hour the body of my friend was found; and a fortnight after my removal I was liberated from prison.

► According to Frankenstein, why does he still live?

► What does Frankenstein think is imminent? How did he feel about the same matter at the time of which he tells?

► What is the result of Franken-stein's trial?

---

2. **assizes.** In England, court sessions held periodically to try civil and criminal cases

Words For Everyday Use

pre • car • i • ous (prē ker´ē əs) *adj.*, insecure; risky

My father was enraptured on finding me freed from the vexations of a criminal charge, that I was again allowed to breathe the fresh atmosphere and permitted to return to my native country. I did not participate in these feelings, for to me the walls of a dungeon or a palace were alike hateful. The cup of life was poisoned forever, and although the sun shone upon me, as upon the happy and gay of heart, I saw around me nothing but a dense and frightful darkness, penetrated by no light but the glimmer of two eyes that glared upon me. Sometimes they were the expressive eyes of Henry, languishing in death, the dark orbs nearly covered by the lids, and the long black lashes that fringed them; sometimes it was the watery, clouded eyes of the monster as I first saw them in my chamber at Ingolstadt.

◀ How does Frankenstein's father feel about his son's acquittal? How does Frankenstein himself feel?

My father tried to awaken in me the feelings of affection. He talked of Geneva, which I should soon visit, of Elizabeth and Ernest; but these words only drew deep groans from me. Sometimes, indeed, I felt a wish for happiness and thought with melancholy delight of my beloved cousin or longed, with a devouring maladie du pays,[3] to see once more the blue lake and rapid Rhone that had been so dear to me in early childhood; but my general state of feeling was a torpor in which a prison was as welcome a residence as the divinest scene in nature; and these fits were seldom interrupted but by paroxysms of anguish and despair. At these moments I often endeavored to put an end to the existence I loathed, and it required unceasing attendance and vigilance to restrain me from committing some dreadful act of violence.

Yet one duty remained to me, the recollection of which finally triumphed over my selfish despair. It was necessary that I should return without delay to Geneva, there to watch over the lives of those I so fondly loved and to lie in wait for the murderer, that if any chance led me to the place of his concealment, or if he dared again to blast me by his presence, I might, with unfailing aim, put an end to the existence of the monstrous image which I had endued with the mockery of a soul still more monstrous. My father still desired to delay our departure, fearful that I could not sustain the fatigues of a journey, for I was a shattered wreck—

◀ What last duty keeps Frankenstein alive?

---

3. **maladie du pays.** Homesickness

Words For Everyday Use

vex • a • tion (veks ā´shən) n., something that causes annoyance or disturbance

tor • por (tôr´pər) n., dullness; apathy

the shadow of a human being. My strength was gone. I was a mere skeleton, and fever night and day preyed upon my wasted frame.

Still, as I urged our leaving Ireland with such <u>inquietude</u> and impatience, my father thought it best to yield. We took our passage on board a vessel bound for Havre-de-Grace,[4] and sailed with a fair wind from the Irish shores. It was midnight. I lay on the deck looking at the stars and listening to the dashing of the waves. I hailed the darkness that shut Ireland from my sight, and my pulse beat with a feverish joy when I reflected that I should soon see Geneva. The past appeared to me in the light of a frightful dream; yet the vessel in which I was, the wind that blew me from the detested shore of Ireland, and the sea which surrounded me told me too forcibly that I was deceived by no vision and that Clerval, my friend and dearest companion, had fallen a victim to me and the monster of my creation. I repassed, in my memory, my whole life—my quiet happiness while residing with my family in Geneva, the death of my mother, and my departure for Ingolstadt. I remembered, shuddering, the mad enthusiasm that hurried me on to the creation of my hideous enemy, and I called to mind the night in which he first lived. I was unable to pursue the train of thought; a thousand feelings pressed upon me, and I wept bitterly.

Ever since my recovery from the fever I had been in the custom of taking every night a small quantity of laudanum;[5] for it was by means of this drug only that I was enabled to gain the rest necessary for the preservation of life. Oppressed by the recollection of my various misfortunes, I now swallowed double my usual quantity and soon slept profoundly. But sleep did not afford me respite from thought and misery; my dreams presented a thousand objects that scared me. Towards morning I was possessed by a kind of nightmare; I felt the fiend's grasp in my neck, and could not free myself from it; groans and cries rang in my ears. My father, who was watching over me, perceiving my restlessness, awoke me; the dashing waves were around, the cloudy sky above, the fiend was not here: a sense of security, a feeling that a truce was established

► *Why is Frankenstein unable to find peace even in sleep?*

---

4. **Havre-de-Grace.** Seaport on the English Channel
5. **laudanum.** Drug containing opium

Words For Everyday Use

in • qui • e • tude (in kwī´ə tyo͞od´) *n.,* restlessness; uneasiness

between the present hour and the irresistible, disastrous future, imparted to me a kind of calm forgetfulness, of which the human mind is by its structure peculiarly <u>susceptible</u>.

Responding to the Selection

Do you think Frankenstein makes a wise decision when he refuses to create a mate for his monster? Is his decision responsible toward other people? toward his creation? Explain your responses.

Reviewing the Selection

Recalling and Interpreting

1. **R:** What does Frankenstein's father fear is the cause of his son's dismal spirits? What is the true cause of these feelings? Why does Frankenstein wish to postpone his marriage to Elizabeth? Why doesn't Frankenstein want to leave his family?

2. **I:** What do Frankenstein's feelings toward his family and toward his new creation suggest about his values?

3. **R:** Where does Frankenstein work on the mate for his first creation? When Frankenstein finally begins work on the new creature, how does he feel about his work? What concerns does he begin to have? What action enrages the creature?

4. **I:** In what way have Frankenstein's feelings about the ability to produce life changed? Why does Frankenstein destroy his creation?

5. **R:** According to the creature, what relationship exists between Frankenstein and him?

6. **I:** Who is more powerful—Frankenstein or his creation? Explain your response.

7. **R:** Of what crime is Frankenstein accused? What evidence is produced against him? What words and actions on his part suggest guilt?

8. **I:** Is Frankenstein responsible for Clerval's death? Would justice have been served if he had been executed for the murder of his friend?

Synthesizing

9. Who has the power to create life in most creation stories? What role is Frankenstein seeking? How does he now feel about usurping this role?

10. Examine the passage on page 161 in which Frankenstein reviews his fears about bringing a mate for his creature into the world. Explain how some of these concerns might be applied to contemporary scientific discovery or exploration.

Understanding Literature (QUESTIONS FOR DISCUSSION)

1. Archetype. An **archetype** is any element that recurs throughout the literature of the world. One archetype is the human quest for knowledge or power beyond human command, and the ensuing destruction. Explain how *Frankenstein* embodies this archetype. What other works do you know that include this archetype?

2. Foreshadowing. Foreshadowing is the act of presenting materials that hint at events to occur later in a story. In chapter 21, the murder of Clerval is disclosed. Find a passage that foreshadows this information.

3. Metaphor. A **metaphor** is a figure of speech in which one thing is spoken or written about as if it were another. This figure of speech invites the reader to make a comparison between the two things. The two things are the writer's actual subject, or the *tenor* of the metaphor, and the thing to which the subject is likened, or the *vehicle* of the metaphor. Identify the tenor and the vehicle of the following metaphor from page 156:

> "I [Frankenstein] am a blasted tree; the bolt has entered my soul; and I felt then that I should survive to exhibit what I shall soon cease to be—a miserable spectacle of wrecked humanity, pitiable to others, and intolerable to myself."

Explain the comparison this metaphor implies.

Chapter 22

The voyage came to an end. We landed and proceeded to Paris. I soon found that I had overtaxed my strength and that I must repose before I could continue my journey. My father's care and attentions were indefatigable, but he did not know the origin of my sufferings and sought <u>erroneous</u> methods to remedy the incurable ill. He wished me to seek amusement in society. I abhorred the face of man. Oh, not abhorred! They were my brethren, my fellow beings, and I felt attracted even to the most repulsive among them as to creatures of an angelic nature and celestial mechanism. But I felt that I had no right to share their intercourse. I had unchained an enemy among them whose joy it was to shed their blood and to revel in their groans. How they would, each and all, abhor me and hunt me from the world did they know my unhallowed acts and the crimes which had their source in me!

My father yielded at length to my desire to avoid society and strove by various arguments to banish my despair. Sometimes he thought that I felt deeply the degradation of being obliged to answer a charge of murder, and he endeavored to prove to me the futility of pride.

"Alas! My father," said I, "how little do you know me. Human beings, their feelings and passions, would indeed be degraded if such a wretch as I felt pride. Justine, poor unhappy Justine, was as innocent as I, and she suffered the same charge; she died for it; and I am the cause of this—I murdered her. William, Justine, and Henry—they all died by my hands."

My father had often, during my imprisonment, heard me make the same assertion; when I thus accused myself, he sometimes seemed to desire an explanation, and at others he appeared to consider it as the offspring of delirium, and that, during my illness, some idea of this kind had presented itself to my imagination, the remembrance of which I preserved in my convalescence. I avoided explanation and maintained a continual silence concerning the wretch I had created. I had a persuasion that I should be supposed mad, and this in itself would forever have chained my tongue. But, besides, I could not bring myself to disclose a secret which would fill my

▶ Why does Frankenstein abhor society? What would people do if they knew what he had done?

▶ For what does Frankenstein claim guilt? What does his father think of these declarations?

▶ Why does Frankenstein continually refuse to reveal his secret? Why would he like to reveal this secret?

Words For Everyday Use

er • ro • ne • ous (ər rō′nē əs) *adj.,* wrong, mistaken, based on error

hearer with consternation, and make fear and unnatural horror the inmates of his breast. I checked, therefore, my impatient thirst for sympathy and was silent when I would have given the world to have confided the fatal secret. Yet, still words like those I have recorded would burst uncontrollably from me. I could offer no explanation of them; but their truth in part relieved the burden of my mysterious woe.

Upon this occasion my father said, with an expression of unbounded wonder, "My dearest Victor, what infatuation is this? My dear son, I entreat you never to make such an assertion again."

"I am not mad," I cried energetically; "the sun and the heavens, who have viewed my operations, can bear witness of my truth. I am the assassin of those most innocent victims; they died by my machinations. A thousand times would I have shed my own blood, drop by drop, to have saved their lives; but I could not, my father, indeed I could not sacrifice the whole human race."

The conclusion of this speech convinced my father that my ideas were deranged, and he instantly changed the subject of our conversation and endeavored to alter the course of thoughts. He wished as much as possible to obliterate the memory of the scenes that had taken place in Ireland and never alluded to them or suffered me to speak of my misfortunes.

As time passed away I became more calm; misery had her dwelling in my heart, but I no longer talked in the same incoherent manner of my own crimes; sufficient for me was the consciousness of them. By the utmost self-violence I curbed the imperious voice of wretchedness, which sometimes desired to declare itself to the whole world, and my manners were calmer and more composed than they had ever been since my journey to the sea of ice.

A few days before we left Paris on our way to Switzerland, I received the following letter from Elizabeth:—

> My dear friend,—It gave me the greatest pleasure to receive a letter from my uncle dated at Paris; you are no longer at a formidable distance, and I may hope to see you in less than a fortnight. My poor cousin, how much you must have suffered! I expect to see you looking even

◄ *What would Frankenstein have done if he could? Explain whether his actions to this point support his assertion. With what enigmatic remark does he conclude his speech? What does he mean by this statement?*

Words For Everyday Use	
in • fat • u • a • tion (in fach´ōͦ ā´ shən) *n.,* affectation of folly; lack of sound judgment caused by strong emotion	
im • pe • ri • ous (im pir´ē əs) *adj.,* overbearing; arrogant	
for • mi • da • ble (fôr´mə də bəl) *adj.,* hard to overcome	

▶ What does Elizabeth hope to see upon Frankenstein's return? Do you think her hope will be realized? Why, or why not?

more ill than when you quitted Geneva. This winter has been passed most miserably, tortured as I have been by anxious suspense; yet I hope to see peace in your countenance and to find that your heart is not totally void of comfort and tranquility.

Yet I fear that the same feelings now exist that made you so miserable a year ago, even perhaps augmented by time. I would not disturb you at this period, when so many misfortunes weigh upon you, but a conversation that I had with my uncle previous to his departure renders some explanation necessary before we meet.

Explanation! You may possibly say, what can Elizabeth have to explain? If you really say this, my questions are answered, and all my doubts satisfied. But you are distant from me, and it is possible that you may dread, and yet be pleased with this explanation; and, in a probability of this being the case, I dare not any longer postpone writing what, during your absence, I have often wished to express to you, but have never had the courage to begin.

You well know, Victor, that our union has been the favorite plan of your parents ever since our infancy. We were told this when young, and taught to look forward to it as an event that would certainly take place. We were affectionate playfellows during childhood, and I believe dear and valued friends to one another as we grew older.

▶ What concern does Elizabeth express? What circumstances lead her to wonder such a thing?

But as brother and sister often entertain a lively affection towards each other without desiring a more intimate union, may not such also be our case? Tell me, dearest Victor. Answer me, I <u>conjure</u> you, by our mutual happiness, with simple truth—Do you not love another?

You have traveled; you have spent several years of your life at Ingolstadt; and I confess to you, my friend, that when I saw you last autumn so unhappy, flying to solitude from the society of every creature, I could not help supposing that you might regret our connection and believe yourself bound in honor to fulfill the wishes of your parents, although they opposed themselves to your inclinations. But this is false reasoning. I confess to you, my friend, that I love you and that in my airy dreams of futurity you have been my constant

---

Words For Everyday Use

con • jure (kun´jər) *vt.,* call upon by an oath

---

friend and companion. But it is your happiness I desire as well as my own when I declare to you that our marriage would render me eternally miserable unless it were the <u>dictate</u> of your own free choice. Even now I weep to think that, borne down as you are by the cruelest misfortunes, you may stifle, by the word honor, all hope of that love and happiness which would alone restore you to yourself. I who have so <u>disinterested</u> an affection for you, may increase your miseries tenfold by being an obstacle to your wishes. Ah! Victor, be assured that your cousin and playmate has too sincere a love for you not to be made miserable by this supposition. Be happy, my friend; and if you obey me in this one request, remain satisfied that nothing on earth will have the power to interrupt my tranquility.

Do not let this letter disturb you; do not answer tomorrow, or the next day, or even until you come, if it will give you pain. My uncle will send me news of your health, and if I see but one smile on your lips when we meet, occasioned by this or any other exertion of mine, I shall need no other happiness.

Elizabeth Lavenza.

◄ What concerns does Frankenstein have about marrying Elizabeth? What fears does Elizabeth have?

This letter revived in my memory what I had before forgotten, the threat of the fiend—"I be with you on your wedding-night!" Such was my sentence, and on that night would the demon employ every art to destroy me and tear me from the glimpse of happiness which promised partly to console my sufferings. On that night he had determined to <u>consummate</u> his crimes by my death. Well, be it so; a deadly struggle would then assuredly take place, in which if he were victorious I should be at peace, and his power over me be at an end. If he were vanquished I should be a free man. Alas! What freedom? Such as the peasant enjoys when his family have been massacred before his eyes, his cottage burnt, his lands laid waste, and he is turned adrift, homeless, penniless and alone, but free. Such would be my liberty except that in my Elizabeth I possessed a treasure, alas, balanced by those horrors of remorse and guilt which would pursue me until death.

Sweet and beloved Elizabeth! I read and re-read her letter, and some softened feelings stole into my heart and dared to

◄ Why does this letter disturb Victor?

◄ What are the possible results of the struggle that Frankenstein thinks will take place on his wedding night?

Words For Everyday Use	
	dic • tate (dik′ tāt′) *n.,* command
	dis • in • ter • est • ed (dis in′ tris tid) *adj.,* not influenced by personal interest or selfish motives
	con • sum • mate (kən sum′it) *vt.,* finish; accomplish

▶ *What barriers exist to Franken- stein's paradisaical dreams?*

▶ *After the monster threatens to be with Frankenstein on his wedding night, why doesn't Frankenstein postpone or forego his marriage?*

whisper paradisaical dreams of love and joy; but the apple was already eaten,[1] and the angel's arm bared to drive me from all hope. Yet I would die to make her happy. If the monster executed his threat, death was inevitable; yet, again, I considered whether my marriage would hasten my fate. My destruction might indeed arrive a few months sooner, but if my torturer should suspect that I postponed it, influenced by his menaces, he would surely find other and perhaps more dreadful means of revenge. He had vowed to be with me on my wedding-night, yet he did not consider that threat as binding him to peace in the meantime, for, as if to show me that he was not yet satiated with blood, he had murdered Clerval immediately after the <u>enunciation</u> of his threats. I resolved, therefore, that if my immediate union with my cousin would conduce either to hers or my father's happi- ness, my adversary's designs against my life should not retard it a single hour.

In this state of mind I wrote to Elizabeth. My letter was calm and affectionate. "I fear, my beloved girl," I said, "little happiness remains for us on earth; yet all that I may one day enjoy is centered in you. Chase away your idle fears; to you alone do I consecrate my life and my endeavors for content- ment. I have one secret, Elizabeth, a dreadful one; when revealed to you, it will chill your frame with horror, and then, far from being surprised at my misery, you will only wonder that I survive what I have endured. I will confide this tale of misery and terror to you the day after our marriage shall take place, for, my sweet cousin, there must be perfect confidence between us. But until then, I conjure you, do not mention or allude to it. This I most earnestly entreat, and I know you will comply."

▶ *To whom will Frankenstein reveal his secret? When will he reveal it?*

In about a week after the arrival of Elizabeth's letter we returned to Geneva. The sweet girl welcomed me with warm affection, yet tears were in her eyes as she beheld my emaci- ated frame and feverish cheeks. I saw a change in her also. She was thinner and had lost much of that heavenly <u>vivacity</u> that had before charmed me; but her gentleness and soft looks of compassion made her a more fit companion for one blasted and miserable as I was.

▶ *What change has come over Elizabeth? Why does this change make her a more appropriate match for Frankenstein?*

---

1. **apple was already eaten.** Refers to the fall of Adam and Eve after eating the fruit of the forbidden tree

Words For Everyday Use	e • nun • ci • a • tion (ē nun´sē a´shən) *n.*, proclamation; announcement vi • vac • i • ty (vi vas´ə tē) *n.*, liveliness of spirit; animation

The tranquility which I now enjoyed did not endure. Memory brought madness with it, and when I thought of what had passed a real insanity possessed me; sometimes I was furious and burned with rage, sometimes low and despondent. I neither spoke nor looked at anyone, but sat motionless, bewildered by the multitude of miseries that overcame me.

Elizabeth alone had the power to draw me from these fits; her gentle voice would soothe me when transported by passion and inspire me with human feelings when sunk in torpor. She wept with me and for me. When reason returned she would remonstrate and endeavor to inspire me with resignation. Ah! It is well for the unfortunate to be <u>resigned</u>, but for the guilty there is no peace. The agonies of remorse poison the luxury there is otherwise sometimes found in indulging the excess of grief.

◄ Why does resignation offer Frankenstein no relief?

Soon after my arrival my father spoke of my immediate marriage with Elizabeth. I remained silent.

"Have you, then, some other attachment?"

"None on earth. I love Elizabeth, and look forward to our union with delight. Let the day therefore be fixed; and on it I will consecrate myself, in life or death, to the happiness of my cousin."

"My dear Victor, do not speak thus. Heavy misfortunes have befallen us, but let us only cling closer to what remains and transfer our love for those whom we have lost to those who yet live. Our circle will be small but bound close by the ties of affection and mutual misfortune. And when time shall have softened your despair new and dear objects of care will be born to replace those of whom we have been so cruelly deprived."

Such were the lessons of my father. But to me the remembrance of the threat returned, nor can you wonder that, omnipotent as the fiend had yet been in his deeds of blood, I should almost regard him as invincible, and that when he had pronounced the words, "I shall be with you on your wedding-night," I should regard the threatened fate as unavoidable. But death was no evil to me if the loss of Elizabeth were balanced with it; and I therefore, with a contented and even cheerful countenance, agreed with my father that if my cousin would consent, the ceremony should take place in ten days, and thus put, as I imagined, the seal to my fate.

◄ Why does Frankenstein feel that the fate promised by the monster is unavoidable?

Words For Everyday Use

re • signed (ri zīnd´) *adj.*, patiently submissive; accepting passively

► What does Frankenstein think the monster's threat means? What do you think the monster actually intends to do?

Great God! If for one instant I had thought what might be the hellish intention of my fiendish <u>adversary</u>, I would rather have banished myself forever from my native country and wandered a friendless outcast over the earth, than to have consented to this miserable marriage. But, as if possessed of magic powers, the monster had blinded me to his real intentions; and when I thought that I had prepared only my own death, I hastened that of a far dearer victim.

As the period fixed for our marriage drew nearer, whether from cowardice or a prophetic feeling, I felt my heart sink within me. But I concealed my feelings by an appearance of <u>hilarity</u> that brought smiles and joy to the countenance of my father, but hardly deceived the ever-watchful and nicer eye of Elizabeth. She looked forward to our union with placid contentment, not unmingled with a little fear, which past misfortunes had impressed, that what now appeared certain and tangible happiness might soon dissipate into an airy dream and leave no trace but deep and everlasting regret.

Preparations were made for the event, congratulatory visits were received, and all wore a smiling appearance. I shut up, as well as I could, in my own heart the anxiety that <u>preyed</u> there and entered with seeming earnestness into the plans of my father, although they might only serve as the decorations of my tragedy. Through my father's exertions, a part of the inheritance of Elizabeth had been restored to her by the Austrian government. A small possession on the shores of Como belonged to her. It was agreed that, immediately after our union, we should proceed to Villa Lavenza, and spend our first days of happiness beside the beautiful lake near which it stood.

► Where will Elizabeth and Frankenstein go after they are married?

In the meantime I took every precaution to defend my person in case the fiend should openly attack me. I carried pistols and a dagger constantly about me and was ever on the watch to prevent <u>artifice</u>, and by these means gained a greater degree of tranquility. Indeed, as the period approached, the threat appeared more as a delusion, not to be regarded as worthy to disturb my peace, while the happiness I hoped for in my marriage wore a greater appearance of certainty as the day fixed for its solemnization drew nearer and I heard it continually spoken of as an occurrence which no accident could possibly prevent.

► What precautions does Frankenstein take? What happens to his fears as his wedding draws closer?

Words For Everyday Use	
ad • ver • sar • y (ad´vər ser´ē) n., opponent, enemy	
hi • lar • i • ty (hi ler´i tē) n., noisy merriment	
prey (prā) vi., have a harmful influence	
ar • ti • fice (ärt´ə fis) n., trickery	

Elizabeth seemed happy; my tranquil demeanor contributed greatly to calm her mind. But on the day that was to fulfill my wishes and my destiny, she was melancholy, and a presentiment of evil pervaded her; and perhaps also she thought of the dreadful secret which I had promised to reveal to her on the following day. My father was in the meantime overjoyed and, in the bustle of preparation, only recognized in the melancholy of his niece the diffidence of a bride.

◀ What is Elizabeth's mood on her wedding day? What different explanations do Frankenstein and his father have for this mood?

After the ceremony was performed a large party assembled at my father's, but it was agreed that Elizabeth and I should commence our journey by water, sleeping that night at Evian[2] and continuing our voyage on the following day. The day was fair, the wind favorable; all smiled on our <u>nuptial</u> embarkation.

Those were the last moments of my life during which I enjoyed the feeling of happiness. We passed rapidly along: the sun was hot, but we were sheltered from its rays by a kind of canopy while we enjoyed the beauty of the scene, sometimes on one side of the lake, where we saw Mont Salêve, the pleasant banks of Montalègre, and at a distance, surmounting all, the beautiful Mont Blanc and the assemblage of snowy mountains that in vain endeavor to emulate her; sometimes coasting the opposite banks, we saw the mighty Jura opposing its dark side to the ambition that would quit its native country, and an almost insurmountable barrier to the invader who should wish to enslave it.

I took the hand of Elizabeth: "You are sorrowful, my love. Ah! If you knew what I have suffered and what I may yet endure, you would endeavor to let me taste the quiet and freedom from despair that this one day at least permits me to enjoy."

"Be happy, my dear Victor," replied Elizabeth; "there is, I hope, nothing to distress you; and be assured that if a lively joy is not painted in my face, my heart is contented. Something whispers to me not to depend too much on the prospect that is opened before us, but I will not listen to such a sinister voice. Observe how fast we move along and how the clouds, which sometimes obscure and sometimes rise above the dome of Mont Blanc, render this scene of beauty

◀ What foreboding does Elizabeth experience?

---

2. **Evian.** Town in France on Lake Geneva

Words For Everyday Use

nup • tial (nup´shəl) *adj.*, of marriage or a wedding

still more interesting. Look also at the innumerable fish that are swimming in the clear waters, where we can distinguish every pebble that lies at the bottom. What a divine day! how happy and serene all nature appears!"

Thus Elizabeth endeavored to divert her thoughts and mine from all reflection upon melancholy subjects. But her temper was fluctuating; joy for a few instants shone in her eyes, but it continually gave place to distraction and reverie.

The sun sank lower in the heavens; we passed the river Drance, and observed its path through the chasms of the higher and the glens of the lower hills. The Alps here come closer to the lake, and we approached the amphitheater[3] of mountains which forms its eastern boundary. The spire of Evian shone under the woods that surrounded it and the range of mountain above mountain by which it was overhung.

The wind, which had hitherto carried us along with amazing rapidity, sank at sunset to a light breeze; the soft air just ruffled the water and caused a pleasant motion among the trees as we approached the shore, from which it wafted the most delightful scent of flowers and hay. The sun sank beneath the horizon as we landed, and as I touched the shore I felt those cares and fears revive which soon were to clasp me and cling to me forever.

▶ *What feelings fill Frankenstein as he reaches shore?*

___
3. **amphitheater.** Level place surrounded by rising ground

Chapter 23

It was eight o'clock when we landed; we walked for a short time on the shore enjoying the transitory light, and then retired to the inn and contemplated the lovely scene of waters, woods, and mountains, obscured in darkness, yet still displaying their black outlines.

The wind, which had fallen in the south, now rose with great violence in the west. The moon had reached her summit in the heavens and was beginning to descend; the clouds swept across it swifter than the flight of the vulture and dimmed her rays, while the lake reflected the scene of the busy heavens, rendered still busier by the restless waves that were beginning to rise. Suddenly a heavy storm of rain descended.

I had been calm during the day, but so soon as night obscured the shapes of objects, a thousand fears arose in my mind. I was anxious and watchful, while my right hand grasped a pistol which was hidden in my bosom; every sound terrified me, but I resolved that I would sell my life dearly and not shrink from the conflict until my own life or that of my adversary, was extinguished.

Elizabeth observed my agitation for some time in timid and fearful silence, but there was something in my glance which communicated terror to her, and trembling, she asked, "What is it that agitates you, my dear Victor? What is it you fear?"

"Oh! Peace, peace, my love," replied I; "this night and all will be safe; but this night is dreadful, very dreadful."

I passed an hour in this state of mind, when suddenly I reflected how fearful the combat which I momentarily expected would be to my wife, and I earnestly entreated her to retire, resolving not to join her until I had obtained some knowledge as to the situation of my enemy.

She left me, and I continued some time walking up and down the passages of the house and inspecting every corner that might afford a retreat to my adversary. But I discovered no trace of him and was beginning to conjecture that some fortunate chance had intervened to prevent the execution of his menaces when suddenly I heard a shrill and dreadful scream. It came from the room into which Elizabeth had retired. As I heard it, the whole truth rushed into my mind, my arms dropped, the motion of every muscle and fiber was suspended; I could feel the blood trickling in my veins and tingling in the extremities of my limbs. This state lasted but for an instant; the scream was repeated, and I rushed into the room.

◄ What change in weather occurs? What effect does this change have on the mood of the scene?

◄ Why does Frankenstein urge Elizabeth to retire?

◄ What happens as Frankenstein is beginning to think that his horrible fate has been averted? What does he realize?

► What does
Frankenstein see
when he enters the
chamber where
Elizabeth had
retired? What does
he wish had then
happened? What
happened to him
instead?

Great God! Why did I not then expire! Why am I here to relate the destruction of the best hope and the purest creature of earth? She was there, lifeless and inanimate, thrown across the bed, her head hanging down and her pale and distorted features half covered by her hair. Everywhere I turn I see the same figure—her bloodless arms and relaxed form flung by the murderer on its bridal bier. Could I behold this and live? Alas! Life is <u>obstinate</u> and clings closest where it is most hated. For a moment only did I lose recollection; I fell senseless on the ground.

When I recovered, I found myself surrounded by the people of the inn; their countenances expressed a breathless terror, but the horror of others appeared only as a mockery, a shadow of the feelings that oppressed me. I escaped from them to the room where lay the body of Elizabeth, my love, my wife, so lately living, so dear, so worthy. She had been moved from the posture in which I had first beheld her, and now, as she lay, her head upon her arm and a handkerchief thrown across her face and neck, I might have supposed her asleep. I rushed towards her and embraced her with ardor, but the deadly languor and coldness of the limbs told me that what I now held in my arms had ceased to be the Elizabeth whom I had loved and cherished. The murderous mark of the fiend's grasp was on her neck, and the breath had ceased to issue from her lips.

► What sign shows
that Elizabeth had
been murdered in the
same manner as
William and Clerval
were murdered?

While I still hung over her in the agony of despair, I happened to look up. The windows of the room had before been darkened, and I felt a kind of panic on seeing the pale yellow light of the moon illuminate the chamber. The shutters had been thrown back, and with a sensation of horror not to be described, I saw at the open window a figure the most hideous and abhorred. A grin was on the face of the monster; he seemed to jeer, as with his fiendish finger he pointed towards the corpse of my wife. I rushed towards the window, and drawing a pistol from my bosom, fired; but he eluded me, leaped from his station, and running with the swiftness of lightning, plunged into the lake.

► When Frankenstein sees the monster at the window,
what does the
creature seem
to be doing?

The report of the pistol brought a crowd into the room. I pointed to the spot where he had disappeared, and we followed the track with boats; nets were cast, but in vain. After passing several hours, we returned hopeless, most of my

► Are the search
parties successful?
What do many of
the searchers begin
to think?

Words
For
Everyday
Use

ob • sti • nate (äb′stə nət) *adj.,* not easily ended

companions believing it to have been a form conjured up by my fancy. After having landed, they proceeded to search the country, parties going in different directions among the woods and vines.

I attempted to accompany them and proceeded a short distance from the house, but my head whirled round, my steps were like those of a drunken man, I fell at last in a state of utter exhaustion; a film covered my eyes, and my skin was parched with the heat of fever. In this state I was carried back and placed on a bed, hardly conscious of what had happened; my eyes wandered round the room as if to seek something that I had lost.

After an interval I arose, and as if by instinct, crawled into the room where the corpse of my beloved lay. There were women weeping around. I hung over it and joined my sad tears to theirs; all this time no distinct idea presented itself to my mind, but my thoughts <u>rambled</u> to various subjects, reflecting confusedly on my misfortunes and their cause. I was bewildered in a cloud of wonder and horror. The death of William, the execution of Justine, the murder of Clerval, and lastly of my wife; even at that moment I knew not that my only remaining friends were safe from the malignity of the fiend; my father even now might be writhing under his grasp, and Ernest might be dead at his feet. This idea made me shudder and recalled me to action. I started up and resolved to return to Geneva with all possible speed.

◄ As thoughts of his past misery swamp his mind, what danger does Frankenstein understand? How does he react to this idea?

There were no horses to be procured, and I must return by the lake; but the wind was unfavorable and the rain fell in torrents. However, it was hardly morning, and I might reasonably hope to arrive by night. I hired men to row and took an oar myself, for I had always experienced relief from mental torment in bodily exercise. But the overflowing misery I now felt, and the excess of agitation that I endured rendered me incapable of any exertion. I threw down the oar, and leaning my head upon my hands, gave way to every gloomy idea that arose. If I looked up, I saw the scenes which were familiar to me in my happier time and which I had contemplated but the day before in the company of her who was now but a shadow and a recollection. Tears streamed from my eyes. The rain had ceased for a moment, and I saw the fish play in the waters as they had done a few hours before;

◄ What is the same as a few hours before? Why is nothing the same?

they had then been observed by Elizabeth. Nothing is so painful to the human mind as a great and sudden change. The sun might shine or the clouds might lower, but nothing could appear to me as it had done the day before. A fiend had snatched from me every hope of future happiness; no creature had ever been so miserable as I was; so frightful an event is single in the history of man.

But why should I dwell upon the incidents that followed this last overwhelming event? Mine has been a tale of horrors; I have reached their acme, and what I must now relate can but be <u>tedious</u> to you. Know that, one by one, my friends were snatched away; I was left desolate. My own strength is exhausted; and I must tell, in a few words, what remains of my hideous narration.

▶ What additional pain does Frankenstein suffer as a result of Elizabeth's murder?

I arrived at Geneva. My father and Ernest yet lived, but the former sank under the tidings that I bore. I see him now, excellent and venerable old man! His eyes wandered in vacancy, for they had lost their charm and their delight—his Elizabeth, his more than daughter, whom he doted on with all that affection which a man feels, who in the decline of life, having few affections, clings more earnestly to those that remain. Cursed, cursed be the fiend that brought misery on his grey hairs, and doomed him to waste in wretchedness! He could not live under the horrors that were accumulated around him; the springs of existence suddenly gave way; he was unable to rise from his bed, and in a few days he died in my arms.

What then became of me? I know not; I lost sensation, and chains and darkness were the only objects that pressed upon me. Sometimes, indeed, I dreamt that I wandered in flowery meadows and pleasant vales with the friends of my youth, but I awoke and found myself in a dungeon. Melancholy followed, but by degrees I gained a clear conception of my miseries and situation and was then released from my prison. For they had called me mad, and during many months, as I understood, a solitary cell had been my habitation.

▶ Why had Frankenstein been in a cell? Why is he released?

▶ What goal consumes Frankenstein after he is released from his confinement?

Liberty, however, had been a useless gift to me, had I not, as I awakened to reason, at the same time awakened to revenge. As the memory of past misfortunes pressed upon me, I began to reflect on their cause—the monster whom I had created, the miserable demon whom I had sent abroad

---

Words For Everyday Use

te • di • ous (tē´dē əs) *adj.,* tiresome or boring

into the world for my destruction. I was possessed by a maddening rage when I thought of him, and desired and ardently prayed that I might have him within my grasp to wreak a great and signal revenge on his cursed head.

Nor did my hate long confine itself to useless wishes; I began to reflect on the best means of securing him; and for this purpose, about a month after my release, I repaired to a criminal judge in the town and told him that I had an accusation to make, and that I knew the destroyer of my family, and that I required him to exert his whole authority for the <u>apprehension</u> of the murderer. The magistrate listened to me with attention and kindness. "Be assured, sir," said he "no pains or exertions on my part shall be spared to discover the villain."

"I thank you," replied I; "listen, therefore, to the deposition that I have to make. It is indeed a tale so strange that I should fear you would not credit it were there not something in truth which, however wonderful, forces conviction. The story is too connected to be mistaken for a dream, and I have no motive for falsehood." My manner as I thus addressed him was impressive but calm; I had formed in my heart a resolution to pursue my destroyer to death, and this purpose quieted my agony and for an interval reconciled me to life. I now related my history briefly but with firmness and precision, marking the dates with accuracy and never deviating into invective or exclamation.

◄ To whom does Frankenstein finally tell his tale? Why does he reveal to this person the secret he had so long guarded?

The magistrate appeared at first perfectly incredulous, but as I continued he became more attentive and interested; I saw him sometimes shudder with horror; at others a lively surprise, unmingled with disbelief, was painted on his countenance.

When I had concluded my narration I said, "This is the being whom I accuse and for whose seizure and punishment I call upon you to exert your whole power. It is your duty as a magistrate, and I believe and hope that your feelings as a man will not revolt from the execution of those functions on this occasion."

This address caused a considerable change in the physiognomy[1] of my own auditor. He had heard my story with that half kind of belief that is given to a tale of spirits and

◄ Does the magistrate believe Frankenstein's tale? Explain.

---

1. **physiognomy.** Facial features

supernatural events; but when he was called upon to act officially in consequence, the whole tide of his <u>incredulity</u> returned. He, however, answered mildly, "I would willingly afford you every aid in your pursuit, but the creature of whom you speak appears to have powers which would put all my exertions to defiance. Who can follow an animal which can traverse the sea of ice and inhabit caves and dens where no man would venture to intrude? Besides, some months have elapsed since the commission of his crimes, and no one can conjecture to what place he has wandered or what region he may now inhabit."

▶ Why does the magistrate refuse to aid Frankenstein?

"I do not doubt that he hovers near the spot which I inhabit, and if he has indeed taken refuge in the Alps, he may be hunted like the chamois[2] and destroyed as a beast of prey. But I perceive your thoughts; you do not credit my narrative and do not intend to pursue my enemy with the punishment which is his desert."

As I spoke, rage sparkled in my eyes; the magistrate was intimidated: "You are mistaken," said he, "I will exert myself, if it is in my power to seize the monster, be assured that he shall suffer punishment proportionate to his crimes. But I fear, from what you have yourself described to be his properties, that this will prove impracticable; and thus, while every proper measure is pursued, you should make up your mind to disappointment."

"That cannot be; but all that I can say will be of little avail. My revenge is of no moment to you; yet while I allow it to be a vice, I confess that it is the devouring and only passion of my soul. My rage is unspeakable when I reflect that the murderer, whom I have turned loose upon society, still exists. You refuse my just demand; I have but one resource, and I devote myself, either in my life or death, to his destruction."

▶ Why will Frankenstein not give in to the disappointment of not capturing the creature?

I trembled with excess of agitation as I said this; there was a frenzy in my manner, and something, I doubt not, of that <u>haughty</u> fierceness which the martyrs of old are said to have possessed. But to a Genevan magistrate, whose mind was occupied by far other ideas than those of devotion and heroism, this elevation of mind had much the appearance of

---

2. **chamois.** Type of small antelope

Words For Everyday Use

in • cre • du • li • ty (in´krə doo´ lə tē) *n.*, disbelief; skepticism

haugh • ty (hôt´ē) *adj.*, arrogant; scornful of others

madness. He endeavored to soothe me as a nurse does a child and reverted to my tale as the effects of delirium.

"Man," I cried, "how ignorant art thou in thy pride of wisdom! Cease; you know not what it is you say."

I broke from the house angry and disturbed, and retired to meditate on some other mode of action.

◄ *To what does the magistrate attribute Frankenstein's tale? Why is Frankenstein angered by the reaction of the magistrate?*

Chapter 24

► By what is Frankenstein driven? What powers does this force give him?

My present situation was one in which all voluntary thought was swallowed up and lost. I was hurried away by fury; revenge alone endowed me with strength and composure; it molded my feelings and allowed me to be calculating and calm at periods when otherwise delirium or death would have been my portion.

My first resolution was to quit Geneva forever; my country, which, when I was happy and beloved, was dear to me, now, in my adversity, became hateful. I provided myself with a sum of money, together with a few jewels which had belonged to my mother, and departed.

► What kind of life does Frankenstein lead?

And now my wanderings began which are to cease but with life. I have traversed a vast portion of the earth and have endured all the hardships which travelers in deserts and barbarous countries are wont to meet. How I have lived I hardly know; many times have I stretched my failing limbs upon the sandy plain and prayed for death. But revenge kept me alive; I dared not die and leave my adversary in being.

When I quitted Geneva my first labor was to gain some clue by which I might trace the steps of my fiendish enemy. But my plan was unsettled, and I wandered many hours round the confines of the town, uncertain what path I should pursue. As night approached I found myself at the entrance of the cemetery where William, Elizabeth, and my father reposed. I entered it and approached the tomb which marked their graves. Everything was silent except the leaves of the trees, which were gently agitated by the wind; the night was nearly dark, and the scene would have been solemn and affecting even to an uninterested observer. The spirits of the departed seemed to flit around and to cast a shadow, which was felt but not seen, around the head of the mourner.

► Where do Frankenstein's wanderings about Geneva lead him? What emotions does he feel upon visiting this site?

The deep grief which this scene had at first excited quickly gave way to rage and despair. They were dead, and I lived; their murderer also lived, and to destroy him I must drag out my weary existence. I knelt on the grass and kissed the earth, and with quivering lips exclaimed, "By the sacred earth on which I kneel, by the shades that wander near me, by the deep and eternal grief that I feel, I swear; and by thee, O

► What oath does Frankenstein make? Who does he call to witness and aid him in his vow?

Words For Everyday Use

com • po • sure (kəm pō´zhər) *n.*, calmness of mind
wont (wänt) *adj.*, accustomed

Night, and the spirits that <u>preside</u> over thee, to pursue the demon who caused this misery, until he or I shall perish in mortal conflict. For this purpose I will preserve my life; to execute this dear revenge will I again behold the sun and tread the green herbage of earth, which otherwise should vanish from my eyes forever. And I call on you, spirits of the dead, and on you, wandering ministers of vengeance, to aid and conduct me in my work. Let the cursed and hellish monster drink deep of agony; let him feel the despair that now torments me."

I had begun my <u>abjuration</u> with solemnity and an awe which almost assured me that the shades of my murdered friends heard and approved my devotion, but the furies possessed me as I concluded, and rage choked my utterance.

I was answered through the stillness of night by a loud and fiendish laugh. It rang on my ears long and heavily; the mountains re-echoed it, and I felt as if all hell surrounded me with mockery and laughter. Surely in that moment I should have been possessed by frenzy and have destroyed my miserable existence but that my vow was heard and that I was reserved for vengeance. The laughter died away, when a well-known and abhorred voice, apparently close to my ear, addressed me in an audible whisper, "I am satisfied, miserable wretch! You have determined to live, and I am satisfied."

◀ How does the fiend respond to Frankenstein's vow?

I darted towards the spot from which the sound proceeded, but the devil eluded my grasp. Suddenly the broad disk of the moon arose and shone full upon his ghastly and distorted shape as he fled with more than mortal speed.

I pursued him, and for many months this has been my task. Guided by a slight clue I followed the windings of the Rhone, but vainly. The blue Mediterranean appeared, and by a strange chance, I saw the fiend enter by night and hide himself in a vessel bound for the Black Sea. I took my passage in the same ship, but he escaped, I know not how.

Amidst the wilds of Tartary[1] and Russia, although he still evaded me, I have ever followed in his track. Sometimes the peasants, scared by this horrid apparition, informed me of his path; sometimes he himself, who feared that if I lost all trace of him I should despair and die, left some mark to guide

◀ How is Frankenstein able to track the creature who can move much faster than he can?

1. **Tartary.** Vast region of Europe and Asia covering land from Russia to the Pacific

Words For Everyday Use

pre • side (prē zīd´) *vi.,* exercise control or authority

ab • ju • ra • tion (ab´jə rā´ shən) *n.,* renunciation; giving up of an opinion or oath

► What difficulties does Frankenstein face? What good does he find during his search?

me. The snows descended on my head, and I saw the print of his huge step on the white plain. To you first entering on life, to whom care is new and agony unknown, how can you understand what I have felt and still feel? Cold, want, and fatigue were the least pains which I was destined to endure; I was cursed by some devil and carried about with me my eternal hell; yet still a spirit of good followed and directed my steps, and when I most murmured would suddenly extricate me from seemingly insurmountable difficulties. Sometimes, when nature, overcome by hunger, sunk under the exhaustion, a <u>repast</u> was prepared for me in the desert that restored and inspirited me. The fare was, indeed, coarse, such as the peasants of the country ate, but I will not doubt that it was set there by the spirits that I had invoked to aid me. Often, when all was dry, the heavens cloudless, and I was parched by thirst, a slight cloud would bedim the sky, shed the few drops that revived me, and vanish.

I followed, when I could, the courses of the rivers; but the demon generally avoided these, as it was here that the population of the country chiefly collected. In other places human beings were seldom seen, and I generally <u>subsisted</u> on the wild animals that crossed my path. I had money with me and gained the friendship of the villagers by distributing it; or I brought with me some food that I had killed, which, after taking a small part, I always presented to those who had provided me with fire and utensils for cooking.

My life, as it passed thus, was indeed hateful to me, and it was during sleep alone that I could taste joy. O blessed sleep! often, when most miserable, I sank to repose, and my dreams lulled me even to rapture. The spirits that guarded me had provided these moments, or rather hours, of happiness, that I might retain strength to fulfill my pilgrimage. Deprived of this respite, I should have sunk under my hardships. During the day I was sustained and inspired by the hope of night, for in sleep I saw my friends, my wife, and my beloved country; again I saw the benevolent countenance of my father, heard the silver tones of my Elizabeth's voice, and beheld Clerval enjoying health and youth. Often, when wearied by a toilsome march, I persuaded myself that I was dreaming, until night should come and that I should then enjoy reality in the arms of my dearest friends. What agonizing fondness

► What sustains Frankenstein during his misery and isolation? In what way does he try to alter reality?

Words For Everyday Use

re • past (ri past′) n., meal

sub • sist (səb sist′) vi., continue to live; remain alive on

did I feel for them! How did I cling to their dear forms, as sometimes they haunted even my waking hours, and persuade myself that they still lived! At such moments vengeance, that burned within me, died in my heart, and I pursued my path towards the destruction of the demon more as a task enjoined by heaven, as the mechanical impulse of some power of which I was unconscious, than as the ardent desire of my soul.

What his feelings were whom I pursued I cannot know. Sometimes, indeed, he left marks in writing on the barks of the trees or cut in stone that guided me and instigated my fury. "My reign is not yet over"—these words were legible in one of these inscriptions—"you live, and my power is complete. Follow me; I seek the everlasting ices of the north, where you will feel the misery of cold and frost to which I am <u>impassive</u>. You will find near this place, if you follow not too tardily, a dead hare; eat and be refreshed. Come on, enemy; we have yet to wrestle for our lives, but many hard and miserable hours must you endure until that period shall arrive."

◄ Why does the creature lead Frankenstein to the far north? Why doesn't he simply kill Frankenstein since he has the power to do so?

<u>Scoffing</u> devil! Again do I vow vengeance; again do I devote thee, miserable fiend, to torture and death. Never will I give up my search until he or I perish; and then with what ecstasy shall I join my Elizabeth and my departed friends, who even now prepare for me the reward of my tedious toil and horrible pilgrimage!

As I still pursued my journey to the northward, the snows thickened and the cold increased in a degree almost too severe to support. The peasants were shut up in their hovels, and only a few of the most hardy ventured forth to seize the animals whom starvation had forced from their hiding-places to seek for prey. The rivers were covered with ice, and no fish could be procured; and thus I was cut off from my chief article of maintenance.

The triumph of my enemy increased with the difficulty of my labors. One inscription that he left was in these words: "Prepare! Your toils only begin: wrap yourself in furs and provide food; for we shall soon enter upon a journey where your sufferings will satisfy my everlasting hatred."

My courage and perseverance were <u>invigorated</u> by these scoffing words; I resolved not to fail in my purpose, and

◄ What effect do the creature's scoffing words have on Frankenstein?

Words For Everyday Use	im • pas • sive (im pas´iv) *adj.*, insensible; not showing pain scoff (skäf) *vt.*, mock in • vig • or • ate (in vig´ər āt´) *vt.*, enliven; fill with energy

► Why is Franken-
stein thankful to
reach the sea of ice?

calling on Heaven to support me, I continued with <u>unabated</u>
fervor to traverse immense deserts until the ocean appeared
at a distance and formed the utmost boundary of the horizon.
Oh! How unlike it was to the blue seas of the south! Covered
with ice, it was only to be distinguished from land by its
superior wildness and ruggedness. The Greeks wept for joy
when they beheld the Mediterranean from the hills of Asia,
and hailed with rapture the boundary of their toils. I did not
weep, but I knelt down and with a full heart thanked my
guiding spirit for conducting me in safety to the place where
I hoped, notwithstanding my adversary's <u>gibe</u>, to meet and
grapple with him.

Some weeks before this period I had procured a sledge and
dogs and thus traversed the snows with inconceivable speed.
I know not whether the fiend possessed the same advantages, but I found that, as before I had daily lost ground in
the pursuit, I now gained on him, so much so that when I
first saw the ocean he was but one day's journey in advance,
and I hoped to intercept him before he should reach the
beach. With new courage, therefore, I pressed on, and in two
days arrived at a wretched hamlet[2] on the seashore. I
inquired of the inhabitants concerning the fiend, and gained

► What prepara-
tions has the crea-
ture made? How do
the villagers feel
about the monster's
course? Why do
Frankenstein's feel-
ings about this
course differ?

accurate information. A gigantic monster, they said, had
arrived the night before, armed with a gun and many pistols,
putting to flight the inhabitants of a solitary cottage through
fear of his terrific appearance. He had carried off their store
of winter food, and placing it in a sledge, to draw which he
had seized on a numerous drove of trained dogs, he had har-
nessed them, and the same night, to the joy of the horror-
struck villagers, had pursued his journey across the sea in a
direction that led to no land; and they conjectured that he
must speedily be destroyed by the breaking of the ice or
frozen by the eternal frosts.

On hearing this information I suffered a temporary access
of despair. He had escaped me, and I must commence a
destructive and almost endless journey across the mountain-
ous ices of the ocean, amidst cold that few of the inhabitants
could long endure and which I, the native of a <u>genial</u> and
sunny climate, could not hope to survive. Yet at the idea that

---

2. **hamlet.** Very small village

Words For Everyday Use	
un • a • bat • ed (un ə bāt′əd) *adj.,* not lessened or diminished
gibe (jīb) *vi.,* jeer or taunt
gen • i • al (jēn′yəl) *adj.,* warm, mild, and healthful

the fiend should live and be triumphant, my rage and vengeance returned, and, like a mighty tide, overwhelmed every other feeling. After a slight repose, during which the spirits of the dead hovered round and instigated me to toil and revenge, I prepared for my journey.

I exchanged my land-sledge for one fashioned for the inequalities of the frozen ocean, and purchasing a plentiful stock of provisions, I departed from land.

I cannot guess how many days have passed since then, but I have endured misery which nothing but the eternal sentiment of a just retribution burning within my heart could have enabled me to support. Immense and rugged mountains of ice often barred up my passage, and I often heard the thunder of the ground sea,[3] which threatened my destruction. But again the frost came and made the paths of the sea secure.

By the quantity of provision which I had consumed, I should guess that I had passed three weeks in this journey; and the continual <u>protraction</u> of hope, returning back upon the heart, often wrung bitter drops of despondency and grief from my eyes. Despair had indeed almost secured her prey, and I should soon have sunk beneath this misery. Once, after the poor animals that conveyed me had with incredible toil gained the summit of a sloping ice-mountain, and one, sinking under his fatigue, died, I viewed the expanse before me with anguish, when suddenly my eye caught a dark speck upon the dusky plain. I strained my sight to discover what it could be and uttered a wild cry of ecstasy when I distinguished a sledge and the distorted proportions of a well-known form within. Oh! With what a burning gush did hope revisit my heart! Warm tears filled my eyes, which I hastily wiped away that they might not intercept the view I had of the demon; but still my sight was dimmed by the burning drops until, giving way to the emotions that oppressed me, I wept aloud.

◄ *What sight erases Frankenstein's despair?*

But this was not the time for delay; I disencumbered the dogs of their dead companion, gave them a plentiful portion of food, and after an hour's rest, which was absolutely necessary, and yet which was bitterly irksome to me, I continued my route. The sledge was still visible, nor did I again lose

---

3. **ground sea.** Deep, broad undulation of the ocean

Words For Everyday Use
pro • trac • tion (prō trak´shən) *n.,* lengthening of duration

► How close does Frankenstein come to his enemy?

► What causes Frankenstein to lose his prey?

sight of it except at the moments when for a short time some ice-rock concealed it with its intervening crags. I indeed perceptibly gained on it, and when, after nearly two days' journey, I beheld my enemy at no more than a mile distant, my heart bounded within me.

But now, when I appeared almost within grasp of my foe, my hopes were suddenly extinguished, and I lost all trace of him more utterly than I had ever done before. A ground sea was heard; the thunder of its progress, as the waters rolled and swelled beneath me, became every moment more ominous and terrific. I pressed on, but in vain. The wind arose; the sea roared; and, as with the mighty shock of an earthquake, it split and cracked with a tremendous and overwhelming sound. The work was soon finished; in a few minutes a tumultuous sea rolled between me and my enemy, and I was left drifting on a scattered piece of ice that was continually lessening and thus preparing for me a hideous death.

In this manner many appalling hours passed; several of my dogs died, and I myself was about to sink under the accumulation of distress when I saw your vessel riding at anchor and holding forth to me hopes of succor and life. I had no conception that vessels ever came so far north and was astonished at the sight. I quickly destroyed part of my sledge to construct oars, and by these means was enabled, with infinite fatigue, to move my ice-raft in the direction of your ship. I had determined, if you were going southward, still to trust myself to the mercy of the seas rather than abandon my purpose. I hoped to <u>induce</u> you to grant me a boat with which I could pursue my enemy. But your direction was northward. You took me on board when my vigor was exhausted, and I should soon have sunk under my multiplied hardships into a death which I still dread, for my task is unfulfilled.

► Why had Frankenstein asked the direction of the ship? What would he have done if the ship had been southward bound?

Oh! When will my guiding spirit, in conducting me to the demon, allow me the rest I so much desire; or must I die and he yet live? If I do, swear to me, Walton, that he shall not escape, that you will seek him and satisfy my vengeance in his death. And do I dare to ask of you to undertake my pilgrimage, to endure the hardships that I have undergone? No; I am not so selfish. Yet, when I am dead, if he should appear, if the ministers of vengeance should conduct him to you,

► What plea does Frankenstein make of Walton? What does he not ask Walton to do? Explain whether you think Walton will honor Frankenstein's request.

| Words For Everyday Use | **crag** (krag) *n.*, steep, rugged rock that rises or protrudes from other rock |
| | **in • duce** (in do͞os´) *vt.*, persuade |

swear that he shall not live—swear that he shall not triumph over my accumulated woes and survive to add to the list of his dark crimes. He is eloquent and persuasive; and once his words had even power over my heart; but trust him not. His soul is as hellish as his form, full of treachery and fiendish malice. Hear him not; call on the names of William, Justine, Clerval, Elizabeth, my father, and of the wretched Victor, and thrust your sword into his heart. I will hover near and direct the steel aright.

Walton, in continuation

August 26, 17—

You have read this strange and terrific story, Margaret; and do you not feel your blood <u>congeal</u> with horror, like that which even now curdles mine? Sometimes, seized with sudden agony, he could not continue his tale; at others, his voice broken, yet piercing, uttered with difficulty the words so replete with anguish. His fine and lovely eyes were now lighted up with indignation, now subdued to downcast sorrow and quenched in infinite wretchedness. Sometimes he commanded his countenance and tones and related the most horrible incidents with a tranquil voice, suppressing every mark of agitation; then, like a volcano bursting forth, his face would suddenly change to an expression of the wildest rage as he shrieked out imprecations on his persecutor.

◄ *What effect has Frankenstein's story had on Walton?*

His tale is connected and told with an appearance of the simplest truth, yet I own to you that the letters of Felix and Safie, which he showed me, and the apparition of the monster seen from our ship, brought to me a greater conviction of the truth of his narrative than his <u>asseverations</u>, however earnest and connected. Such a monster has, then, really existence! I cannot doubt it; yet I am lost in surprise and admiration. Sometimes I endeavored to gain from Frankenstein the particulars of his creature's formation, but on this point he was impenetrable.

◄ *Does Walton believe Frankenstein's story? Why, or why not?*

"Are you mad, my friend?" said he. "Or whither does your senseless curiosity lead you? Would you also create for yourself and the world a demoniacal enemy? Peace, peace! Learn my miseries, and do not seek to increase your own."

◄ *What information does Frankenstein refuse to share with Walton? Why might Walton press Frankenstein for this information even after hearing Frankenstein's horrifying tale?*

Words For Everyday Use

con • geal (kən jēl´) vt., thicken; coagulate

as • sev • er • a • tion (ə sev´ə rā´ shən) n., assertion; serious or positive statement

Frankenstein discovered that I made notes concerning his history; he asked to see them and then himself corrected and augmented them in many places, but principally in giving the life and spirit to the conversations he held with his enemy. "Since you have preserved my narration," said he, "I would not that a mutilated one should go down to <u>posterity</u>."

Thus has a week passed away, while I have listened to the strangest tale that ever imagination formed. My thoughts and every feeling of my soul have been drunk up by the interest for my guest which this tale and his own elevated and gentle manners have created. I wish to soothe him, yet can I counsel one so infinitely miserable, so <u>destitute</u> of every hope of consolation, to live? Oh, no! The only joy that he can now know will be when he composes his shattered spirit to peace and death. Yet he enjoys one comfort, the offspring of solitude and delirium: he believes that when in dreams he holds converse with his friends and <u>derives</u> from that communion consolation for his miseries or excitements to his vengeance, they are not the creations of his fancy, but the beings themselves who visit him from the regions of a remote world. This faith gives a solemnity to his reveries that render them to me almost as imposing and interesting as truth.

Our conversations are not always confined to his own history and misfortunes. On every point of general literature he displays unbounded knowledge and a quick and piercing apprehension. His eloquence is forcible and touching; nor can I hear him, when he relates a pathetic incident or endeavors to move the passions of pity or love, without tears. What a glorious creature must he have been in the days of his prosperity, when he is thus noble and godlike in ruin! He seems to feel his own worth and the greatness of his fall.

"When younger," said he, "I believed myself destined for some great enterprise. My feelings are profound, but I possessed a coolness of judgment that fitted me for <u>illustrious</u> achievements. This sentiment of the worth of my nature supported me when others would have been oppressed, for I deemed it criminal to throw away in useless grief those talents that might be useful to my fellow creatures. When I reflected on the work I had completed, no less a one than the creation of a sensitive and rational animal, I could not rank myself with the herd of common projectors. But this

▶ *What is Frankenstein's only comfort? What is his only hope for consolation?*

▶ *What opinion does Frankenstein seem to hold of himself? What opinion does Walton hold of him?*

▶ *In what way are Frankenstein's early aspirations similar to Walton's expectations?*

Words For Everyday Use	
pos • ter • i • ty (päs ter´ə tē) *n.*, all succeeding generations
des • ti • tute (des´tə to͞ot´) *adj.*, lacking; being without
de • rive (di rīv´) *vi.*, come; originate
il • lus • tri • ous (i lus´trē əs) *adj.*, famous; distinguished

thought, which supported me in the commencement of my career, now serves only to plunge me lower in the dust. All my speculations and hopes are as nothing, and like the archangel who aspired to omnipotence,[4] I am chained in an eternal hell. My imagination was vivid, yet my powers of analysis and application were intense; by the union of these qualities I conceived the idea and executed the creation of a man. Even now I cannot recollect without passion my reveries while the work was incomplete. I trod heaven in my thoughts, now exulting in my powers, now burning with the idea of their effects. From my infancy I was imbued with high hopes and a lofty ambition; but how am I sunk! Oh! My friend, if you had known me as I once was, you would not recognize me in this state of <u>degradation</u>. Despondency rarely visited my heart; a high destiny seemed to bear me on until I fell, never, never again to rise."

◀ To whom does Frankenstein compare himself? In what way are the two similar?

Must I then lose this admirable being? I have longed for a friend; I have sought one who would sympathize with and love me. Behold, on these desert seas I have found such a one, but I fear I have gained him only to know his value and lose him. I would reconcile him to life, but he repulses the idea.

◀ Why does Walton loathe the idea of Frankenstein's death?

"I thank you, Walton," he said, "for your kind intentions towards so miserable a wretch; but when you speak of new ties and fresh affections, think you that any can replace those who are gone? Can any man be to me as Clerval was, or any woman another Elizabeth? Even where the affections are not strongly moved by any superior excellence, the companions of our childhood always possess a certain power over our minds which hardly any later friend can obtain. They know our infantile dispositions, which, however they may be afterwards modified, are never eradicated; and they can judge of our actions with more certain conclusions as to the integrity of our motives. A sister or a brother can never, unless indeed such symptoms have been shown early, suspect the other of fraud or false dealing, when another friend, however strongly he may be attached, may, in spite of himself, be contemplated with suspicion. But I enjoyed friends, dear not only through habit and association, but from their

◀ Why are childhood friends and early family connections important?

---

4. **archangel . . . omnipotence.** Refers to Satan, the fallen archangel who wanted to be more powerful than God

Words For Everyday Use	**deg • ra • da • tion** (deg´rə dā´shən) *n.*, being lowered in rank, status, or condition

own merits; and wherever I am, the soothing voice of my Elizabeth and the conversation of Clerval will be ever whispered in my ear. They are dead, and but one feeling in such a solitude can persuade me to preserve my life. If I were engaged in any high undertaking or design, <u>fraught</u> with extensive utility to my fellow-creatures, then could I live to fulfill it. But such is not my destiny; I must pursue and destroy the being to whom I gave existence; then my lot on earth will be fulfilled and I may die."

My beloved Sister, September 2nd.

I write to you encompassed by peril and ignorant whether I am ever doomed to see again dear England and the dearer friends that inhabit it. I am surrounded by mountains of ice which admit of no escape and threaten every moment to crush my vessel. The brave fellows whom I have persuaded to be my companions look towards me for aid, but I have none to bestow. There is something terribly appalling in our situation, yet my courage and hopes do not desert me. Yet it is terrible to reflect that the lives of all these men are endangered through me. If we are lost, my mad schemes are the cause.

And what, Margaret, will be the state of your mind? You will not hear of my destruction, and you will anxiously await my return. Years will pass, and you will have visitings of despair, and yet be tortured by hope. Oh! My beloved sister, the sickening failing of your heartfelt expectations is, in prospect, more terrible to me than my own death. But you have a husband and lovely children; you may be happy. Heaven bless you and make you so!

My unfortunate guest regards me with the tenderest compassion. He endeavors to fill me with hope and talks as if life were a possession which he valued. He reminds me how often the same accidents have happened to other navigators who have attempted this sea, and in spite of myself, he fills me with cheerful auguries. Even the sailors feel the power of his eloquence; when he speaks they no longer despair; he rouses their energies and, while they hear his voice they believe these vast mountains of ice are mole-hills which will vanish before the resolutions of man. These feelings are transitory; each day of expectation delayed fills them with fear, and I almost dread a mutiny caused by this despair.

▶ *Describe the situation in which Walton and his crew find themselves. What is Walton willing to risk?*

Words For Everyday Use	**fraught** (frôt) *adj.,* filled; charged or loaded

September 5th.

A scene has just passed of such uncommon interest that, although it is highly probable that these papers may never reach you, yet I cannot forbear recording it.

We are still surrounded by mountains of ice, still in imminent danger of being crushed in their conflict. The cold is excessive, and many of my unfortunate comrades have already found a grave amidst this scene of desolation. Frankenstein has daily declined in health; a feverish fire still glimmers in his eyes, but he is exhausted, and when suddenly roused to any exertion, he speedily sinks again into apparent lifelessness.

I mentioned in my last letter the fears I entertained of a mutiny. This morning, as I sat watching the wan countenance of my friend—his eyes half closed and his limbs hanging listlessly—I was roused by half a dozen of the sailors, who demanded admission into the cabin. They entered, and their leader addressed me. He told me that he and his companions had been chosen by the other sailors to come in <u>deputation</u> to me to make me a requisition which, in justice, I could not refuse. We were <u>immured</u> in ice and should probably never escape, but they feared that if, as was possible, the ice should dissipate and a free passage be opened, I should be rash enough to continue my voyage and lead them into fresh dangers after they might happily have surmounted this. They insisted, therefore, that I should engage with a solemn promise that if the vessel should be freed I would instantly direct my course southward.

◄ What do the sailors demand?

This speech troubled me. I had not despaired, nor had I yet conceived the idea of returning if set free. Yet could I, in justice, or even in possibility, refuse this demand? I hesitated before I answered, when Frankenstein, who had at first been silent, and indeed appeared hardly to have force enough to attend, now roused himself; his eyes sparkled, and his cheeks flushed with momentary vigor. Turning towards the men he said,

"What do you mean? What do you demand of your captain? Are you then so easily turned from your design? Did you not call this a glorious expedition? And wherefore was it glorious? Not because the way was smooth and <u>placid</u> as a southern sea, but because it was full of dangers and terror, because at every new incident your fortitude was to be called forth and

◄ What is the purpose of Frankenstein's speech? What does he urge the sailors to do?

Words
For
Everyday
Use

dep • u • ta • tion (dep′yo͞o tā′shən) *n.*, group of persons appointed to represent others

im • mure (im yo͝or′) *vt.*, confine; shut up within

plac • id (plas′id) *adj.*, tranquil; calm

your courage exhibited, because danger and death surrounded it, and these you were to brave and overcome. For this was it a glorious, for this was it an honorable undertaking. You were hereafter to be hailed as the benefactors of your species, your names adored as belonging to brave men who encountered death for honor and the benefit of mankind. And now, behold, with the first imagination of danger, or, if you will, the first mighty and terrific trial of your courage, you shrink away, and are content to be handed down as men who had not strength enough to endure cold and peril; and so, poor souls, they were chilly and returned to their warm firesides. Why, that requires not this preparation; ye need not have come thus far and dragged your captain to the shame of a defeat merely to prove yourselves cowards. Oh! Be men, or be more than men. Be steady to your purposes and firm as a rock. This ice is not made of such stuff as your hearts may be; it is mutable and cannot withstand you if you say that it shall not. Do not return to your families with the stigma of disgrace marked on your brows. Return as heroes who have fought and conquered, and who know not what it is to turn their backs on the foe."

He spoke this with a voice so modulated to the different feelings expressed in his speech, with an eye so full of lofty design and heroism, that can you wonder that these men were moved? They looked at one another and were unable to reply. I spoke; I told them to retire and consider of what had been said: that I would not lead them farther north if they strenuously desired the contrary; but that I hoped that, with reflection, their courage would return.

They retired, and I turned towards my friend; but he was sunk in languor and almost deprived of life.

How all this will terminate I know not; but I had rather die than return shamefully—my purpose unfulfilled. Yet I fear such will be my fate; the men, unsupported by ideas of glory and honor, can never willingly continue to endure their present hardships.

September 7th.

The die is cast; I have consented to return if we are not destroyed. Thus are my hopes blasted by cowardice and indecision; I come back ignorant and disappointed. It requires more philosophy than I possess to bear this injustice with patience.

▶ *What promise does Walton make? How does he feel about his decision?*

stig • ma (stig´mə) *n.*, mark of disgrace or reproach

September 12th.

It is past; I am returning to England. I have lost my hopes of <u>utility</u> and glory; I have lost my friend. But I will endeavor to detail these bitter circumstances to you, my dear sister; and while I am wafted towards England, and towards you, I will not despond.

September 9th, the ice began to move, and roarings like thunder were heard at a distance as the islands split and cracked in every direction. We were in the most imminent peril, but as we could only remain passive, my chief attention was occupied by my unfortunate guest, whose illness increased in such a degree that he was entirely confined to his bed. The ice cracked behind us and was driven with force towards the north; a breeze sprung from the west, and on the 11th the passage towards the south became perfectly free. When the sailors saw this and that their return to their native country was apparently assured, a shout of tumultuous joy broke from them, loud and long-continued. Frankenstein, who was dozing, awoke and asked the cause of the tumult. "They shout," I said, "because they will soon return to England."

"Do you, then, really return?"

"Alas! yes; I cannot withstand their demands. I cannot lead them unwillingly to danger, and I must return."

"Do so, if you will; but I will not. You may give up your purpose, but mine is assigned to me by heaven, and I dare not. I am weak, but surely the spirits who assist my vengeance will endow me with sufficient strength." Saying this, he endeavored to spring from the bed, but the exertion was too great for him; he fell back and fainted.

◄ *Why won't Frankenstein give up his goal?*

It was long before he was restored, and I often thought that life was entirely extinct. At length he opened his eyes; he breathed with difficulty and was unable to speak. The surgeon gave him a composing draught and ordered us to leave him undisturbed. In the meantime he told me that my friend had not many hours to live.

His sentence was pronounced, and I could only grieve and be patient. I sat by his bed, watching him; his eyes were closed, and I thought he slept; but presently he called to me in a feeble voice, and bidding me come near, said, "Alas! the strength I relied on is gone; I feel that I shall soon die, and

Words For Everyday Use

u • til • i • ty (yōō til´ə tē) *n.*, usefulness

► *What deathbed opinion does Frankenstein hold of his work and his decisions regarding his work? What conflicting responsibilities did he face? Which responsibility does he feel was stronger?*

► *Why does Frankenstein think the creature deserves to die? What plea to Walton does he renew?*

► *What last advice does Frankenstein give Walton?*

he, my enemy and persecutor, may still be in being. Think not, Walton, that in the last moments of my existence I feel that burning hatred and ardent desire of revenge I once expressed; but I feel myself justified in desiring the death of my adversary. During these last days I have been occupied in examining my past conduct; nor do I find it blamable. In a fit of enthusiastic madness I created a rational creature and was bound towards him to assure, as far as was in my power, his happiness and well-being. This was my duty; but there was another still <u>paramount</u> to that. My duties towards the beings of my own species had greater claims to my attention because they included a greater proportion of happiness or misery. Urged by this view, I refused, and I did right in refusing, to create a companion for the first creature. He showed unparalleled malignity and selfishness in evil: he destroyed my friends; he devoted to destruction beings who possessed exquisite sensations, happiness, and wisdom; nor do I know where this thirst for vengeance may end. Miserable himself, that he may render no other wretched, he ought to die. The task of his destruction was mine, but I have failed. When <u>actuated</u> by selfish and vicious motives I asked you to undertake my unfinished work, and I renew this request now when I am only induced by reason and virtue.

"Yet I cannot ask you to renounce your country and friends to fulfill this task; and now that you are returning to England you will have little chance of meeting with him. But the consideration of these points, and the well balancing of what you may esteem your duties, I leave to you; my judgment and ideas are already disturbed by the near approach of death. I dare not ask you to do what I think right, for I may still be misled by passion.

"That he should live to be an instrument of mischief disturbs me; in other respects, this hour, when I momentarily expect my release, is the only happy one which I have enjoyed for several years. The forms of the beloved dead flit before me, and I hasten to their arms. Farewell, Walton! Seek happiness in tranquility and avoid ambition, even if it be only the apparently innocent one of distinguishing yourself in science and discoveries. Yet why do I say this? I have myself been blasted in these hopes, yet another may succeed."

| Words For Everyday Use | **par • a • mount** (par´ ə mount´) *adj.*, ranking higher than another in power or importance |
| | **ac • tu • ate** (ak´ choo̅ āt´) *vt.*, put into action or motion |

His voice became fainter as he spoke; and at length, exhausted by his effort, he sank into silence. About half an hour afterwards he attempted again to speak, but was unable; he pressed my hand feebly, and his eyes closed forever, while the irradiation of a gentle smile passed away from his lips.

Margaret, what comment can I make on the untimely extinction of this glorious spirit? What can I say that will enable you to understand the depth of my sorrow? All that I should express would be inadequate and feeble. My tears flow; my mind is overshadowed by a cloud of disappointment. But I journey towards England, and I may there find consolation.

I am interrupted. What do these sounds portend? It is midnight; the breeze blows fairly, and the watch on deck scarcely stir. Again there is a sound as of a human voice, but hoarser; it comes from the cabin where the remains of Frankenstein still lie. I must arise and examine. Good night, my sister.

Great God! What a scene has just taken place! I am yet dizzy with the remembrance of it. I hardly know whether I shall have the power to detail it; yet the tale which I have recorded would be incomplete without this final and wonderful catastrophe.

I entered the cabin where lay the remains of my ill-fated and admirable friend. Over him hung a form which I cannot find words to describe; gigantic in stature, yet uncouth and distorted in its proportions. As he hung over the coffin, his face was concealed by long locks of ragged hair; but one vast hand was extended, in color and apparent texture like that of a mummy. When he heard the sound of my approach he ceased to utter exclamations of grief and horror and sprung towards the window. Never did I behold a vision so horrible as his face, of such loathsome yet appalling hideousness. I shut my eyes involuntarily and endeavored to recollect what were my duties with regard to this destroyer. I called on him to stay.

◀ *What reaction does the creature have as he stands over the coffin of Frankenstein?*

He paused, looking on me with wonder; and again turning towards the lifeless form of his creator, he seemed to forget my presence, and every feature and gesture seemed instigated by the wildest rage of some uncontrollable passion.

"That is also my victim!" he exclaimed. "In his murder my crimes are consummated; the miserable series of my being is wound to its close! Oh, Frankenstein! generous and self-devoted being! What does it <u>avail</u> that I now ask thee to

◀ *What has wound to a close? How does the creature feel about what it has done?*

Words For Everyday Use

a • vail (ə vāl´) vi., help; be of use

pardon me? I, who irretrievably destroyed thee by destroying all thou lovest. Alas! He is cold, he cannot answer me."

His voice seemed suffocated and my first impulses, which had suggested to me the duty of obeying the dying request of my friend, in destroying his enemy, were now suspended by a mixture of curiosity and compassion. I approached this tremendous being; I dared not again raise my eyes to his face, there was something so scaring and unearthly in his ugliness. I attempted to speak, but the words died away on my lips. The monster continued to utter wild and incoherent self-reproaches. At length I gathered resolution to address him in a pause of the tempest of his passion: "Your repentance," I said, "is now <u>superfluous</u>. If you had listened to the voice of conscience and heeded the stings of remorse before you had urged your diabolical vengeance to this extremity, Frankenstein would yet have lived."

"And do you dream?" said the demon. "Do you think that I was then dead to agony and remorse? He," he continued, pointing to the corpse, "he suffered not in the consummation of the deed. Oh! Not the ten-thousandth portion of the anguish that was mine during the lingering detail of its execution. A frightful selfishness hurried me on, while my heart was poisoned with remorse. Think you that the groans of Clerval were music to my ears? My heart was fashioned to be susceptible of love and sympathy, and when wrenched by misery to vice and hatred, it did not endure the violence of the change without torture such as you cannot even imagine.

"After the murder of Clerval I returned to Switzerland heartbroken and overcome. I pitied Frankenstein; my pity amounted to horror: I abhorred myself. But when I discovered that he, the author at once of my existence and of its unspeakable torments, dared to hope for happiness, that while he accumulated wretchedness and despair upon me he sought his own enjoyment in feelings and passions from the indulgence of which I was forever barred, then impotent envy and bitter indignation filled me with an insatiable thirst for vengeance. I recollected my threat and resolved that it should be accomplished. I knew that I was preparing for myself a deadly torture, but I was the slave, not the master, of an impulse which I detested yet could not disobey. Yet when she died! Nay, then I was not miserable. I had cast off all feeling, subdued

▶ For what does Walton condemn the creature?

▶ What tortures does the creature say he has suffered? What remorse does he feel Frankenstein should have suffered?

▶ Does the creature take responsibility for his actions? Why, or why not?

Words For Everyday Use

su • per • flu • ous (sə pur´floo əs) *adj.*, excessive; unnecessary

all anguish, to riot in the excess of my despair. Evil thenceforth became my good. Urged thus far, I had no choice but to adapt my nature to an element which I had willingly chosen. The completion of my demoniacal design became an insatiable passion. And now it is ended; there is my last victim!"

I was at first touched by the expressions of his misery; yet, when I called to mind what Frankenstein had said of his powers of eloquence and persuasion, and when I again cast my eyes on the lifeless form of my friend, indignation was rekindled within me. "Wretch!" I said. "It is well that you come here to whine over the desolation that you have made. You throw a torch into a pile of buildings, and when they are consumed, you sit among the ruins and lament the fall. Hypocritical fiend! If he whom you mourn still lived, still would he be the object, again would he become the prey, of your accursed vengeance. It is not pity that you feel; you lament only because the victim of your malignity is withdrawn from your power."

"Oh, it is not thus—not thus," interrupted the being. "Yet such must be the impression conveyed to you by what appears to be the purport of my actions. Yet I seek not a fellow feeling in my misery. No sympathy may I ever find. When I first sought it, it was the love of virtue, the feelings of happiness and affection with which my whole being overflowed, that I wished to be participated. But now that virtue has become to me a shadow and that happiness and affection are turned into bitter and loathing despair, in what should I seek for sympathy? I am content to suffer alone while my sufferings shall endure; when I die, I am well satisfied that abhorrence and opprobrium should load my memory. Once my fancy was soothed with dreams of virtue, of fame, and of enjoyment. Once I falsely hoped to meet with beings who, pardoning my outward form, would love me for the excellent qualities which I was capable of unfolding. I was nourished with high thoughts of honor and devotion. But now crime has degraded me beneath the meanest animal. No guilt, no mischief, no malignity, no misery, can be found comparable to mine. When I run over the frightful catalogue of my sins, I cannot believe that I am the same creature whose thoughts were once filled with sublime and transcendent visions of the beauty and the majesty of goodness. But

◄ In what way had the creature changed by the time of Elizabeth's murder?

◄ What is Walton's first reaction to the creature's story? To what do these feelings change?

◄ What change in himself does the creature have difficulty accepting? To what does he compare himself and the change he has undergone?

Words For Everyday Use	**hyp • o • crit • i • cal** (hip´ə krit´ i kəl) *adj.*, pretending to be better than one really is **op • pro • bri • um** (ə prō´brē əm) *n.*, anything bringing disgrace or shame

it is even so; the fallen angel becomes a malignant devil. Yet even that enemy of God and man had friends and associates in his desolation; I am alone.

"You, who call Frankenstein your friend, seem to have a knowledge of my crimes and his misfortunes. But in the detail which he gave you of them he could not sum up the hours and months of misery which I endured wasting in impotent passions. For while I destroyed his hopes, I did not satisfy my own desires. They were forever ardent and craving; still I desired love and fellowship, and I was still spurned. Was there no injustice in this? Am I to be thought the only criminal when all human kind sinned against me? Why do you not hate Felix who drove his friend from his door with <u>contumely</u>? Why do you not execrate the rustic who sought to destroy the savior of his child? Nay, these are virtuous and <u>immaculate</u> beings! I, the miserable and abandoned, am an abortion,[5] to be spurned, and kicked at, and trampled on. Even now my blood boils at the recollection of this injustice.

"But it is true that I am a wretch. I have murdered the lovely and the helpless; I have strangled the innocent as they slept and grasped to death his throat who never injured me or any other living thing. I have devoted my creator, the select specimen of all that is worthy of love and admiration among men, to misery; I have pursued him even to that irremediable ruin. There he lies, white and cold in death. You hate me, but your abhorrence cannot equal that with which I regard myself. I look on the hands which executed the deed; think on the heart in which the imagination of it was conceived, and long for the moment when these hands will meet my eyes, when that imagination will haunt my thoughts no more.

"Fear not that I shall be the instrument of future mischief. My work is nearly complete. Neither yours nor any man's death is needed to consummate the series of my being and accomplish that which must be done, but it requires my own. Do not think that I shall be slow to perform this sacrifice. I shall quit your vessel on the ice raft which brought me thither and shall seek the most northern extremity of the globe; I shall collect my funeral pile and consume to ashes

▶ What injustices does the being note? Explain whether you agree that these actions are unjust.

▶ What last action does the creature deem necessary to end his work?

---

5. **abortion.** Here, an immature, unsuccessful creature

this miserable frame, that its remains may afford no light to any curious and <u>unhallowed</u> wretch who would create such another as I have been. I shall die. I shall no longer feel the agonies which now consume me or be the prey of feelings unsatisfied, yet <u>unquenched</u>. He is dead who called me into being; and when I shall be no more, the very remembrance of us both will speedily vanish. I shall no longer see the sun or stars or feel the winds play on my cheeks. Light, feeling, and sense will pass away; and in this condition must I find my happiness. Some years ago, when the images which this world affords first opened upon me, when I felt the cheering warmth of summer and heard the rustling of the leaves and the warbling of the birds, and these were all to me, I should have wept to die; now it is my only consolation. Polluted by crimes, and torn by the bitterest remorse, where can I find rest but in death?

> ◄ What emotions would the thought of death have previously aroused? What does the creature now feel upon the prospect of death?

"Farewell! I leave you, and in you the last of human kind whom these eyes will ever behold. Farewell, Frankenstein! If thou wert yet alive and yet cherished a desire of revenge against me, it would be better satiated in my life than in my destruction. But it was not so; thou didst seek my extinction that I might not cause greater wretchedness; and if yet, in some mode unknown to me, thou hast not ceased to think and feel, thou wouldst not desire against me a vengeance greater than that which I feel. Blasted as thou wert, my agony was still superior to thine, for the bitter sting of remorse will not cease to rankle in my wounds until death shall close them forever.

"But soon," he cried, with sad and solemn enthusiasm, "I shall die, and what I now feel be no longer felt. Soon these burning miseries will be extinct. I shall ascend my funeral pile triumphantly and exult in the agony of the torturing flames. The light of that conflagration will fade away; my ashes will be swept into the sea by the winds. My spirit will sleep in peace, or if it thinks, it will not surely think thus. Farewell."

He sprang from the cabin window as he said this, upon the ice raft which lay close to the vessel. He was soon borne away by the waves and lost in darkness and distance.

> ◄ What is the last image Walton has of the creature?

THE END

Words
For
Everyday
Use

un • hal • lowed (un hal´ōd) *adj.,* not holy or sacred
un • quenched (un kwencht´) *adj.,* not satisfied

Responding to the Selection

Whose story do you find more compelling, Frankenstein's or the creature's? For which character do you feel more sympathy? Why? Do you think Walton shares your opinion? Explain.

Reviewing the Selection

Recalling and Interpreting

1. **R:** What concerns does Frankenstein have about marrying Elizabeth? What emotions does Elizabeth display on her wedding day? Why does Frankenstein ask Elizabeth to retire to their chamber? What does Frankenstein think the creature plans to do? What does the creature do instead?

2. **I:** Why are Frankenstein's preparations for the creature's attack unsuccessful? Explain whether the creature's act of revenge is a worse punishment than the action that Frankenstein expected.

3. **R:** What loss is added to the loss of Elizabeth? To whom does Frankenstein finally tell his tale? How is his tale received? Does he achieve his end by telling the story? What does Frankenstein vow to do?

4. **I:** Explain how Frankenstein's losses strengthen him. Does Frankenstein fulfill his vow? Explain.

5. **R:** Why does the creature lure Frankenstein to the far north? What preparations does Frankenstein make to follow the creature? What natural event causes Frankenstein to lose sight of his prey? Why had he asked where the ship was bound when the sailors attempted to rescue him? What warning does he give Walton?

6. **I:** Is Frankenstein a rational human being? Should he pursue his quest for revenge? Does Walton take Frankenstein's warning to heart? Explain your responses.

7. **R:** What promise does Frankenstein beg of Walton? What does Walton say when he sees the creature? In what way do the stories of the creature differ from those told by Frankenstein? How do these stories move Walton?

8. **I:** Why does Walton lose his sympathy for the creature? Explain whether he fulfills Frankenstein's expectations.

Synthesizing

9. In what ways are Walton and Frankenstein similar? How do you think Walton would have reacted if he were in Frankenstein's position?

10. In her introduction, Shelley says that she wanted to write a story which would speak to the mysterious fears of our nature and awaken thrilling horror. To what fears of our nature do you think she refers? Do you think she has succeeded in creating this type of story? Why, or why not?

Understanding Literature (QUESTIONS FOR DISCUSSION)

1. **Allusion, Metaphor, and Simile.** An **allusion** is a rhetorical technique in which reference is made to a person, event, object, or work from history or literature. A **metaphor** is a figure of speech in which one thing is spoken of or written about as if it were another. A **simile** is a comparison using *like* or *as*. Identify each of the following allusions as a metaphor or a simile and explain the comparison made in each case.

- I . . . dared to whisper paradisaical dreams of love and joy; but the apple was already eaten, and the angel's arm bared to drive me from all hope.
- Like the archangel who aspired to omnipotence, I am chained in an eternal hell.

2. **Setting and Mood.** The **setting** of a literary work is the time and place in which it occurs, together with all the details used to create a sense of a particular time and place. **Mood**, or **atmosphere**, is the emotion created in the reader by part or all of a literary work. In your own words, describe the setting created at the beginning of chapter 23. What mood is created by the details of this setting?

Plot Analysis of *Frankenstein*

The following diagram, known as Freytag's Pyramid, illustrates the main plot of *Frankenstein*. For definitions and more information on the parts of a plot illustrated below, see the Handbook of Literary Terms.

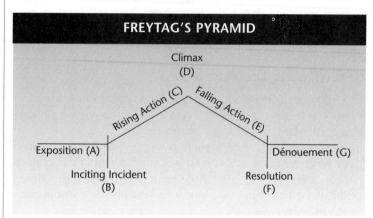

The parts of a plot are as follows:

The **exposition** is the part of a plot that provides background information about the characters, setting, or conflict.

The **inciting incident** is the event that introduces the central conflict.

The **rising action**, or complication, develops the conflict to a high point of intensity.

The **falling action** is all the events that follow the climax.

The **resolution** is the point at which the central conflict is ended, or resolved.

The **dénouement** is any material that follows the resolution and that ties up loose ends.

Exposition (A)

Walton's letters at the beginning of the novel set the story in the isolated arctic regions of Europe and identify Walton, the narrator, as a scientist bent to excess on his mission. The beginning of Frankenstein's story provides background information about Frankenstein's family and childhood, introducing his parents, Elizabeth, and Clerval. The early chapters also present Frankenstein's ambition and interest in science.

Inciting Incident (B)

Frankenstein attends the university and becomes overly zealous in his studies and experiments, culminating in the creation of the monster. As soon as the creature comes to life, Frankenstein deserts him.

Rising Action (C)

The monster leaves Frankenstein's chambers. After spending time in the woods, he arrives at a village and is driven out by the villagers. He arrives at the De Lacey cottage and makes his home in a nearby hovel. The creature learns to speak and read by listening to the De Laceys, especially to the lessons Felix gives to Safie, a young Turkish woman. The lessons also teach him about history, human society, and human nature. The creature tries to befriend the cottagers but he is shunned and driven off. The creature is also repulsed by a young man who thinks the creature killed his beloved. The creature is even rejected by a young child whom he assumes will not yet have formed prejudices. When the being learns that the child is the brother of Frankenstein, he begins to wreak his revenge by murdering the child. When Justine, the former servant of the Frankensteins, is tried and executed for the murder, Frankenstein is plagued by guilt. Frankenstein meets his creation, hears his tale, and agrees to create a female companion for him. Frankenstein travels with Clerval to England where he begins to create the monster's companion. Becoming disgusted with his work, Frankenstein destroys the new creature. His first creation is enraged and threatens that he will be with Frankenstein on his wedding night. After spending a night drifting in his boat, Frankenstein lands in Ireland where he is accused of Clerval's murder. Frankenstein is cleared of the charges and returns to Geneva with his father.

Climax (D)

Frankenstein marries Elizabeth. He is on his guard for an attack of the monster and is prepared to kill the creature or die trying. He is unprepared, however, when the monster seeks vengeance by killing Elizabeth. Frankenstein finally reveals his secret and tries to enlist help in his efforts to destroy the creature. The magistrate finds the story unbelievable and suggests that Frankenstein's quest is in vain. Frankenstein vows to follow the creature, seeking revenge for his murdered family and friends, vowing that this quest will end when either he or the creature dies.

Falling Action (E)

Frankenstein's quest takes him into the arctic regions where the seas are frozen over. After coming within miles of the creature, nature intercedes, breaking up the ice and separating the two. Frankenstein is picked up by Walton's crew, bringing the story back to the beginning of the novel. Frankenstein grows weaker and continues to share his story with Walton. Knowing that he is dying, he asks Walton to continue his quest against the monster.

Resolution (F)

Frankenstein insists on continuing after the creature despite his ill health and the fact that Walton has turned his ship to the south. He dies aboard the ship, ending his quest for revenge.

Dénouement (G)

Walton encounters the creature looking at Frankenstein's dead body. He condemns the creature for his actions. After the creature makes a last plea for his cause and says he will kill himself in a great funeral pyre, he disappears.

Creative Writing Activities

Creative Writing Activity A: Letters

Frankenstein begins and ends with letters from Walton to his sister. In fact, the whole story is told in letters. How do you think Margaret Saville would react upon receiving these letters? Examine the letters to try and gain a better understanding of Mrs. Saville. Then write one or more letters from Margaret Saville in response to the letters Walton has written.

Creative Writing Activity B: Science Fiction Story

Science fiction is highly imaginative fiction containing fantastic elements based on scientific principles, discoveries, or laws. Often science fiction deals with the future, the distant past, or with worlds other than our own, such as other planets, parallel universes, and worlds under the earth or the sea. The genre allows writers to suspend or alter certain elements of reality in order to create fascinating and sometimes instructive alternatives. *Frankenstein* asks us to consider the implications of human exploration into the life creating force. Write your own story in which you use scientific principles, discoveries, or laws to explore some aspect of human nature or of the reality of our world today.

Creative Writing Activity C: Newspaper Article

Imagine the story of Frankenstein and his creature is true. Write a newspaper account about some aspect of the story. You may wish to work with your classmates to create a newspaper that presents several different aspects of the story. Some possibilities include an interview with Frankenstein, an interview with the monster, a psychological profile of the killer, an editorial about scientific exploration, or an article about the pursuit of the killer. You may decide to write for a sensational tabloid or for a respected newspaper.

Creative Writing Activity D: Travelogue

There are many passages in which Frankenstein provides descriptions of his travels along the Rhine, through the Alps, or in the northern regions of Britain. Begin by choosing as a subject a place where you have traveled or lived. Find aspects of this location that you find interesting visually, particularly powerful or moving, or exceptionally attractive. Describe these places using vivid images for somebody who may not have seen or experienced these areas.

Creative Writing Activity E: Gothic Elements

Gothic works, like *Frankenstein*, include elements of horror, suspense, mystery, and magic, and often contain dark, brooding descriptions of settings and characters. Write a description of a Gothic setting. Begin by freewriting about Gothic settings in stories or movies you have seen. You may wish to extend your description into a Gothic story.

Creative Writing Activity F: Adaptation

Frankenstein has been adapted many times to a wide variety of artistic forms. Create your own adaptation of the novel. Your adaptation might take the form of a film screenplay, a children's picture book, a comic book, or a narrative poem. To begin, you may wish to outline the main points of the plot and identify the key themes you would like to develop in your work. You may make any changes to the original text that you feel are necessary, add to the story, or take out parts of the story that do not suit your purpose.

Critical Writing Activities

Critical Writing Activity A: Modern Prometheus

Mary Shelley originally subtitled this work "The Modern Prometheus," alluding to Greek mythology (see "The Story of Prometheus" in Selections for Additional Reading, page 229). In a brief essay, explain why Frankenstein is a modern Prometheus. In what way do his actions reflect both stories about Prometheus? Is his fate similar to Prometheus's? Prepare a thesis which explains the relationship you see between the two stories. Then use examples from the text to support your opinion.

Critical Writing Activity B: Science Fiction and the Relevance of *Frankenstein*

Science fiction is highly imaginative fiction containing fantastic elements based on scientific principles, discoveries, or laws. *Frankenstein* was one of the first science fiction stories, yet it is still powerful today. In an essay, explain why *Frankenstein* is a science fiction novel and examine why a novel written about scientific ideas popular in 1818 is still relevant today.

Critical Writing Activity C: *Frankenstein* and the Ancient Mariner

Shelley alludes often to "The Rime of the Ancient Mariner" (see page 230). If you have not already done so, read this poem by Samuel Taylor Coleridge. Then compare and contrast the theme and structure of the poem with the theme and structure of *Frankenstein*. To do so, you may wish to consider the following questions: Who is the narrator or speaker in each work? What has the narrator or speaker of each work wrongly done? What are the consequences of these actions? Why is the narrator or speaker of each work intent upon telling his tale? What theme in *Frankenstein* is reinforced by the allusions to the ancient mariner?

Critical Writing Activity D: Feminist Criticism

Two main issues on which feminist criticism of *Frankenstein* has focused are the role of women in the novel and the theft of a woman's role of giving birth. Choose one of the prompts on the next page on which to focus your essay.

- Who are the women in the novel? What roles do women play in the novel? What are the characteristics of the women who are portrayed or mentioned? Why do you think that Mary Shelley chose three male voices to narrate this story? In what way might these considerations reflect Shelley's own experience as a woman?

- The seizing of a woman's power takes two forms in *Frankenstein:* in giving life to the monster, Frankenstein takes over a woman's role of giving birth and at the same time steals the power of Nature, which in the novel is portrayed as a female force. In what way might this reflect Shelley's sense of a woman's role and male attitudes toward and treatment of women in her society?

Critical Writing Activity E: Comparing and Contrasting Characters

Choose one of the following sets of characters to compare and contrast: Frankenstein and Walton, Frankenstein and the monster, and Frankenstein and Clerval. In your essay, you may want to address some of the following subjects in relation to each character: ambition and goals, relationships with others, inner goodness or evil, anger and revenge. Begin by setting up a Venn diagram to organize your ideas. Use the names of the two characters as the heading for the chart. Then fill in the chart with the similarities and differences between the two characters. Use specific examples from the text.

Projects

Project A: Reviewing a Film Adaptation

Many film adaptations have been made of *Frankenstein*. In fact, many people are more familiar with cinematic versions of the story than they are of Shelley's novel. Some of these films are listed in the Selected *Frankenstein* Film List on page xiii. View one movie about Frankenstein. Then discuss with others the films you have seen. You may wish to examine the following questions: How do the films differ from the novel in structure? in plot? in characterization? What themes do the films explore? Are these themes explored in a different way than they are in the novel? In what way do the films reflect the social and political atmosphere of the period in which they were produced?

Project B: Depictions of the Monster

Many people have an image of the monster from *Frankenstein* that is based on a movie adaptation. Create depictions of the monster, based solely on the text of the novel. You may picture the monster in any activity described in the book, but pay special attention to the physical characteristics of the creature.

Project C: Storytelling Contest

According to Mary Shelley, *Frankenstein* was created as part of a contest to see who among a group of friends could tell the best ghost story. Host your own storytelling contest. Choose a theme, such as the good and evil in all people, the limitations of human knowledge, or the fear of failure. Each person should try to come up with a story on this theme. In small groups share your stories. Each group should choose their favorite, and then have the winner from each group present his or her story to the class.

Project D: Helpful and Destructive Scientific Discoveries

Frankenstein critiques overzealous scientific exploration and presents some of the dangers of experimentation gone awry. In recent years we have learned the problems many scientific or technological wonders have caused to the environment or to human beings. Choose any current scientific issue, such as experimental drugs, genetic engineering, or cloning. Research the subject and present your own opinion about it. In what way might your subject be positive for humanity? What dangers might it present? What legal or ethical rules should govern your subject?

Project E: Mapping

The story begins in the arctic regions of the far north. Other parts of the story take place in Switzerland, Germany, and England. Using an atlas as a source, construct your own map of Europe in the eighteenth century. Then mark significant places in the story, including the trip Frankenstein takes with Clerval and the route of his pursuit of the monster. Illustrate the map with scenes that occur at some of the places you have marked on the map.

Project F: Mock Trial

Imagine that the monster is captured and brought to trial for the deaths of William, Henry, and Elizabeth. With your classmates take the roles of the prosecution, the defendant, the judge, jury, and witnesses. Consider what evidence is available about the murders and what possible defenses might be made.

Selections for Additional Reading

"The Story of Prometheus"
Anonymous, retold by Sara Hyry

In Greek mythology, Prometheus is a Titan who created and championed humankind. His name means forethought, while his brother's name, Epimetheus, means afterthought. Prometheus is portrayed as a hero in Aeschylus's Prometheus Bound *and in Percy Shelley's* Prometheus Unbound.

Prometheus and Epimetheus were given the task of creating animals and humans. As usual, Epimetheus did not plan his work, and proceeded to give all of the gifts he had to the animals. He gave out swiftness and cunning and warming fur and protective shells. He realized he had no way of making humans special. Then Prometheus took charge, fashioning humans out of mud to walk upright like the gods. Zeus, who breathed life into these creatures, praised Prometheus for his fine job,. but he was afraid that these beings might one day become strong enough to challenge the gods. He smiled in relief when he saw that the people did not have fire and could not cook their food, make strong weapons or tools, or create vessels such as bowls and pots.

Prometheus saw what Zeus saw, but he sympathized with the beings he had shaped. Defying Zeus's orders, Prometheus contrived to bring fire to people. Stealing fire from heaven, he hid it in a reed and carried it to the humans. After Prometheus showed humans the many uses of fire, they prospered. Zeus was consumed with rage when he saw that humans had fire, fuming that humans would one day challenge the gods. Prometheus answered that humans would not revolt if they were loved and taught as they should be. Zeus, however, would not be calmed. He ordered that Prometheus should be chained to a rock on Mt. Caucasus and that everyday a powerful eagle would feed on his liver. Prometheus's liver regenerated each day, and this torture continued for thirty thousand years. Mighty Hercules finally released Prometheus from his suffering.

Zeus's revenge did not end with his punishment of Prometheus. He wanted vengeance on the human race as well. He had Hephastus mold a girl of clay. This girl, who was named Pandora, was taught to be skilled, desirable, and cunning. Zeus gave her a beautiful container as a gift but told her she must never open it. He then sent Pandora to Epimetheus to be his bride, warning Epimetheus that Pandora's box must not be opened. Flattered by Zeus's attention, Epimetheus gladly wed Pandora and locked her box away that she might not be tempted to open it. Pandora's curiosity got the best of her, and one day while Epimetheus was sleeping, she took the key to the closet where he had placed the box for safe keeping. As she opened the box to peek inside, she heard a loud whirring sound and felt the rush of many tiny wings against her face. She tried to close the lid, but it was too late. The contents, all the evils that now plague the world, were released and spread over the earth. Zeus's revenge would have been complete, but Pandora managed to trap one thing—hopelessness. The last evil contained in the box was the most powerful of all, for without hope the other evils would have taken root and claimed the world as their own.

"The Rime of the Ancient Mariner"
by Samuel Taylor Coleridge

Samuel Taylor Coleridge (1772–1834) was born in rural Devonshire, England. He attended school in London and later in Cambridge. A sensitive, intelligent, but often rather lonely student, he left school in debt, dissolution, and disgrace to enlist in the Light Dragoons, a mounted military unit. Not suited to military life, he was soon rescued by friends and returned to the university, although he never graduated. Coleridge suffered from rheumatism and took laudanum, following the standard medical procedures of the day. He became addicted to the drug around 1800, soon after becoming estranged from his wife. Perhaps because of his tragic addiction, many of Coleridge's most intense work efforts remain unfinished and exist only in the form of scrawled notes. Nonetheless, Coleridge is considered one of the great poets of his era.

"The Rime of the Ancient Mariner" was based on a dream that one of Coleridge's friends shared with him. The poem was intended as a collaboration between Coleridge and his friend, William Wordsworth. Wordsworth contributed to the poem but did not complete the project. In this poem the Mariner kills an albatross and is punished for doing so. From this poem comes the phrase "an albatross around one's neck," meaning a distressing burden or sense of guilt.

"The Rime of the Ancient Mariner"
by Samuel Taylor Coleridge

IN SEVEN PARTS

"I readily believe that there are more invisible than visible Natures in the universe. But who will explain for us the family of all these beings, and the ranks and relations and distinguishing features and functions of each? What do they do? What places do they inhabit? The human mind has always sought the knowledge of these things, but never attained it. Meanwhile I do not deny that it is helpful sometimes to contemplate in the mind, as on a tablet, the image of a greater and better world, lest the intellect, habituated to the petty things of daily life, narrow itself and sink wholly into trivial thoughts. But at the same time we must be watchful for the truth and keep a sense of proportion, so that we may distinguish the certain from the uncertain, day from night."

—Adapted by Coleridge from Thomas Burnet,
Archaeologiae Philosophicae (1692).

ARGUMENT

How a Ship, having first sailed to the Equator, was driven by storms to the cold Country towards the South Pole; how the Ancient Mariner cruelly and in contempt of the laws of hospitality killed a Seabird and how he was followed by many and strange Judgments: and in what manner he came back to his own Country.

PART I

It is an ancient Mariner
And he stoppeth one of three.
—"By thy long gray beard and glittering eye,
Now wherefore stopp'st thou me?

An Ancient Mariner meeteth three Gallants bidden to a wedding feast, and detaineth one.

5   The Bridegroom's doors are opened wide,
And I am next of kin;
The guests are met, the feast is set:
May'st hear the merry din."

He holds him with his skinny hand,
10   "There was a ship," quoth he.
"Hold off! unhand me, graybeard loon!"
Eftsoons[1] his hand dropped he.

---

1. **Eftsoons.** At once

He holds him with his glittering eye—
The Wedding-Guest stood still,
15 And listens like a three years' child:
The Mariner hath his will.[2]

The Wedding-Guest is spell-bound by the eye of the old seafaring man, and constrained to hear his tale.

The Wedding-Guest sat on a stone;
He cannot choose but hear;
And thus spake on that ancient man,
20 The bright-eyed Mariner.

"The ship was cheered, the harbor
    cleared,
Merrily did we drop
Below the kirk,[3] below the hill,
Below the lighthouse top.

25 The Sun came up upon the left,
Out of the sea came he!
And he shone bright, and on the right
Went down into the sea.

The Mariner tells how the ship sailed southward with a good wind and fair weather, till it reached the Line.

Higher and higher every day,
30 Till over the mast at noon[4]—"
The Wedding-Guest here beat his breast,
For he heard the loud bassoon.

The bride hath paced into the hall,
Red as a rose is she;
35 Nodding their heads before her goes
The merry minstrelsy.

The Wedding-Guest heareth the bridal music; but the Mariner continueth his tale.

The Wedding-Guest he beat his breast,
Yet he cannot choose but hear;
And thus spake on that ancient man,
40 The bright-eyed Mariner.

"And now the STORM-BLAST came, and he
Was tyrannous and strong;
He struck with his o'ertaking wings,
And chased us south along.

The ship driven by a storm toward the South Pole.

45 With sloping masts and dipping prow,

---

2. **He holds . . . his will.** The mariner has hypnotized or mesmerized the Wedding-Guest.
3. **kirk.** Church
4. **Higher . . . noon.** The location of the ship is told by the sun. Here, it has reached the equator.

As who pursued with yell and blow
Still treads the shadow of his foe,
And forward bends his head,
The ship drove fast, loud roared the blast,
50 And southward aye we fled.

And now there came both mist and snow,
And it grew wondrous cold:
And ice, mast-high, came floating by,
As green as emerald.

55 And through the drifts the snowy clifts   *The land of ice,*
Did send a dismal sheen: *and of fearful*
Nor shapes of men nor beasts we ken[5]—   *sounds where no*
The ice was all between.   *living thing was*
                                                                  to be seen.

The ice was here, the ice was there,
60 The ice was all around:
It cracked and growled, and roared and
          howled,
Like noises in a swound![6]

At length did cross an Albatross,   *Till a great sea*
Thorough the fog it came;   *bird, called the*
65 As if it had been a Christian soul,   *Albatross, came*
We hailed it in God's name.   *through the*
                                                                  snow-fog, and
                                                                  was received
It ate the food it ne'er had eat,   *with great joy*
And round and round it flew.   *and hospitality.*
The ice did split with a thunder-fit;
70 The helmsman steered us through!

And a good south wind sprung up   *And lo! the*
          behind;   *Albatross*
The Albatross did follow,   *proveth a bird of*
And every day, for food or play,   *good omen, and*
Came to the mariners' hollo!   *followeth the*
                                                                  ship as it
                                                                  returned north-
75 In mist or cloud, on mast or shroud,[7]   *ward through fog*
It perched for vespers nine;   *and floating ice.*
Whiles all the night, through fog-smoke
          white,
Glimmered the white Moon-shine."

---

5. **ken.** Know
6. **swound.** Swoon
7. **shroud.** Ropes that support a mast

"God save thee, ancient Mariner!
80 From the fiends, that plague thee thus!—
Why look'st thou so?"—With my cross-
    bow
I shot the ALBATROSS.

PART 2

The Sun now rose upon the right:[8]
Out of the sea came he,
85 Still hid in mist, and on the left
Went down into the sea.

And the good south wind still blew
    behind,
But no sweet bird did follow,
Nor any day for food or play
90 Came to the mariners' hollo!

And I had done a hellish thing,
And it would work 'em woe:
For all averred, I had killed the bird
That made the breeze to blow.
95 Ah wretch! said they, the bird to slay,
That made the breeze to blow!

Nor dim nor red, like God's own head,
The glorious Sun uprist:
Then all averred, I had killed the bird
100 That brought the fog and mist.
'Twas right, said they, such birds to slay,
That bring the fog and mist.

The fair breeze blew, the white foam flew,
The furrow followed free;
105 We were the first that ever burst
Into that silent sea.

Down dropped the breeze, the sails
    dropped down,
'Twas sad as sad could be;
And we did speak only to break
110 The silence of the sea!

All in a hot and copper sky,
The bloody Sun, at noon,

The ancient Mariner inhospitably killeth the pious bird of good omen.

His shipmates cry out against the ancient Mariner, for killing the bird of good luck.

But when the fog cleared off, they justify the same, and thus make themselves accomplices in the crime.

The fair breeze continues; the ship enters the Pacific Ocean, and sails northward, even till it reaches the Line.

The ship hath been suddenly becalmed.

---

8. **The Sun . . . right.** Now the ship is heading north into the Pacific Ocean.

234 FRANKENSTEIN, OR THE MODERN PROMETHEUS

Right up above the mast did stand,
No bigger than the Moon.

115 Day after day, day after day,
We stuck, nor breath nor motion;
As idle as a painted ship
Upon a painted ocean.

Water, water, everywhere,
120 And all the boards did shrink;
Water, water, everywhere,
Nor any drop to drink.

The very deep did rot: O Christ!
That ever this should be!
125 Yea, slimy things did crawl with legs
Upon the slimy sea.

About, about, in reel and rout
The death-fires[9] danced at night;
The water, like a witch's oils,
130 Burnt green, and blue and white.

And some in dreams assurèd were
Of the Spirit that plagued us so;
Nine fathom deep he had followed us
From the land of mist and snow.

135 And every tongue, through utter drought,
Was withered at the root;
We could not speak, no more than if
We had been choked with soot.

Ah! well-a-day! what evil looks
140 Had I from old and young!
Instead of the cross, the Albatross
About my neck was hung.

PART 3

There passed a weary time. Each throat
Was parched, and glazed each eye.
145 A weary time! a weary time!
How glazed each weary eye,
When looking westward, I beheld
A something in the sky.

The Albatross begins to be avenged.

A Spirit had followed them; one of the invisible inhabitants of this planet, neither departed souls nor angels; concerning whom the learned Jew, Josephus, and the Platonic Constantinopolitan, Michael Psellus, may be consulted. They are very numerous, and there is no climate or element without one or more.

The shipmates, in their sore distress, would fain throw the whole guilt on the ancient Mariner: in sign whereof they hang the dead sea bird round his neck.

The ancient Mariner beholdeth a sign in the element afar off.

9. **death-fires.** Saint Elmo's fire is an electric discharge often seen on a ship's mast. Superstitious sailors believe it is an omen of danger.

At first it seemed a little speck,
150 And then it seemed a mist;
It moved and moved, and took at last
A certain shape, I wist.[10]

A speck, a mist, a shape, I wist!
And still it neared and neared:
155 As if it dodged a water-sprite,[11]
It plunged and tacked and veered.[12]

With throats unslaked, with black lips
baked,
We could nor laugh nor wail;
Through utter drought all dumb we
stood!
160 I bit my arm, I sucked the blood,
And cried, A sail! a sail!

At its nearer approach, it seemeth him to be a ship; and at a dear ransom he freeth his speech from the bonds of thirst.

With throats unslaked, with black lips
baked,
Agape they heard me call:
Gramercy![13] they for joy did grin,
165 And all at once their breath drew in,
As they were drinking all.

A flash of joy;

See! see! (I cried) she tacks no more!
Hither to work us weal;[14]
Without a breeze, without a tide,
170 She steadies with upright keel!

And horror follows. For can it be a ship that comes onward without wind or tide?

The western wave was all aflame.
The day was well nigh done!
Almost upon the western wave
Rested the broad bright Sun;
175 When that strange shape drove suddenly
Betwixt us and the Sun.

And straight the Sun was flecked with bars,
(Heaven's Mother send us grace!)
As if through a dungeon grate he peered
180 With broad and burning face.

It seemeth him but the skeleton of a ship.

---

10. **wist.** Knew
11. **water-sprite.** A supernatural being in control of the natural elements
12. **tacked and veered.** Changed direction
13. **Gramercy!** Great thanks, from the French *grand-merci*
14. **weal.** Benefit

Alas! (thought I, and my heart beat loud)
How fast she nears and nears!
Are those *her* sails that glance in the Sun,
Like restless gossameres?

And its ribs are seen as bars on the face of the setting Sun.

185 Are those *her* ribs through which the
     Sun
Did peer, as through a grate?
And is that Woman all her crew?
Is that a DEATH? and are there two?
Is DEATH that woman's mate?

The Specter-Woman and her Deathmate, and no other on board the skeleton ship.

190 *Her* lips were red, *her* looks were free,
Her locks were yellow as gold:
Her skin was as white as leprosy,[15]
The Night-mare LIFE-IN-DEATH was she,
Who thicks man's blood with cold.

Like vessel, like crew!

195 The naked hulk alongside came,
And the twain were casting dice;
"The game is done! I've won! I've won!"
Quoth she, and whistles thrice.

Death and Life-in-Death have diced for the ship's crew, and she (the latter) winneth the ancient Mariner.

The Sun's rim dips; the stars rush out:
200 At one stride comes the dark;
With far-heard whisper, o'er the sea,
Off shot the spectre-bark.

No twilight within the courts of the Sun.

We listened and looked sideways up!
Fear at my heart, as at a cup,
205 My lifeblood seemed to sip!
The stars were dim, and thick the night,
The steersman's face by his lamp
     gleamed white;
From the sails the dew did drip—
Till clomb above the eastern bar
210 The hornèd Moon, with one bright star
Within the nether tip.[16]

At the rising of the Moon,

One after one, by the star-dogged Moon,
Too quick for groan or sigh,
Each turned his face with a ghastly pang,
215 And cursed me with his eye.

One after another,

---

15. **leprosy.** A characteristic of leprosy is white, scaly skin.
16. **hornèd Moon . . . nether tip.** This is considered an omen of evil.

Four times fifty living men,
(And I heard nor sigh nor groan)
With heavy thump, a lifeless lump,
They dropped down one by one.

*His shipmates
drop down dead.*

220 The souls did from their bodies fly—
They fled to bliss or woe!
And every soul, it passed me by,
Like the whizz of my crossbow!

*But Life-in-
Death begins her
work on the
ancient Mariner.*

PART 4

"I fear thee, ancient Mariner!
225 I fear thy skinny hand!
And thou art long, and lank, and brown,
As is the ribbed sea-sand.
I fear thee and thy glittering eye,
And thy skinny hand, so brown."—

*The Wedding-
Guest feareth
that a Spirit is
talking to him;*

230 Fear not, fear not, thou Wedding-Guest!
This body dropped not down.

*But the ancient
Mariner assureth
him of his bodily
life, and pro-
ceedeth to relate
his horrible
penance.*

Alone, alone, all, all alone,
Alone on a wide wide sea!
And never a saint took pity on
235 My soul in agony.

The many men, so beautiful!
And they all dead did lie:
And a thousand thousand slimy things
Lived on; and so did I.

*He despiseth the
creatures of the
calm,*

240 I looked upon the rotting sea,
And drew my eyes away;
I looked upon the rotting deck,
And there the dead men lay.

*And envieth that
they should live,
and so many lie
dead.*

I looked to heaven, and tried to pray;
245 But or ever a prayer had gushed,
A wicked whisper came, and made
My heart as dry as dust.

I closed my lids, and kept them close,
And the balls like pulses beat;
250 For the sky and the sea, and the sea and
the sky
Lay like a load on my weary eye,
And the dead were at my feet.

The cold sweat melted from their limbs,
Nor rot nor reek did they:
255 The look with which they looked on me
Had never passed away.

*But the curse
liveth for him in
the eye of the
dead men.*

An orphan's curse would drag to hell
A spirit from on high;
But oh! more horrible than that
260 Is the curse in a dead man's eye!
Seven days, seven nights, I saw that
    curse,
And yet I could not die.

The moving Moon went up the sky,
And nowhere did <u>abide</u>:
265 Softly she was going up,
And a star or two beside—

*In his loneliness
and fixedness he
yearneth towards
the journeying
Moon, and the
stars that still
sojourn, yet still
move onward;
and everywhere
the blue sky
belongs to them,
and is their
appointed rest,
and their native
country and their
own natural
homes, which
they enter unan-
nounced, as
lords that are
certainly expected
and yet there is a
silent joy at their
arrival.*

Her beams bemocked the sultry main,
Like April hoar-frost spread;
But where the ship's huge shadow lay,
270 The charmèd water burnt alway
A still and awful red.

Beyond the shadow of the ship,
I watched the water snakes:
They moved in tracks of shining white,
275 And when they reared, the elfish light
Fell off in hoary flakes.

Within the shadow of the ship
I watched their rich attire:
Blue, glossy green, and velvet black,
280 They coiled and swam; and every track
Was a flash of golden fire.

*By the light of
the Moon he
beholdeth God's
creatures of the
great calm.*

*Their beauty and
their happiness.*

O happy living things! no tongue
Their beauty might declare:
A spring of love gushed from my heart,
285 And I blessed them unaware:
Sure my kind saint took pity on me,
And I blessed them unaware.

*He blesseth them
in his heart.*

The self-same moment I could pray;
And from my neck so free
290 The Albatross fell off, and sank
Like lead into the sea.

*The spell begins
to break.*

PART 5

Oh sleep! it is a gentle thing,
Beloved from pole to pole!
To Mary Queen the praise be given!
295 She sent the gentle sleep from Heaven,
That slid into my soul.

The silly buckets on the deck,
That had so long remained,
I dreamt that they were filled with dew;
300 And when I awoke, it rained.

By grace of the holy Mother, the ancient Mariner is refreshed with rain.

My lips were wet, my throat was cold,
My garments all were dank;
Sure I had drunken in my dreams,
And still my body drank.

305 I moved, and could not feel my limbs:
I was so light—almost
I thought that I had died in sleep,
And was a blessed ghost.

And soon I heard a roaring wind:
310 It did not come anear;
But with its sound it shook the sails,
That were so thin and sere.[17]

He heareth sounds and seeth strange sights and commotions in the sky and the element.

The upper air burst into life!
And a hundred fire-flags sheen,
315 To and fro they were hurried about!
And to and fro, and in and out,
The wan stars danced between.

And the coming wind did roar more loud,
And the sails did sigh like sedge;[18]
320 And the rain poured down from one
      black cloud;
The Moon was at its edge.

The thick black cloud was cleft, and still
The Moon was at its side:
Like waters shot from some high crag,
325 The lightning fell with never a jag,
A river steep and wide.

17. **sere.** Dried up
18. **sedge.** A plant that grows in wet ground or water

The loud wind never reached the ship,
Yet now the ship moved on!
Beneath the lightning and the Moon
330 The dead men gave a groan.

The bodies of the ship's crew are inspirited, and the ship moves on;

They groaned, they stirred, they all uprose,
Nor spake, nor moved their eyes;
It had been strange, even in a dream,
To have seen those dead men rise.

335 The helmsman steered, the ship moved on;
Yet never a breeze up-blew;
The mariners all 'gan work the ropes,
Where they were wont to do;
They raised their limbs like lifeless tools—
340 We were a ghastly crew.

The body of my brother's son
Stood by me, knee to knee:
The body and I pulled at one rope,
But he said nought to me.

345 "I fear thee, ancient Mariner!"
Be calm, thou Wedding Guest!
'Twas not those souls that fled in pain,
Which to their corses[19] came again,
But a troop of spirits blest:

But not by the souls of the men nor by demons of earth or middle air, but by a blessed troop of angelic spirits, sent down by the invocation of the guardian saint.

350 For when it dawned—they dropped their
    arms,
And clustered round the mast;
Sweet sounds rose slowly through
    their mouths,
And from their bodies passed.

Around, around, flew each sweet sound,
355 Then darted to the Sun;
Slowly the sounds came back again,
Now mixed, now one by one.

Sometimes a-dropping from the sky
I heard the sky-lark sing;
360 Sometimes all little birds that are,
How they seemed to fill the sea and air
With their sweet jargoning![20]

---

19. **corses.** Corpses
20. **jargoning.** Singing

And now 'twas like all instruments,
Now like a lonely flute;
365 And now it is an angel's song,
That makes the heavens be mute.

It ceased; yet still the sails made on
A pleasant noise till noon,
A noise like of a hidden brook
370 In the leafy month of June,
That to the sleeping woods all night
Singeth a quiet tune.

Till noon we quietly sailed on,
Yet never a breeze did breathe:
375 Slowly and smoothly went the ship,
Moved onward from beneath.

Under the keel nine fathom deep,
From the land of mist and snow,
The spirit slid: and it was he
380 That made the ship to go.
The sails at noon left off their tune,
And the ship stood still also.

The lonesome Spirit from the South Pole carries on the ship as far as the Line, in obedience to the angelic troop, but still requireth vengeance.

The Sun, right up above the mast,
Had fixed her to the ocean:
385 But in a minute she 'gan stir,
With a short uneasy motion—
Backwards and forwards half her length
With a short uneasy motion.

Then like a pawing horse let go,
390 She made a sudden bound:
It flung the blood into my head,
And I fell down in a swound.

How long in that same fit I lay,
I have not to declare;
395 But ere my living life returned,
I heard and in my soul discerned
Two voices in the air.

The Polar Spirit's fellow demons, the invisible inhabitants of the element, take part in his wrong; and two of them relate, one to the other, that penance long and heavy for the ancient Mariner hath been accorded to the Polar Spirit, who returneth southward.

It "Is it he?" quoth one, "Is this the
    man?
By him who died on cross,
400 With his cruel bow he laid full low
The harmless Albatross.

The spirit who bideth by himself
In the land of mist and snow,
He loved the bird that loved the man
405 Who shot him with his bow."

The other was a softer voice,
As soft as honeydew:
Quoth he, "The man hath penance done,
And penance more will do."

PART 6

FIRST VOICE
410 "But tell me, tell me! speak again,
Thy soft response renewing—
What makes that ship drive on so fast?
What is the ocean doing?"

SECOND VOICE
"Still as a slave before his lord,
415 The ocean hath no blast;
His great bright eye most silently
Up to the Moon is cast—

If he may know which way to go;
For she guides him smooth or grim.
420 See, brother, see! how graciously
She looketh down on him."

FIRST VOICE
"But why drives on that ship so fast,
Without or wave or wind?"

SECOND VOICE
"The air is cut away before,
425 And closes from behind.

The Mariner hath been cast into a trance; for the angelic power causeth the vessel to drive northward faster than human life could endure.

Fly, brother, fly! more high, more high!
Or we shall be belated:
For slow and slow that ship will go,
When the Mariner's trance is abated."

430 I woke, and we were sailing on
As in a gentle weather:
'Twas night, calm night, the moon was
    high;
The dead men stood together.

The supernatural motion is retarded; the Mariner awakes, and his penance begins anew.

All stood together on the deck,
435 For a charnel-dungeon[21] fitter:
All fixed on me their stony eyes,
That in the Moon did glitter.

The pang, the curse, with which they
        died,
Had never passed away:
440 I could not draw my eyes from theirs,
Nor turn them up to pray.

And now this spell was snapped: once
        more
I viewed the ocean green,
And looked far forth, yet little saw
445 Of what had else been seen—

*The curse is
finally expiated.*

Like one, that on a lonesome road
Doth walk in fear and dread,
And having once turned round walks on,
And turns no more his head;
450 Because he knows, a frightful fiend
Doth close behind him tread.

But soon there breathed a wind on me,
Nor sound nor motion made:
Its path was not upon the sea,
455 In ripple or in shade.

It raised my hair, it fanned my cheek
Like a meadow-gale of spring—
It mingled strangely with my fears,
Yet it felt like a welcoming.

460 Swiftly, swiftly flew the ship,
Yet she sailed softly too:
Sweetly, sweetly blew the breeze—
On me alone it blew.

Oh! dream of joy! is this indeed
465 The lighthouse top I see?
Is this the hill? is this the kirk?
Is this mine own countree?

*And the ancient
Mariner behold-
eth his native
country.*

We drifted o'er the harbor bar,
And I with sobs did pray—

---

21. **charnel-dungeon.** Cemetery

470 O let me be awake, my God!
   Or let me sleep alway.

   The harbor bay was clear as glass,
   So smoothly it was strewn!
   And on the bay the moonlight lay
475 And the shadow of the Moon.

   The rock shone bright, the kirk no less,
   That stands above the rock:
   The moonlight steeped in silentness
   The steady weathercock.

480 And the bay was white with silent light,
   Till rising from the same,
   Full many shapes, that shadows were,
   In crimson colors came.

   A little distance from the prow
485 Those crimson shadows were:
   I turned my eyes upon the deck—
   Oh, Christ! what saw I there!

   Each corse lay flat, lifeless and flat,
   And, by the holy rood!²²
490 A man all light, a seraph²³ man,
   On every corse there stood.

The angelic spirits leave the dead bodies,

And appear in their own forms of light.

   This seraph band, each waved his hand:
   It was a heavenly sight!
   They stood as signals to the land,
495 Each one a lovely light;

   This seraph band, each waved his hand,
   No voice did they impart—
   No voice; but oh! the silence sank
   Like music on my heart.

500 But soon I heard the dash of oars,
   I heard the Pilot's cheer;
   My head was turned perforce away
   And I saw a boat appear.

   The Pilot and the Pilot's boy
505 I heard them coming fast:

---

22. **rood.** Cross
23. **seraph.** The highest order of angels

Dear Lord in Heaven! it was a joy
The dead men could not blast.

I saw a third—I heard his voice:
It is the Hermit good!
510 He singeth loud his godly hymns
That he makes in the wood.
He'll shrieve[24] my soul, he'll wash away
The Albatross's blood.

PART 7

This Hermit good lives in that wood
515 Which slopes down to the sea.
How loudly his sweet voice he rears!
He loves to talk with marineres
That come from a far countree.

The Hermit of the Wood,

He kneels at morn, and noon, and eve—
520 He hath a cushion plump:
It is the moss that wholly hides
The rotted old oak-stump.

The skiff-boat neared: I heard them talk,
"Why, this is strange, I trow!
525 Where are those lights so many and fair,
That signal made but now?"

"Strange, by my faith!" the Hermit said—
"And they answered not our cheer!
The planks looked warped! and see those
      sails,
530 How thin they are and sere!
I never saw aught like to them,
Unless perchance it were

Approacheth the ship with wonder.

Brown skeletons of leaves that lag
My forest-brook along;
535 When the ivy tod is heavy with snow,
And the owlet whoops to the wolf below,
That eats the she-wolf's young."

"Dear Lord! it hath a fiendish look,"
(The Pilot made reply)
540 "I am a-feared"—"Push on, push on!"
Said the Hermit cheerily.

---

24. **shrieve.** Absolve

The boat came closer to the ship,
But I nor spake nor stirred;
The boat came close beneath the ship,
545 And straight a sound was heard.

Under the water it rumbled on,
Still louder and more dread:
It reached the ship, it split the bay;
The ship went down like lead.

The ship sud-
denly sinketh.

550 Stunned by that loud and dreadful sound,
Which sky and ocean smote,
Like one that hath been seven days
drowned
My body lay afloat;
But swift as dreams, myself I found
555 Within the Pilot's boat.

The ancient
Mariner is saved
in the Pilot's
boat.

Upon the whirl, where sank the ship,
The boat spun round and round;
And all was still, save that the hill
Was telling of the sound.

560 I moved my lips—the Pilot shrieked
And fell down in a fit;
The holy Hermit raised his eyes,
And prayed where he did sit.

I took the oars: the Pilot's boy,
565 Who now doth crazy go,
Laughed loud and long, and all the while
His eyes went to and fro.
"Ha! ha!" quoth he, "full plain I see,
The Devil knows how to row."

570 And now, all in my own countree,
I stood on the firm land!
The Hermit stepped forth from the boat,
And scarcely he could stand.

"O shrieve me, shrieve me, holy man!"
575 The Hermit crossed his brow.
"Say quick," quoth he, "I bid thee say—
What manner of man art thou?"

The ancient
Mariner ear-
nestly entreat-
eth the Hermit
to shrieve him;
and the penance
of life falls
on him.

Forthwith this frame of mine was
        wrenched
With a woeful agony,
580 Which forced me to begin my tale;
And then it left me free.

Since then, at an uncertain hour,
That agony returns:
And till my ghastly tale is told,
585 This heart within me burns.

And ever and anon throughout his future life an agony constraineth him to travel from land to land;

I pass, like night, from land to land;
I have strange power of speech;
That moment that his face I see,
I know the man that must hear me:
590 To him my tale I teach.

What loud uproar bursts from that door!
The wedding-guests are there:
But in the garden-bower the bride
And bride-maids singing are:
595 And hark the little vesper bell,
Which biddeth me to prayer!

O Wedding-Guest! this soul hath been
Alone on a wide wide sea:
So lonely 'twas, that God himself
600 Scarce seemèd there to be.

O sweeter than the marriage feast,
'Tis sweeter far to me,
To walk together to the kirk
With a goodly company!—

605 To walk together to the kirk,
And all together pray,
While each to his great Father bends,
Old men, and babes, and loving friends
And youths and maidens gay!

610 Farewell, farewell! but this I tell
To thee, thou Wedding-Guest!
He prayeth well, who loveth well
Both man and bird and beast.

And to teach, by his own example, love and reverence to all things that God made and loveth.

He prayeth best, who loveth best
615 All things both great and small;
For the dear God who loveth us,
He made and loveth all.

The Mariner, whose eye is bright,
Whose beard with age is hoar,
620 Is gone: and now the Wedding-Guest
Turned from the bridegroom's door.

He went like one that hath been stunned,
And is of sense forlorn:
A sadder and a wiser man,
625 He rose the morrow morn.

Glossary

PRONUNCIATION KEY

VOWEL SOUNDS

a	hat	ō	go	ʉ	burn
ā	play	ô	paw, born	ə	extra
ä	star	o͞o	book, put		under
e	then	o͞o	blue, stew		civil
ē	me	oi	boy		honor
i	sit	ou	wow		bogus
ī	my	u	up		

CONSONANT SOUNDS

b	but	l	lip	t	sit
ch	watch	m	money	th	with
d	do	n	on	v	valley
f	fudge	ŋ	song, sink	w	work
g	go	p	pop	y	yell
h	hot	r	rod	z	pleasure
j	jump	s	see		
k	brick	sh	she		

ab • hor • rence (ab hôr´əns) *n.*, hatred; aversion

ab • ject (ab´jekt´) *adj.*, miserable, wretched

ab • ju • ra • tion (ab´jə rā´shən) *n.*, renunciation; giving up of an opinion or oath

ab • so • lu • tion (ab´sə lo͞o´shən) *n.*, formal freeing from guilt; remission from sin

ab • stain (əb stān´) *vi.*, voluntarily do without

ab • struse (ab stro͞os´) *adj.*, hard to understand; deep

a • byss (ə bis´) *n.*, deep chasm

ac • cede (ak sēd´) *vi.*, consent; agree to

ac • qui • esce (ak´wē əs´) *vi.*, agree without protest but without enthusiasm

ac • tu • ate (ak´cho͞o āt´) *vt.*, put into action or motion

a • cute • ness (ə kyo͞ot´nis) *n.*, shrewdness; severity

ad • duce (ə do͞os´) *vt.*, give as a reason; cite as an example

ad • junct (a´junkt´) *n.*, a thing added to something else, but not essential to it

ad • ver • sar • y (ad´vər ser´ē) *n.*, opponent, enemy

af • fa • bil • i • ty (af´ə bil´ə tē) *n.*, gentleness; friendly and pleasant manner

ag • i • tate (aj´i tāt´) *vt.*, move violently

al • lege (ə lej´) *vt.*, declare; offer as an excuse

al • le • vi • ate (ə lē´vē āt´) *vt.*, lighten or relieve; reduce or decrease

al • lure (ə lo͞or´) *vt.*, tempt, attract, entice

a • mel • io • rate (ə mēl′yə rāt) *vt.*, improve; make better

an • guish (aŋ′gwish) *n.*, great suffering; distress

an • i • ma • tion (an′i mā′shən) *n.*, life; liveliness

an • ni • hi • la • tion (ə nī′ə lā′shən) *n.*, destruction; nullification

an • tip • a • thy (an tip′ə thē) *n.*, aversion; strong dislike

ap • a • thy (ap′ə thē) *n.*, lack of interest or emotion

ap • pa • ri • tion (ap′ə rish′ən) *n.*, anything that appears unexpectedly or in an extraordinary way

ap • pease (ə pēz′) *vt.*, satisfy

ap • per • tain (ap′ər tān′) *vt.*, relate; have to do with; pertain

ap • pre • hen • sion (ap′rē hen′shən) *n.*, capture or arrest

ap • pro • ba • tion (ap′rə bā′shən) *n.*, commendation; official approval

ar • bi • ter (är′bət ər) *n.*, judge

ar • dent (ärd′′nt) *adj.*, intensely enthusiastic

ar • dent • ly (ärd′′nt lē) *adv.*, passionately; eagerly

ar • ti • fice (ärt′ə fis) *n.*, trickery

as • cribe (ə skrīb′) *vt.*, attribute

as • sail (ə sāl′) *vt.*, attack; assault

as • sev • er • a • tion (ə sev′ə rā′shən) *n.*, assertion; serious or positive statement

as • suage (ə swāj′) *vt.*, lessen; allay

a • sy • lum (ə sī′ləm) *n.*, refuge; place where one is safe

a • tro • cious (ə trō′shəs) *adj.*, appalling or dismaying; unpleasant and offensive

au • gu • ry (ô′gyo͞o rē) *n.*, indication

a • vail (ə vāl′) *vi.*, help; be of use

a • verse (ə vʉrs′) *adj.*, not willing; opposed

a • vid • i • ty (ə vid′ə tē) *n.*, eagerness; enthusiasm

balm • y (bäm′ē) *adj.*, mild and pleasant

bar • bar • i • ty (bär ber′ə tē) *n.*, cruel behavior; inhumanity

bar • ren (bar′ən) *adj.*, dull; unproductive

base (bās) *adj.*, contemptible; inferior

be • nev • o • lence (bə nev′ə ləns) *n.*, kindness

be • siege (bē sēj′) *vt.*, harass or beset with questions

blight (blīt) *n.*, that which destroys growth, causes devastation

buf • fet (buf′it) *vt.*, thrust about

ca • dence (kād′′ns) *n.*, inflection; rhythmic flow of sound

cal • lous (kal′əs) *adj.*, unfeeling

can • vas (kan′vəs) *vt.*, examine or discuss in detail

ca • pa • cious (kə pā′shəs) *adj.*, able to contain or hold much

ca • pit • u • late (kə pich′yo͞o lāt′) *vi.*, give up; stop resisting

ca • price (kə prēs′) *n.*, whim; sudden, impulsive change of mind or emotion

chi • mer • i • cal (kī mer′i kəl) *adj.*, imaginary; unreal

com • mence • ment (kə mens′mənt) *n.*, beginning

com • mis • er • ate (kə miz′ər āt′) *vt.*, feel or show sorrow or pity

com • pla • cen • cy (kəm plā′sən sē) *n.*, quiet satisfaction com • po • sure (kəm pō´zhər) *n.,* calmness of mind

con • ceive (kən sēv´) *vt.,* form or develop in the mind

con • cil • i • at • ing (kən sil´ē āt´iŋ) *adj.,* soothing; placating

con • de • scen • sion (kän´di sen´shən) *n.,* patronizing manner or behavior

con • du • cive (kən dŏŏ´siv) *adj.,* tending or leading to

con • fide (kən fīd´) *vt.,* entrust to someone; tell confidentially

con • geal (kən jēl´) *vt.,* thicken; coagulate

con • ge • ni • al (kən jēn´yəl) *adj.,* suited to one's needs or disposition; agreeable

con • jure (kun´jər) *vt.,* call upon by an oath

con • ster • na • tion (kän´stər nā´shən) *n.,* great fear or shock that makes one feel confused

con • sum • mate (kən sum´it) *vt.,* finish; accomplish

con • sum • ma • tion (kän´sə mā´shən) *n.,* completion; fulfillment

con • tem • plate (kän´tem plāt´) *vt.,* study carefully

con • tu • me • ly (kän´tyŏŏ mel´ē) *n.,* haughty and contemptuous rudeness

con • va • les • cence (kän´və les´əns) *n.,* recovery after illness

con • vul • sive (kən vul´siv) *adj.,* having the nature of involuntary spasms

cor • dial (kôr´jəl) *adj.,* warm and friendly; hearty

coun • te • nance (koun´tə nəns) *n.,* face

crag (krag) *n.,* steep, rugged rock that rises or protrudes from other rock

crev • ice (krev´is) *n.,* narrow opening caused by a crack

cull (kul) *vt.,* select

cur • so • ry (kʉr´sə rē) *adj.,* superficial

daunt • less (dônt´lis) *adj.,* fearless

de • bar (dë bär´) *vt.,* keep a person from some right or privilege; exclude

de • clam • a • to • ry (dē klam´ə tôr´ē) *adj.,* marked by artificial eloquence

de • fer (dē fʉr´) *vt.,* postpone or delay

def • er • ence (def´ər əns) *n.,* respect

deg • ra • da • tion (deg´rə dā´shən) *n.,* being lowered in rank, status, or condition

de • lin • e • ate (di lin´ē āt´) *vt.,* depict, draw, or describe

de • note (dē nōt´) *vt.,* indicate

de • nounce (dē nouns´) *vt.,* condemn; criticize

dep • o • si • tion (dep´ə zish´ən) *n.,* testimony

de • prav • i • ty (dē prav´ə tē) *n.,* corruption; wickedness

dep • re • cate (dep´rə kāt) *vt.,* feel and express disapproval of

de • prive (dē prīv´) *vt.,* take something away from forcibly; keep from having, using, or enjoying

dep • u • ta • tion (dep´yŏŏ tā´shən) *n.,* group of persons appointed to represent others

de • rive (di rīv´) *vi.,* come; originate

des • pi • ca • ble (des´pi kə bəl) *adj.,* deserving to be despised; contemptible

de • spond • ence (di spän´dəns) *n.,* dejection; lack of hope de • spond • en • cy (di spän´dən sē) n., dejection; loss of courage or hope

des • ti • tute (des´tə tool´) adj., lacking; being without

di • a • bol i • cal • ly (dī´ə bäl´ik lē) adv., wickedly; fiendishly

dic • tate (dik´tāt´) n., command

dif • fi • dent (dif´ə dənt) adj., shy

di • late (dī´lāt´) vi., discourse; comment on at length

dil • a • to • ri • ness (dil´ə tôr´ē nəs) n., delay

dil • a • to • ry (dil´ə tôr´ē) adj., slow or late; intending to cause delay

dil • i • gence (dil´ə jəns) n., constant, careful effort; perseverance

dis • con • so • late (dis kän´sə lit) adj., dejected; inconsolable

dis • dain (dis dān´) vt., treat as unworthy; reject with scorn

dis • in • ter • est • ed (dis in´tris tid) adj., not influenced by personal interest or selfish motives

dis • po • si • tion (dis´pə zish´ən) n., nature or temperament; customary frame of mind

dis • qui • si • tion (dis´kwi zish´ən) n., formal discussion

dis • si • pate (dis´ə pāt´) vt., make disappear; drive away

dis • sol • u • ble (di säl´yoo bəl) adj., capable of being dissolved or broken up

dis • suade (di swād´) vt., turn away from by persuasion or advice

di • vine (də vīn´) vt., find out by intuition

doc • ile (däs´əl) adj., easy to manage; submissive

dor • mant (dôr´mənt) adj., alive but not moving; sleeping

dot • ing (dōt´iŋ) adj., foolishly or excessively fond

ear • nest • ness (ʉr´nist nəs) n., seriousness

ec • cen • tric • i • ty (ek´sen tris´ə tē) n., deviation from what is ordinary or customary; oddity

el • o • quence (el´ə kwəns) n., graceful and persuasive speech

e • lude (ē lood´) vt., avoid or escape

e • ma • ci • ate (ē mā´shē āt´) vt., cause to become abnormally thin, as by starvation

em • bark (em bärk´) vi., begin a journey

em • i • nent • ly (em´ə nənt lē) adv., outstandingly; remarkably

em • u • la • tion (em´yoo lā´shən) n., desire to equal or surpass

en • deav • or (en dev´ər) vt., strive; attempt with great effort

en • dow • ment (en dou´mənt) n., gift of nature; inherent ability

en • er • vat • ing (en´ər vāt´iŋ) adj., weakening; devitalizing

en • fran • chise (en fran´chīz´) vt., free

en • ig • mat • ic (en´ig mat´ik) adj., perplexing; baffling

en • nui (än´wē´) n., boredom

e • nounce (ē nouns´) vt., enunciate; announce or proclaim

en • ter • prise (ent´ər prīz) n., bold or dangerous undertaking or project

en • tice • ment (en tīs´mənt) n., allurement; temptation

en • treat (en trēt´) vt., implore

en • treat • y (en trēt´ē) n., earnest request; plea

e • nun • ci • a • tion (ē nun´sē ā´shən) n., proclamation; announcement

e • phem • er • al (e fem´ər əl) adj., short-lived; fleeting

ep • i • thet (ep´ə thət´) *n.*, disparaging word or phrase

eq • ui • ta • ble (ek´wit ə bəl) *adj.*, characterized by equity; fair; just

er • ro • ne • ous (ər rō´nē əs) *adj.*, wrong, mistaken, based on error

er • ro • ne • ous • ly (ər rō´nē əs lē) *adv.*, mistakenly; wrongly

e • vince (ē vins´) *vt.*, indicate; show plainly

ex • alt (eg zôlt´) *vt.*, fill with pride or joy

ex • cul • pate (əks kul´pāt´) *vt.*, prove guiltless

ex • e • crate (ek´si krāt´) *vt.*, curse; denounce

ex • e • cra • tion (ek´si krā´shən) *n.*, cursing

ex • hor • ta • tion (eg´zôr tā´shən) *n.*, urging plea

ex • or • di • um (eg zôr´dē əm) *n.*, opening part of a statement

ex • pe • dite (eks´pə dīt´) *vt.*, speed up; facilitate

ex • pos • tu • late (eks päs´chə lāt´) *vi.*, reason with earnestly

ex • qui • site (eks´kwi zit) *adj.*, beautiful and of highest quality

ex • tort (eks tôrt´) *vt.*, get from somebody through threats or violence; extract

ex • ul • ta • tion (eg´zul tā´shən) *n.*, act of rejoicing; jubilation

fac • ile (fas´il) *adj.*, easy

fa • cil • i • tate (fə sil´ə tāt´) *vt.*, make easy or easier

fas • tid • i • ous (fas tid´ē əs) *adj.*, hard to please; oversensitive

feint (fānt) *n.*, sham; false show

fer • vent • ly (fʉr´vənt lē) *adv.*, passionately; earnestly

fet • ter (fet´ər) *vt.*, confine; restrain

fi • del • i • ty (fə del´ə tē) *n.*, loyalty; devotion to duty

fla • grant (flā´grənt) *adj.*, outrageous

fluc • tu • ate (fluk´cho͞o āt´) *vi.*, rise and fall

fore • bod • ing (fôr bōd´iŋ) *n.*, prediction, especially of something bad

for • mi • da • ble (fôr´mə də bəl) *adj.*, hard to overcome

for • sake (fôr sāk´) *vt.*, abandon

for • ti • tude (fôrt´ə to͞od´) *n.*, strength to bear misfortune or pain calmly

fraught (frôt) *adj.*, filled; charged or loaded

fruit • less (fro͞ot´lis) *adj.*, unsuccessful; futile

fu • tile (fyo͞ot´´l) *adj.*, ineffective; unimportant

gall (gôl) *n.*, something that is distasteful

gen • i • al (jēn´yəl) *adj.*, warm, mild, and healthful

ges • tic • u • la • tion (jes tik´yo͞o lā´shən) *n.*, energetic gesture

gibe (jīb) *vi.*, jeer or taunt

grat • i • fi • ca • tion (grat´i fi kā´shən) *n.*, cause of satisfaction

guile (gīl) *n.*, slyness and cunning

hag • gard (hag´ərd) *adj.*, having a wild, worn look, caused by sleepless-ness or grief

haugh • ty (hôt´ē) *adj.*, arrogant; scornful of others

hav • oc (hav´ek) *n.*, great destruction and devastation

hi • lar • i • ty (hi ler´i tē) *n.*, noisy merriment

hov • el (huv´əl) *n.*, hut; miserable dwelling

hyp • o • crit • i • cal (hip´ə krit´i kəl) *adj.*, pretending to be better than one really is

ig • no • ble (ig nō´bəl) *adj.*, not noble; common; base

ig • no • min • y (ig´nə min´ē) *n.*, disgrace; shame; loss of reputation

il • lus • tri • ous (i lus´trē əs) *adj.*, famous; distinguished

im • bibe (im bīb´) *vt.*, take into mind and keep

im • bue (im byo͞o´) *vt.*, permeate or inspire

im • mac • u • late (im ak´yo͞o lit) *adj.*, pure; innocent; without sin

im • mure (im yo͝or´) *vt.*, confine; shut up within

im • mu • ta • ble (im myo͞ot´ə bəl) *adj.*, unchangeable

im • pas • sive (im pas´iv) *adj.*, insensible; not showing pain

im • pel (im pel´) *vt.*, force; urge

im • pend • ing (im pend´iŋ) *adj.*, threatening; about to happen

im • per • cep • ti • ble (im´pər sep´tə bəl) *adj.*, not easily perceived or seen

im • pe • ri • ous (im pir´ē əs) *adj.*, overbearing; arrogant

im • per • ti • nent (im pʉrt´'n ənt) *adj.*, disrespectful; insolent

im • po • tence (im´pə təns) *n.*, weakness; powerlessness

im • pre • cate (im´pri kāt´) *vt.*, invoke

im • pru • dent • ly (im pro͞od´'nt lē) *adv.*, without thought to the consequences

in • an • i • mate (in an´ə mit) *adj.*, not endowed with life

in • ar • tic • u • late (in´är tik´yo͞o lit) *adj.*, unable to be understood

in • cal • cu • la • ble (in kal´kyo͞o lə bəl) *adj.*, too great to be calculated

in • cite (in sīt´) *vt.*, urge; stir up

in • clem • en • cy (in klem´ən sē) *n.*, storminess or severity

in • com • mode (in´kə mōd´) *vt.*, bother; inconvenience

in • cre • du • li • ty (in´krə do͞o´lə tē) *n.*, disbelief; skepticism

in • de • fat • i • ga • ble (in´di fat´i gə bəl) *adj.*, untiring

in • del • i • ble (in del´ə bəl) *adj.*, permanent; lasting

in • dig • nant (in dig´nənt) *adj.*, feeling or expressing anger or scorn

in • dis • crim • i • nate • ly (in´di skrim´i nit lē) *adv.*, randomly; without making sound choices

in • do • lence (in´də ləns) *n.*, idleness, laziness

in • duce (in do͞os´) *vt.*, persuade

in • dulge (in dulj´) *vt.*, satisfy (a desire); gratify

in • dul • gence (in dul´jəns) *n.*, leniency; act of giving in to the wishes of another

in • es • ti •ma • ble (in es´tə mə bəl) *adj.*, too great or valuable to be measured; invaluable

in • ex • or • a • ble (in eks´ə rə bəl) *adj.*, unrelenting; unalterable

in • fal • li • bly (in fal´ə blē) *adv.*, without error; reliably

in • fa • my (in´fə mē) *n.*, disgrace, dishonor; bad reputation

in • fat • u • a • tion (in fach´o͝o ā´shən) *n.*, affectation of folly; lack of sound judgment caused by strong emotion

in • fer • ence (in´fər əns) *n.*, conclusion drawn by reasoning from known facts

in • fuse (in fyo͞oz´) *vt.*, put into; fill

in • ge • nu • i • ty (in´jə no͞o´ə tē) *n.*, cleverness; originality and skill

in • hos • pi • ta • bly (in häs´pit ə blē) *adv.*, without kindness or friendliness toward guests

in • junc • tion (in juŋk´shən) *n.*, command

in • qui • e • tude (in kwī´ə tyo͞od´) *n.*, restlessness; uneasiness

in • sti • gate (in´stə gāt´) *vt.*, urge on or spur to some action

in • su • per • a • ble (in so͞o´pər ə bəl) *adj.*, insurmountable

in • teg • ri • ty (in teg´rə tē) *n.*, uprightness, honesty, and sincerity

in • tri • ca • cy (in´tri kə sē) *n.*, complexity

in • tu • i • tive (in to͞o´i tiv) *adj.*, having to do with perceptions or knowledge that are not based on conscious reasoning

in • ure (in yo͞or´) *vt.*, make accustomed to

in • vig • or • ate (in vig´ər āt´) *vt.*, enliven; fill with energy

in • vin • ci • ble (in vin´sə bəl) *adj.*, unconquerable

ir • ra • di • ate (ir rā´dē āt) *vt.*, illuminate; light up; make bright

ir • rep • a • ra • ble (ir rep´ə rə bəl) *adj.*, not able to be repaired, mended, or remedied

ir • re • proach • a • ble (ir´ri prō´chə bəl) *adj.*, blameless; faultless

ir • res • o • lute (ir rez´ə lo͞ot´) *adj.*, wavering in decision or purpose

ir • rev • o • ca • bly (ir rev´ə kə blē) *adv.*, unalterably

la • bo • ri • ous (lə bôr´ē əs) *adj.*, involving or calling for much hard work; difficult

la • ment (lə ment´) *vi.*, feel or express deep sorrow; mourn

lan • guid (laŋ´gwid) *adj.*, without vitality or spirit; dull

las • si • tude (las´i to͞od´) *n.*, listlessness; weariness

liv • id (liv´id) *adj.*, discolored like a bruise; grayish-blue

loath • some (lōth´səm) *adj.*, disgusting; detestable

lus • trous (lus´trəs) *adj.*, bright; shining

mach • i • na • tion (mak´ə nā´shən) *n.*, secret plot or scheme with evil intent

ma • lig • ni • ty (mə lig´nə tē) *n.*, quality of being very harmful or dangerous

man • i • fest (man´ə fest´) *vt.*, show plainly

man • i • fold (man´ə fōld´) *adj.*, many and varied

me • di • a • tion (mē´dē ā´shən) *n.*, diplomatic intervention to settle differences

mel • an • chol • y (mel´ən käl´ē) *adj.*, sad and depressed; gloomy

mer • ce • nar • y (mur´se ner ē) *adj.*, motivated by desire for money; greedy

mien (mēn) *n.*, bearing; way of carrying oneself

min • is • ter (min´is tər) *vi.*, give help; attend to needs

mor • ti • fi • ca • tion (môr´tə fi kā´shən) *n.*, humiliation; loss of self-respect

mul • ti • far • i • ous (mul´tə far´ē əs) *adj.*, diverse; having many kinds of parts

myr • i • ad (mir´ē əd) *n.*, indefinitely large number

noi • some (noi´səm) *adj.*, foul smelling and unhealthy

nov • el • ty (näv´əl tē) *n.*, freshness; unusualness

nup • tial (nup´shəl) *adj.*, of marriage or a wedding

ob • du • rate (äb´do͝or it) *adj.*, inflexible; hardened and unrepenting

o • blige (ə blīj´) *vt.*, make indebted for a favor or kindness done

ob • lit • er • ate (ə blit´ər āt´) *vt.,* blot out; destroy

ob • liv • i • on (ə bliv´ē ən) *n.,* condition of being forgotten or over-looked

ob • sti • nate (äb´stə nət) *adj.,* not easily ended

o • di • ous (ō´dē əs) *adj.,* disgusting; deserving hatred

om • ni • po • tent (äm nip´ə tənt) *adj.,* having unlimited power

op • pro • bri • um (ə prō´brē əm) *n.,* anything bringing disgrace or shame

pal • pa • ble (pal´pə bəl) *adj.,* easily perceived by the senses

pal • pi • tate (pal´pə tāt´) *vi.,* beat rapidly or flutter

pan • e • gyr • ic (pan´ə jir´ik) *n.,* formal speech or writing in praise of a person or event; tribute

par • a • mount (par´ə mount´) *adj.,* ranking higher than another in power or importance

par • ox • ysm (par´əks iz´əm) *n.,* sudden convulsion or outburst

par • ti • al • i • ty (pär´shē al´ə tē) *n.,* tendency to favor unfairly; bias

ped • ant • ry (ped´´n trē) *n.,* ostentatious display of knowledge

pen • sive (pen´siv) *adj.,* thinking deeply or seriously

pen • u • ry (pen´yo͞o rē) *n.,* poverty; destitution

per • am • bu • la • tion (pər am´ byo͞o lā´shən) *n.,* walk

per • di • tion (pər dish´ən) *n.,* loss of the soul; damnation

per • pe • trate (pʉr´pə trāt´) *vt.,* commit; perform something evil

per • se • vere (pur´sə vir´) *vi.,* continue in some course of action despite difficulty; be persistent

per • ti • nac • i • ty (pʉr´tə nas´ə tē) *n.,* stubborn persistence

per • turb (pər turb´) *vt.,* agitate, upset

pe • ruse (pə ro͞oz´) *vt.,* read carefully; examine

per • ver • si • ty (pər vʉr´sə tē) *n.,* contrariness

pet • ty (pet´ē) *adj.,* unimportant; small-scale

pit • tance (pit´´ns) *n.,* small amount; barely sufficient sum of money

plac • id (plas´id) *adj.,* tranquil; calm

plat • i • tude (plat´ə to͞od´) *n.,* commonplace quality

poign • ant (poin´yənt) *adj.,* sharply painful; evoking pity; emotionally touching

pol • i • tic (päl´i tik´) *adj.,* prudent; shrewd

pos • ter • i • ty (päs ter´ə tē) *n.,* all succeeding generations

pre • car • i • ous (prē ker´ē əs) *adj.,* insecure; risky; uncertain

prec • i • pice (pres´i pis) *n.,* steep cliff

pre • cip • i • tate (prē sip´ə tāt´) *vt.,* throw headlong; hurl downward

pre • cip • i • ta • tion (prē sip´ə tā´shən) *n.,* rash haste

pre • side (prē zīd´) *vi.,* exercise control or authority

pre • tense (prē tens´) *n.,* false reason; unsupported claim

pre • vail (prē vāl´) *vi.,* persuade; induce; produce or achieve the desired effect

prey (prā) *vi.,* have a harmful influence

pro • cure (prō kyo͝or´) *vt.,* get by some effort

pro • fane (prō fān´) *adj.,* not consecrated; secular

pro • fun • di • ty (prō fun´də tē) *n.,* great depth

prog • e • ny (präj´ə nē) *n.,* offspring

prog • nos • ti • cate (präg näs´ti kāt) *vt.,* foretell or predict; indicate beforehand

prom • on • to • ry (pram´ən tôr´ē) *n.,* headland; peak of land that juts into the water

prop • a • gate (präp´ə gāt´) *vt.,* reproduce

pro • tract (prō trakt´) *vt.,* draw out; lengthen

pro • trac • tion (prō trak´shən) *n.,* lengthening of duration

prov • o • ca • tion (präv´ə kā´shən) *n.,* something that excites a strong feeling, especially resentment or irritation

pru • dence (prōō d´ns) *n.,* cautiousness; discretion

pur • loin (pər loin´) *vt.,* steal

quell (kwel) *vt.,* subdue; put an end to

ram • ble (ram´bəl) *vi.,* roam or move about without direction or connection

ran • kling (raŋ´kliŋ) *adj.,* causing anger or resentment

rap • tur • ous • ly (rap´chər əs lē) *adv.,* with ecstasy; as if carried away with love or joy

rash • ly (rash´lē) *adv.,* recklessly; hastily

rav • ish (rav´ish) *vt.,* transport with joy

re • ca • pit • u • la • tion (rē´kə pich´ə lā´shən) *n.,* summary or brief restatement

re • dress (rē´dres´) *n.,* compensation for wrong done

re • lin • quish (ri liŋ´kwish) *vt.,* give up; abandon

re • miss • ness (ri mis´nəs) *n.,* carelessness; negligence

re • mon • strate (ri man´strāt´) *vi.,* protest, object

ren • der (ren´dər) *vt.,* cause to be or become; make

re • nowned (ri nound´) *adj.,* famous

re • past (ri past´) *n.,* meal

re • pine (ri pīn´) *vi.,* complain; fret

re • plete (ri plēt´) *adj.,* well-filled

re • pose (ri pōz) *n.,* rest

rep • ro • bate (rep´rə bāt) *vt.,* condemn; reject

re • pug • nance (ri pug´nəns) *n.,* extreme dislike or distaste

req • ui • si • tion (rek´wə zish´ən) *n.,* formal request

re • signed (ri zīnd´) *adj.,* patiently submissive; accepting passively; yielding and uncomplaining

ret • ro • spect (re´trə spekt´) *n.,* contemplation or survey of the past

re • ver • ber • ate (ri vʉr´bə rāt´) *vt.,* echo or resound

rev • er • en • tial (rev´ə ren´shəl) *adj.,* showing or caused by deep respect, love, or awe

rev • er • ie (rev´ər ē) *n.,* dreaming

sa • gac • i • ty (sə gas´ə tē) *n.,* shrewdness; wisdom and good judgment

sal • ly (sal´ē) *n.,* sudden start into activity

sa • lu • bri • ous (sə lōō´brē əs) *adj.,* healthful; wholesome

san • gui • na • ry (saŋ´gwi ner´ē) *adj.,* accompanied by or eager for bloodshed

sa • ti • ate (sā´shē āt´) *vt.,* satisfy or gratify completely

sa • vor • y (sā′vər ē) *adj.*, appetizing; salty

sci • on (sī′ən) *n.*, shoot or bud

scoff (skäf) *vt.*, mock

scourge (skurj) *n.*, cause of serious trouble or affliction

sed • u • lous (sej′ oo ləs) *adj.*, persistent

se • ren • i • ty (sə ren′ə tē) *n.*, calmness; tranquility

slough (slōō) *n.*, bog or swamp

so • lic • i • tude (sə lis′ə tōōd) *n.*, excessive care or concern

som • ber (säm′bər) *adj.*, dark and gloomy

spec • ter (spek′tər) *n.*, ghost or apparition

spent (spent) *adj.*, worn out; physically exhausted

spurn (spʉrn) *vt.*, refuse or reject with contempt

squal • id (skwäl′id) *adj.*, wretched; miserable

squal • id • ness (skwäl′id nəs) *n.*, wretchedness

stig • ma (stig′mə) *n.*, mark of disgrace or reproach

sub • lime (sə blīm′) *adj.*, majestic; awe-inspiring

sub • sist (səb sist′) *vi.*, continue to live; remain alive on

suc • cor (suk′ər) *n.*, aid, help, or relief

suf • fice (sə fīs′) *vi.*, be enough; be sufficient

su • per • flu • ous (sə pur′flōō əs) *adj.*, excessive; unnecessary

sup • pli • ant (sup′lē ənt) *n.*, petitioner; person who makes a request

sup • po • si • tion (sup′ə zish′ən) *n.*, assumption

sur • mount (sər mount′) *vt.*, overcome

sus • cep • ti • ble (sə sep′tə bəl) *adj.*, easily influenced or affected by

te • di • ous (tē′dē əs) *adj.*, tiresome or boring

tim • or • ous (tim′ər əs) *adj.*, timid; full of fear

tor • por (tôr′pər) *n.*, dullness; apathy

tran • si • to • ry (tran′sə tôr′ē) *adj.*, temporary; not permanent

tra • verse (trə vʉrs′) *vt.*, cross

treach • er • y (trech′ər ē) *n.*, betrayal of trust or faith; disloyalty

tri • fling (trī′fliŋ) *adj.*, trivial; of little value or importance

tu • mul • tu • ous (tōō mul′chōō əs) *adj.*, wild and noisy; greatly agitated

un • a • bat • ed (un ə bāt′əd) *adj.*, not lessened or diminished

un • al • lied (un′ə līd′) *adj.*, not united

un • bound • ed (un boun′did) *adj.*, unlimited

un • couth (un kōōth′) *adj.*, awkward; crude

un • du • la • tion (un′dyōō lā′shən) *n.*, wavy motion

un • gen • i • al (un jēn′yəl) *adj.*, unpleasant

un • hal • lowed (un hal′ōd) *adj.*, not holy or sacred; evil

un • in • tel • li • gi • ble (un in tel′i jə bəl) *adj.*, incomprehensible; that cannot be understood

un • quenched (un kwencht′) *adj.*, not satisfied

un • re • mit • ting (un ri mit′iŋ) *adj.*, not stopping or relaxing; incessant

u • til • i • ty (yōō til′ə tē) *n.*, usefulness

vac • il • lat • ing (vas′ə lāt′iŋ) *adj.*, wavering

var • i • e • gat • ed (ver′ē ə gāt′id) *adj.*, varied; diversified

ve • he • ment (vē′ə mənt) *adj.*, characterized by intense feelings; forceful

ven • er • a • ble (ven´ər ə bəl) *adj.,* worthy of respect by reason of age, dignity, character, or position

venge • ance (ven´jəns) *n.,* revenge

ves • tige (ves´tij) *n.,* trace, bit

vex • a • tion (veks ā´shən) *n.,* something that causes annoyance or disturbance

vis • age (viz´ij) *n.,* face

vi • vac • i • ty (vi vas´ə tē) *n.,* liveliness of spirit; animation

wan • ton • ly (wän´tən lē) *adv.,* deliberately; recklessly

wont (wänt) *adj.,* accustomed

writhe (rīth) *vi.,* twist, contort, squirm

yearn (yʉrn) *vi.,* be filled with longing

zeal (zēl) *n.,* enthusiastic devotion in pursuit of an ideal

Handbook of Literary Terms

Allusion. An **allusion** is a rhetorical technique in which reference is made to a person, event, object, or work from history or literature. In the subtitle of her work, Mary Shelley alludes to the legend of Prometheus from Greek mythology.

Archetype. An **archetype** is any element that recurs throughout the literature of the world. An archetypal element in *Frankenstein* is the human quest for knowledge and power.

Biographical Criticism. **Criticism** is the act of evaluating or interpreting a work of art or the act of developing general guidelines or principles for such evaluation or interpretation. **Biographical criticism** attempts to account for elements of literary works by relating them to events in the lives of their authors.

Character. A **character** is a person (or sometimes an animal) who figures in the action of a literary work. A *protagonist*, or *main character*, is the central figure in a literary work. An *antagonist* is a character who is pitted against a protagonist. *Major characters* are those who play significant roles in a work. *Minor characters* are those who play lesser roles. A *one-dimensional character*, *flat character*, or *caricature* is one who exhibits a single dominant quality, or *character trait*. A *three-dimensional, full*, or *rounded character* is one who exhibits the complexity of traits associated with actual human beings.

Dramatic Irony. **Irony** is a difference between appearance and reality. In **dramatic irony**, something is known by the reader or audience but unknown to the character.

Epistolary Novel. An **epistolary novel** is a work of imaginative prose that tells a story through letters, or epistles. The letters at the beginning of *Frankenstein* tell the story of the stranger picked up by Walton's crew.

Foreshadowing. **Foreshadowing** is the act of presenting materials that hint at events to occur later in a story. Frankenstein's dream about Elizabeth foreshadows her death.

Frame Tale. A **frame tale** is a story that itself provides a vehicle for the telling of other stories. Robert Walton's letters to Mrs. Saville act as a frame for Frankenstein's tale.

Imagery. An **image** is a word or phrase that names something that can be seen, heard, touched, tasted, or smelled. The images in a literary work are referred to, collectively, as the work's **imagery**.

Metaphor. A **metaphor** is a figure of speech in which one thing is spoken or written about as if it were another. This figure of speech invites the reader to make a comparison between the two things. The two "things" involved are the writer's actual subject, the *tenor* of the metaphor, and another thing to which the subject is likened, the *vehicle* of the metaphor. In chapter 19, when Frankenstein says, "I am a blasted tree," he is using a metaphor:

TENOR	VEHICLE
I (Frankenstein)	blasted tree

Mood. **Mood,** or **atmosphere**, is the emotion created in the reader by part or all of a literary work. A writer creates a mood through judicious use of concrete details.

Narrator. A **narrator** is one who tells a story. The narrator in a work of fiction may be a central or minor character or simply someone who witnessed or heard about the events being related.

Romanticism. **Romanticism** was a literary and artistic movement of the eighteenth and nineteenth centuries that placed value on emotion or imagination over reason, the individual over society, nature and wildness over human works, the country over the town, common people over aristocrats, and freedom over control or authority. Mary Shelley was part of the Romantic movement.

Science Fiction. **Science fiction** is highly imaginative fiction containing fantastic elements based on scientific principles, discoveries, or laws. It is similar to fantasy in that it deals with imaginary worlds but differs from fantasy in having a scientific basis. Mary Shelley's *Frankenstein* was an early precursor of modern science fiction. She based her idea of the creation of artificial life on nineteenth-century experiments with so-called animal magnetism, the electrical charge believed by some people in those days to be the force motivating living things and distinguishing them from nonliving things.

Setting. The **setting** of a literary work is the time and place in which it occurs, together with all the details used to create a sense of a particular time and place. Writers create setting by various means. In fiction, setting is most often revealed by means of description of such elements as landscape, scenery, buildings, furniture, clothing, the weather, and the season. It can also be revealed by how characters talk and behave.

Simile. A **simile** is a comparison using *like* or *as*. A simile is a type of *metaphor*, and like any other metaphor, can be divided into two parts, the tenor (or subject being described), and the vehicle (or object being used in the description). In chapter 2, Frankenstein describes "the saintly soul of Elizabeth" as shining "like a shrine-dedicated lamp in our peaceful home." Elizabeth's soul is the tenor, and a "shrine-dedicated lamp" is the vehicle. They can be compared because they share certain qualities such as radiance and purity. See *metaphor*.

Theme. A **theme** is a central idea in a literary work. *Frankenstein* explores a number of themes, including the conflict between good and evil, and the tragic consequences of unrestrained power and knowledge.